Larry Brown was in the Vietnam War

1st Short Stories that made it was "Big Bad Love"
theme is love gone wrong writes about
men without purpose

Essential methpor is "backroads of ms"
Cooler of beer in front of truck

aimless, lost character

novel "Joe" got sent to prision but it rehabilitated
him

What is the protrayal of women in
the novel? Is it a good one?
What makes a woman character
a woman?

Choose a progression of some
Sort that you want to talk about.
 - Silences (extended conversations)
   What is unspoken, hidden

# PRAISE FOR *FATHER AND SON* AND LARRY BROWN

"*Father and Son* is so vividly written it is almost cinematic."
—*Chicago Tribune*

"Professors will be, or at least ought to be, teaching *Father and Son* as an extraordinary example of fine writing."—*USA Today*

"Larry Brown is a master."—*Newsday*

"Larry Brown will cause you to be disappointed with every other novel you may pick up this year."—Thom Jones

"Brown succeeds triumphantly in his most wise, humane, and haunting work to date."—*Publishers Weekly* (starred review)

"A book so good you have to call it great."—*Men's Journal*

"This is the novel that will live with you day and night."
—Kaye Gibbons

"Riveting."—*Vanity Fair*

"*Father and Son* is that most valuable of novels: a truly important work, a resounding achievement by an author at the peak of his form."—*The State* (Columbia, SC)

"A powerful tale of love and betrayal, family ties and brutal revenge."—*Atlanta Journal-Constitution*

"Larry Brown writes like a force of nature."—Pat Conroy

"Another great and durable book from Larry Brown, and the rawness of emotions in it will stay raw within you for a long time."—Rick Bass, *The Boston Globe*

FATHER AND SON

**AN OWL BOOK**
**HENRY HOLT AND COMPANY    NEW YORK**

# FATHER
## AND SON

A NOVEL BY

**LARRY**

**BROWN**

FATHER AND SON

Henry Holt and Company, LLC
*Publishers since 1866*
115 West 18th Street
New York, New York 10011

Henry Holt® is a registered trademark of
Henry Holt and Company, LLC.

Published in Canada by Fitzhenry & Whiteside Ltd.,
195 Allstate Parkway, Markham, Ontario L3R 4T8.

Grateful acknowledgment is made to *Reckon* magazine, where an excerpt from this
novel first appeared.

Library of Congress Cataloging-in-Publication Data
Brown, Larry
Father and Son: a novel / by Larry Brown.
p.   cm.
ISBN 0-8050-5303-4
1. Ex-convicts—Mississippi—Fiction. 2. Fathers and sons—Fiction
3. Mississippi—Fiction
PS3552.R6927F38   1997                          97-15382
813'.54—dc21                                    CIP

Henry Holt books are available for special promotions and
premiums. For details contact: Director, Special Markets.

First published in hardcover in 1996 by Algonquin Books
of Chapel Hill, a division of Workman Publishing.

First Owl Books Edition 1997

Designed by Bonnie Campbell

Printed in the United States of America

10  9  8  7  6  5  4  3  2

FATHER AND SON

It was Saturday when they drove the old car into town, returning him, passing by the big houses with their blankets of dark grass beneath the ancient oaks. Midday. A hot wind blew in the car windows and rattled papers on the dash as they went up the wide and shaded avenue toward the square. It was cooler here in the hills than it had been in the Delta that morning, though not by much.

"It's been dry," Puppy said. "Daddy's well quit on him again. I'm afraid it dried up."

Glen scratched at a tick bite behind his ear and crossed his legs in the seat.

"What's he do for water?"

"I hauled him some. His pump may be messed up again, I don't know. I guess you can see about it when you get out there. You are gonna go out there, ain't you?"

"I don't know if I'll make it out there today or not," Glen said. "I don't see nobody here to meet us."

"What'd you expect? A parade? Why don't you go on out there and see him?"

"I'll go see him sometime."

"He ain't in real good shape, you know."

"I ain't in real good shape myself," Glen said.

Puppy slowed for the intersection, pulled up almost under the traffic light and stopped. "You hungry?"

"Yeah. Let's go over to Winter's and get a hamburger."

Puppy glanced at him and studied the traffic light. "I kind of hoped you wouldn't want to go over there right off the bat. Lunchtime and all. Crowd in there."

Glen looked out over the square and the brick buildings that ringed it, the old whitewashed courthouse in the center where they had sentenced him. The dusty automobiles were parked at an angle against the deep curbing and people were moving on the sidewalks.

"I ain't had any breakfast."

The light changed and the battered old vehicle rolled forward.

"You should have told me. We could have stopped somewhere."

"I was in a hurry."

"Afraid they'd change their minds?"

"It wouldn't have surprised me."

Puppy nodded and turned the wheel to the right and eased along until he saw an open space. He guided the car in. The bumper scraped against the concrete and he shut the motor off. They got out and Puppy stopped at the parking meter and put a nickel in it and bumped it with his hand until the needle came up. He stepped up on the sidewalk, hitching at his baggy pants, tucking in the sweaty surplus of his shirttail.

"Well, hell, come on," he said, and held the door of the cafe open for Glen. The screen door flapped shut behind them and they stood in a room floored with boards worn smooth from years of shoe leather. Slow fans hanging from the peeling wooden ceiling stirred the warm air.

"You want to set at the counter?" Puppy said. "Or do you want to get a table?"

"It don't matter." Glen was looking around to see who he knew in there.

"Hey Puppy," said a man at the back. He was wearing overalls and he had one black lens in his eyeglasses. He nodded gravely to Glen and Glen returned it with a sparse movement of his head, but he didn't say anything.

"Hey Woodrow," Puppy said.

"Who's that stranger you got with you?"

"You know who that is," Puppy said. "Let's just set at the counter, Glen."

They eased onto a pair of round padded stools. The linoleum of the counter was so worn it had no pattern. They could see hamburger patties sizzling on the grill behind the register. The room smelled of smoke, onions, grease.

"Where's Jewel?" said Glen.

"I don't know." Puppy was looking around. "I guess she's in the back." He nudged Glen in the ribs and gazed past his shoulder. "How'd you like to have you a little of that?"

Glen turned his head and saw a young woman reading a magazine and smoking a cigarette at one of the tables. She had on a white dress and she wore some colored plastic bracelets on her wrists. She looked oddly familiar to him, like some child he might once have known or merely spoken to.

"Uh-huh," he said.

She rocked slightly in her seat to some tune in her head and mouthed silently the words she was reading.

"Who is that?"

"Erline Price."

"Naw. That ain't her, is it?"

"She's growed up some, ain't she?"

She must have heard them talking about her or sensed it. She looked up and squinted behind her glasses. She touched the frames to see better and nodded. "Hey Randolph. Hey Glen. I didn't know you were home."

"Yeah," Glen said, smiling. "I just got in."

She nodded, grinned, and went back to reading her magazine. After they turned away she looked back up at him again.

Jewel stopped halfway through the kitchen doors with a carton of hamburger patties in her hands. She set them on the counter and wiped the hair out of her eyes and came down to stand in front of Glen. She looked like she was about to cry.

"Don't do that," he said. She reached out and put her hand on his arm. He let it stay there but he kept watching her face. She looked around at the people studying them.

"I've got to turn these hamburgers," she said. "I'll be right back."

She went to the grill and started flipping hamburgers, glancing back at him, edging something out of her eye with the corner of her apron.

"Right in front of the whole goddamn town," Puppy said in a low voice, and Glen turned to stare at him.

"You think I give a shit what these people think?"

Puppy put his elbows on the counter and laced his fingers together. He shifted on the stool and peered up at a ceiling fan for a moment. "Far as I know you never did care what anybody thought."

"What y'all want to eat, Glen?" Jewel said.

"Just give us a couple of hamburgers apiece. And some Cokes. Make em to go."

She came back over to where they sat. "Why don't you eat in here? I want to talk to you. I got a lot I want to tell you." She was trying to smile, trying to be cheerful. She didn't seem to know what to do with her hands.

"We got to go out to the cemetery," Puppy said. "Glen ain't been out there yet."

4

"Oh," she said, watching him, glancing back at the grill where the smoke was rising thicker. "Well. I'll hurry up and fix em then. I got some almost ready." She turned away and stood at a table and began setting out buns from a cellophane pack. "Have you seen your daddy yet?"

"We just got in. Just this minute."

"It sure don't seem like three years now. Seems like it went by in a hurry. I sure was sorry to hear about your mama."

Glen didn't say anything. He pulled out a cigarette and lit it, plucked a bit of tobacco off his tongue.

"Let me get your Cokes," she said. She opened the drink box and reached in for a pair of short bottles, then pried their caps off and set them up on the counter. An old man in a suit walked up and leaned on it.

"You ain't got my dinner ready yet?"

She snapped her face up and her eyes got bright and hard.

"I'm fixin em fast as I can, mister. You'll just have to wait your turn like everbody else."

The old man blinked and backed up. He looked at Glen and Puppy with a hostile glare and sat down, then leaned back in his chair and muttered to himself.

Jewel was stuffing a white sack full of hamburgers wrapped in waxed paper. Glen stood up and reached for some money but she said, "Don't worry about that. I'm sorry I'm so busy right now. I'll talk to you later. Okay?"

She watched his face for an answer.

"Okay?"

She started to turn away but he reached over and touched her arm. A small cloud of smoke was wafting up from the grill, spreading out along the ceiling, loud sizzling and grease burning. A few people stood up to see better. He took the neck of the sack and folded it down, not looking at her. But finally he did.

"I'll see you," he said.

"I hope so. You hardly ever wrote."

"I got some stuff I got to take care of. You know. I got to see some people."

"Let it go. Don't go lookin for trouble. I can't take no more of that."

"Well," he said.

She leaned close and whispered, "Things has changed, Glen. We got to have a talk."

"Come on, Glen," Puppy said. He was standing at the door with his hand on it.

Glen waved the hamburger sack at her. They went out. She went back to the grill and started scraping off the scorched meat and flinging it viciously into the garbage can. She cried a little but nobody said anything. They just watched her like an audience.

The gravel road curved away to a green and grassy hill bright and hot beneath the afternoon sun. They pulled up in the shade of the oaks and ate with the car doors open, the radio playing.

"You gonna start back up with her, I guess."

Puppy wasn't looking at him. He was staring out through the windshield, cupping his hamburger in both hands close to his lap. Glen balled up the waxed paper and started to throw it out the door, but dropped it on the floorboard instead. He turned slightly to watch his brother.

"What did you figure I'd do?"

"I don't know. I thought you might want to go out to the place and stay with Daddy. Maybe try to stay out of trouble."

"Bullshit, Randolph." He watched a little breeze riffle through the leaves and turn their pale undersides up. A bird sang in the distance. "I ain't gonna stay with Daddy. I got a house of my own. Even if I didn't have a house of my own I wouldn't stay with him."

"You could try it and see how you like it."

"I already know how I'd like it. If you so damn crazy about somebody to stay with him why don't you go out there and stay with him?"

Puppy shook his head. "I'm just your brother. I just want to look out for you."

7

"Naw, you just want to run my goddamn business for me."

Puppy didn't say anything. His stubbled jaw moved slowly as he chewed. Out past the dusty hood of the car the gravestones seemed to march away to the trees, the deep shade and cool of the bordering timber.

"Where's she at?" said Glen.

"Over yonder on the right. Next to . . . well, close to Aunt Eva."

They sat looking at the stones until Glen made a little motion with his hands.

"Is that where Theron is?"

Puppy studied him.

"Yeah, he's over there too," he said slowly. "I'd about decided you never would ask."

Glen got out and stood in the gravel and looked back inside, holding on to the door handle.

"Well I'm gonna go on. See if I can find her."

"I may walk out there after while."

Glen let the door fall to and went up the road in front of the car. He walked fifty or sixty yards in the gravel and then stepped over a hog-wire fence, holding the wire down behind his buttocks with one hand and fending off the stands of briars with the other and stomping at them and swinging his legs over one at a time. A lizard rustled over a hot stone and the tall, dry sage grass sang softly in a short breath of wind. He stopped and looked for a moment at the stones. So many of them and where to start. The unbroken peace that place invoked. He went slowly, stepping between the headstones and pausing to read one here and there. He kept looking ahead for new earth. But it wouldn't be new now. Not after a year. It would probably have grass growing on it by now. Each time he saw fresh dirt he went to it, but it was never hers. He was sweating a little under the sun, in the open glare of it, and he wondered what shape the house would be in after three years. He'd have to clean it all up, fix what was broken, get the electricity turned on. He had to see about his car and try to get it running, then look for a way to make some money. He had to see Jewel.

He stopped in the middle of the graveyard and looked around. Puppy had said next to Aunt Eva, but he wasn't even sure where she was, and she'd been dead so long. Eva's was an old funeral, barely remembered. Kids in ties and crying women, mud on their shoes. He was little then. A Davis or a Clark, she'd be next to them. He started reading the names on the stones and working his way right and suddenly found himself in the middle of them. They were all buried together, had been for the last hundred years. Fathers, mothers, children, the grandfathers and the dead from three wars. He found the grave but he couldn't believe it. There was no stone, only a small metal shield with a white card clamped to it and the name of the funeral home embossed on it to mark her resting place. He squatted and peered at the card, the typewritten words of ink almost bled away. No flowers, plastic or any other kind. Not even the withered stems. Just a rough patch of ground with blue and red clay. He knew that she had probably been buried in the cheapest casket they could find.

He got on his knees there next to the little metal marker and tried to read the tiny words and numbers printed there. He looked back to see if his brother was coming. He could see Puppy's feet sticking out a window of the car. Faint music drifted on the summer air. He felt close to these dead here with their stones and the finality of the earth that bound them together. There was a stone there he'd never visited and he finally turned his head and read it:

## THERON DAVIS
### Gone But Not Forgotten

He cried then, rocking on his heels, watching the small brown striped bees hovering nearby in the scattered clover. After a while he stopped crying and wiped the wetness away from his face with his fingers and sat there, hardening his face, changing it so that his brother would not know that he had cried. He went out the gate and back down over the gravel to the car.

Puppy was lying on the seat, his eyes closed, his fingers intertwined peacefully on his chest. Glen slapped his feet down from where they were propped on the door, and when Puppy opened his eyes and started up he told him, "I ought to whip your ass. You and Daddy's both."

"You ain't changed a damn bit."

"What'd you do with her money? Spend it?"

Puppy held on to the back of the seat with one hand and the steering wheel with the other and struggled to pull himself upright.

"I ain't seen the damn money. Daddy took care of all that stuff."

"Why ain't there a stone?"

Puppy glared at him and then came on out the door.

"Why don't you ask him? They ain't no need in gettin mad at me over it. I didn't have nothin to do with it."

Puppy stepped past him and pulled a cigarette out. Glen kicked at the rocks he stood on and looked again out over the grass. "How much you reckon one costs?"

Puppy lit his cigarette and sighed a lungful of smoke. He motioned helplessly. "I don't know. I figure you could get one for a couple hundred if it ain't too fancy. If you want, we can ride over to Tupelo one day and see."

Glen leaned against the car and put his hands on the hood. "I like to never found her. All her brothers and everybody out here and you can't even hardly find her place. I want us to ride over there one day before long and price one. You reckon they'd finance it?"

"I guess they would. They financed the funeral. We ain't never paid for that yet."

Puppy turned to the car and rested his arms on the roof, smoking his cigarette and tapping softly with the tips of his fingers on the faded paint and just waiting for the rest of the questions, a small annoyance showing on his face.

"So how much was the funeral?"

"I think it's about twelve hundred dollars all told. It costs a right smart to get buried these days."

"Well? Have you paid any on it?"

Puppy was evading his eyes. He was clearly troubled, but he began nodding.

"Sure. I made a few payments on it. When I could. Here and there."

"How much?"

"Well goddamn, Glen, I got three kids to feed and bills to pay just like everbody else. Shit, I ain't made out of money."

"How much have you paid on it?"

"I don't know exactly."

"How much would you guess?"

"Aw. I guess about thirty dollars."

"Shit," Glen said. He walked around the hood and got in the car on the other side. "Take me out to the house. I got a lot to do."

Puppy got in the car and closed the door. "Well you don't have to get pissed off about it. I've had a lot on me. It ain't been easy for me neither." He cranked the car and turned it around under the trees, backing up in the gravel and scraping his tailpipe on the bank.

"Damn," he said. "This old car's about wore out. I wish I had the money to buy me a new one. I went out there and cranked yours once in a while."

"How long's it been since you cranked it?"

Puppy started to answer and then saw a white car pull in off the highway and block the road. There was a six-pointed gold star emblazoned on the door. He hit the brakes and the right front wheel grabbed in the gravel so that the front slewed a little and they came to a sudden halt, sliding in the rocks. Dust flew up around them and came in through the windows.

"Son of a bitch," Glen said. He put his hand on the door handle but Puppy grabbed his arm. He tried to get loose and out the door but Puppy held him tighter.

"Now wait a minute," Puppy said.

"Wait's ass. I want to talk to that bastard."

"Hell. Don't get sent back the first day you get home. You know he ain't gonna take no shit off you."

"But I'm supposed to take some off him?"

"Just wait and see what he wants."

"I know what he wants. He wants to rub my nose in it."

"Well don't get out. Just stay in the car. Hear?"

Glen turned loose of the door handle and jerked his arm loose from Puppy, then eased back in the seat.

"I ain't scared of him. I did my time."

The sheriff got out of the car with his sunglasses on and left the door open. They could see a racked shotgun above and behind the front seat. When Puppy switched off his ignition they could hear the cruiser idling, the rough stutter of the cam. Bobby Blanchard wore blue jeans and a blue checked shirt. He wasn't wearing a gun. He stopped about four feet away from the car and nodded to them.

"Hey Randolph. Hello Glen."

Glen didn't answer, just stared into the dark glasses on Bobby's face. Bobby's pants were wet below the knees.

"I ain't come to give you a hard time, Glen." He crossed his arms over his chest and studied the ground, toed at the gravel with his cowboy boot. "There's not anything I can say that'll make you feel better."

"You got that right," Glen said.

Bobby looked off to one side, looked up at the sky, then looked back. "I was just headed home to change clothes and I saw the car. I sure am sorry about your mama."

"He's just upset cause we ain't got her a stone yet," Puppy said.

"If it means anything from me, I hate it all happened like it did," Bobby said. "I wish a lot of times I had a crystal ball. I could stop a lot of stuff before it starts." He put his hands in his pockets and he seemed uncertain of what he was saying.

"I'm gonna make sure he stays out of trouble," Puppy said.

"Why don't you shut the hell up, Puppy?" Glen told him, and pointed to Bobby. "All he wants is somebody to kiss his ass."

"The man just wants to talk to you."

"I've done served my time, I told you. I don't have to talk to nobody. You can set here and lick his ass all day if you want to but I ain't."

The man who'd sent him up pulled his sunglasses off. He flicked them lightly along his thigh. He hadn't shaved and he rubbed unhappily at the black bristles on his jaw.

"I tell you what I'm gonna do, Glen. Just for today. While it's just you and me and Puppy here. I'm gonna take a little shit off you so we can get it all straight."

"I figured you'd get around to that."

"I try to do my job. If somebody calls me up at two o'clock in the mornin, I get up and go. If it's Saturday night and I got the fights on television, I get up and go. I been over at Spring Hill all night draggin a pond for a boy that drowned yesterday afternoon. We found him about an hour ago. Eleven years old. I just went and told his mama."

"What in the hell's that got to do with me?"

"Well, I'll tell you. I get paid to do whatever needs to be done. I try my best to keep the drunks off the road and the troublemakers in line. Now

I'll be the first one to admit that you had some bad breaks. But it don't excuse what you did."

"I told you he run out in front of me."

"You were drunk."

"I spent three years of my life in that goddamn shit hole you put me in."

"Which a lot of folks think wasn't near long enough. Ed and Judy Hall would have loved to seen you rot down there. If you'd killed my kid I'd probably feel the same way. But I'm not the judge. I'm just the sheriff. You're out now. All you got to do is act right. I know we ain't never gonna be friends. You never did like me anyway."

Glen was trembling and he didn't trust his voice. He said, "Well let me just tell you a few things. I don't want to be your friend. And I don't need no lecture from you. Now what do you think about that?"

Bobby nodded and put his glasses back on.

"That's about what I thought. But I tried. You got two years' probation, right?"

"Eighteen months."

"Who's your probation officer?"

"I don't know. I'm to go to the office."

"It's probably Dan Armstrong. When are you supposed to report?"

Glen made Bobby wait before he answered.

"Monday mornin."

Bobby nodded a little more and he seemed to weigh this information while he watched the ground. He looked up quickly.

"Okay. He's gonna tell you everything, so you don't need to hear it from me. Your brother there could probably talk a little sense into you if you'd let him. Long as you stay straight, you won't hear a word out of me. I don't want you to think you got to carry a chip around on your shoulder. Now if you want to, we'll shake hands like grown men. Put all this behind us."

And he stepped closer and held his hand out, a big strong hand with freckles and fine black hair on his arm. He offered it and stood in the hot silence waiting. Glen spat out the window.

"I'll tell you what I'll do," he said. "Since it's just us three out here. Just you and me and Puppy? You take that badge off for five minutes and I'll stomp your ass in the ground. Then we'll see if you want to be friends or not. See if you want to shake hands then."

Bobby drew his hand back slowly and said, "You wouldn't win." He turned and walked back to his cruiser and got in and shut the door and turned around.

"Boy that was real smart," Puppy said. "Man try to do you a favor and you. . . . Boy," he said. He cranked the car. "I don't believe you sometimes."

"Why don't you just carry me somewhere I can get a beer and shut up?" Glen said.

"You start any shit with him you'll be right back in the pen."

"He ain't gonna send me back to the pen. He'll have to kill me first."

"If you don't act right he will. And I didn't think you was supposed to go in a bar while you're on probation anyway. I thought you wanted to go home."

"I don't now."

After Puppy had pulled out into the road and they were moving again, Glen said, "Hell, you can go in a store and buy me some, can't you?"

"I guess I can. Have you got any money?"

"Hell yes, I've got some money. You ain't got any on you?"

Puppy shook his head sadly. "Ain't got much."

"Didn't you get paid yesterday?"

"I did. And I lost most of it in a card game. And I had to put gas in the car this mornin. Reckon I could get that back from you?"

Glen was already reaching for his billfold. "How much?"

"Aw. I guess about ten dollars. Ten or twelve."

Glen gave him fifteen. They bumped over the rough old highway through the afternoon sun past stretches of timber and by yards with wrecked cars parked in orderly rows. He saw familiar things, a solitary tree in a field, the rotting hulk of a wooden wagon sinking its way into the ground. He watched everything until they pulled into a place near Abbeville, a little county joint with beer signs in the windows. Puppy parked and got out.

"What you want and how much?"

"Get a case and make sure it's cold. Here."

Glen handed him some more money and watched him climb the steps, could see him through the windows going to the big cooler. Cars and trucks passed down the road beside him. Finally Puppy came back out with the case slanted against his hip under one arm. Glen reached and opened the back door. Puppy slid the beer onto the seat, then took a six-pack around to the front.

Glen looked at the beer. He placed his hand on it. Cold in the hot air, clean little bright cans beginning to sweat. He tore one loose and opened it with the church key that was on the dash and turned it up to his mouth and let it stand there until he drained it. He took the can down, belched.

"That was pretty good," he said, and got another one.

"Damn, Glen, they don't allow you to drink on the premises. Got a sign right there."

"I don't give a shit. Now carry me over to Barlow's."

"You ain't got no business over there. He'll be drunk and you'll be into it before you know it."

"You sound like a old woman, Puppy. I got some unfinished business with him."

Puppy turned the wheel and looked out the window to see if anything was coming.

"You had any sense you'd let it slide, too. You don't need to go over there. Let's go see Daddy."

"I'll go see him when I git goddamn good and ready. If you don't want to take me I can find somebody else to run me over there."

Puppy studied him for a few seconds, resigned to it.

"Hell, I'll carry you. You gonna go anyway. Just don't blame me if he whips your ass again."

"Ain't no son of a bitch gonna get me down and kick me and get away with it."

"Yeah, and if you hadn't cut him he probly wouldn't've got you down and kicked you. Somebody cut me I'd kick him too. You lucky he didn't shoot you. I would've."

Puppy pulled out to the stop sign, then hit the gas. They didn't talk for a while. The few houses alongside the road rapidly gave way to plowed or planted fields and spotted cows with outsized horns and barns with roofs of brown tin and gray rotting sides. Glen turned the vent so that the hot wind rushed in to ruffle his shirt, his hair. He opened a pack of Camels and dropped the wrapper out the window.

Puppy looked at him briefly, then turned his face back to the road.

"What's the first day like down there?"

Glen didn't look around. "Call you out on the grass. What they call the grass. Ain't no grass, just dirt. Call you out to fight and if you don't fight they take you down and fuck you in the ass."

"You fight?"

"You goddamn right."

"Ever day?"

"Till they left me alone."

"How long did that take?"

"Bout a week."

"You gonna give me one of them beers?"

Glen reached down and got him one and handed it to him. Puppy steered with his knees and got the opener and punched two holes in the can. Foam spurted from the top and he sucked at it. He drove with one hand, the beer between his legs, glancing out the window from time to time.

"He might not even be up," he said. "This early."

"He still got that monkey?"

"Last time I was over there he did. That's about a ugly son of a bitch. You ever seen the way he acts around a woman that's on her period?"

"Goes crazy, don't he?" said Glen.

"Shit. Worse than that. Jumped on some old gal over there one night, had his dick run out. She like to had a goddamn fit. He's bit several people."

Glen finished his beer and threw the can out the window. He reached down for another just as they crossed the county line. "He better not bite me."

After an eighth of a mile Puppy let off the gas and slowed the car, checking the rearview mirror, shifting down into second, and turning into a rutted dirt road where a weathered sign on a leaning post pointed a crooked red arrow toward BARLOW'S COLD BEER DANCING POOL.

The place wasn't visible from the highway at all. It was hidden in a thicket of loblolly pine and the dried needles had coated the roof with a carpet of brown. On the front porch sat a Coke machine, several chairs, two big Walker hounds with slatted ribs and hanging tongues. The dogs rose to their feet with lifted hackles and snarled briefly before leaving the porch. There were no cars in the yard. Puppy eased to a stop against one of the peeled logs there. He cut off the motor. The hounds melted into the surrounding underbrush and were seen no more. Glen set his beer on the floor and opened the door.

"Watch them dogs," Puppy said.

"I ain't worried about them dogs."

He got out and closed the door and stood there for a moment, then crossed the yard with its litter of bottle caps and cigarette butts and stepped up on the porch. He tried the door. The knob turned silently in his hand. He looked back at Puppy, who was raising a beer to his mouth. Glen stepped inside.

The bar was dimly lit by the sunlight that came through the dirty windows. All the chairs were turned upside down on the tables and the floor had been swept clean. The room seemed heavy with menace, as if all the bottles broken over heads and all the shots fired into human bodies had condensed into a thick and heavy presence of uneasiness and waiting.

He walked quietly to the bar and stood listening. There was no sound. Even the ceiling fans were stilled. The ranked bottles at the back of the bar held a muted gleam, familiar labels. He thought about pouring a drink.

The monkey climbed up on the bar ten feet away and sat silently, baring its teeth at him. It was nearly two feet tall, dark hair, a long tail. Long yellow canines dulled by tobacco juice. It grimaced and hissed at him.

"You nasty son of a bitch," Glen said.

In one leap it was on him and biting his hand. The fear came up in his throat the same way it had the day he almost jumped off the barn. The monkey was clawing at him, the little leathery black fingers clutching at his clothes with terribly surprising strength. He managed to get his other hand around its throat and it began to make a dreadful noise, crying almost like a child. The tail curled around his forearm and gripped it tight. He pulled his mangled fingers free and blood spattered over them. Blood on its teeth. He slammed the monkey against the dark wood of the bar, the furry body twisting and writhing at the end of his arm and the teeth bared in that fiendish grin and all the while the scared wailing and screeching. He slammed it again and he could feel the fine bones smashing, the strength going out of it. The monkey was shaking its head and

19

shitting on him. He gagged and threw it down and staggered back, looking at his hand. Deep lacerations, the fingers torn, vein and muscle. The
monkey lay on its side until in a sudden rage he kicked it. It landed heavily against the bar and dropped back to the floor. It lay dazed, blinking.
He watched it. One of its legs was bent beneath it. It passed a fist over its
face almost wearily and rolled over onto its belly and put its knuckles on
the boards and started trying to crawl away from him.

"Bite me now you son of a bitch," Glen panted. He kicked it again and
it fell over on its back with the black hands trembling. He looked into its
eyes and he saw shock and revelation there.

There was one empty beer bottle sitting on the bar. He leaned over
and picked it up, bent low over the monkey, and knocked a huge dent
in its skull. It trembled and shook the way a clubbed fish will and then
it relaxed and was still. He dropped the bottle on the floor and straightened. Blood was dripping off his middle finger, had seeped under the
nail. The bar was quiet once again. The same silent chairs. He saw his
harried reflection looking back at him from the mirror behind the bar,
the bottles like old friends. He stepped back there and took a fifth of
whiskey down.

He turned and walked across the floor, opened the door, and looked at
his brother sitting in the car. He blinked in the sunlight as the blood
dripped onto the porch.

He went down the steps. Puppy started out of the car when he saw the
blood, but Glen waved him back. He walked around to the other side and
got in.

"What in the hell?"

"That monkey. Let's get out of here. Quick."

"What? Did it jump on you?"

"Yeah. Let's go."

Puppy cranked the car but could hardly take his eyes off the mangled hand. It was webbed with trails of blood that were starting to dry. He kept looking at the hand while he backed up. He stopped and turned the car around in the gravel.

"Damn, boy, you gonna have to see the doctor about that. Ain't no tellin what kind of filth that thing had on its teeth."

Glen got his beer from the floor and started drinking it. When they got to the highway, Puppy stopped and looked both ways hurriedly. "Did anybody see you?"

"Wasn't nobody in there."

"Did you kill it?"

"Hell yes I killed it."

Puppy pulled out into the road, going through the gears rapidly, getting it up to sixty as fast as he could.

"Well at least nobody saw you."

They rode in silence for a while then. They went across the levee and saw people fishing in the river far below the bridge, their boats and their long glossy canepoles.

"If he knew I was fixin to get out, he'll know it was me," Glen said. "Did you tell anybody?"

"A few. I didn't figure it was no secret."

Glen lifted his beer and drank. Puppy watched his mirror.

"Just take me out to my house and help me get my car cranked, then. That's all I'll ask of you."

"You not going to see Daddy?"

"Fuck him."

"Aw shit, Glen."

"You heard me. I said fuck him."

"Now listen, Glen. It ain't right to not go see him. He's missed you."

"He don't miss nothin but a whiskey bottle when he ain't got one in his hand."

Puppy found a cigarette in his pocket and got it lit and opened the other beer that was on the seat and took a big drink from it, wiping his mouth with the back of his hand, still watching behind them.

"Hell, I'll help you get your car cranked. I brought another battery just in case. Pour some gas in the carburetor it ought to crank. But let's go over to Daddy's first and see him just a minute anyway."

"Didn't even put her down a headstone."

"He looked at some. I know he looked at some."

A long black car loomed down the road. The driver was opening it up coming into the river bottom. The sun gleamed on the chrome bumper and the car came toward them at some incredible rate of speed. Puppy's old car rocked with a blast of wind as the thing shot by and hurtled down the road behind them.

"Was that him?" Said Glen.

"Yeah. That was him. Headed home."

"He'll come after me. You know that, don't you?"

"Naw, I don't know that."

"Well. I do."

That was all he said about it. They stopped in town and bought alcohol and bandages. Glen sat in the car with his feet in the street, leaning out the open door, pouring the alcohol over the cuts, closing his eyes for the way it burned. He drenched it good and wrapped the whole thing in gauze and while he was sitting there thinking everything over, he figured he might as well go ahead and finish it, now that it was started.

Virgil was sitting on the porch when they pulled up. A Redbone puppy with long legs and big feet was lying beside him. It raised its head sleepily and got up, looking around to see who had come. It wagged its tail appeasingly as it got out of the way, head turned to look sideways apologetically or just to be careful. It disappeared around the side of the house.

The place looked pretty much as it always had, the old unpainted house nestled in the weeds and the tin of the roof rusted to a mottling of gray and brown. The abandoned '48 Chevy coupe was still parked out to the side with four flats, and his father was there in the chair just as he had been the last time Glen saw him, as if time had warped and nothing had moved these three years he'd been locked down.

Puppy had his door halfway open, looking back at Glen. "Well? There he is. You gonna get out?"

Glen muttered something and stepped out. They stood in the thin grass of the yard looking up at their daddy. He was still a big man and the cane he held seemed out of place and too small for him. His hair was grayer now, but his hands and his arms still looked strong. His skin was dark from the summer sun.

Glen opened the back door of the car and brought out the rest of the beer. He walked across the yard and set it on the porch at his father's feet. Virgil watched him for a few moments and then reached down slowly and got one. There was an opener hanging from a nail driven into a post. He opened the can, his big hands flexing, and white foam spewed out. He waited for it to stop, holding the opener out for somebody to take. Glen took it, opened two more beers, handed one to Puppy, and stood in the yard drinking silently, looking around. In the garden out by the coupe, turnips the size of softballs rested their purple heads against the dry ground. Rotted bean stakes still leaned against a rusted piece of barbed wire, sheathed in dead vines. Dried catfish heads littered the dirt.

Glen's daddy finally set the can on the porch beside his cane and then moved the cane between his knees as he pulled makings from his shirt pocket and set to rolling Prince Albert. He did it swiftly, from long practice. His fingers were steady and soon he was done. With the cigarette between his lips he glanced up.

"Well," he said. "You don't look no worse for wear."

Glen didn't answer right away. He was thinking of the days he had worked in this garden with his mother, of wandering its rows of tomatoes with a jar in his hand for the worms that crawled over the young green globes. He would pick them off and put them in his jar. She punched holes in the top for air. Or she would send him every other day to cut the okra with the small dull paring knife. When they needed beanpoles she would drive them down a dirt road into the creek bottom and they'd walk around the edges of the freshly plowed fields to the stands of cane that bordered the banks. He remembered lashing big racks of them to the top of the car, their long and limber ends. Gathering extra ones for set hooks in the river, wet foggy mornings clambering up and down the muddy banks with his father, the catfish breaking the surface and gasping for water on the ends of their lines. Virgil's hair was still black then, and his wounds had not slowed him down so much. No bad car wrecks yet. He wrestled a catfish out of a hole in the bank one morning and it weighed forty pounds. They still had the picture somewhere, Glen guessed, but he didn't need to see it. He could remember Virgil sitting beside the thing fifty feet back from the bank, smoking his ready-rolleds then, the muscles of his broad back showing through his wet shirt, the fish breathing steadily in her new world and the sleek thickness of her shining flanks. And the fish fry that weekend, his mother cooking in the kitchen and their cousins and uncles drinking beer with his father at the table. Old voices and old times gone by and the memories of them like faded photos on a screen.

He looked up at his daddy. "You still just look like an old drunk to me," he said.

Puppy swelled up. His face went red. Glen watched him for a second and then told his father, "You too sorry to even put her a headstone up. And he wanted me to come see you. Well. I've seen you."

Virgil met his eyes with a level gaze and drew calmly on his smoke. He never even blinked. The Redbone puppy poked his head out from the side of the house and watched them hopefully, wagging his tail briefly. He seemed not to want to offend anybody. It was quiet for a moment.

Puppy sat down on the steps. He stared at the ground. He looked as if all the air had gone out of him.

"That trip down there didn't do you a damn bit of good," he said sadly. He lifted his beer and drank.

Virgil didn't say anything. He just sat there in his chair and looked out across the road.

Glen turned away. Off to the fields and past the trees where the clouds drifted in the sky. He reached in his pocket for a smoke, took one out of the pack, and put it to his lips. "Welcome fuckin home, huh?" he said. He lit the cigarette with a battered gold Zippo, snapped the lighter shut, and returned it to his pocket.

The house was one of the few things Glen had salvaged from his marriage. It had five rooms and brick siding with a tin roof. Weeds had grown up in the yard and one corner of the porch was sagging. Striped wasps threaded the air over his head as he turned the knob and pushed the front door open. Inside lay the silence of a house long empty. She had taken very little, only her clothes it looked like. The furniture was coated with dust and the television sat in one corner black and dead. Somebody had been in the house walking around, footprints proving it in the solid coating of dust on the floor.

He walked back to the kitchen. Dirt daubers had built nests on the walls and in the sink lay some dead bugs, a few encrusted plates. He went back outside and closed the door behind him. Puppy was standing in the yard and he was a little drunk. He had taken the fresh battery out of the trunk and it was sitting at his feet. A few wrenches stuck out of his pocket. They opened the doors of the car shed and pulled them back so that the late-afternoon sun glowed dully on the rusted chrome of the bumper. The hood was up. Puppy looked inside and glanced at his brother.

"Good thing we brought one," he said.

Glen looked inside the engine compartment and saw the positive and negative cables lying inside the battery box. His hand was hurting and he wished the monkey was still alive so he could kill it again.

"I be damn," he said. "I'd like to know who in the hell did that."

"It was in there last time I was out here," Puppy said. "Get the gas out of the trunk, Glen, and I'll stick this battery in and we'll see if she'll turn over. I need to get on home."

It took fifteen minutes to get it running. Puppy adjusted the timing and the carburetor until it would idle and advance. They bled the brakes.

"I'd put some plugs in it first chance I got and some points too," Puppy said. "I believe I'd get some new water hoses. They'll rot when one sets up this long."

Glen got behind the wheel and cranked it, revving it a little. He drove it into the yard and cut it off. His brother leaned in the window opposite. "What's your plans?"

"I don't know. Get something to eat. I may go see Jewel. She still live where she did?"

"She ain't moved. I wouldn't get in no trouble if I was you."

"You ain't me, though, are you?" Glen said.

Puppy just shook his head and looked down at the seat.

"Naw, Glen. I sure ain't you."


He stopped at a station two miles down the road for fresh gas, then went inside for cigarettes and two little Cokes. He mixed a drink from the bottle of whiskey he'd stolen and rode around for a while. He didn't want to get over to her house before dark. The sun was going down and there was mown hay raked in the fields. He hung his arm out the window and smoked a cigarette, cruising past the houses set back from the road with their amber lights showing through the front windows. Suppertime. He drank from the Coke bottle and it warmed his stomach. He finished that one pretty quick and opened the other bottle and mixed another drink.

At the red light in town he came to a stop and waited for it to turn and drove through it once it did and eased along the storefronts, looking at the cafe. The lights were off and the door was shut. He circled the square twice. A few produce vendors were still doing business. On Saturdays they sold vegetables from the back ends of their trucks, the vehicles nosed into the high sidewalks and little roofs of wood and tin built over them to shade their goods from the sun, big watermelons and bushel baskets of purple hull peas and yellow squash, bright red tomatoes. At one time that was his lot, too, rising early with his mother to go out to the truck patch and pick the produce from vines still wet with dew, loading them into the truck and getting to the square early to set up and hang the scales and lay out the paper sacks, sitting there all day to earn money that his father would drink up that weekend.

He sipped his whiskey and glanced at the vendors a last time and then headed out of town, reading the signs in the store windows, looking at the cheap furniture on the sidewalks, the lamps and dressers, driving slow and thinking about his old man. He had first fought him when he was twelve and he had fought him five times before he whipped him the first time when he was fifteen, a prolonged battle that went all through the house with both of them knocking over furniture, breaking tables, his mother down on the floor with her hands tangled in her hair screaming for it to stop. That day he had knocked his father all the way through the screen door onto the porch, but it hadn't resolved anything, since what they had between them could not be resolved then in that place. And maybe couldn't be now. He smoked and drove and thought about his father, who had survived the long march at Bataan but had come away crippled, having been bayoneted through the hands and the back and the right thigh. In his childhood, Glen had heard him moan and toss and plead through his dreams, and had seen him give himself to long periods of silence when he stared off into the sky and maybe relived old memories that he would talk about only when he was drinking. He wondered if he still did that. He wondered why the Japs hadn't just gone ahead and killed him when they had the chance. It would have made things a hell of a lot easier for everybody. He could have had a different daddy then, instead of the one he had now.

Jewel's room was nearly dark, but he could see the old dresser and the bureau, a tiny rocking chair and some toys scattered over the rug. The lace curtains that had flared out billowing in a black and storm-crazed spring night of his memory when the strobic lightning illuminated them struggling against each other on the bed now hung still and unmoving. There didn't seem to be a breath of air in the room tonight.

He stripped off the condom and went down the hall to the bathroom where a small light was plugged into the wall socket and flushed it down the commode. Then he went back into the bedroom and lay down beside her again. The whiskey was sitting on the bedside table and he reached and got it and tilted a drink down his throat. She put her hand on his leg.

"Can you stay the night?" she said.

"Not tonight."

They listened to each other breathing in the darkness.

"Lord that was good," she said. "It's been so long. You don't have to go."

"I got to."

"Will you come back?"

He didn't answer that. He found his clothes in a pile on the floor and he sorted through them for a sock or an undershirt. They were tangled with her things.

"Don't you want to see him?"

He paused and looked over his shoulder at her. "See him?"

"Yeah. I bet he'd like to see you."

He pulled on his socks and slipped his shorts over his hips, remembering a big baby in a crib who had stared up at him with dark eyes beneath a cheap mobile that spun slowly, blue fairy horses with knurled horns on their heads, orange suns and yellow stars, little pink bunny rabbits. A silent child who looked like him.

He sat there and buttoned his shirt.

"Hell, he don't know me."

"He's four. He knows you. I showed him the picture."

"What the hell did you go and do that for?"

"I'll go see if he's awake," she said. The lamp came on and he saw her arm pull back from it. She got up from the bed naked and pulled her robe off the chair nearby. She put it on and went barefoot out the door, down the darkened hall. He took another drink. It felt like something near death in here to him. He put the rest of his clothes on and combed his hair in front of the dresser next to the bed. When he turned to face a small noise at the bedroom door she was standing there holding the boy on her hip.

"There's Daddy, see Daddy?" she said to him softly. He was not a baby anymore yet he looked small for his age. He fixed Glen with a look of intense interest and rubbed at one eye with a dimpled fist to see him better maybe.

"Ain't he growed?" she said. "Look what a big boy."

Watching this Glen reached and got the whiskey off the bedside table.

"Put him back in bed. It's late."

"I just wanted you to see him."

"Take him back."

She spun quickly and went down the hall almost running. Glen walked through the living room and out the front door. He stood on the porch and took another drink of the whiskey. Then he went and sat in the car and waited for her to come out.

He heard a noise. The screen door flapped faintly and she was a pale form moving rapidly across the black grass toward him. She bent down to the window and her voice had turned cold.

"Are you not going to stay with us? After all this time? I want you to see him. You get back out of that car."

He didn't turn to her, just looked out across the hood.

"I ain't ready for that. I was still at Parchman last night if you know what I mean."

She put her hand on his arm and he felt the strength in her fingers when she tightened her grip.

"I told you I need to talk to you. Does all this time I've waited not mean nothin to you? Trying to raise this baby by myself?"

"I got to go."

"Don't you leave me like this, Glen. You come back in here and you sit down and talk to me."

He leaned back in the seat and looked at her. Her hair was loose and wild and the gown she'd slipped on was open at the top so that he could see her full breasts and her big nipples. All the nights he had dreamt of her and gone to sleep thinking about her, all the days in the cotton patches when only the thought of this night got him through, commanded him to get out of the car and take her hand and fall back into her bed and sleep with her and smell her hair and skin.

He reached forward and cranked the car, pulled the headlights on.

"I'll see you later, Jewel," he said, and let out on the clutch. She stepped back from the car and said some things, but by then he was going down the driveway and he didn't bother to listen to whatever they were.

Virgil was asleep. He was naked in his bed and turned on his side. The Redbone puppy whined through the screen door and a lamp with a few moths batting around it showed the cigarette butts knocked from the ashtray and empty beer cans on the floor, a chewed paper. The news played on the TV screen unheard and the light flickered on his mangled body, the scars that ran up his back and the hole in the side of his leg where they had twisted the bayonet and probed his living flesh with wide grins to his howls for mercy. The marred hands composed now, at rest.

Glen crossed the room without looking at him much and turned on the hall light and went back to his old room. The Winchester was still there, leaning in the corner. He went to it and picked it up. The receiver and the barrel had some rust showing, but he pushed the release and shucked the slide halfway back easily. A green Remington showed itself at the ejection port, the brass softly shining in the breech. He rechambered it and turned the gun toward the bed and pumped it, the shells tossing and flipping onto the quilt with little muted thumps. He sat down and looked at them. Birdshot mostly, but the first one that had come out was 00 buckshot.

"Shit," he said quietly. He stuck the buckshot back in and chambered it and uncocked the hammer and laid it on the bed. He got up and walked into the kitchen and turned on the light. Dirty plates and ruined scraps. Bugs crawling away. He started opening drawers. The first one had a broken glass in it, some bent spoons, a box of matches. He shut it and opened another one. What looked to be an ancient rubber and some big red shells. One was a 10-gauge. Two were three-inch magnums, 12-gauge. His gun was a 12 but it was an old 12 and he didn't want to blow it up in his own face. He figured that'd be worse than getting shot.

"What do you want with these damn things?" he said to the room. He slammed the drawer and opened another one. Some old green bread was in there and a plate somebody had eaten off several years ago, looked like.

"Goddamn," he said, and slammed that one too.

He moved to the other side of the sink where some of his mother's dish towels were hanging on a little wooden rack. He took one and stuck it in his pocket and opened the last drawer. There were four rounds of 12-gauge buckshot in there on a saucer. He picked them up and looked at them. They looked like they'd shoot. There was some dried dog shit on the floor. He guessed the Redbone puppy had been coming in some. The linoleum was torn and scuffed, ripped loose in places. The room was full of dead plants in pots. He turned the light off and walked out.

In the bedroom he picked up the gun by the stock and slipped the shells in one at a time, pushing them up with his thumb. He checked it one more time to see that one was in the chamber, then turned off the light and went back up the hall.

In his sleep, his father looked like some huge broken mannequin. Glen studied the gun in his hands and remembered when it used to hang above the kitchen door. It had been in canebrakes and the deep jungle woods of coons on steaming nights with spotted dogs leaping and howling and trying to climb the trees with their toenails, men standing in water amid cypress knees, men with flashlights in their hands searching in the vine-choked growth of leaves and poison ivy above for two red eyes. It had been in river bottoms on mornings when ice cracked underfoot and the sudden yammering of dogs came through the woods gaining decibels and the deer broke free from the cover and rocketed forty feet in a second. It had been held beneath beech trees on foggy mornings when the squirrels moved and shook the dew from the branches or paused in profile to hull a hickory nut with their rasping teeth, little showers of shredded matter pattering softly down through the leaves to scatter on the forest floor. Or mornings when nothing came and the cold was a vivid pain that held him shivering in its grip and the gun was an ache in his naked hands where he sat huddled with misery in some gloomy copse of hardwood timber.

He cocked the hammer now and swung the barrel up to his father's head and held the black and yawning muzzle of it an inch away. He tightened his fingers on the checkered pistol grip. The old man slept on, father and son. Some sense of foreboding told him to pull back and undo all of this before it was done. Yet he put his finger on the trigger, just touched it. He already knew what it would look like.

Virgil moved in his sleep, made a small sound almost like a cough. The puppy whined outside. The house was quiet but for that.

He raised the barrel and caught the hammer with his thumb and eased back on the trigger, letting it down. He went out the door, lighting a cigarette, hurrying.

Sometime during the night somebody had pinned the monkey to the bar with an ice pick through the thorax and it lay there atrophied with its palms upward like Christ in His final agony. Several people had put out cigarettes on it. Somebody had bought it a drink. Somebody had cut off its tail.

Barlow had two whores and an old fisherman left. The whores were trying to get the fisherman to put them up in the hotel in Pine Springs but the fisherman had to go fishing at six in the morning and Barlow was getting tired of hearing about it. He'd sent Rufus out to the road with the garbage and now Rufus came back through the door and walked straight to the bar.

"Somebody out by the road," he said.

"Who?"

"It look like Glen Davis. Can you pay me?"

"Pay you?" Barlow stirred himself erect and glared at him. "Goddamn. Pay you?"

Rufus nodded. "It's been since last Friday."

Barlow reached over for a fifth of Wild Turkey and poured some in his glass. He reached into a tub of ice at his knee and dumped some in the whiskey. He pointed.

"You see my damn monkey?"

Rufus looked at the thing with distaste. "I see him. He ain't gone bite nobody else."

"He bit you one time, didn't he?"

"That's right, he did."

"I bet you ain't even sorry the son of a bitch is dead. Are you, Rufus?"

"Naw. I ain't sorry."

"You probly glad the son of a bitch is dead. Ain't you, Rufus?"

"That's right, I am."

"Well I ain't," Barlow said, and threw back about half the drink. "You sure it's him?"

"I know it's him."

Rufus watched the people in the bar and leaned his elbows next to the whiskey. He leaned a little closer and lowered his voice. "I'll go eat me some supper. I'll come back later but I need to get paid fore I go home."

The whores and the fisherman were still arguing. Barlow looked at the monkey for a while and then opened the register. He went into the tens and pulled out five of them and folded the money and passed it to Rufus, who stuck it in his pocket and then slipped out the side door with one high backward wave of his hand.

"Well, well," Barlow said in a quiet voice. There was a little shelf right beneath the register that had been specially built. He eased out the gun and opened the cylinder and checked that all six chambers were loaded. He did these things unseen, below the level of the bar. It had been a slow day anyway. The Corps of Engineers had opened the gates of the dam at Sardis and people were yanking the catfish out around the clock. He spun the cylinder and closed it, then cocked the weapon and held it on the fat whore, who looked at it and saw it like a snake coiled at her elbow.

"Get the hell out of here," he said. "Git."

They cleared out fast. Their cars cranked outside and gravel crunched under the tires. He heard them leave and then there was nothing but silence. He lifted his drink and held the pistol. He listened hard. A few minutes passed. He thought he saw movement on the porch and he raised the pistol and pointed it. There was only silence. The lights were on all around him. He jumped up to knock them out with the barrel of the pistol and the window exploded in upon him.

Glen waited in the weeds for the longest time. He saw Rufus come down the drive with the garbage in the truck and he stepped back out of the headlights' glare but maybe not far enough. Rufus got out of the truck, dumped the garbage, came back. Glen thought about shooting him then, even drew down on him for a moment, then realized he couldn't do it and pulled the shotgun down. He watched Rufus drive back, saw him walk in, saw him talking, saw him leave. Straight across the cotton patch walking. Then the other cars left. He lay flat while they drove past.

The dogs said nothing as he came up, just moved out of the way, tails down. He stepped soundlessly up on the porch and moved toward the window as Barlow raised the pistol. He stepped back and Barlow reached up with the barrel as if to shoot out the lights a few feet above him. He stepped back in front of the window and cocked the hammer and let off the first shot, which pulverized the window and blew Barlow back against the ranked bottles behind the bar and shattered the mirror. Barlow hung there for a second, then his gun hand came down and a bullet blew by Glen's ear. Glen pumped his and fired and pumped it and fired and Barlow fired a shot into the floor and sagged down out of sight. A shard of glass swung, tinkled, fell.

Rufus had a small shack across the bottom and up the hill and he had a regular trail that he used to go back and forth from his house to the beer joint. The trail wound beside a big cotton patch and through part of a pasture and there was a footlog he used to cross a shallow creek where bullfrogs sat and sang and he was jogging like a dog now in a slow lope, his feet raising dust in the black air. There was a ridge off to the southwest that was covered with pines and as he ran he could see the porch light from his house shining between the trees. He slowed to cross the footlog and hushed the singing frogs and turned up the hill, his tennis shoes dropping softly in the needles and on the little stones that littered the path. He ran easily, breathing steadily, the sweat coiling down his back and his arms slowly pumping. His dog yapped once and growled and he yelled for it to be quiet as he drew nearer. At the crest of the hill he slowed to a walk and put his hands on his hips. He could see Lucinda on the porch still shelling peas. She'd been there all day and there was some ungodly number of peas in a washtub beside her.

He walked up to the porch and stood there for a second. She didn't look up.

"You still shellin them peas?"

She sat with her dark legs spread and a big dishpan nestled in the hollow sling her dress made between her massive thighs. She was throwing the hulls into some grocery sacks scattered around her.

"Ain't had nobody to help me," she said.

"What about them younguns?"

"Them younguns in the bed."

Her lower lip was pooched out and she gave an enormous sigh but her fingers never stopped their steady motions. He knew she'd heard the shots.

"What's all that mess down there?" she said.

He turned his head and looked into the black woods for a moment.

"White folks' business," he said, and stepped up on the porch and went inside. The dog came up out of the yard and climbed the porch and sniffed at the peas and sniffed at the hulls and then it sniffed at Lucinda's bare toes and licked one of her feet.

"Git on outta here you old soup bone," she said, and the dog sat. Rufus came back out with a glass of iced tea and sat down on the top step with his pipe and a small tin of Prince Albert. Lucinda sat there shelling their peas.

"I wish you'd git some other place to work," she said. "All them drunks down there. He don't do nothin but lay drunk hisself. Don't pay you nothin."

Rufus was loading his pipe. "I know it," he said. He got it loaded and pulled a kitchen match from his pocket and struck it on a board beside him and lit the pipe, drawing deep on it, holding the flame over it, until he shook the match out and dropped it in the yard. He reached into his pocket and pulled out the money and kept ten and handed the rest to her. She took it and looked at it. He puffed on his pipe and scratched the back of his head.

"Is that it?"

"That's it."

"Huh. You think we gonna feed them younguns on that? You bed not go back down yonder tonight neither. You hear me?"

Rufus didn't answer. He had heard the separate and distinct concussions of the pistol and the shotgun as they spoke to each other. It was plain to him that the shotgun had spoken loudest and he knew he had to go back.

The door was open and the lights were on when Rufus mounted the porch. He looked past the dead monkey whose fur was speckled with glass dust, tiny points of light shining, saw the blood on the wall and the holes in the wall and the shattered bottles and mirror. He looked at the front of the bar and saw the splintered wood. There was no sound and he began to wish he had listened to his woman.

He went forward into the room on quiet feet, but he was very conscious of the noise he made as the floorboards creaked. The register was opened and robbed, the chrome clamps that held the bills pressed down all standing straight up. He was afraid to lean over and see what was behind the bar because he knew already what he would find. Knowing didn't help because he still had to look at him, so he looked. Barlow was on the floor behind the bar. He couldn't see all of him. He could see the bloodied sleeve on one arm, and part of his bloody head, and one twisted leg.

A board groaned behind him, a chair kicked over.

Rufus froze and said, "I don't mess in no white folks' business."

A strange moan came from behind the bar. He heard with full clarity the cocking of a hammer, the thin tiny click that was loud in that hushed place, like the tick of the clock in your room just before sleep.

Barlow's eyes were full of blood and he couldn't find his gun. Things were still dripping on him and he could feel the blood cooling on his clothes. Blood sucked in and out of one nostril with a little congested sound. Some splinters on one of the boards were digging into his cheek, but he didn't move. He heard the door open, the steps come closer. He lay still, his eyes open. He held his breath.

Something hard prodded his shoulder, his head. He felt two feet straddle him. Then the bell on the register rang and he heard the drawer roll open, the flicking of the little metal arms, the feet removing themselves from over him. The lid on one of the coolers opened and somebody lifted a beer out and didn't close it. He heard the bottle being opened, a long sucking bubbling. Must have really hit the spot. Then the steps moved away and around in front of the bar and off to the left of the door where one table sat back almost hidden in a corner. He let his breath out. His fingers explored the sticky wood but still they felt no weapon and he was weak and laboring by now to breathe so he concentrated on lying still and listening. For a while there was nothing to hear, but then a chair creaked, a body settled. The light was bright over him and it was a puzzle to him how he knew that.

His last thoughts were memories, a time in 1956 when he got two flats on his car and had to walk four miles. He stopped at a house for a drink of water and a blind old man was there on the front porch in a rocker. The blind man wouldn't talk to him. He asked for water and the old man simply lifted his hand and pointed to a log shed beside the house. There was a pump with a long handle in there and a sluice and some canned goods arrayed on shelves. It was cool and dark in there and on a stone slab stood a quart fruit jar of water with which to prime the pump. It primed easily: he could remember the water welling up out of the earth into the pipe and rising up from the spout into the sluice and cascading down the trough, clean, clear, cold. He bent his sweating face to the water and drank long from it, wetted his head and his neck and hands and arms. In the deep shade of the trees in the yard he looked around. There were birds and a breeze. Sanctuary. He thanked the old man before resuming his walk in the sun but the old man only sat there with his opaque eyes and his impassive face like somebody made out of wood.

He wished now for another drink of that good water. He heard somebody come in and he moaned, couldn't help it, heard Rufus say he didn't mess in white folks' business and then he died.

The night was cool now and Glen had all the windows down so that a steady breeze blew through the car. It was a little past midnight. He drank from a warm beer and eyed his speed, not hurrying, not weaving, just going on home. The road swarmed with bugs and the night spoke to him in the voices of frogs and crickets. The black water alongside the road lay still and choked with bits of driftwood and empty beer bottles whose necks leaned out above the surface debris of twigs and bark, the trash thrown from passing cars.

He stared at the road that unfolded before him, guided the car gently around the curves and past the lightless houses where dogs slept too and over little railed bridges barely wide enough for two vehicles to meet. A quarter moon rode high and pale among the stars that showed their cold fire through the black infinity that stretched above the trees, their dark green tops wheeling past the windshield.

He slowed, checked his mirror, slung the bottle out, and turned onto a sand road that wound for miles through a vast forest of pines and oaks and the gullied wastes of loggers, splintered remnants of saplings lean-ing at crazy angles, past sleeping hulks of machinery, John Deere, Massey-Ferguson, going slowly, the tires whispering in the sand, the road turning and rising into hills and ridges where there was no traffic but himself. There was one beer left on the seat and he groped about on the dash for the opener and held the car to the road with his elbow while he pried off the cap. He tossed it out the window and took a sip from the bottle, shifting his left foot around on the floorboard and then resting the bottle between his legs.

He drove unmolested through those quiet increments of the night to the edge of the forest and onto a blacktop road, turned at the mailbox, and eased up the drive to halt in front of his father's house, where he pushed off the headlights and killed the ignition. Long moments there on the seat with the blackness looming through the glass and his hands shaking just a little. The dim light in the front room beckoning him to rest from his labors. He could not see his face in the rearview mirror, could not see what his eyes thought. He got out and took the keys to the back of the car and unlocked the trunk. The bulb in the trunk was burned out but he could see the shotgun across the spare tire. He picked it up and closed the trunk and went through the dark yard, up the steps and into the house through the torn screen door. He stopped in the living room suddenly. The television was still on and Virgil had turned onto his stomach in his sleep. The Redbone puppy still whined at the back door. He walked in the half dark back to his old room, leaned the gun in the corner, and undressed quickly. He hadn't slept in this house in a very long time.

He could smell the must of the sheets when he pulled the covers back, but he slipped in under them and turned the pillow over and punched it with his fist and put his head down on it. The house was quiet. He could see the dim glow of the television up the hall. There was a scratching at the back door and then some more whining and finally toenails clicking over linoleum. He raised up in the bed and saw the puppy slink up the hall, tail slowly wagging, and disappear into the living room. He lay back down and closed his eyes still working the pump slide in his mind's eye, still hearing the silent explosions in his brain, wondering if he'd be able to get to sleep. But after a while the puppy came in and nosed at him and he didn't know anything about that.

Morning. Bobby fanned at a fly that rose from his cheek and opened his eyes and looked at the green walls around him. He sat up. His back was hurting from sleeping on the couch again. The clock on the wall showed 6:15. His boots were on the floor beside the couch and he pulled them on and got up. There was a small bathroom just outside his office and he went in there to look in the mirror. He needed a shave, always did. He turned the water on in the sink and ran his comb under it and started running it through his hair. A door opened somewhere in the jail and then closed.

"That you, Jake?"

"Yeah," came the answer. "Good mornin."

"Mornin. We got any coffee?"

"I'll make it. You been here all night?"

"I laid down about two."

He put his comb back in his pocket and went into his office and opened the top drawer of his desk. There was an electric razor in there and he plugged it in next to the lamp and started shaving. After a while Jake came to the door with a paper cup of coffee and leaned in the door-way. "How come you to spend the night?"

"I didn't mean to. Laid down to close my eyes for a minute and I just now woke up. What about Byers?"

Jake hooked a thumb in his belt and blew on his coffee. He had to think about it before he spoke.

"Not much. Did two years in the army and worked in Detroit for six months. What time you want to go down there?"

Bobby unplugged the razor and put it away. There was a small closet in the corner and he stripped off his shirt and threw it into a gym bag on the floor and pulled a clean uniform shirt off a hanger. He put it on and started buttoning it up.

"Let me get some coffee and we'll head out. Is Harold here?"

"Not yet. You gonna try to go to church?"

"I don't know."

Jake moved aside as Bobby went past him out the door and down the hall and he followed him, his gun belt creaking. The sheriff sat down at the desk in the dayroom and started rummaging through some drawers.

"I ain't had time to go in a month. Hell, she had the preacher over for dinner last Sunday and I couldn't even make that. Have you seen that . . . here it is. Is that coffee ready yet?"

He pulled out a card with some new brass and began clipping it to his shirt. Jake was pouring him a cup at the table. He put a spoonful of sugar into it and stirred it and shook off the spoon and laid it down and brought the cup to him all steaming.

"Thanks."

He leaned back in his swivel chair and put his feet up on the desk and took a drink of his coffee. There was a pack of Lucky Strikes on the desk and he shook one out. Jake took his own chair across the room and slid down in it until he was resting on his backbone. "You think he really did it?"

"I guess if we dig him up he did."

"Who's gonna do the diggin?" Jake wanted to know.

Bobby just smiled at him.

"Why don't we take a trusty down there with us?"

"Which one you trust?"

Jake thought about it. He pushed the brim of his hat up off the front of his head.

"We could take Willowby. He's got that bad leg and couldn't run off from us."

Bobby sipped his coffee and slid an ashtray closer. He waggled the toe of his boot.

"He probably couldn't dig too good either. We got to take Byers down there anyway, we can just let him do it."

Jake took his hat off and laid it on the chair beside him as a troubled look crossed his face.

"Goddang, Bobby, you gonna make a feller dig up his own daddy?"

Bobby got up and refilled his cup and smiled over his shoulder. "I am unless you'd rather do it. Go stick him in the car and see if you can find a shovel. I'll be ready in a few minutes."

Jake took his coffee with him and pulled out a big ring of keys and went down a hall to a closed door. He entered through it and the door swung shut behind him.

Bobby sat back down at the desk and stubbed out his smoke and lit another one almost immediately. He wished folks would do all their meanness on Thursday nights instead of Saturday so he wouldn't have to work Sunday every weekend. The phone was there beside him and he picked up the handset and dialed the first three digits of his mother's number and then put it back in the cradle. She was probably still in bed this early.

He leaned back in the chair again and looked at his watch. He smoked and just waited for the noise that would be Jake bringing out the prisoner. The things that people did to each other didn't surprise him anymore, ever since he'd learned they were capable of doing any thing you could imagine and some things you couldn't.

The coffee was growing cold in the cup. He finished it and set the cup on the desk and got up. Harold was coming through the front door with his lunch box and a couple of paperbacks.

"Mornin, Sheriff."

"Mornin. Me and Jake's going down below Taylor to see about this mess. Stick around the radio in case we need you, okay?"

"Sure thing, Sheriff."

Bobby went back to his office and picked up his revolver by the belt that held the holster and carried it back through the dayroom, but he didn't strap it on. The steel door down the hall slammed and a bandaged black prisoner came shuffling out with his wrists manacled, looking neither left nor right, Jake following. Harold was pouring coffee at the table. After he got his cup he turned on the television and started watching it.

They went out and Bobby held the back door of the car open for the prisoner, then got behind the wheel of the cruiser and put the gun on the seat. He cranked the car and turned up the volume on the radio. Jake got in beside him and they pulled out.

Traffic was slow this Sunday morning. Churchgoers rising to leisurely breakfasts and dressing in their good clothes, lawns mown, clean cars parked neatly in their drives. The streets lined with big oaks that gave a welcome shade. He eyed the prisoner through the rearview mirror, but Byers never lifted his head. Jake tapped his fingers on the roof.

"We ought to go fishin sometime, Bobby."

Bobby glanced at him and pulled up at a stop sign, looked both ways, and drove on through. "Fishin?" he said. "If the county would hire me about four more deputies I might have time to. Hell. I'd settle for a day off once in a while."

They drove around the square, the shops closed, the sidewalks empty, as if nobody lived there. Easing around it Bobby saw a pint whiskey bottle standing beside a curb. He pulled up next to it and halted the car, then stepped out and picked it up. It still had a drink or two left in it. He got back in the car with it and turned to look at his prisoner.

"You want a drink?" he said. Byers nodded and mumbled something softly and Bobby passed him the bottle and watched him twist off the top with his cuffed hands and turn it up. Bobby looked at Jake. "Might be the last one he gets for a while."

Jake didn't answer. Bobby shut the door and they drove on.

There was a patch of plowed ground furred with young grass out by the old house and there was a clean low mound of dirt humped up in the center of it. A good crop of turnips in a row along one side. Jake was looking at the turnips and Bobby was looking at the dirt. Byers stood still handcuffed and looking off into the distance somewhere.

"Them's some pretty turnips," Jake said.

"Where's the shovel?" Bobby said. It was hot out there under the sun and he wanted to get it over with.

Jake winced a little and said, "Shit."

Byers had put a dreamy look on his face and he pointed toward the side of the house. Bobby walked over there and found a shovel so worn the blade was thin like a knife, fresh dirt caked in dull brown clots. He got it by the handle and walked back out to the plowed ground where Jake was still admiring the little patch.

"I swear them is some pretty turnips."

"Get over here and uncuff him, Jake."

Bobby stood holding the shovel until the bracelets were off and then he handed it to Byers.

"Dig," he said.

The prisoner walked the few steps to the mound of earth and studied it for a moment. He looked up at Bobby with nothing showing on his face and then he sank the blade into the ground. He lifted a spadeful of dirt and threw it backward and without pausing reached in for another one. Bobby squatted on his heels and fished a cigarette from his pocket and watched him dig. He hadn't dug long before the shovel hit something soft. Byers stopped digging and stared down into the dirt for a few moments. Then he dropped the shovel and went to his knees and started pulling at the soil with his hands, piling it to one side. Jake made a move to come forward but Bobby stopped him with his hand. Byers stayed on his knees, clawing with his fingers as he started breathing faster and moving his hands more rapidly. He began to resemble a dog digging his way beneath a fence as the dirt flew back and landed on his clothes. He moaned as he dug and he kept shaking his head and muttering so that Bobby had cause to wonder who he was talking to.

The head and face emerged first, closely cropped coils of gray wire encrusted with dirt, small pockets of dirt cupped on the eyelids. Byers brushed it away gently, gently, a bone hunter exhuming fossils. He had stopped moaning now. He paused and looked up at Bobby.

"Shit fire," Jake said quietly.

Byers was crying without making any sound as he went down the length of his father's body, uncovering the arms, the hands. At last he stood up and bent over and grabbed the wrists. He pulled hard, straining against the earth that had temporarily claimed this cadaver. He dragged the body from the shallow grave. They could see blood on the shirt, knife cuts on the throat that were coated with dirt. There was a light smell of rot about him already, that and the fragile pungency of the earth, reminding Bobby of spring somehow, the freshly turned dirt in the rows, small green things growing.

Byers released his hold and the arms dropped stiffly. He squatted and looked at them each in turn for instructions as to what came next.

"Cuff him," Bobby said. "Give him a cigarette and I'll go call the coroner down here."

He got up to walk over to the car and Jake pulled the cuffs from his pocket and snapped them back on the prisoner. He was pulling his smokes out when Bobby opened the door and sat down on the seat of the cruiser. He watched Jake bend over Byers and he picked up the mike and called up to the jail. Harold answered and Bobby told him they needed the coroner, and he was thinking that he should have told Jake to find something to cover the old man with, a blanket, something. It didn't seem right to have him lying out in the sun like that. He keyed the mike again and told Harold to call over to his house and tell his mother that it didn't look like he was going to be able to make it to church and probably not dinner either. Harold said he'd take care of it and Bobby thanked him.

He hung up the mike and looked out. Byers was sitting on the ground right in front of the car, smoking, talking to the body. Bobby didn't see his deputy.

"Jake?"

"I'm over here."

Bobby got out of the car and turned around. Jake was over in the turnip patch, digging with the shovel. He walked over there.

"What in the hell are you up to?"

The deputy paused in his work only for a moment. He already had a good-sized pile heaped up in a growing mound.

"It'd be a shame to leave these good turnips down here. Ain't gonna be nobody here to eat em now."

"Have you lost your rabbit-assed mind?"

"Naw. I just like a good mess of turnips once in a while."

Virgil was sitting on the top step eating a biscuit and smoking a cigarette when Glen walked out on the back porch and stepped to the end where a wringer washing machine and a tub full of car parts and empty dog food sacks rested. The boards were dangerous with decay and Virgil watched him place his feet carefully on the joists where there were nail heads and then start peeing off the end of the porch into a flower bed made out of an old tractor tire that now held only grass and weeds.

"You got any coffee in this house?" Glen said.

"Look in there next to the sink."

Virgil turned his head away and just sat there gazing out across what he called a yard. There were several junked cars back there with cardboard boxes full of hay and they were inhabited primarily by scrubby chickens. Virgil would go out there and get an egg or two once in a while. There was a car battery on the porch and it was wired to a headlight. Whenever he heard a ruckus among the chickens at night he would go out with a little Sears single-shot .22 and flip a wall switch for the battery and with the whole pastoral scene illuminated he would ventilate whatever house cat coon fox or possum was making off across the yard with one of his squawking fowl. He rarely hit the birds and they could usually be returned minus a few feathers to their nests. The coons he roasted in deep pans covered with tin foil and stuffed with carrots and sweet potatoes and feasted on them, dividing the bones for gnawing with the Redbone puppy.

Glen finished and leaned on the post there and fished his cigarettes and lighter from his pants pocket.

"Why don't you cut that TV off when you go to bed? Ain't nothin on that time of night anyway."

His daddy tossed the rest of the biscuit to the puppy, who had come from under the porch. He sniffed it, picked it up delicately, then trotted back out of sight wagging his tail.

"It's just company. I didn't even know you was here till I got up. What time did you get in?"

Glen came back down the porch with a cigarette in his mouth and stopped to stretch near the steps.

"I don't know. Twelve-thirty or one."

"You go see Jewel?"

"I went over there and fucked her."

Virgil got still and didn't move. He'd almost given up on trying to get along with Glen but never had given up on blaming himself for not unloading the gun that morning. He didn't know how one man could keep so much hate inside him. Especially his own boy, especially for his own father. Puppy was right. Going down there didn't do him any good.

"I don't see how you can talk about her like that. Like she ain't nothin."

Glen snorted. "What you gonna do about it, whip my ass? You got too old for that a long time ago."

It was getting hot already. The bright spots of a thousand drops of dew gleamed in the grass and with the sun risen the spans of new webs stretched down from the clothesline and over the rusted fence and the vines of morning glory threaded through the wire.

"I just think she deserves a little more consideration than what you give her."

"Consideration?"

"Yeah."

Glen hooked a ladder-back chair with his toe and slid it close enough to sit down. He crossed his legs.

"Okay, old man. Lay your wisdom on me. What do you consider I ought to do about her?"

"She's in the mess she's in cause of you."

"Ain't you a good one to talk about stuff like that? A man who never made a mistake. Seems like I talked to one of your mistakes yesterday."

Virgil half turned and leaned his shoulder against a post, then looked into the eyes that studied him with such contempt. A face so like his own mocking him.

"When I was sick last year she come by here and cleaned this house. Fed me too."

"I never asked her to do a thing for me. You neither."

"She brought that boy over here too."

"She better not bring him no more." Glen flicked his ashes idly on the porch and slumped in the chair and stretched his legs out. "I know what she wants. Same thing ever woman wants. Get married. I've done tried that and it don't work. Does it? You tell me."

Virgil stood up and hitched up his pants. He walked a couple of steps and caught hold of the door. "It's what most folks do. I didn't blame Melba when she left you. You the cause of that, too. Only good thing about it was you didn't have any kids. And I'm damn glad of it, too. Cause I don't know what the hell they'da eat for the last three years."

Virgil stepped inside and went to the stove and got the coffeepot and took off the lid. He was shaking. There was some mold on the grounds inside. He took out the strainer and knocked it against the garbage can and refilled the pot with water from a gallon wine jug that was sitting on the kitchen table. The coffee was in a blue can beside the sink and he fixed it all and clapped the lid over it and set it on the burner and lit it with a match.

"You ever feed this dog anything besides a biscuit?"

Virgil picked up a small bag of dog feed and pushed the screen door open. The puppy was walking around on the porch with his tongue hanging out. He poured some of the feed into a plate and the puppy started eating. They watched him. Occasionally he'd lift his head and crunch his breakfast loudly to let them know how it was going, look around, wag his tail.

"What's your plans?" Virgil said.

Glen flipped the cigarette butt out into the yard and stood up. He locked his fingers behind his head and stretched again.

"I don't know. I got to work on my car some more. I might see if I can get my job back."

"If you go to town sometime I wish you'd pick me up a contact switch for my pump. I can straight-wire it to run but I don't want to burn it up."

"I thought it run dry."

"It ain't run dry. They's thirty foot of water in it."

"That's what Puppy said."

"Puppy don't know shit about a well."

Glen opened the door and went into the kitchen with his father following him. The coffee was perking on the stove.

"Why don't you clean this place up?" Glen said. "Looks like a bunch of pigs lives here or somethin."

He looked through the cabinets for two clean cups and it took a while. Virgil picked up a dish towel and grabbed the pot and poured. Glen opened the refrigerator to see a hunk of dried cheese, some rancid bacon, a can of evaporated milk.

"I'll get around to it," Virgil said. He spooned sugar from a bag into his cup and tossed the spoon into the sink. Glen poured milk the viscosity of motor oil into his cup and looked at it.

"Damn," he said. "What do you do for food around here?"

"I got some chili and stuff in that cabinet. Puppy's good to bring stuff over. I can always walk down to the store."

"Where's your cane at?"

"It don't hurt every day. Just some days."

"Does it hurt today?"

"Naw."

They sat down at the table and lit cigarettes. The Redbone peered through the ragged screen door and then flopped down against it. It sagged in and out with his breathing. Glen looked above the door. The two bent horseshoes were still hanging there on their rusty nails. He blew on his coffee and stared at nothing.

"How's it feel to be out?" his daddy said.

"What do you care?"

"How'd they treat you?"

"Keep you in a pen about like a cow. Can't sleep. Always somebody yellin some crazy shit at night."

Virgil looked at the dog lying against the screen door. He seemed to sleep about twenty-three hours a day.

"How you like my dog?" he said.

"Looks like a shit-eater to me. Where'd you get that bag of bones?"

"He ain't no shit-eater," Virgil said. "That's a pure-blood registered Redbone. He's Purple Ribbon bred, by God. That there's a good dog."

Glen picked up his coffee and sipped on it and said, "Good for what? Run rabbits probly. He's pore as a damn snake."

"He just needs a good wormin. I'm gonna worm him soon as I get me some worm medicine. Clean him out good he'd gain some weight."

Glen shook his head and made a face at the puppy. The puppy stretched his legs out on the porch boards and yawned before he lowered his head.

"What do you want with a coon dog? You ain't no coon hunter."

"He's just company," Virgil said. He made a little motion with his cigarette. "Gets kinda quiet around here sometimes."

"Did you drink up the money for Mama's headstone?"

Virgil raised his eyes. "Who said I drank it up?"

"Nobody. But I know you."

Virgil turned away from him in the chair and watched the dog. This was no time to tell him about his mother. Not with him already starting in like this.

"You ain't even gonna say you sorry are you?"

Virgil didn't look up. He couldn't reason with him. Not when he got things in his head and kept them that way. It wasn't any use to try. He was worn down and he'd had a long rest but now his rest was over and he didn't know if he could take this all over again. Even Theron would have said enough by now. If he knew what he'd gone through. Did the dead see? Did they know? Did they take pity on what the living did? Did Emma?

He turned back around in the chair and got up.

"I'm gonna go up front and watch TV and lay down. I don't want to get into it with you. Whether you believe it or not I'm glad to see you."

He put his cup in the sink. The puppy raised his head and looked at him, then sat up and pulled a hind foot to his head and started scratching his ear. Virgil glanced at him and walked out of the kitchen and up the hall. He thought he'd watch a little of the church music on television. He didn't go to church except for funerals but he liked to turn it on on

Sunday mornings and not be completely heathen. The television had a tall wooden cabinet and a round screen about a foot in diameter. He turned it on and sat down on his chair right in front of it and waited for it to warm up. Saturday afternoons he got the Slim Rhodes show out of Memphis with Dusty Rhodes and Speck Rhodes. He liked to sit there and have a drink and listen to that before he went down to the VFW.

He heard Glen come into the room behind him but he didn't pay any attention to him. The picture was starting to come on and it was rolling. He got up and opened a panel in front and adjusted a knob until the picture settled down. Some choir was singing. He sat down. Glen sat down on the couch with his coffee.

"Your mama used to like this show," Virgil said.

Glen didn't say anything. Virgil wished he'd just stay in the kitchen if he was going to be hateful. The choir finished its number and the camera moved to the preacher. Virgil laced his fingers across his stomach and stretched his legs out.

"What you want to watch this crap for?" Glen said. "All that fucker wants is you to send him some money."

"I don't send him no money. I just watch him preach."

"Why don't you see if there's some cartoons on?"

"They don't show em on Sunday mornin."

"They used to."

"They don't no more."

"Turn it over on another channel."

"I want to watch this."

"I want to see if the goddamn cartoons is on."

Glen got up and moved toward the television and Virgil started to get up but then decided he'd just let him see for himself. Glen flipped the channels, bent over the set with a cigarette hanging from his mouth. More preaching. More preaching. Bugs Bunny.

FATHER AND SON

Glen settled back on the couch.

"Told you."

"This is my TV," Virgil said.

"This is Mama's TV."

"It's in my house."

"This ain't even your house. Uncle Lavester give you this house."

"It's mine, though."

"Yeah, till he dies and Catherine decides to boot your ass out. Then where you gonna stay?"

Glen turned his attention back to the set and Virgil watched him watching it. Then he got up and walked back to the bedroom.

His shoes were sitting beside a chair and he sat down to put them on. Glen was laughing up front. He wished he'd just go on and leave, let him alone. He tied his shoes and got up to comb his hair. There wasn't much black left now, just a streak here and there. It didn't take long to get old and he wondered where all the time got to. Like the war. It seemed so far back but still so close. It didn't seem possible for that much time to have passed and left him like this. All the stuff you were going to do tomorrow turned into today's stuff. You could screw around all your life and it looked like he had. Glen was right. He didn't even own the linoleum he was standing on.

The closet was still full of Emma's clothes and he pawed through the hangers on his side, looking for a clean shirt. He thought he'd just get out of the house for a while, maybe walk over to the store. His leg felt okay today and he liked to get out whenever he could. Sitting around the house got old.

He found a shirt that wasn't too dirty and he put it on and buttoned it up, tucked the shirttail inside. His money was on the dresser and he stuck it in his pocket. When he went back to the living room, Glen was still sitting there, watching a commercial.

"I'm gonna walk down to the store," Virgil said. "You gonna be here when I get back?"

"I don't know." Glen didn't look up, just sprawled there on the couch in his bare feet.

"Well. I'll see you sometime."

"Right."

He went on out the door and the Redbone came trotting around the corner of the house to meet him.

"C'mere," he told him. The puppy followed him over to a little tree by the end of the porch and Virgil bent to pick up a tattered dog collar that was wired to a piece of Emma's clothesline. He put the collar around the puppy's neck and snapped the clothesline into an eye hook he'd threaded into the tree and left him there. There was a pan of water with a few dead bugs floating on the surface and the shade of the porch was close enough for him to get in under it if he wanted to. He glanced up at the house. The television was still going and he could hear Glen laughing at the cartoons again. There wasn't any need in talking to him.

The heat seemed to turn up a few degrees as he walked the dirt road. Deep green ridges lay thickly wooded in the distance and cows stared at him from behind their fences as he went along. The cotton was tall everywhere in spite of the dry spell. Once in a while a vehicle passed him, folks dressed up and going to church in their pickups and rusty cars, rattling through the gravel and spreading a cloud of light brown dust that washed over him and went into his nose and settled over the ditches and roadside grasses. He was a man seen often walking at odd hours of the night or day and those passersby mostly ignored him as he did them.

On this fine day the pale clouds hung far and near in their slowly changing shapes, now flat and unbunched or colliding softly as the sun rose higher and gaining height, folding and refolding their masses to recombine in new banks that climbed the sky and built and drifted. He walked beneath the sky and on top of the land, a tiny figure moving like an ant.

He was sitting on a stump at the corner of a property line where a big sycamore shaded his cigarette-rolling when a '54 Chevy sedan came easing around the curve just above an idle. The car had originally been blue and white but now it sported a red front fender and a green hood. Above the grill a chrome-winged nymph leaned swimming into the wind. Virgil licked the length of his paper tube and stuck one end into his mouth as the car jerked to a halt beside him and died.

"Good God," he said. Woodrow was grinning behind the steering wheel. His teeth were splayed out in front but only two or three showed. Virgil crossed his legs on the stump and leaned one wrist on top of the other. "You out mighty early."

"I ain't been to bed yet. We went huntin last night and I just got in. I lost old Nimrod and I still got Naman in the backseat. Come on and get in, where you headed?"

"I'm just out for my daily exercise," Virgil said. He got up and stepped across the shallow ditch and walked around behind the car. In passing he looked in at what appeared to be an enormous dead Bluetick stretched out across the backseat, all four legs straight out, huge feet. He opened the door and got in the front seat and rolled the window down.

"Old Naman's plumb give out," Woodrow said. "He run a coon for three hours straight by the watch. He was still treein his ass off when I finally put the leash on him. Here, get you a drink."

He held up a half pint of whiskey. Virgil took the bottle and looked at it.

"It's awful early," he said. "But I reckon I will."

He twisted the cap off and turned a good drink down his throat. Woodrow cranked the car and pulled it down into low and they crept off.

He got up a little speed, shifted it into second, and left it there. Virgil took one more drink and then capped it and put it on the seat between them.

"You headed the wrong way, Woodrow. I was gonna walk over to the store."

"I'll run you by there. I'm just out lookin for old Nimrod."

"Where did y'all turn out?"

"Hell." Woodrow hung his arm out the window and pointed. "Five or six miles from here. I reckon he jumped a deer. He may be in Stone County by now for all I know. I just thought he might be out on the road somewhere. If I can find the son of a bitch I'm gonna sell him."

"I thought he was a good coon dog."

"He is when he runs a coon."

Virgil smoked his cigarette and flipped the ashes down the outside of the door. The car smelled like wet dogs and spilled whiskey.

"I saw your boys yesterday," Woodrow said. He had the habit of poking the black lens of his eyeglasses once in a while as if to see better. His hammer had tried to drive a nail that glanced off a sunny roof on a summer day. Virgil had seen that gray and vacant eye.

"You did? Where at?"

"They come in Winter's and stayed a little bit. I spoke to em. Is he glad to be out?"

Virgil scratched his leg. He drew on his cigarette and rested his elbow on the window frame.

"I can't tell if he is or not. He's over at the house when I left. I spect he's still pissed off at the whole world. He always was."

Woodrow steered the car carefully down the sandy road and through curves laned with thick timber, a lush canopy overhead that was a haven for squirrels and birds.

"Did you tell him about his mama?"

"Naw. I was going to but he started in on me about her not having a headstone. You can't talk to him when he gets like that."

"What's he gonna do about that youngun?"

"Probably nothin."

"Let me pull over up here and see if I can hear anything out of old Nimrod. He'll tree a squirrel in the daytime ever once in a while but he's probably asleep or headed back home by now."

Woodrow eased to a stop in the middle of the road and shut off the car. Virgil took the last drag from his smoke. He let it drop out the window and glanced over his shoulder at the hound on the backseat. There was only the rise and fall of his ribs to mark any life within him. The motor ticked and popped. Virgil leaned his head out the window and listened.

"You ever killed any squirrels with him?"

"A couple. He'll tree possums too. He'll run the livin shit out of a fox."

The woods were mostly still. There was a weak wind high in the very tops of the oaks and hickories. A crow called once in the distance. A tree frog sang. The sun dappled patterns of light and dark over the hood. There was the barely audible bark of a dog somewhere far off and muted in those wooded hills.

"Damn," Woodrow said, and leaned back in the seat from where he'd been cupping his ear to the world. He pointed toward the back of the car. "He's back over there on Miss Hattie's place, sounds like. Let me turn this thing around."

He started the car and drove up to the place where a grassy old logging road met the one they were on. He stopped there and turned around, going back the way they'd come, still moving at a crawl.

"I wish he'd just sit down and talk to me some," Virgil said. He looked at the whiskey on the seat and turned his head away from it. "I reckon he'd rather watch them damn cartoons."

A big doe bolted from the undergrowth and cleared the road in one bound, a long flow of bunched muscles sailing over in a gray flash. Woodrow had made to touch the brake but said Damn softly and kept going. They both looked after where the deer had penetrated the solid wall of leaves without a sign but for one single quaking frond.

"I wish I knew what to tell you," said Woodrow. The car rocked and swayed a little on its bad shocks as he sped up and shifted into third. "Maybe after he stays home for a while he'll appreciate it. You think it did him any good?"

"I doubt it."

The trees began thinning a little as they went on and in places it looked as if a bomb had been dropped except for the lack of any craters, the land open and catching full sun and dotted with stumps and shattered tree trunks, the tracks of dozers that like some gargantuan beast had devoured the shade. Then the woods closed around them again.

They drove into a deep hollow with a sharp curve and met a pickup right in the bottom of it. Woodrow steered carefully on the very edge of the road, gravel rattling against the underside of the car, rocks flying into the ditches. Virgil looked out and saw a six-foot pit alongside them. It was bone dry and coated with dust, littered with scrubby weeds and pebbles. Up on the banks the remnants of old fences hung on some of the trees. The road was washboarded in places and the car bucked hard when they ran over it, the windows jarring as if they would break in their frames. Virgil looked over his shoulder but it wasn't bothering the sleeping hound.

"How's your puppy?" Woodrow said.

"He's all right. I need to worm him sometime."

"I got some over at the house I can let you have. If we catch old Nimrod we'll take him and Naman back over to the house and put em up and feed em and I'll let you have some of it."

"I appreciate it, Woodrow."

"You in a hurry to get to the store? It ain't much further over here to Miss Hattie's place."

"I ain't in no hurry."

They came down out of the hills and rattled along a steep cut that had been graded with mule-drawn equipment back in the thirties and they leveled out in a small creek bottom where cotton was planted. Big patches of it stretched away to stands of trees and the sky opened before them boundless but for those trees, a deep blue where hawks feathered the thermal drifts or rode low over the fence rows or perched on posts holding lengths of barbed wire along the road. They went over a shallow branch by a shoddy bridge floored with timbers that rumbled loosely under the tires of the car.

"Ain't you glad you don't have to pick that cotton?" Woodrow said.

Virgil nodded, watching it, the sun warm on his arm where he rested it on the window frame.

"Yep," he said.

"Did Glen have to pick any?"

"He ain't said. I guess he had to do whatever they told him. Said he couldn't sleep at night for all the noise."

They were on a pretty good road now and Woodrow sped up a little, raising a dust cloud behind them. They went a long way across the bottom and Virgil pulled his makings out and rolled another smoke.

"You been up all night?" he said.

"I slept a little right before daylight. I had a fire built to keep the mosquitoes off me and I curled up next to it for a while."

They started slowing down just before the crossroads and Woodrow came nearly to a stop, glancing both ways before he turned to the right and went on along another short straightaway and climbed a hill. Virgil lit his smoke with the wind flaring the flame. At the top of the hill

Woodrow slowed the car, shifted down, and turned onto a side road past planted pines and a few old abandoned houses. They went across a wooden bridge and through a cattle gap and out into a pasture full of wildflowers that brushed at the sides of the car. He stopped near a line of sweet gums that bordered the creek.

"Let's see what we can hear now," he said.

Virgil sat with his legs crossed and listened. The wind was delicately wafting the heavy branches of the gums and the leaves shimmered a little, rested, then lifted in brilliance again. A cow bawled up near the barn and they could hear a tractor running somewhere. But no dogs barked.

"I'll be damn," Woodrow said. "I would have swore he was right in here somewhere. Let's get out and walk down here where we was last night."

They walked and walked, Woodrow cupping his hand around his mouth once in a while and hooting for the dog. It was pretty there along the creek and Virgil could see a distant herd of black cows resting under a clump of oaks in the middle of the pasture. They stopped after a bit and squatted on the ground. Woodrow called the dog but there was just the wind blowing to answer.

"Well damn," he said. "I hate to go off and leave him. I know that was him. Hell, he may be headed home by now."

"That's a pretty good walk."

"Main thing I'm scared of is somebody'll pick him up or he'll get run over by a car."

Virgil got up and walked over to the nearest tree and started taking a leak. He tried to read something carved into the tree but time had rendered it into a mottled scar in the bark. It took him a long time to finish and only when he was sure he was through did he tuck it back inside and zip his trousers. It always took longer now than it used to.

"You havin trouble with your prostrate gland again, Virgil?"

"Yeah. I reckon I need to go back to the doctor and let him stick his finger up my ass again."

He walked back over to Woodrow and Woodrow stood up.

"Ain't no need to wait around on him. If he ain't back by this afternoon I'll ride over here again and check on him. Come on and I'll run you by the store and then I guess I'll go home and get some sleep."

They turned around in the pasture and drove back up to the blacktop road and turned right. At the top of the next hill they passed the church and its yard full of cars and trucks. Virgil saw Jewel's car there parked under a big tree and a small pang of longing to see the boy went through him. Maybe before too much longer. There was still a good bit of water in the river. The catfish were hard to catch when it was this hot but he thought he knew where there might be some bream biting. If nothing else just an afternoon on the riverbank with the boy. The two of them together, he liked that, liked answering his questions except when they were about Glen. *Went over there and fucked her.* He kept looking out the window long after the church had gone past.

"What you shakin your head about Virgil?"

"Aw hell. Just that boy. I just feel real bad about him. He's a good little old boy."

"He loves to fish, don't he?"

"Yep."

They were back in the hills now and more houses appeared and there were mailboxes by the road and fenced yards and barns and field equipment in sheds, the post office, and finally the store. Woodrow pulled in and parked. The dog in the backseat raised his head, maybe thinking he was home. They got out and slammed the doors. Some folks were sitting around the storefront on crates and drink boxes, empty cotton poison cans.

"Let me get old Naman out," Woodrow said. "He may need to use the bathroom."

He opened the back door and found a leash on the floorboard and snapped the catch into a big ring on the dog's collar and let him out. The hound was large even for his breed. He leaned his hips back and opened his mouth and lowered the front half of his body and stretched in the sunshine.

"Come on, Naman."

Woodrow walked him around the side of the store and the dog raised his leg over the air compressor, looking around sleepily.

"That's a big dog," somebody said. Virgil turned to see who had spoken. The voice sounded familiar.

It was a boy about eighteen, barefooted with blue jeans and a T-shirt.

"Yeah, he is," Virgil said. He couldn't figure out who the boy was. "How's it goin?"

"Pretty good, Mr. Virgil, how you?"

The name still wouldn't come to him and then he remembered a smaller version of him in shorts, trying not to cry, a fishing lure hung in his hand.

"Tommy Babb," he said. "I like to not recognized you, boy. Where you been?"

The boy smiled then and leaned back against the wall. Virgil hadn't seen him in years and his short body was now packed with muscle. He used to see him on the river bridge fishing all the time, his bicycle leaning against the rail. He'd always wave to Virgil when he went by.

"I'm in the army now," he said. "I just come home on leave. How's old Puppy these days?"

Virgil wouldn't have thought the boy was old enough to be in the army. It didn't seem possible that this child could be a soldier.

"He's all right, I guess. Got three kids. He works for the county now."

Virgil stood there for a moment and then he bent over and pulled up a Coke case and sat down. "How long you been in the army?"

"About six months. I'm through with all my schools. They're gonna ship me out before long so I thought I'd come home for a while. See Daddy and them. You remember when you took that lure out of my hand?"

Virgil nodded. It was a day long ago. "That was pretty bad, wasn't it?"

"I thought it was. You remember how it was?" Tommy held up his hand to illustrate and Woodrow brought the hound back around to the front. "It was in this thumb and this first finger, had em stuck together. They was four of em in past the barb and you took some needle-nose pliers and cut the hooks off and pushed em on through."

"I remember," Virgil said. "You didn't shit in your britches, did you?"

Tommy grinned and an old man beside him smiled.

"I might near did."

"You want a Coke, Virgil?" Woodrow said. "I'm gonna take this dog on and go to bed, I guess, get up this evenin and go check on old Nimrod. See if I can find him before somebody runs over him."

Virgil scratched his jaw. "I'll get me one in a minute. I think I'm just gonna sit over here for a while."

"You don't want me to run you on home?"

"Naw. I can walk or catch a ride with somebody later on."

Woodrow was loading the dog back into the car and after he closed the door he paused beside it. "I'll run that wormer over one of these days before long. Let's go drink a beer sometime."

"All right. I'll see you, Woodrow. Thanks for the ride."

Woodrow got in his car and he cranked it up and left. The dog was standing in the backseat looking out the window. Virgil moved his Coke case in out of the sun and pulled out his makings, then stuck them back in his pocket and got up.

"I remember what I come over here for now," he said.

He put one foot on the low step and stopped for a moment.

73

"Y'all want a cold drink?"

"No thanks, Mr. Virgil."

"Not me, Virgil."

He went on inside and opened the door on the drink box and peered into the darkness and got a little green glass Coke and opened it on the box. He took a sip and looked at the vacant counter. There was a rack of cakes and bread midway down the floor and he walked over and stood looking at the things displayed there. Banana pies, oatmeal cookies, Moon Pies. He got a Moon Pie and a small bag of chips and carried his things over to the counter and put them all down.

"Hey Junior," he said. A door opened at the back and then a cloth curtain parted as a man came through on a pair of crutches. His left foot was bound in a thick cast and it went up nearly to his knee. It was coated with greasy handprints.

"Hey Virgil. Hold on, I'm slow today." He made his progress in a series of stops and starts, hitching himself along by degrees.

"I thought you'd have that thing off by now."

"Aw hell, the doctor said it needed to stay on another week and be sure that bone's healed."

When he got to the counter he took the crutches from under his arms and leaned them against the wall. He gripped the counter and eased himself onto the high stool behind the register.

"Whew," he said. "Althea went to church and left them younguns here and I can't hardly watch em by myself. What else for you, Virgil?"

"Let me have a pack of Camels."

He sipped his Coke while Junior reached high and propped himself with one arm for the cigarettes and then started punching buttons on the register.

"I heard Glen was back home," he said.

"Yeah. Puppy drove down and got him yesterday and they got in about dinnertime."

The storekeep was squinting through his glasses at each item as he rang it up.

"You gonna drink that Coke here, Virgil?"

"Yeah. Let me have a box of matches, too."

Junior tossed them on the counter and pecked at his machine with a bony forefinger. A little bell rang and the cash drawer slid open. He peered at the tape and leaned forward to hold it with his fingers, glancing at the items and nodding to the tape until apparently he was satisfied with what it said.

"Dollar and a half, Virgil."

Virgil handed him the money and put the cigarettes in his pocket. He picked up the chips and the Moon Pie and Junior gave him his change. The drawer rolled shut and Virgil heard a car go down the road, but it was headed toward the church. Junior scratched his ear and leaned on the counter.

"I sure hate it you've had such troubles, Virgil. I wouldn't wish it on a enemy."

Virgil didn't know what to say. He stood there uneasily sipping his Coke. Other people had said stuff like that to him and all it did was make him feel worse.

"I saw Jewel one day a while back," the storekeep said.

"Is that right?"

"Yeah. That's a cute little old boy she's got. Just cute as he can be."

Virgil just nodded. He looked out to the road.

"Yeah he is," he said. "Well. I'm gonna go out there and talk to these boys. I'll see you, Junior."

"You come back, Virgil."

"Yeah."

He stepped back outside. His face was burning just a little. He sat back down on the Coke case and stuck the cigarettes in his shirt pocket. The old man had gone. He was a veteran of the first world war and Virgil had heard him speak of the Argonne Forest and how the shells landed first to the west, then to the east, and that you had to run to either side once you knew the coordinates because the next one was coming right down the middle.

It was hot even in the shade. He didn't have a watch but he guessed it wasn't dinnertime. Nobody was leaving the church yet. There was an old store across the road that had been closed for a long time but he could remember it being open from the time he was a boy, long before he went to the war. The windows were boarded shut now, the planks on the front porch gapped and broken, the whole building leaning a little to the left. It looked like a good push would bring the whole thing down.

A car came down the road and slowed, pulled in. A door slammed. Mary Blanchard came around the back end of the car and stepped into the shade of the porch. She had on a dark blue dress. She was still a good-looking woman. She stopped when she saw him.

"Why hey, Virgil," she said.

He turned slightly and nodded at her. "Hey Mary. How you been?"

She pulled a little cigarette holder from the pocket of her dress and tapped one out of the pack, then looked back up at him.

"Pretty good, but I haven't seen you in a while. I heard Glen was home. How is he?"

Virgil didn't look at her much. He just glanced at her and reached for his Coke. "He's all right, I guess."

She lit the cigarette and he wondered if she'd sit down, but she didn't. She just kept standing there and looking at him. "Bobby said he saw him."

She leaned an elbow on top of one of the gas pumps. The Babb boy was watching something across the road. She drew on her cigarette and ran one hand distractedly through her hair. Virgil thought she looked better than ever.

"Is he gonna stay with you?"

"I don't know. He was over at the house a while ago. He went by his house yesterday I reckon and got his car. I don't look for him to stay with me, though."

She watched the boy sitting there and put one hand in her pocket. Another car came by. Virgil looked up at her again. "Has church let out?"

"Yeah." She glanced at her watch. "I just stopped to get some milk and some bread before I went home. They called and said Bobby wasn't coming for dinner. He doesn't hardly have time to sit down and eat sometimes. He stays so busy most of the time. Why don't you come eat with me? It'll just be me and you."

"Well. I don't know," he said.

"I got fried chicken. Chocolate pie."

He looked up at her and she was smiling at him. He knew she wouldn't have asked if anybody besides that boy had been sitting there. And he wanted to. But Bobby might come in. You never could tell about him. He was apt to show up most anywhere at any time.

"I appreciate it, Mary. I don't guess I better."

She didn't stop smiling. She dropped her smoke and stepped on it and touched him lightly on the shoulder as she came by, heading in.

"Well don't be a stranger. You hear?"

"Okay," he said. He could feel the boy watching him. He heard her steps on the floor inside, heard her talking to Junior.

"You caught any fish lately, Mr. Virgil?" The boy had turned back toward him.

"Not lately. It's been so hot. We need a rain."

"Yessir. I been over in Georgia. It's hot over there."

"How you like the army?" Virgil said. He opened the Moon Pie and took a bite of it.

"It's all right, I guess. It ain't bad now that I'm out of basic. You was in the army, wasn't you?"

"Yeah. World War II."

"Daddy said you were a prisoner of war."

He nodded and took a sip of his drink. Almost every day the ax came down and Lt. Roberts tried to catch his head when it went rolling away, like something that had happened yesterday or was still happening. How they'd yipped and squealed with delight at the pumping stream of blood and how the eyes in the head fixed and stared at the sun.

"Yes I was," he said. "They held me nearly three years."

"Where was that?"

He heard the register ring inside and wished he could just get in the car with her and go. It wasn't too late to say yes. But he didn't want to cause any talk about her. He didn't care what anybody said about him.

"That was in the Philippines," he said. "Forty-two. April, I think. We surrendered after three months. I was on Bataan Peninsula. Roosevelt sent MacArthur over to Australia and General King came in."

"I heard it was rough."

He looked at the boy's earnest and sober face. He couldn't tell him how it really was. There was too much of it, too many bad things that wouldn't go away even now.

"It was that," he said. "It ain't nothin to be proud of. I wish it hadn't happened."

"It wasn't your fault, though."

"Well. We was cut off. Food, ammunition. Lots of boys got malaria and there wasn't any medicine. A jungle's a bad place to have to live."

He picked up his Coke and leaned over and dropped the rest of the Moon Pie into the trash.

"That thing's kind of stale," he said. "You ain't headed into that mess overseas, are you?"

The boy rocked back on his seat and lowered his head. He nodded slowly and then looked up warily.

"Yessir. I reckon I am."

"When you got to leave?"

"Two more weeks. They sent me on home cause I'll be over there for a year."

Mary came out the door but she didn't stop. "Bye, Virgil. Hope I see you sometime."

"Bye."

He didn't watch her get into her car, but he watched it when it pulled off. She waved at him.

"I was sorry to hear about Miss Emma," the boy said.

Virgil stared at the bottle caps and the cigarette butts on the ground in front of him.

"I appreciate that," he said.

They got quiet. He didn't want to talk about Emma. He kept thinking that maybe Jewel would come by the store now that church was over. Once in a while a car came down the road but nobody stopped. He didn't much want to go back home if Glen was still there.

"How's your leg?" the boy said. "You used to have some trouble with it, didn't you?"

"It's okay most of the time. I have to use a cane once in a while but most days I can get around pretty good. I get out and walk regular, try to keep it in shape. You get old as me everything starts to kind of fall apart on you."

"You need a ride back home? I can give you a ride if you need one."

"I think I'm gonna sit around here for a while. I get tired of settin around the house."

He lit another cigarette and looked at the car. It was sitting behind the boy, a new Chevy, bright red, flashy hubcaps.

"That your car there?"

"Yeah. How you like it?" The boy turned around and faced the car. "I just got it. I'm gonna leave it here for Mama to drive and it probably won't have too many miles on it by the time I get back."

"Is it a new one?"

"Yeah. I mean yessir. They changed the body style. It's got a 327 in it and it'll shit and git. You want to take a ride?"

The boy was already off his seat and putting his empty bottle in the rack.

"Where you gonna ride to?"

"I don't care. Up the road and back. Come on and go with me."

"Well. I ain't rode in a new car in a while."

Virgil put his bottle away too and opened the little bag of chips as they walked out to the car.

"Hop in."

Virgil got in. It had bucket seats and a shifter on the floor and the letters SS emblazoned on the steering wheel. The boy got in with the keys and cranked it up. It rumbled gently when he tapped the gas with his foot.

"This is a nice car," Virgil said.

"Thank you. I've done waxed it twice. She'll do nearly ninety through a quarter."

"Quarter?"

"Quarter mile. She'll lay a strip of rubber from here to the curve yonder. Daddy's scared to set down in it it's so fast."

"Well don't get it up too fast with me in here. How fast will it go?"

The boy eased out on the clutch and they swung out. He pressed the gas and Virgil was pulled back in the seat a little.

"I don't know," the boy said. He popped second and a rear tire barked. "I ain't had it up as fast as it'll go yet. I been tryin to break it in easy, except I run a few people. Ain't nobody beat me yet."

He went up into third gently and they went around the curve beyond the store and out past the cotton gin and up the road toward Paris. The blacktop road was patched and cracked and low grass stood up along both sides of it. The boy dropped the car into high gear and the wind rushed in through the windows.

"She's nice," Virgil said.

"I saved my money the whole six months. Didn't go out much, just stayed in and shined my shoes." He grinned. "I got some cold beer in the cooler if you want one. You want one?"

"I might drink one if you got plenty."

"I got plenty. I bought some the other night over at Barlow's. You ever been over there?"

Virgil reached for a cigarette and pulled his matches out as the car slowed. The boy took a lot of pleasure in shifting the gears. He tromped on it a little and then started edging toward the side of the road.

"I used to go over there some," Virgil said. "I ain't been over there in a while now. He still got that monkey?"

"Yessir. He was settin right there on the bar the other night. I've heard that thing would bite you if he don't like your looks. He didn't pay no attention to me, though."

He stopped the car in the grass and shut off the motor. He pulled the keys out and said, "I'll be right back."

Virgil lit his cigarette and looked at the woods lining the road. He'd squirrel-hunted all through here when he was a boy. He had a mule he used to ride over here. He'd tie him to a tree and find his way back to him at dark and ride him home with the stars shining. This road was nothing but a wagon trail then. Cars would get mired on it and mules would have to pull them out. That was when he first met Mary. He still remembered how she looked then, how she'd wear a ribbon in her hair when she came to meet him under an old oak that had been gone for many years now. The trunk lid went up, then it slammed, and the boy came back around with two beers in his hands. He got in and handed one to Virgil.

"It's cold," he said. "I hope you like Pabst."

"This is fine, thanks. You got an opener?"

"Yessir. He give me three I believe."

He found one in the glove box and opened the cans. Virgil took a sip and it tasted cold as ice.

"Damn," he said. "That's pretty good."

A car came by that looked like Jewel's. He looked down the road where it had gone and thought about the things Glen had said. But it was out of his hands. Never had been in them.

"Yep," the boy said, and cranked the car. "You want to ride around awhile? You got time?"

"Sure," Virgil said. "I got plenty of time."

The boy grinned, gunned the motor, and they swung out into the road. Virgil couldn't help but smile, watching him.

Clancy's old pickup climbed the dusty hill through stunted pines and snarled growths of honeysuckle and briars, bumping along in low gear over the rough spots and whining past the dump where Rufus threw their garbage to keep from hauling it off somewhere. Clancy had already raised his own children and they were scattered now to Chicago, Flint, West Texas, and Tampa. His pickup had some wire chicken cages in the back end that were rattling around and he'd thrown some milk crates back there for Lucinda's children to ride on to church. His shoes were shined and he had on his tie and a starched white shirt, a snap-brim hat he'd paid eighteen dollars for in Memphis. The crease is his trousers was sharp and defined. He'd dusted off the seat and slid the jumble of tools to one corner on the floor before he left his house and he wasn't early, so he couldn't figure why Lucinda would be sitting on the front porch the way she was in her robe instead of being dressed for church. He pulled up in the yard with the chickens scattering and clucking and the dog barking in the dust. He switched the key off. The door didn't have a handle on the inside, nothing but an open panel that revealed the simple mechanism of the window and the sheet of glass itself that rested within it. He reached out for the door handle and pushed it down. The dog came up waving his tail as he got out. Clancy was a patient man but he was getting close to sixty, and the first emotion he felt was a quick nagging one of aggravation that they weren't ready. He put out one hand to keep the dog from jumping on him as he stepped over the tree roots and the chicken shit and the pine needles that formed the yard.

"I thought y'all gone be ready," he said, and then he took a good look at his sister's face. She was wringing a grimy piece of tissue between her hands and swaying a little, back and forth, and she wouldn't look at him. She'd been crying and she was crying still. The screen door pushed open a crack and a small face peered out.

"Shut that door, Queenola," she said, and the small face withdrew. Inside a shriek of laughter that didn't sound quite right, rising boys' voices, rapid running steps. Clancy stopped on the first step, leaned over, and grabbed a post and eased himself up on the porch.

"What's wrong now," he said.

She slowly turned her face to him. "He ain't come home."

Clancy lowered himself into a chair and sat gingerly, leaning forward. He took his hat off and with a handkerchief he pulled from its safe-keeping inside mopped at his face. He sat there holding the hat and the handkerchief.

"Huh," he said. "Where then reckon is he?"

"I know where he's at. He still down yonder."

She tipped her head toward the wall of pines that rimmed the north side of the house. The noise of the children inside dropped to silence and he looked through the screen door to see them grouped in a dim huddle, listening.

"Well," he said. "What you want me to do?"

"Go down there and see. I'll send Derek down to the road."

He sat there and looked out across the yard. He put his handkerchief back inside his hat and put his hat back on.

"Well," he said. "I don't reckon we goin to church."

84

He raised himself from the chair, leaned forward for the post, eased down the steps. For a moment he stood in the yard and looked at her. He remembered the night she was born by the light of a coal-oil lamp in a blood-soaked bed where his mother screamed curses down on the house and damned his daddy for ever putting it in her. Then he went to the truck and got in. The chickens scattered again, feathers fluttering and settling in the little dusty clouds they stirred.

Clancy had never been to Barlow's but he knew where it was. His drinking days were long over, his people had their own places anyway, up in the forests and back roads of Stone County, little roadhouses where the Kimbroughs and the Burnsides played their guitars on the weekends and rocked the old buildings until dawn.

He turned in at the sign, having made a short but bumpy journey around the base of the ridge that Rufus and his family lived on, traveling the main highway briefly and rocking along with cars passing at what were reckless speeds to him. These young people driving so fast scared him. The road to the joint was littered with beer cartons and trash, the sides high with weeds. There was a curve in the road and he slowly rounded it and saw the place sitting there in a grove of pines, a highly polished black car pulled around to one side. He slowed and shifted down. He felt bad already, had begun to know something inside himself like grief. It just felt like trouble. His old truck ground to a halt and he sat there looking everything over before he killed the engine. Now that he was here he didn't know what to do. In the yard it was quiet but on the highway behind the joint the cars were flying by, trucks with their heavy loads whining. He got the door open and stepped down from the truck, holding on to the door frame and slipping off the seat to stand in the heat still watching. He heard a murderous low growl that reached cold fingers into his heart and found a big snarling hound crouched

within thirty feet of him, its tail tucked and all the hair on its back standing up. As he watched, another one joined it and they began to stalk
toward him like lions, with their unwavering eyes fixed firmly on his.

"Lord have mercy," he said, and turned, trying to get back in the truck
and almost falling, but he made a lunge and got in and pulled the door
shut. He kept a pair of pliers on the dash to roll up the window but the
spline gear of the window mechanism was worn from just that type of
use and it slipped first in his hands and then under the pliers as he
worked feverishly at it, the dogs up against the truck now, acting crazy
and growling. He got it up halfway and then leaned across the seat and
rolled the other window all the way up. It sounded like the dogs were
circling the truck, making ragged sounds of wet rumbling in their
throats. He'd never seen dogs act so. He'd been bitten by white men's dogs
and white men had been bitten by his, but he had never questioned it
and even understood it. But there was something wrong with these two
besides the fact that he was black. These two were ready to kill somebody.
Anybody.

Maybe if he were younger, or maybe if he were younger and had a
club. But two at once. He'd never seen rabies but he didn't think it was
that.

One of the hounds reared suddenly against the window and Clancy
was faced with its terrible white fangs and maddened eyes and the drool
it slobbered on the glass as it snarled and glared at him. He pulled back
from it. He didn't think it could get in. It stayed there for a while and it
began to whine a little, licking at the glass. After a bit it dropped back to
the ground.

Clancy hauled out his pocketwatch and looked at it. Church was going
to start in twenty minutes but that didn't matter now. He felt kind of
embarrassed. More than anything he wanted to see Rufus walk out that
front door that was standing so wide open and if he was drunk it would

be all right, he'd take him on home and put him to bed. He'd done stuff like this himself a long time ago and a young man was entitled to some mistakes. Just as long as everything was all right. But the reason Rufus wasn't going to walk out that door was the reason the dogs were acting the way they were. He wondered if maybe he should just crank his pickup and turn it around and drive out of here, go over to Mr. Wylie's store and use the phone to call the sheriff. And what would the sheriff do? Come over here and shoot these dogs? Or would he just hear an old fool babbling about some dogs keeping him in his truck at a white man's beer joint and making him late for church and hang up on him? But it was simple, really: he couldn't leave and he couldn't get out. He had to do something. If something was wrong with Rufus, he had to do something. Rufus wasn't home so something was wrong with Rufus. The simplicity and the puzzlement of it played around and around in his head but he couldn't figure what move to make. The main thing was to see about Rufus without letting the dogs take him down, because if they did . . . What was wrong with them dogs?

He couldn't even hear them now. He knew they had to be lying in front of the truck. Just waiting. He couldn't get out and he couldn't leave. If that log wasn't lying in front of the truck, he could turn the truck sideways somehow and get up close to the porch, maybe get in that way, make a jump for the door . . . but the log was in the way. And the window was blown out.

Old fool, he told himself. Rufus in there and you got to do something. That window blowed out the way it was, Rufus probably dead in there. Do something, but what?

There was that jumble of things on the floorboard of the truck: a tattered pair of leather gloves, some braided wire, a claw hammer with one broken claw, loose nuts and bolts, a sack of fence staples. He didn't see anything for a weapon but the hammer, and if they both came at him again, same time . . . it was pitiful to be old and still  scared. But Clancy had been scared just about all his life. The white man. The uncrossable lines of things you could do and things you couldn't. The water fountains and the bathrooms and the places to eat. He'd been born in 1906 and the old men from the old war still sat around the stores and talked when he was a boy. He'd seen hangings, the corpses of men burned alive. One of his uncles had been run down and caught by a bunch of white men because a white woman said he hadn't tipped his hat to her on his mule. He'd never seen that uncle again and he'd been scared of things like that all his life and now just when it looked like things might be going to change, now when the president himself had helped get that colored boy into school over there at Oxford, here he was faced with this. Two dogs belonging to a white man. It didn't seem right. And he didn't have anything against the dogs. It wasn't their fault that they were owned by a white man who owned a place he had to get into. They were just living on the place. They were just in their dogs' way looking after what was theirs and they were scared because of something that happened and he hated to have to do it but he needed to get out of the truck and go in there. He couldn't leave. And he couldn't get out if they were going to take him down.

It wasn't that hard, really, not as hard as he'd thought it might be. He put the gloves on and took the pliers and twisted a short noose from one end of the wire so that he could make a sort of slipknot and when the dogs came snarling and snapping to the window he slipped the noose around their necks one at a time and hauled them strangling and screaming to the one-eared claw hammer and delivered the killing blows, blood running from their ears and their limp bodies underfoot when he stepped from the truck to see at last whatever in the world had happened to his brother-in-law.

. . .

Later in the day there were people standing in the yard wanting to buy beer, the ones who had come early, before the law blocked the road off, parked in their cars and pickups with cane poles sticking out the back ends of trucks and out the windows of cars with all the gear of fishermen, tackle boxes, minnow buckets, coolers, and chain stringers. There were two hearses since there were two funeral homes involved, one in the county and one in Pine Springs, shiny old Cadillacs with twelve-ply tires and white satin curtains and gleaming dusty hoods. The dogs were there in their dried blood like sleepers, flies clambering over them and busily depositing their larvae, a quick hatch coming in this weather. There was one minor altercation between a deputy and two drunks who became irate when they found they couldn't buy any beer today. They were told to either be nice or leave and one did leave but was arrested for drunk driving before he ever made it back to the highway. The other one said something witty to the deputy and was clapped quickly in irons and taken to a patrol car and, when nobody was looking, rapped professionally upside his head with a heavy slapstick and rendered meek as a lamb on the stifling backseat of the cruiser. Smart motherfucker should have keep his mouth shut.

There was much speculation among the spectators, it was a robbery, it was a crime of passion or a crime of drink, the dogs had been killed first, the dogs had been killed last. They could see the window shot out so most figured it was a shootout.

The sun rose higher and those onlookers with enough sense to stay out of the way moved back into the shade of the loblollies to view the proceedings from the relative cool of that vantage point, where they were comfortable with their cigarettes and the occasional snuck slurp of a saved-over beer retrieved from the melting ice of their coolers.

The deputies moved in and out of the building with bags of equipment and cameras and wheeled gurneys and as they worked their militarily pressed tan wool shirts sported dark wet circles beneath their armpits and across the center of their backs. The sheriff stayed inside.

When the investigation was complete, when the photographs had all been taken and the shotgun shells gathered and all the evidence dusted for fingerprints, there was a general huddle of licensed officials near the front door and the first body was brought out. It was wrapped in white sheets like a body prepared for burial at sea and they did tilt it slightly bringing it off the porch into the full glare of the sun so that the large patches of blood were very bright and wet with a kind of patina showing as they carried it across the yard to the opened door of one of the waiting hearses. The spectators noted that that one went to the white funeral home. All hands returned to the bar. They stayed inside so long it was openly speculated that the law might be having a cold one themselves.

The second body was brought out much like the first with the exception that all the bloodstains were concentrated on what was left of the head. The black embalmers received this one in their hearse. For a while the deputies stood around. Then they went back in.

The last victim was not brought out on a gurney. He was carried in a cardboard box that had formerly housed twelve fifths of Austin Nichols Wild Turkey, 101 proof. This small and hairy primate was placed on the backseat of the sheriff's car and the driver of that vehicle finally emerged dressed in a white sport coat with a brown fedora, leading an aged black man in handcuffs by the cloth of his sleeve. He was placed in the backseat and the doors closed upon him.

The procession pulled out, lights winking, radios squawking, and it wended its way out of the yard and around the curve and up the road toward the highway, toward the distant whine of the trucks on the bridge that spanned the Potlockney River, the final destination of the little tailless gnome that lay stiff on the floorboard of the sheriff's car, and that could not speak for the innocent either.

It was still hot in the kitchen and Jewel put the dinner dishes in the sink to wash later. She hadn't slept well after Glen left and four o'clock in the morning found her at the stove in her robe, frying chicken. What remained of it was lying on a plate now over a cold burner. She set a few glasses in the soapy water and looked out the window to check again on David. He was in the swing that Virgil had hung for him and his cat was sitting there as usual, watching him. She ran some more hot water over the dishes and filled her glass with iced tea again. Sometimes there was a breeze out on the back porch and she thought she'd go sit there for a while. She needed to talk to Glen and she needed to talk to him soon.

There was a little clump of trees in the backyard near the fence, an old picnic table back there, a mildewed hammock hung from two of the trees. The yard was small and neat with flowers and a vegetable garden, tomatoes, some corn, a few clean rows of purple hull peas. She chopped the grass on weekends in her swimming suit, barefooted, dust coating her red toenails.

She sat down in a rocker that had been her mother's. Some sweat had beaded at her temples and she mopped at it with the back of her hand and eased back into the chair, rocking a little, watching her son.

"You want some Kool-Aid?" she said.

"No ma'am," he called, and kept swinging.

She thought about all those people watching yesterday, knowing about Glen, knowing about David. She hated that she'd cried.

She had on a pair of short shorts and she raised her feet and propped them on a post, pushing herself back and forth slowly with her toes. A breeze blew gently, cooling her.

"You have to take your nap after while," she said.

"I know it." He was like a metronome, never varying his speed, endlessly rising and falling, in and out of the shade.

She sat there in the breeze, listening for traffic on the road. Once in a while a car would come by and then wind out of hearing. After he played in the yard with the cat following him she told him that if he'd go on and take his nap she'd fill the little plastic pool for him and he could play in it when he got up. He was an obedient child and he went without arguing, inside the house through the screen door. She heard him pull a chair up to the sink and fill a glass with water and she could see him in her mind, standing there on the chair, drinking it, silent, his hair plastered down on the back of his neck. Ten minutes later she checked on him and he was curled up on the bed, the fuzzy tiger beside him, the breeze blowing the curtains out. She went back to the porch.

She kept on rocking, looking at her watch every few minutes. After a while she went into her bedroom and pulled her clothes off slowly and put on the swimming suit.

The hoe was hanging from a tree limb and she got it down and went into the garden, chopping at the grass that was coming up around the corn, turning the dry dirt over and wishing it would rain. She hoed for thirty minutes and then went inside and pulled the suit off and knelt naked by the tub, drawing it full of warm water and then stretching out with her toes sticking out over the front of the tub and her head propped on the rim, her hair hanging down outside it. Thinking about last night. She didn't get to say any of the things she'd meant to. It all happened so fast and then he was gone. He'd barely looked at David. He didn't even say when he'd be back or if he would be. She didn't know what to do now. It looked like nothing had changed except that he was home again. Things couldn't keep going the way they were. She drew a deep breath and sighed. She stared at the tile on the wall. A car slowed on the road, pulled in, stopped. She got up and grabbed a towel as she looked out the window but it wasn't Glen. It was Bobby.

She shut the bathroom door and dried herself rapidly, stepping into her panties and shorts and fastening the top half of the swimming suit around her. When she heard his boots on the porch she reached for the doorknob and slipped on the wet floor, just barely catching herself on the knob and the edge of the sink.

"Shit," she said. She'd jammed her toe into the bottom of the door. He was knocking. She hobbled out through the living room, limping past the toys that were scattered on the rug. He was standing back a little from the door and he'd taken his hat off. He still had his uniform on.

With one finger to her lips she pushed open the screen door and let him in.

"David's asleep. Let's go out on the back porch."

"What'd you do to your foot?" he said, following her, his heavy frame making a loose board creak.

"I slipped down in the bathroom. I was in the tub when you pulled up."

She saw him glance at the chicken on the stove as he was coming through.

"Have you had anything to eat?"

"Naw, but don't worry about me. I'll go over to the house after while."

She pushed him out the door and told him to sit down and she'd fix him a plate.

"Don't fix me nothin to eat. I just stopped by."

"Go on and sit down. You want tea or milk?"

"Milk."

She got a plate from the safe and put three pieces of chicken on it. There was potato salad in the Frigidaire and she scooped a round clump of it and put it next to the chicken. Plump red tomatoes were on the windowsill and she peeled one over the garbage can with her little paring knife. Three thick red slices slid onto the plate from her dripping fingers. She poured a big glass of milk and salted the tomatoes lightly, then got him a fork and a cloth napkin and pushed the door open with her hip. He was sitting in the rocker next to hers, smoking a cigarette and watching her with his calm brown eyes. He stubbed the fire from his cigarette on the post and dropped the dead butt in his shirt pocket.

"We ate all the rolls," she said. "I can get you a piece of loaf bread." She bent over and set the plate in his lap and saw him trying not to look at her breasts and that made her smile a little smile.

"This is fine," he said, reddening a bit. "You didn't have to go to all this trouble."

She handed him the milk and slid the other rocker back a bit and went inside for her cigarettes. When she came out he was chewing a mouthful of chicken and cutting the tomatoes with his fork.

She sat down with her knees together, holding her elbows with opposite hands and leaning forward to watch him eat.

"You go to church?" he said.

"Yeah. I saw your mama. She said you never did come home last night. You have some trouble?"

He nodded with a full mouth, looking out across the yard while he chewed. He reached for the milk and took a big drink and mopped at his forehead with the back of his hand.

"Yeah. I wish I'd been in church stead of where I was." He held the plate balanced on his knees and forked up some of the potato salad.

"Was it bad?"

"Bad enough. Sure is some good chicken."

She leaned back in her chair and lit one of her cigarettes. She pulled her feet up underneath her.

"Don't you get tired of it?"

He leaned back too. He was still sweating. The radio said something in the car out front, some man talking in static.

"Is that for you?"

"Naw. I checked out for a while." He paused. "Of course I get tired of it."

"That sure was bad about that little boy that drowned."

"It's been a bad weekend all around," he said.

The bones were piling up on his plate and she stepped inside for the milk carton and came back out with it to pour him another glass. He nodded his thanks and kept on eating. She went back in and put the milk up. He'd just about cleaned his plate when she came back out and she stood waiting for him to finish. When he did she took the plate and the napkin and carried them inside.

He'd stretched his legs out and was smoking another cigarette when she sat down beside him again. She hugged her knees and watched him.

"I didn't know whether to come by," he said. "I saw him yesterday." He wouldn't look at her much. She raised her head and put her chin on her knee and watched the breeze in the trees.

"I guess he's been over," he said finally.

"You knew he would be."

She looked at him and saw what that had done to him. She almost got up and went to him, but the look on his face stopped her. He drew on his cigarette and picked up his hat. "Well? What did he say?"

"Not much."

"Did you think he would?"

"All I know is I told him I'd wait for him three years ago. And I waited."

He seemed to be gathering himself for something. His whole body was braced in the chair and somehow she could see him pulling up strength from deep inside himself in the way he looked at her, like a dog that had been whipped but still refused to yield. His eyes were shining and he spoke softly.

"I can give you and David a good life. I didn't drive by here last night. I wanted to. I figured I owed you one chance to get things settled with him. But I can't . . . I won't live like this."

He put his hat on and then he stood up. She still had her chin on her knees when he bent over to kiss her cheek. She turned her lips to him too late and he didn't wait. He went down the steps and stopped for just a moment there in the yard between the little pecan trees they'd planted that spring. A car went down the road slowly out front. She listened but he didn't.

"I enjoyed my dinner. You can call me when you make up your mind."

Then he went across the yard and around the corner of the house. There was a tiny noise behind her and she looked around still sitting in the chair. David was standing inside the kitchen watching her through the screen door. He wanted to know if that was his daddy and she told him it wasn't.

There was a scanner hung beneath the radio in his cruiser and he was getting some traffic from the highway patrol and some more from another county, he thought maybe Stone. He hadn't been listening that close and he couldn't tell what they had going on. He didn't really care either. There was plenty for him to worry about in his own county and it seemed like it got worse all the time. Always somebody fucking up. He knew he needed a vacation but he didn't know when he'd ever get the time to take one.

It was still hot and he had all the windows down and his hat was on the seat again. It would have been nice to stay over at Jewel's for a while. Sit there and talk. He guessed he should have just kept his mouth shut. But he couldn't stand not knowing.

There was probably a crowd of people up at Dorris Baker's house but he thought he ought to swing by there, just let them know he was thinking about them. There were some bad days ahead. He picked up the radio mike and told Harold where he was going. Harold said that was a ten-four and the radio was silent again. The scanner kept chattering. There was a bad wreck on 30 East about four miles out of New Albany. They were calling for an ambulance and a wrecker. He turned the volume down on the scanner and lit another cigarette.

It wasn't like the could just run him off. Keep some more things from happening. There wasn't any doubt in his mind that Ed Hall was going to try something sometime. Maybe he needed to go and have a little talk with him, too. Some people you couldn't tell about. Ed went to church and coached Little League and all that good shit, but that didn't mean he might not load up his 30-30 one day and go find Glen and stick the muzzle in his ear. It wouldn't bring his little boy back but it would probably make him feel a hell of a lot better, at least until they sent him to the same place Glen had just come out of.

He turned up County Lake Road. He got up pretty close to the house and started seeing vehicles pulled over next to the ditches.

"Boy boy," he muttered, guiding the cruiser carefully between the cars. They'd damn near blocked the road. He never knew what to say at these things. Stuff like this where nobody was really to blame for it. Nobody to punish for it. Nobody really guilty of anything except maybe carelessness, or just being young.

He eased past the house to see a throng of people in the yard. There was an empty space at the end of the driveway as if they'd left it just for him and he swung in and parked. He shut the car off and got out and put his hat on. Folks nodded and spoke as he walked up.

"Hey Bobby."

"How you doing, Sheriff?"

He shook a few hands, being quiet and respectful, lifting a hand to wave at faces here and there. They parted for him and he went up the wide brick steps past the potted flowers onto the porch. It was crowded, people gathered still in their church clothes and kids not playing but sitting mutely on the porch boards with their feet hanging above the flower beds, behaving like they'd been told to. He took his hat off and pulled open the screen door and stepped inside the living room. People in chairs eating, a low murmur of conversation. He could see the women gathered in the kitchen and he headed back there quietly, speaking soft hellos as faces turned toward him. He was caught by the arm at the opened French doors and arrested by the seamed face of Miss Lula, who was already old when she taught him in the eighth grade.

"Why don't you set down and let me fix you a plate, Bobby?" She had already begun steering him toward a chair but he just stood still and bent over to her.

"I've already eaten, thanks. I wanted to speak to Dorris and Sue just a minute. Are they here?"

Miss Lula was a small thing in a black lace dress. Her hair was a pale blue with little whorls of coiled webs sprayed and tightly packed.

"Sue's laying down in the bedroom but Dorris is down at the barn. You want me to get her up?"

He glanced at the people watching him. There was food on every available surface in the kitchen, table and countertop laden with fried chicken and deviled eggs, sliced hams and casseroles, pies, cakes, dishes of vegetables and sweet potatoes.

"No ma'am," he said. "Don't get her up. I'll go out and see Dorris. Do you know if they need anything?"

She gazed around and shook her head as if she were lost in all this and then looked up at him. "Do you know I've taught just about everbody in this house?"

"I don't doubt that, Miss Lula." He smiled down at her. She still had her hand on his arm.

"When you gonna find you a nice girl and get married? You can't live with your mama your whole life."

"I'm workin on it," he said, already turning his attention away from her. "I'm gonna ease on out here. I'll see you, Miss Lula."

"He's took it hard, Bobby."

"I know he has."

He moved away from her and began to try and make his way through the kitchen to the back door, people jostling a little and shifting to allow his passage and all of them eating, forks moving toward mouths and fingers holding rolls and pickles. He knew this was just the preliminary. The actual funeral would be much worse.

"Hello, Bobby."

"Hey. Scuse me, ma'am."

They'd all have to watch and listen to the screaming and the wailing and the gnashing of teeth. Then they'd all come over here and eat again and trickle out one by one leaving the clean dishes stacked on the tables with their names written on tape beneath them and the leftover food crammed into the refrigerator. The dogs would eat good for a few days. All these people would bind together for a number of hours or days in the way that only great tragedy wrought. And then their lives would have to go on and the loss would diminish for all those except the ones who lived in this house. They would wake to it every day, sleep by it every night. It would infiltrate their meals and their lovemaking and their trips to take out the garbage. The slightest thing would remind them of it. It might grow gradually dimmer with a great passage of time but it would never fully leave or be closed out like the shutting of a door. That's what he hated about it. He didn't blame them for eating, but he wouldn't have even if Jewel hadn't fed him.

He breathed an open sigh when he stepped out on the back porch. He nodded to some wide-eyed boys who viewed him with mute admiration, their mouths slack with awe.

"How you boys?"

Dorris had his tractors and his combine and his two cotton-pickers parked under the big shed he'd built three years ago and Bobby could see the fields of cotton stretching away behind the house, a vast acreage of green that lay shimmering in the heat. A group of men were sitting in some lawn chairs in the shade beside a cotton trailer. He walked across the yard toward them and a man standing a little apart from the group came out from under the shed to meet him. He could see that Dorris was shaking his head and crying before he got to him and he felt like crying himself because it was so unfair. He reached his hand out.

"God, Bobby," Dorris said.

They didn't hug but they shook hands hard. Dorris had been in the boat when Bobby hooked the boy's leg with the gambrel. Standing in that muddy water and feeling that cold slick limb come into his hand. Having to raise his face and look at Dorris in the boat.

They dropped their hands and watched each other. Bobby asked him how he was doing.

"Not worth a shit. I thought I could take it better than this but I can't. Come on out here and get you a chair."

Birds were moving in the branches of the trees. From inside the house came the steady babble of voices. They walked side by side to the end of the yard and across a patch of gravel that was stained with oil or grease and sunlit. Broken gaskets and flattened cans.

"I had to get out of the house for a while," Dorris said. "All them people. You know. I mean they mean well. They've brought a ton of food."

"I saw it. Have you made arrangements yet?"

"We picked out the casket this mornin. He's out at the funeral home tonight and the funeral's at two tomorrow."

Bobby nodded but he couldn't think of much to say. He knew all the people sitting out there: Sammy Brewer, Carlton Thomas, Lewis Foster, and there looking up at him with something like personal insult on his face was Ed Hall. It made sense that he would be here since he had something in common with Dorris now. Bobby spoke to them all and they all said hello or nodded except Ed. They were sitting at the edge of the shade among drums of oil and sacks of seed and fertilizer, weather-browned men who with their hats off showed a white line of demarcation above their foreheads where the sun never touched them. Farmers, carpenters who never took their shirts off if they were outside.

"We was just talking," Dorris said. "About that old pond. I never had fished in it but Lewis said he had."

Lewis leaned forward enthusiastically to tell his fish story in a high and rapid voice.

"I caught a bass out there one day weighed eight pounds," he said. "Caught him on a weedless worm and the son of a bitch fought like a motherfucker. Caught him over there on the back side right next to an old log that was in there."

"I didn't know they was goin," Dorris said. "I wished I'd knowed they was goin."

Bobby looked at the toes of his boots and said to himself, But you wouldn't have done anything different, Dorris, you would have stayed on your tractor or worked on a fence or whatever you were doing. They were just going fishing.

"Course I don't blame myself for it," he went on. "He'd told me he could swim a little. Said he was gettin pretty good. I was gonna take off one Saturday and me and him go. Course I always stay so busy. I'm always so busy," he said.

Yeah, and hindsight, and what if? You could do that forever and drive yourself crazy with it when the simple truth was that they had been fishing, and his boy had suddenly stood up on the transom of the boat and told the other two to watch him cut a back flip. He had gone into the water and he never had come up. Bobby thought he might have hit a log down there. It was full of logs, always had been, and in truth there had been a swelling low on the base of the skull. It was his right as the sheriff to order an autopsy, but with the body lying under a tarpaulin on the bank with a small crowd of the grieving already gathered, Dorris had led him a few steps away and whispered fiercely into his ear that he couldn't stand to think about them cutting him apart, that he was dead and nothing was going to change that, and please don't let them do that to his baby, Bobby, not the one who fed the bottle calf Omar Junior and whose rabbits housed in hutches he could almost reach out and touch from where he was standing now in the shade of the shed.

They stood or sat in silence for a moment. Dorris leaned up against his cotton-picker. He was massaging his left hand with his right. Bobby could feel Ed watching him and he knew why.

"How you doing, Ed?"

Ed wasn't doing okay. He was braced in his chair and a tumble of words was trying to come out of him but he was nearly strangling on his rage.

"He's out."

"What?"

Bobby knew then he'd made a mistake by not taking a good look at Ed when he'd first walked up, because now he could see the tears shining in his eyes and how his body was shaking and then he was coming out of the chair and standing and openly crying and trying to form words.

"They don't get no older," he finally said, and he took little half-shuffling steps forward. Bobby looked at the faces watching them and he put one hand out to try and stop this from happening.

"Hold it, Ed. Dorris don't . . ."

"Dorris knows what I'm talking about."

Bobby glanced at Dorris. He was slowly folding up, his face breaking into lines and caving in on itself. The other men just sat there.

"Ed. Don't do this to Dorris."

"Why not? He's gonna have to learn it like I had to learn it. My boy would be nine today if that drunk son of a bitch hadn't run over him. And he is out?"

He was heaving by then and he had crouched lightly as if he were going to jump him and Bobby didn't know that he wouldn't. And what would he do if he did? Whole house full of folks looking out the windows? Their elected official. A grieving constituent. Rolling over the ground duking it out at this somber gathering. Uncool.

"You get ahold of yourself, Ed. You walk on out here with me and I'll listen to whatever you got on your mind."

"You know what I got on my mind, I want to know how come you let that sorry bastard out."

Sometimes in his job he didn't know what to do and this was suddenly one of those times. He hated to coldcock him right here with his slapstick.

"Let's go get in my car, Ed."

"I don't have to go get in no car. I ain't done nothing wrong."

"You're upsetting Dorris."

"Dorris was already upset."

"Yeah, well, you're not helping things any. You either shut up or you come on with me."

He could see him thinking everything over, could see his eyes slowly shifting sideways to where Dorris stood.

"Come on, Ed. For God's sake think about this family."

Bobby walked closer and took him by the elbow the way somebody might take an aged relative or feeble shut-in. He spoke over his shoulder as he walked him away. "I'll be back, Dorris."

He started to add that he was sorry but he was already sorry and it was probably too late for that. Ed shook off his hand and they walked around the side of the house, past the cars in the yard. He opened the passenger door of the cruiser for Ed and walked around. He got in on his side and took his hat off, laid it on the seat between them. The revolver was still under the seat where he'd put it when he left Grinder's Switch.

He pushed the door out to the second notch in the hinge and propped one boot between the windshield and the top of the door. He pulled out one of his smokes. Ed had already lit one of his and was puffing hard.

"Fellow needs to be careful what he says at a time like this," Bobby said. "Things stick in people's minds."

"You talking about me?"

"I'm talking about Dorris. He's got a lot of hard times ahead of him. That little scene back there didn't help him none."

A few cars had already left. He hoped he didn't have anybody blocked in who would need to get out anytime soon. But all of a sudden he didn't want to stay much longer himself if he could help it.

"How'd you know he was out, Ed?"

"Uncle Albert saw him in town yesterday. But the judge had done called me and told me he was coming home. What the hell happened? I thought they gave him eight years."

Bobby bent his head and lit his smoke. He snapped the lighter shut and dropped it in his shirt pocket. There was a long sigh in him and he went ahead and let it out. The workings of the law and probation and parole and he didn't even want to start talking about it.

"First let me say this. I'm sorry for what happened. I was sorry before and I still am."

"Yeah, and maybe if you'd been out patrolling more you could have picked him up before he had a chance to kill my boy."

He had it now. Ed was going to do his best to piss him off. So why didn't he just shut up since there wasn't any sense in talking to him?

"Let me ask you this, Ed. If they'd took Glen Davis and put him in the gas chamber, would you be happy?"

He could almost see the wheels in his head turning. Ed was drawing thoughtfully on his cigarette, one knee crossed comfortably over the other and one hand supporting his elbow while he smoked in a gesture that was almost feminine. Finally he shook his head.

"Naw. I don't guess so. I'd feel a little better maybe. Knowing the son of a bitch was dead."

"But you wouldn't be happy."

"No."

"What would make you happy, Ed?"

Ed turned and looked at him like he was crazy.

"Why goddamn, that's simple. Have my boy back."

Bobby drew hard on his cigarette and rested the hand that held it on the steering wheel. A lot of people were still standing around in the yard, some watching them.

"Come on, Ed, be reasonable. You're not gonna get your little boy back."

"Right, because that drunk son of a bitch runs loose and the damn law won't do nothing to him."

"He was shut up for three years."

"My boy's dead."

"I had a talk with him."

"I'm gonna have a talk with him."

It got quiet in the car.

"You better not do nothing stupid."

"If the goddamn law won't take up for me I'll take up for myself."

"What's that supposed to mean?"

Ed flipped his cigarette out the window and opened his door, but he stared at Bobby for just a moment before he got out.

"I guess it means blood's thicker than water," he said, and then he was out and the door had slammed and he was walking away without looking back.

What was it Glen had said? Take that badge off for five minutes? He just wished he could.

Glen was on the road again. The cartoons had only lasted a few more minutes but he'd gotten bored with watching them before then anyway. There were a few clothes in the backseat and he was trying to decide what to do next. He didn't want to go back to his house because there was nothing there for him and the weather was too nice to stay inside. He had all this freedom now. He didn't want to waste any of it.

His stomach said it was time to eat but they had taken his wristwatch away from him at Parchman and had given him one back that wasn't his and was broken. He complained but it didn't do any good. The only thing a complaint would get you down there was a good ass-whipping, and he never did ask for another one.

He thought about heading to the store for some cigarettes, but the old man had said he was going over there, and he didn't want to run into him again this soon. He'd driven by Puppy's trailer but his car wasn't there.

His own car wasn't running too good. It missed a little when he pressed hard on the gas and Puppy was probably right about the points and plugs. He never had learned to work on one the way Puppy had, didn't like all that grease under his fingernails and having to mess with all those nuts and bolts, bust your knuckles on something. Long as they got him where he was going he was satisfied.

He drove past his house and glanced at the yard. The doors of the car shed were still standing open and he could see where he and Puppy had trampled the grass in the yard the day before. He wondered if Puppy had a lawn mower that was running. It was mighty hot to get out there and cut it, though. What he needed worse than anything was some money. He frowned, thinking about a job. There was always the stove factory and he figured he could probably get on out there again. Stand out there and put screws in holes or something. The work wasn't hard but it was eight hours on your feet and a concrete floor. Puppy might know if there was anything. The money he had wasn't going to last long, and he needed to get the lights turned on in his house and buy some groceries. He guessed he could eat at the cafe for a few days, or maybe even over at Jewel's if he could get over there after her kid was in bed. He didn't like looking at him.

There wasn't much traffic on the road. Once in a while he'd meet a car and raise a languid hand. He wondered how long it would take him to run into Ed Hall somewhere. And what would happen when he did. He still remembered him yelling in the courtroom when they were leading him out after the sentencing. Deputies holding Ed back. He'd probably have to be dealt with sooner or later, but Glen hoped it would be later. He needed to lay low now, be sitting there in the probation office in the morning right on time, yessir and nosir the whole time. Show them that he'd learned his lesson. He hated to be under their thumb but it was a lot better than staying down at Parchman. The days were long down there when you had a hoe in your hands. All he had to do was be careful. All he had to do was not get caught doing anything wrong for a while and then they'd let him off probation. It wouldn't be that hard a thing to do.

He finished the cigarette and flipped the butt out the window. The gas gauge showed half full. He could do some riding around this afternoon, find something to eat, maybe head down to the VFW and see if it was open. He could always ride across the river and get a six-pack, maybe drop by Jewel's later. The more he thought about her, the more he wanted to do that, but there was the kid to deal with. She'd probably want him to play with him or something, and he didn't want to do that. He was a little troubled to know that she'd been over to see Virgil, and had taken the boy, too. He hoped Virgil wasn't trying to act like some grandfather or something. That could come to a screeching halt. Virgil didn't have any business coming between them. There wasn't any need for him to poke his nose in it.

But it probably wouldn't hurt anything to just go by there for a little while. He didn't have to go in. He could just get her to come out to the car for a while. She'd probably do that. It had been a long time. He just didn't want to have to talk to her about the kid right now. He didn't want her to start making him feel bad about it again. It wasn't all his fault anyway. It took two to tango.

It was easy to get careless after you went with a woman for a while. He'd never liked rubbers anyway. It didn't feel as good. She'd always tried to get him to use the damn things, kept them, even, who knows where she'd gotten them. A single woman in this town didn't just walk into the drugstore and buy a pack of rubbers. Maybe her doctor got them for her. Maybe they had rubber machines in the women's bathrooms in the gas stations and beer joints. He didn't know. Maybe she drove up to Memphis and bought them where nobody knew her. He could remember them arguing about it, all that crying she'd do amid declarations of love. But then she'd get hot and forget about it when he promised not to leave it inside her. But then it would get to feeling so good . . . it was just a mistake. Just one of those things. There wasn't anything he could do about it now.

He drifted along and eyed the countryside and wondered if she'd fucked anybody while he was in the pen. She might have, the way she was. No telling how many times she'd been propositioned right there in the cafe while he was gone. It was natural. She was a pretty woman. Men were attracted to her. But he didn't want to marry her. He didn't know why he'd ever married Melba anyway. She said he drank too much and ran around all the time but he'd done all that before they got married so she should have known that he wasn't going to change his life for her. He didn't know what women expected you to do anyway. Work like a dog forty hours a week stay home on Saturday night go to church on Sunday and give them all your money he guessed. Not even go out and drink a beer? To hell with that. He was glad she was gone and he hoped he never saw her again. The few times he'd hit her she'd been asking for it anyway. *Where you been, who you been out with, what's that on you?* He got tired of listening to that shit. If Jewel wanted him to keep coming around she could take him the way he was. If she didn't like it she wasn't the only woman around.

Erline Price had sure grown up. He wondered just how grown-up she was. Maybe he'd see.

He drove into the city limits and pulled up to the stop sign. The heat was bad coming off the sidewalks and the street. Nobody much stirring. He went on through the stop sign and tooled up the street looking to see what was open. The gas stations would be, some of the little stores or maybe a hamburger joint. It was past time to find something to eat. Where a big restaurant had once stood there was a paved parking lot and he didn't know what had happened there. Fire maybe. So many things would have changed in three years. There was probably lots of news he'd missed. Old folks he'd known now dead. He felt a twinge of sadness for what he'd lost and would never know. He still had all the letters from his mother. She'd written every week but he knew she couldn't have told him everything in her world. Never spoke of her hurts, was always cheerful for him. She'd sent cookies, cakes, at Christmas little packages of gifts, small wrapped presents, the fried apple pies he'd always loved. And she had gotten sicker and sicker with the cancer and the letters had slowed down coming and then one day a guard came in and told him she was dead.

But they wouldn't let you out for that. Even if your mother died they wouldn't let you go bury her. When he got some money he'd go find a flower shop and buy some and take them out there. He had to see about that headstone. There was a lot to do.

He went on up the street and drove through the light just as it turned green. Just a few cars were parked around the square. Some kids in a convertible were talking to some more kids in another car. A truck that was still sitting where it had been yesterday. The benches under the oaks were empty but for a few pigeons perched there or pecking along the ground. The water fountains marked COLORED and WHITE. A slow and sleepy Sunday afternoon. Folks resting on their beds after big dinners, sitting on front porches, company pulling up. He could remember when it was like that at his house. Long years ago. Before everything went bad and he found out how the world really was, how it was unforgiving and cruel to children and adults alike, that you couldn't count on anything being the way it was supposed to be, that grown people made mistakes just like everybody else, and how some of those mistakes were forever lasting and would follow you to your grave. There was no use thinking of how things could have turned out. They had turned out the way they had, like the dead old history he had studied in those battered books in Mary Blanchard's classroom all those years ago.

He had slowed down way below the speed limit and somebody blew a horn behind him. He glanced up quickly into the rearview mirror, hot words ready or the middle digit of his unbandaged hand, but he saw a face and glasses behind a steering wheel, a hand waving, and he smiled, waved back, started looking for a place to pull over and talk to Erline.

She was driving a little green Mercury Comet and she followed him into the parking spaces in front of the bank. She pulled up next to him against the curb. He was going to talk to her from where he was but she got out of her car and into his.

"What are you doing all by yourself on a Sunday afternoon?" she said.

"Lookin for you."

"I thought you already had a girlfriend."

She was a little on the skinny side but she was cute. He liked the way her arms and legs looked, solid and browned. While he'd toiled chopping at his endless cotton patch with armed riders watching him she'd probably lain on a beach towel in her father's yard, her skin glistening with sweat and baby oil, the radio playing surfing songs.

"She's in church."

"And you ain't."

"That's right. Where can you get something to eat around here today?"

"That depends on what you want to eat."

She took him to a place about five miles out of town, a rib shack that sold beer. There was a jukebox blaring inside and some college students were shooting pool on some battered tables in a room off to the side. Business was kind of slow. He put a few quarters into the box and got a pair of beers. Leaning on the long bar he studied a menu written in chalk on the wall and ordered a side of ribs with slaw and loaf bread. The sullen counterman who took his order scratched figures with a pencil nub on a small yellow tablet. The beer was cold and dripping. With a gentle hand on a tiny waist he steered her into a booth and then stretched out with his back propped comfortably. He offered her a cigarette but she had some of her own. She didn't know how to inhale and she laughed too much and too loud at his stories of drinking and driving fast, the thrills of his youth. She wasn't used to drinking either and by the time he'd gnawed all the bones clean she was downright silly from two more beers. He bought some cigarettes and got her back in the car. She seemed to be feeling pretty good and sat close to him in the seat. A little kiss on his ear, the tracings of cool nails on the black hairs of his arm.

"What's your daddy gonna say when you come in like this?"

"I guess I better sober up fore I go home."

"I guess you better."

She didn't know what was happening even after he got her inside his house, having been lulled with the lie of stopping for a clean shirt and the promise of letting her use the bathroom. He didn't change shirts but he did take off the one he was wearing. She stayed in the bathroom for a long time. There was some of the whiskey left and he sipped it lying on his bed, which smelled to him just like the one at his father's house. Half reclining there among the peeling walls in the dusty house, sipping slowly and smoking a cigarette and silently stoking his anger, eyeing the closed bathroom door. He wondered if she'd tell anybody. Her father's wrath, her mother's shame, the pain of their knowledge, all things to be weighed and considered gravely in the dark of her bedroom where maybe later the nightmares would come, raving black horses with foam blowing from their mouths and their withers slathered with flecks of slobber. How hard a story to tell, how even to begin to recant her guilt, that the secret flower which must be kept safe and sacred now lay drowned in a sea of swimming sperm, their little mustard-seed heads and their tails lashing for the moat that guards the cell. Daddy I got fucked and he just got out of the pen.

She came out of the bathroom slowly, a little woozy, maybe a little apprehensive. Maybe she'd thought everything over in there. Where she was and what was going on here. He patted the side of the bed for her, his smile frozen and his eyes glazed, but not with whiskey.

She didn't want to get on the bed with him and he got up and tried to kiss her but she made sounds of wanting to leave so he stopped playing around with her and just threw her on the bed. He climbed on top of her while she kicked him. She was strong for being so small but he forced her head still and smothered her mouth with his, licking her whole face and trying to unfasten his pants with the bad hand. She was a little demon of flashing eyes and surging limbs that seemed to undulate beneath him and move in all directions at once. He started to hit her and did double up his fist but he didn't want to mark what the world could see. In that one moment of hesitation she slapped his right eye and kicked him hard in the throat. With the quickness of something raised in the woods she was off the bed and across the room and would have been out the front door but for the thirty-cent hardware bolt he'd slid shut when she went into the bathroom. He caught her by the hair and walked her backwards to the bed, watchful for kicks to the balls, keeping the hurt hand behind him to protect it. She was screaming but there was nobody to hear and whoever it was that drove by a time or two probably just saw an old car parked beside an old house, high grass in the yard, nothing more, nothing to report here, all secure. He pushed her back down on the bed with her entire body fighting against him, every muscle and fiber, her fingernails seeking his eyes and her own eyes wild like a trapped animal. He pinned both her wrists behind her head with one hand while she tried to bite him with her flashing white teeth. He laughed at that and they struggled and shook the frame of the bed. It was hard to stop her from moving.

He was careful not to tear her clothes but sometime before they were both naked she gave up and started crying. Each little button and buttonhole he manipulated with a grandmother's touch. She seemed to want to hug him for protection against what was happening to them. Tears leaked from her eyes and ran down to her ears. She begged him to stop and she never really stopped begging and just before he rose up over her he put one hand over her mouth and watched her eyes as they widened and then went glassy. He forced his way inside her a few millimeters at a time and then rode her hard down into the pillows where she bucked and gagged and snorted. Her eyes fluttered and he thought she was dead. He told her things, the names of the parts of her body, how they felt, what he was doing to her, how much he liked it. After a while she seemed to stop listening. He did it slow and long and hard and even when he saw that she was bleeding he kept on. Dust rising from the sheets and drifting over into bars of sunlight that slanted across a vacant spot on the wall where a picture had hung. The headboard making its mindless thumping, the springs in the old bed passed down from some dead member of his family squeaking and keeping time. He pulled out and shot it onto her belly, her ribs. He got off her and went to find something with which to clean himself. When he came back with a sheet he'd found under a cabinet she was lying on her side with her legs together and she'd puked a small neat puddle of vomit onto the floor. He didn't try to talk to her. After he wiped himself off he pitched the sheet at her and put on his clothes and took the whiskey out to the front porch where a rusted kitchen chair sat against the brick siding. There was never a sound from within. He smoked cigarettes and drank the whiskey. It was twenty minutes before she came out, for the first time the way she would so often look the rest of her life, head lowered, eyes downcast. He examined her critically. She didn't look much different. But she wouldn't look at him and she went straight to the car and opened the door and got in.

On the way in to town he tried to talk to her but she wouldn't talk. No laughter at his dirty jokes now. Just the wind coming in the windows and the dregs of the whiskey in the bottle on the seat between them. He thought it odd that she took a drink of that but with no more notice of him and his presence than if the car had been driving itself.

It was early afternoon still. He didn't take her back to her car. Nobody saw him stop on a street just off the square and let her off there. He told her that if she wanted some more she knew where he lived. She had already turned her face away and she got out without a word, closed the door softly, then walked slowly away. He drove past her, smoking, drove past her car and noted the heat of the day and eyed his gas gauge and then headed out of town, toward cool rooms and dark paneled wood, those jukebox lights and those sad country songs about cheating and a woman and love fucked up.

Bobby parked the cruiser next to one of the big pin oaks that cooled his mother's front porch. He got the revolver from under the seat but left his hat in the car. Her Buick wasn't in the car shed and he figured she was probably heading to the house from where he'd come. The swing looked inviting, freshly painted and filled with pillows, and he went up the steps and got his key from his pocket. She locked it even when he was sleeping there, which wasn't every night but often enough that he still called it home. He unlocked the door and stepped inside.

He dropped the gun in a chair and took off his shirt. When he got back to his room he pulled off his T-shirt, wadding it and pitching it and getting a fresh one from the drawer. The phone rang one time and quit. He stood listening. It didn't ring anymore. He sat down on the bed and took off his boots and his socks, the shiny hardwood floor cool and clean under his bare feet.

The hall was wide and the walls were hung with pictures of old relatives long dead and gone, uncertain girls in ruffled dresses holding sprays of flowers or the reins of spotted ponies. Outdated wear on a slim boy in knickers who was his mother's husband. He stopped and looked at him again and studied him, then the brown-tone image beside it of that grown child in barracks cap and captain's bars. Shot down over Africa, his bones maybe bleached beneath the shifting sands of a distant continent and the flaming wreckage he rode down burning alive leaching slowly back into the substratum. A man he never got to know. Charles Blanchard, deceased stranger.

She'd already cleaned up from dinner and out of habit he looked in the refrigerator to see what she'd left him. Cold pork chops and a tossed salad. He reached back for a beer and grabbed a pork chop and nibbled it while he opened the bottle. A long cold draught, a fly humming near the ceiling. He pushed the icebox door shut with his foot and wandered to the back door, then remembered his cigarettes and went back to his room for them. It was bad that he'd left the way he had. He couldn't explain it to Dorris, but he probably already knew. Sometimes he thought everybody did.

His cigarettes and lighter were on the dresser. He shoved them in his pocket and walked back through the kitchen. The clock was ticking softly on the wall. He looked around the room. Everything was neat and orderly, the bread stashed in the corner of the counter, the floor with its dull shine, the table holding only the salt and pepper shakers. A dead and empty room. He got out the back door holding the beer and the pork chop and stepped to the edge of the porch, looking out over the yard. It was filled with flowers and their brightly colored blossoms were stirring in the breeze. He saw the old man's body in the dirt again and he couldn't understand what could have happened between Byers and his father to bring them to that. Maybe it was nothing more than whiskey.

Bobby could see his cows grouped under a big scalybark just beyond the fence and he went down the steps and walked out there. Omar looked around and saw him, turned his massive head up and sniffed the wind. Bobby leaned on the fence, gnawing the scraps of meat from the bone. He tossed it over the fence and the bull came toward him, his tail lashing the flies away from his hindquarters.

"Hey big boy," Bobby said. He took a long drink from the beer and set the bottle on the ground. He bent a little more and reached under the bottom board of the fence for a corncob that was lying there and he waited with it, his arms resting on the top board. The bull came up, all two thousand pounds of him, all sleek black muscle with a hide that rolled and shifted as he walked. He stopped just short of the fence and his heavy bag swung gently between his legs.

"Come on up here and I'll scratch your old head. Come on."

He hadn't had a halter on him in a long time but he was still pretty tame. He stood there watching Bobby.

"I ain't got nothing to eat. Come on up here."

The bull turned and walked down the fence a few steps and then turned again and came back. He stopped with his head near Bobby's hand. He extended his head and sniffed. A big horsefly was feeding on his shoulder and Bobby reached out and smacked it flat with his hand. It lay crushed in a patch of black hair matted with blood.

"Hurts don't it?"

He reached out with the corncob and started rubbing it between Omar's ears and the bull stood there swinging his tail. The cows watched them on their knees, quietly working their jaws and twitching their ears at the flies that constantly tormented them. In the pond down in the pasture they sometimes walked to their knees and then up to their hips and lifted the clouds of flies from their backs, coming all wet and slick from the water, wearing leggings of rank mud that dried and cracked later.

The bull closed and opened his eyes and turned his head aslant on his neck and Bobby smiled watching him.

"You like that, don't you? Like getting that old head scratched."

He patted Omar a final time and dropped the corncob. The beer was half full and he picked it back up and got out his cigarettes and lit one.

The grass felt good on his toes. He went back across the yard, just looking around. Just killing time. Mary had cut the grass the day before and
that didn't need doing. She'd hired three painters for the house in May
and they had scraped it and put on two coats, repainted all the trim, so
that didn't need doing. There was always something on the stove. If a cow
got sick she called the vet out. He didn't worry about her staying by herself because she was better with a pistol than he was and she had one in
her nightstand, a little chrome .380 with black plastic grips. He didn't
even know why she kept that picture in the hall. It had to be for herself
because surely it wasn't for him. Maybe it was just a little reminder of
what could have been. But that picture didn't do him any good. It didn't
make it any easier to grow up with only a mother to show him things. He
still didn't know anything about working on a car. Still didn't know how
to slip up on a squirrel. He knew she'd done the best she could. And she
never had lied to him about who his father was. There wasn't any need to.
All anybody had to do was take a good look at him. But it still didn't stop
him from asking her: Why didn't you just get married again? To somebody. Anybody. So I could have had somebody to show me the stuff I
needed to know. So you could have had somebody too. But he knew the
answer to that. She didn't want anybody else. She never had and never
would. He guessed that was real love, the real thing. To wait for years and
years and sleep alone and grow old waiting. Like Jewel had been waiting.
The thought of her with Glen was too awful and the image was something he'd managed to keep out of his head so far.

He wandered around the side of the house and out across the front
yard. The trees were old and big. There was always a breeze out there and
he stood in it. A car came down the road and he waved. The horn blew.

"Yep, the sheriff's drinking a beer in his own front yard," he said to
it. And he turned the bottle up and finished it.

He stood there debating, holding the bottle with one finger down inside the neck of it, gently tapping it against his thigh. It was only four o'clock. He didn't like to drink more than a couple since the phone could always ring.

"Hell," he said, and went back into the house for another beer. This time he stretched out on the swing with the paper, his head propped against a bank of pillows, the chains creaking slowly and the breeze wafting over him. News of the world far off and near. Beetle Bailey and Snuffy Smith. Once in a while he lifted the beer and took a cold sip. But the paper couldn't hold his interest. He reclined there with the pages scattered over the painted boards of the porch and watched the trees. He could see them in the bed together now and the things that occurred there in his mind were horrible. He sat up in the swing and looked out across the road to the crops under the sun and the sky that lay beyond them.

"God," he said softly. "Help me."

She didn't come in until nearly six. He was still in the swing and the ashtray beside him was filled with cigarette butts. She pulled in fast like she always did and put the Buick in the car shed. He'd told her over and over that she was going straight out the back end of it one day and he didn't like to ride with her. The door slammed. He heard the crunch of her feet on the gravel and she came up the side steps with her purse in her hand.

"What you doing, Maw?" he said without looking at her. She sat down in a rocker next to him, taking off her shoes and stretching out her legs.

"I been over at Sue's. Lord that was pitiful."

"Wasn't it, though."

"They said you'd been by but they didn't know where you went. I hated to leave and I hated to stay and watch it. Did you find something to eat?"

"Yes'm. All them people still over there?"

"A lot of em's left. We washed all the dishes and cleaned up her kitchen. I never saw the like of food in one house in my life." She rocked a little and crossed her fingers over her stomach. "How long you been home?"

"Couple of hours."

"What about all that mess you had to go to?"

"Well," he said. "It's a damn mess all right."

He rolled over on his back and gripped the swing chain with his toes.

"I don't see how Sue's gonna live through it," she said. "I swear they have the worst luck. It's only been two years since their house burnt down."

The sun was sinking a little lower in the sky and the oaks were letting a few rays through, tiny spots of light winking as the limbs shifted in the breeze.

"You going out to the funeral home?" she said.

"I don't know. Are you?"

"I hadn't decided. I know it'll be full of people. I hate not to go. I need to fix you some supper."

He pushed the swing chain with his toes and let it rock back and forth. The chains creaked a little.

"Don't worry about me. I'll probably take a cruise after while anyway. I got to go by the jail and fill out some papers. Make sure nobody's escaped. I can fix me a sandwich when I get in. I wish they'd let me get a night's sleep tonight. I've bout had it."

"I saw Jewel at church," she said.

"That's what I heard."

She took this in silence for a while, just rocking. He wasn't going to volunteer anything. He would have told her himself that he didn't need her advice if she'd offered it but he guessed she knew better than to try that. He stayed where he was, waiting.

"Where'd you see her?"

"Over at her house."

"You went by there?"

"Yep. Sure did."

"In your patrol car."

"I didn't turn the siren on."

More silence. More waiting and rocking.

"Well. It's your business."

"That's right. It sure is."

"Was he over there?"

"Nope."

"What would you have done if he had been?"

"I guess one of us would have left, Mama."

She just shook her head. She picked up her shoes and her purse and she got up and started toward the door. She stopped halfway across the porch. "You coming home tonight?"

"I'm planning on it. Nothing don't happen."

She shook her head some more but she didn't say anything, just went on inside the house and left him out there by himself.


Things were quiet at the jail when he went by there around seven. Harold had gone off duty an hour before and Elvis Murray was watching "Lassie." He was an old man and he'd been the jailer there long years before Bobby ever had thoughts of running for sheriff. There was some coffee in the pot and Bobby got a cup and sat down at the table with him.

"How's it going, Elvis?" he said.

Elvis swiveled around in Bobby's chair and pulled at his nose. "Everything's fine, I reckon."

"Everybody get fed?"

"Yep. They had a good supper. Chicken-fried steak and mashed pota-toes and gravy. I had a plate myself."

Bobby lit a cigarette and looked at Lassie for a minute. She was bark-ing frantically and trying to tell Timmy something.

"You heard anything out of Byers?"

"He wouldn't eat his supper and I heard him crying one time."

"You talk to him?"

"Tried to. I asked him did he need anything and he said yeah, a hack-saw blade. How come him to kill his daddy?"

Bobby looked into his cup. "I don't know."

They sat there for a little bit. Bobby really didn't have any reason for coming by. He was just in the habit of checking on things. Elvis went back to watching his show and Bobby sat there thinking about Jewel. Wondering what this night would bring her. He was so deep into his thoughts that when Elvis spoke again it didn't register for a moment. He raised his head. "What?"

"I said that was bad about Frankie Barlow, wasn't it?"

He suddenly felt like he had been asleep for a while and the mention of that name was something that had lain buried, something he should have been keeping an eye on.

"What about Frankie Barlow?"

"You ain't heard?"

"Naw, I ain't heard. What?"

"Well I just figured you knew. It's been on the scanner all day might near. Hell. Somebody killed him last night. Killed that nigger that worked for him too."

All the things he'd worried about and now they were here. All this time just waiting for him to get out and for it to start all over again. He put both feet flat on the floor and set the coffee cup down. Elvis was star-ing at him. "Damn, boy, you white as a sheet."

"Did they call over here?"

"Naw. I just figured you knew it. My nephew come by the house and told me. I got that scanner in the bedroom and I turned it up. Hell, Bobby, it ain't in our county and I just figured . . ."

"How'd your nephew know about it?"

"He was coming back from fishing, stopped by there to get some beer, said the place was crawlin with cops and somebody told him Barlow got his head blowed off."

He wasn't even seeing the jail anymore. He was seeing the inside of that beer joint that he himself had been in many times years ago. The tall stools and the little baby monkey that clambered over the place like a squirrel and swung from rafter to rafter like a trapeze artist, how Barlow fed it peanuts one at a time and the patrons gave it beer.

"What's the matter?" Elvis said. He reached over and turned the TV down. Bobby got the logbook and flipped it open. Harold had gone home and Jake had started his vacation at four o'clock. That left Cecil on call and Jerry on the road somewhere patrolling.

"Nothing. I was just wondering about something." He closed the logbook and put it back on the desk. "You know if they picked up anybody?"

"Yeah."

"Who?"

"Some nigger."

It wasn't quite dark when he drove his cruiser into the parking lot of the jail in Pine Springs and pulled in among the black-and-tan patrol cars gathered there. He'd called ahead to tell them he was coming but he didn't see the sheriff's new brown Galaxie parked near the front door. He shut off the car and got out. A few bats were fluttering over the parking lot.

There was a short concrete landing outside the door and he went up the steps to it. He reached for the doorknob but the door opened and swung out before he could turn it. A surprised deputy who narrowed his eyes at first and then looked at Bobby's badge and did a quick recovery. "Evening, Sheriff, how you doing?"

"Fine. You?"

The deputy nodded and went on down the steps. Bobby went inside. There was nobody in the dayroom, but a television was playing.

"Hey Vinnie."

Nobody answered him but he could hear people talking somewhere. There were WANTED posters from the FBI hanging on a bulletin board. Somebody was laughing down the hall. He walked back there. A deputy was leaning over a partition talking to the dispatcher. The deputy was grinning and telling her some things in a low voice and he didn't look around immediately. The dispatcher looked at Bobby and nodded. She finally pointed to him and the deputy turned his head, then straightened up and nodded affably.

"Yessir. Can I help you?"

"I'm here to see Vinnie. He in?"

The deputy looked at the dispatcher. "You know if he's in?"

She was a pretty young black woman with a gold tooth and she looked a little flustered.

"I'm not sure," she said to Bobby. "His office is back there. Right down the hall. Just go on back."

"Thank you ma'am."

He stepped around the deputy, who had already turned his attention back to the woman. Bobby glanced at her as he went by and she smiled. He nodded. The office was at the end of the hall and there was a pane of rippled glass in the top half of the door. He rapped on it.

"Hey Vinnie."

Somebody inside said for him to come on in and he opened the door. Two deputies were leaning over a table looking at some papers. One of them was named Jones and Bobby had talked to him at a roadblock one night.

"Hey Sheriff," he said, and came over with his hand out. They shook. "How's the world treating you?"

"About the same, I guess. I was looking for Vinnie."

"Yessir. He's stepped out for a minute. Come on and have a seat. This is Jimmy Douglas here."

Bobby nodded to him but kept standing. They seemed to be waiting for something, but his business wasn't with them.

"Can we get you something, cup of coffee maybe?"

"That'd be fine, thanks."

"How about getting him some coffee, Jimmy?"

"Sure."

The other man went out the door and closed it behind him. Bobby took the chair that was offered and sat down. He saw an ashtray on Vinnie's desk and he lit up and crossed his legs, took off his hat. Jones leaned back against the table and pulled a piece of lint off his pants.

"Well we had a busy day," he said.

"That right?"

"Yeah, if it ain't drunks it's car wrecks and thieves. Somebody beating the shit out of his old lady. Is Hughie still out there talking to Juliet?"

"You mean the dispatcher?"

"Yessir. I wish she'd go on and give him some so he'd stop talking about it. Vinnie's done told him he's going to fire his ass if he don't stop talking to her on the radio. And when he ain't around her it's nigger this and nigger that. Beats anything I ever seen."

"She's a pretty woman," Bobby said.

"Yessir she is. Vinnie said you wanted to talk to him about that thing today."

Bobby shifted in the chair. The deputy wasn't smiling anymore.

"He did?"

"Yessir."

Bobby leaned over holding his hat and slid the ashtray closer.

"I'm chief deputy now," Jones said. "I can tell you what happened. Or what we found."

"Did you go out there today?"

"I was the first one there. Last one to leave. We ain't got the pictures developed yet but it was one hell of a mess."

"What time was that?"

"This morning about ten o'clock."

The other deputy came back in with the coffee and set it on the desk close to the ashtray. Bobby thanked him and he went back out. It was hot in the office and papers lay on the dirty floor. Bobby took a sip of the coffee and nearly scalded his tongue. He set it down.

"I heard y'all picked up somebody."

The deputy shook his head and looked at a picture of Lyndon Johnson on the wall.

"We done turned him loose. He didn't have nothin to do with it. He was just over there lookin for his brother-in-law. He found him, too. With his whole head blowed off. He didn't have no gun, nothin. And they was both dead a long time before he got there. Coroner said that himself."

Bobby picked up the coffee and tried another sip. It tasted like it was about three days old. They hadn't put any sugar in it, either.

"You know what time it happened?"

"Around midnight maybe. Maybe a little later. It looked like somebody shot Barlow through the window and then shot him a few more times."

"What with?"

"Shotgun. A twelve. We picked up four shells."

Bobby stared at the wall and smoked his cigarette. He could imagine how it looked and what that much lead would have done to a man.

"Did they take anything?"

"Cleaned out the register except for the change. But Barlow had about eighteen hundred dollars in his billfold. I don't guess they thought to check for that."

"And what about the other guy?"

"That was Rufus Tallie. He worked for him, had for years. I figure he was killed later. His house was close to there. Probably heard all the racket and came in at the wrong time. I went over and talked to his wife. It was real bad. They got about five kids."

Bobby leaned back in the chair and puffed on his cigarette, then bent forward and stubbed it out.

"So," he said. "You don't think it was a robbery."

"It's hard to say. I imagine he's made a lot of enemies over the years. You can't deal with a bunch of drunks seven days a week and not have trouble."

"Ain't that the damn truth," Bobby said.

"Could be somebody just had something against him and went over there and settled it. I doubt we'll ever know who did it. We ain't got a thing to go on. We ain't got a single witness. Less somebody ups and confesses that's probably the end of it."

He was probably right. It was all a question of whether you could live with something like that and be able to keep your mouth shut about it. Byers could have probably gotten away with killing his daddy. But he sobered up and he couldn't live with it. And if Glen had done this, could he? As bad as Bobby hated to think it, he probably could.

"Do you think there's a lot of people who'd like to see Barlow dead?"

The deputy considered this for a moment.

"He never done nothing to me," he said finally. "But there was always a lot of trouble out there."

Bobby set the coffee down and stood up and put his hat on. "Well. I appreciate you talking to me."

"I'm sorry Vinnie ain't here. You could wait on him if you want to."

"I better get on back. I got to go to a funeral tomorrow and I got to get some sleep."

The deputy came away from the desk and shook hands with Bobby once more. Bobby stood there for a second and then he looked into the deputy's eyes.

"Is he drunk again?"

The deputy was hurt by the question, but he turned his head away and nodded at the floor.

"It's got to where it's every weekend's business. I don't know how much longer I can cover for him. He give me a job seven years ago. I'm grateful to him for that. But I reckon he just don't care no more." He looked up at Bobby. "You think you'll ever get like that? Where you just don't care no more?"

"Ask me in twenty years," Bobby said, and he straightened his hat as he started out. But then he thought of something and he stopped. "What about the monkey?"

"Shit. They got him, too."

Tommy Babb had gone on down the road in his shiny red car a few hours before, but Virgil was still sitting on a bar stool under the winking blue lights of the VFW. There was a long uneven bar top that had been sawn out of the center of a tree and its glossy surface was marred from the burns of a thousand cigarettes and thousands of nights. Not many faces resided there in the back mirror, just his and Woodrow's and that of a weathered whore named Gloria who was about sixty. The bartender was watching Ed Sullivan on the television and he'd already rung the bell for last call. Sunday nights he closed early unless it was a holiday or somebody's birthday or some other special event. Anything would do, but there was nothing special going on tonight. Virgil had a six-pack in a sack on the stool beside him for the ride home and after.

"Y'all drank up, now," the bartender said.

Woodrow raised his bottle and drank from it. Gloria was trying to weave her bottle into his to make some kind of a toast. Virgil was glad Woodrow was sitting between them since he'd seen her give somebody a blow job on one of the pool tables one night and figured she was probably diseased.

"I'll be ready in a minute, Virgil," Woodrow said.

"I ain't in no hurry."

The boy had come in for a while with him, where he was welcomed by the drunk and the sober alike, bought beers, told tales of war, and given advice. Don't pat em on the head. Don't fuck em if they cough cause they got TB. That old thing about it being sideways is just a bunch of bullshit. Virgil had talked fishing with him in those few hours and he hoped him well in his distant war.

"Y'all come on, now, I got to go home and eat supper," said the bartender.

"Me too," Virgil said. It was probably going to be something out of a can. That was about all he had, beef stew or soup. He guessed he could make some tuna fish. All evening he'd thought about that fried chicken and the one who'd fried it. He'd had some vague hope earlier that maybe the afternoon would somehow take him by there, but that had died now. It had been a long time since he'd seen her. He'd held himself back and today at the store there had been those questions in her eyes. He guessed it had been close to a year. And there had been no way for her to see him as long as he stayed at home since she wouldn't come by there. The few times she'd called him he was still feeling guilty over Emma. Maybe she'd gotten to hurting so bad she couldn't stand it.

Woodrow lifted his bottle again and emptied it, set it down. He picked up a fresh one already opened.

"All right, come on, let's let Fred go home," he said.

They got off their stools and said their good-byes. Woodrow had to take Gloria's arm to steady her because her hipbones weren't good and she was weary with drink. Virgil followed them out the door, his sack tucked up under his arm, watching his step out in the dark gravel lot, making his way behind them over to the car. He got in the backseat with the dog, who was sitting there looking around.

"Old Nimrod ain't took a shit back there has he?" Woodrow was poking his head in the window at him.

"I can't smell it if he has."

"Good. If he tries to bite you or anything, just knock the shit out of him."

Woodrow went around and got Gloria into the front seat. She turned around, smiled at Virgil with her hag's smile.

"I'll suck you off for two bucks, Virgil."

"I'll pass."

"Woodrow won't get it in good till he'll shoot off. Grown man like him."

"Well I guess you just look so good Gloria he can't control himself."

"I guess so."

She seemed happily satisfied with that and turned back around. Woodrow came over to Virgil's side and got in behind the wheel. He turned that last beer up and then stuck it between his legs. Then he reached forward and cranked the car and they pulled out. He turned the lights on and Virgil looked at the dog next to him. An immeasurably sad hound with his long drooping face and ears that hung way down. He looked big enough to bite your hand off.

"You still gonna sell this dog, Woodrow?"

"Hell yes. I'm gonna take him to Ripley first thing in the mornin. Trade him for a crate of chickens or maybe a goat. Trade him for a good goat and he'd keep my pasture cleaned up."

Virgil borrowed the opener from the dash and took the top off one of the beers and then passed it back. He took a good sip and settled back in the seat. The headlights carved a tunnel of light through the black woods that surrounded them, high sage grass in the ditches on either side and the road twisting through hills and curves where sometimes deer stood stark and gray with their big ears and electric eyes. Sometimes they froze where they were and sometimes they put their tails up and leaped fluidly away, bounding over downed logs and brush piles with their tails waving like banners.

Gloria had moved closer to Woodrow and she was saying something to him in a low voice. Woodrow was nodding and listening and Virgil wondered what she was telling him. What she was going to do to him maybe. Probably nothing that mattered. Just drunk talk. He'd said plenty of it himself more times than he cared to remember.

He sipped his beer and looked at the dog. The hound had curled up on the seat with his head hanging over the edge, jostling slowly inside his skin as the old car bumped and rocked over the road. Woodrow drove slowly and the radio played country tunes at a low level, songs by an angel of the earth whose soul had been freed on the side of a mountain.

He got one of the last Camels from his pocket and lit it, resting his elbow on the armrest and leaning against the door as they began to be bathed softly in a pulsing red light that seemed to have drifted upon them from out of the sky.

"Damn," Woodrow said. "The law's got us."

Virgil turned around and looked at the car tailing them and the dust rising against the headlights so that they were steadily emerging from a cloud of tiny particles that threatened to cover them, put them out.

"Hell, I guess I better pull over."

Woodrow came to a stop in the middle of the road and left the motor running. Virgil turned back around to face the front and watched Woodrow looking into the rearview mirror.

"He's comin up here," Woodrow said. "Stick this beer in between us, Gloria."

She took it and did something with it, maybe secreted it away somewhere in the folds of her dress. Woodrow had his window down and Virgil heard a car door slam behind them.

"It's Bobby."

Virgil turned his head and looked at him as he came up beside the car.

He had his gun on and he looked in at Virgil first, then at Woodrow and Gloria.

"Hey Bobby," Woodrow said.

"Hey Woodrow. What are y'all up to?"

"Aw, we just been down to the VFW for a little bit. We was takin Virgil home."

"That right?"

"Yeah."

Virgil didn't say anything but he wondered why he'd stopped them. The car was still running and Gloria was looking straight ahead. Bobby just stood there for a second like he was trying to think of what to say. Then he bent over and put his hands on his knees.

"I need to talk to Virgil," he said. "I thought I might run into y'all down here somewhere."

He moved down to the window where Virgil was sitting and leaned over to him. "You mind getting in with me for a little bit? I'll take you on home after while."

It wasn't like he could say no. But there was nothing unreasonable about it. Bobby'd picked him up before. And even seemed glad to see him sometimes.

"I guess I can. Let me get my beer."

Bobby reached and opened the door for him. The headlights of the cruiser behind them made little shadows stretch ahead of the rocks in the road.

"Sure. I just need to talk to you for a little bit."

"Ain't nothin wrong is it?"

Bobby shook his head and looked down on him with a face that was full of sadness.

"Ain't nothin wrong, Virgil. Come on and let's take a little ride."

The dog had been watching this but now he settled back down on the seat and closed his eyes. Virgil gathered up his sack and got out of the car holding the single beer bottle in his hand, the cigarette in his mouth. Bobby shut the door behind him when he stepped away from the car and he turned to look back at Woodrow. He looked worried. Gloria was still sitting woodenly beside him.

"I'll see you later, Woodrow."

Woodrow nodded and lifted one hand and gave a little wave good-bye to him. He pulled the car down in gear and sat there for a moment.

"Take it easy, Virgil."

"Okay."

Bobby had already started walking back toward his car and Virgil blinked, glancing into the headlights. He took a drink of his beer and started walking. Woodrow pulled off and waved again. Bobby had already gotten in and was sitting behind the wheel lighting a cigarette. The interior light was on and Virgil saw that Bobby had left his door open until Virgil could get around to the other side. He opened the door to the front seat and hesitated, not knowing whether to set the rest of the beer in there or not. But he got on in and set the sack between his feet and closed the door. Bobby closed his door and the light went out.

"You don't mind taking a little ride with me, do you, Virgil?"

He had taken his hat off and it was lying on the seat between them. Bobby seemed to be studying him with something almost like worry on his face.

"Naw. I don't mind. I don't mind at all."

"Well," Bobby said softly. "That's good." And they pulled off.

"You want one of these beers?" Virgil said. He offered the bottle but Bobby just shook his head.

"I better not. Not tonight."

There was a small green light burning on the radio that was under the dash but the radio was silent. They drove slowly. He pushed a switch and the red light outside went off. He started picking up a little speed and Virgil sipped his beer. The car was nearly new and it leveled most of the bumps out of the road.

"When'd you get this car?"

"About a month back. I gave my old one to Jake and Harold got his."

They kept driving and Bobby steered the car with a casual hand. On a long straightaway they encountered dust drifting across the road and through the darkness ahead one single red taillight that was Woodrow. Bobby slowed down.

"What y'all been up to?" he said.

"Nothing. Drinking a beer."

"I thought you quit."

Virgil thought about it for a moment.

"Well. Not exactly," he said. "I try to stay off that whiskey. Hurts my liver to drink it."

Bobby nodded. The dust was thicker and they were closer to Woodrow now. At an intersection where they could see the red light still moving down the road ahead of them Bobby turned right and got out of the dust. He pushed it up to about forty and left it there.

"I talked to Glen yesterday," he said.

"I heard you did. I saw your mama at the store today."

"What was she doing?"

"She just stopped in for a minute. Wanted me to come eat dinner with her."

Bobby glanced over at him.

"Well? Did you?"

"Naw. I didn't know whether you'd want me to or not."

"Why do you think I'd care?"

"I don't know."

Virgil raised the beer bottle and took a long drink from it. Bobby stared at the road.

"Goddamn, Virgil, I don't care for you eating dinner. If it makes her happy. If it makes you happy. If you think I spend my time worrying about that you're wrong."

Virgil didn't say anything. He guessed he'd finally get around to whatever he had on his mind, but he thought he knew what that was.

"I mean it ain't like we ever have a family dinner or anything," Bobby said. "Half the time she ends up eating by herself cause I'm off somewhere. She'd probably like to have some company besides me sometime anyway. Or a bunch of old women puttin a quilt together."

Bobby slowed the car a bit and he seemed to relax. He watched things all around him as he drove, the fence at the side of a pasture, a rabbit frozen in the weeds, the lights of houses far off in the dark.

"You know Frankie Barlow, don't you, Virgil?"

"Yeah, I know him. I ain't seen him in a long time. I used to go over to his place some. Long time ago when he was just a boy. I knew his daddy. It didn't do to cross him."

"How you know that?"

Virgil took a drink of his beer and looked out the window for a moment, then watched the needle on the speedometer hovering around thirty-five.

"I just do."

"You ever see anybody who did?"

"Not exactly."

Bobby smiled at him for a second, like maybe he didn't believe him. "How you know it didn't do to cross him then?"

Virgil crossed his legs and reached for the last cigarette in his pocket. He lit it and rested the beer bottle on his leg.

"I went over there early one day to get some beer. I had some lines out in the river, that was back when I was still commercial fishin. There was a window there by the side and the old man slept on a cot in there. Somebody come by in the middle of the night, he'd get up and sell em some beer. But he come to the door and let me in that day and there was a big puddle of blood on the floor. I like to stepped in it. Hell, I looked down, knowed what it was, but I asked him what it was and he said it wasn't nothin, just where he had to kill some son of a bitch the night before. Went on and sold me my beer."

Bobby nodded and the car slowed even more. "I never did know him. That was before my time, I guess. I've known Frankie a long time. Glen used to go over there a lot. I did, too, years ago. Them two never did seem to like each other. Always figured they'd eventually get into it. Both of em bad to fight when they got to drinkin."

"Puppy told me that Glen was drunk before he ever got over there."

"They got into it about Jewel, didn't they? Wasn't that what it started over?"

"I think Barlow offered to buy her a drink was all it was."

"Yeah, I finally got that much out of her," Bobby said. "She don't like to talk about it much. I reckon she tried to talk him into lettin her drive home but he wouldn't do it. Got mad. Dropped her off then rode around all night long. Have you seen her lately?"

"Not in a while," Virgil said, and took another drink of his beer. "My car's been tore up and I can't hardly walk over there. Some days I can make it to the store and back. That's about it."

Bobby looked out his window and turned his head back.

"Glen tell you I had a talk with him?"

*Seems like I talked to one of your mistakes yesterday.*

"Yeah. Come to think of it he did. But he's mad at me. He thinks I drank up the money for his mama's headstone."

"Did you?"

"Nope. I just ain't went and got it yet. Ever damn penny of it's still right there in the cabinet where she kept it."

Bobby loosened his hold on the steering wheel a little and eased back in the seat, relaxing just a bit.

"Jewel said you helped her buy some stuff for David. Some Christmas presents and stuff last year. It's good of you to help her, Virgil."

"Somebody's got to. Glen won't."

"Tell me something, Virgil. Does he just blame the whole world for all his problems? Does he even care what he does to you?"

"I don't know what's in his head. I thought he was a good boy at one time. But he's been this way ever since Theron died. If I could take it all back and change it I would. But I can't."

"What does he say about Jewel?"

"You don't want to hear it."

Bobby closed up on him again and just kept driving. With him it was hard to tell when he was mad. But if he didn't want him to tell the truth what the hell did he pick him up for? He had a ride home to start with. Minding his own business.

"Did he spend the night with you last night?" Bobby said.

"Yeah."

"What time did he get in?"

"I don't know. I laid down about eleven, I guess. He come in sometime after that. He was in his bed asleep when I got up. I guess he come in after he went to see her. But I don't know. And I ain't gettin in the middle of it."

Bobby turned his head and looked at Virgil hard.

"What do you mean? You're already in the middle of it. You been taking him fishin and puttin up swings for him. What do you call that if it ain't right in the middle of it?"

"That's all right, by God. If his own daddy won't take care of him I will. And dare any damn body to try and stop me."

Bobby turned his face back to the road and drove in silence for just a moment, and then he looked at Virgil again.

"Don't get all upset, now."

"I ain't upset. But he's gonna find out you been seeing Jewel. And then what's gonna happen?"

"Me and Jewel ain't done nothing wrong," Bobby said.

"Yeah, but he never will believe it and you know it. You better go on and tell him. Or get her to."

"She don't know what the hell to do."

"I know what he ain't gonna do."

It got quiet in the car. He guessed Bobby was getting pissed off but he didn't care. He was about to get the same way. None of this was his fault and he wished they'd just leave him out of it. Nobody ever listened to him anyway, never had. All this was just as hard on him as it was on them. Maybe harder. He took a few more pulls on his cigarette and then flipped it out the window. They were all still young and they thought they would be forever. They didn't know how fast their lives would go by, how one day they'd turn around thirty years from now and wonder how it had managed to pass so quickly. They didn't know that the things they did now were important and would matter when those thirty years were up. He didn't want to try and tell Bobby any of that. He couldn't take sides in this. They were going to have to work all this out for themselves. And all he could do was watch, and hope for the best.

"How come he hates me so bad, Virgil? I ain't such a bad guy, am I? I always got along with Theron. And Randolph, too. Even after I got elected and caught Glen doing something wrong, I'd cut him all the slack I could."

"Why?" Virgil said. "Why would you cut him some slack? You grew up with him. You know how he is."

Bobby seemed embarrassed. He didn't look around. "I don't know. I guess partly cause of you. Probly partly cause of what happened to Theron. I always felt sorry for him after that. Tried to be nice to him. But he never would let me."

Virgil took a small sip from his beer and glanced out the window for a moment. The houses along the road were dark now and there was a sad wonder in Bobby's voice. Virgil wished he could give him the answers to his questions, and he knew there must have been a lot of them down through the years. There had been so many times when he would have given anything to be able to just take him fishing one afternoon, to let him know that he cared about him and that he was sorry for the way things had to turn out sometimes, but there never had been any chance of that. Emma had seen to that. That crazy jealousy she had for Mary had driven a wedge between them, and the lies she had told Glen when he was too young to know better had eventually convinced him they were truth. All the nights out drinking and fishing on the river. All the car wrecks and the times in jail. He wondered what he could have been thinking of in those years when she was poisoning his mind against him. It was all such a waste. Way too late to fix now.

"How old was you when you and Glen got in that fight?"

"I don't remember, Virgil. He's a good bit younger than me. Course he was as big as me. I reckon he's about four years younger than me, ain't he?"

"Yeah. You were born while I was still on Corregidor."

"Forty-two."

"Right. If I could have got a leave and come home, I would have married your mama. I mean if your granddaddy would have let me. But after they bombed Pearl Harbor they wadn't no leaves. Then four months later

I was captured. I don't blame her for marrying Charles. She had to do somethin."

"Yeah," Bobby said. "But Charles was killed in '43. Why didn't you marry her when you got out? When was that? Forty-five?"

"Yeah. But I couldn't hardly walk for nearly a year. I had that infection in my spine. I didn't figure she wanted a cripple. How could I have even supported y'all?"

"How come you married Emma then?"

"She got pregnant."

"That don't seem like much of an answer, Virgil."

Bobby stopped the car and killed the motor and got out. He left the lights on and went to the trunk with the keys. When he came back he cranked the car and passed a bottle over.

"Here. I took this off a drunk the other night. Drink it if you want it."

Virgil lifted the bottle and looked at it. It was a pint of good whiskey and it was nearly full. It warmed his stomach when he twisted the cap off and took a drink. The car moved forward and when Bobby started speaking again he never looked around. He might have been talking to the road.

"Somebody killed Frankie Barlow over at his place last night. They think around midnight. That's why I asked you what time he got in. I can't prove nothin. It ain't even my county. And I damn sure can't watch him all the time. I ain't trying to sound like an asshole. I just know how he is. I don't want to see Jewel hurt no more. So if you see him before I do, tell him that he better be careful."

He didn't say anything else. He sped up and drove fast, powering the car into the curves and eating the miles away. He slowed a little when he got close to Virgil's house and then he turned into the drive and pulled up next to the porch. The Redbone puppy was lying there on his chain. Virgil got his beer and his whiskey gathered up and got out and shut the door. The car backed away and turned around, and then it went out of the yard and up the road, dust swirling behind it, the red taillights growing smaller and the sound of the car diminishing to a low roar that went on and on through the hills so that he could hear it for a long time, standing there under the stars, sipping from the whiskey and listening to the puppy whine and whine.

Mary was reading a book in the big armchair when he opened the door and stepped in. He turned the lock behind him and put the gun and the keys on a ledge in the hall, dropped the hat on the coffee table.

"You're out late," she said.

"The wheels of justice got to keep on rollin, Maw." He flopped into a green recliner and pushed the footrest out on it. "What you got? Another one of them trashy romance novels?"

"It's a book about Africa," she said. "I always wanted to go to Africa. Ever since Charles got killed I've always wanted to."

"Well I don't. Missippi's wild enough for me."

"Don't sit there. You'll go to sleep."

"I may do it but I'm too damn tired to move. You go to the funeral home?"

"I was just about the last one to leave. I kept waiting around on you. I just knew you'd show up. Where you been?"

"I had to go somewhere."

She got up and went into the kitchen. It was dark in there and he saw the light in the icebox come on, her robe moving in front of it. He heard her open the bottle and she came back in and handed him the beer. He took it and nodded his thanks and took a good long drink of it, lowered the contents by a third.

"And I went and talked to Virgil."

She greeted this with silence, just sat with one finger stuck up across her bottom lip the way she did and studied him. He had to be in her class when he was in the sixth grade. She watched them all that way while they did their lessons and that was when he learned that when she did that her mind was a million miles away.

"I took him home," he said. "Been down at the VFW again, drinking with Woodrow and that old Parks woman."

He took another sip of the beer. He kind of wanted to eat something but he kind of wanted to get to bed, too.

"What time you going out there tomorrow?" he said.

"I think they open at twelve. But I thought I'd get up early and make some sandwiches and take them by the house first."

"I got to go in early, too. We got to do that escort and Jake's on vacation. We're shorthanded. Hell, we're always shorthanded."

She looked down at her hands and examined her nails with her fingers straight out.

"What'd you have to talk to Virgil about?"

"I just wanted to have a little talk with him."

"About Glen?"

"About Glen and some other things, too. Can you get me up about six?"

"I reckon so. You want me to fix you some breakfast?"

"How about fixing me about three eggs and some ham and make me some biscuits? I'll take you out for an ice cream cone sometime in my cop car, give you a thrill."

"You just get up when I holler at you."

"I'm going to bed right now. Soon as I finish this beer."

They sat there for a little while. The big clock in the call ticked its slow minutes. And a little bit later she woke him, had already taken the bottle from his hand. She told him to go to bed and he did. That night he dreamed of Jewel sleek and wet on a sand dune, waves breaking behind her and a bucket and pail standing in the wash. He was building a house and he watched from the roof. The sun was hot and gulls were crying in the air. There was a grave nearby, just a wooden cross stuck up in the sand, and she was picking flowers to place around it. She was sad but he knew it would pass. He laid shingles one by one under the sun and the day was long and boats tacked in the bright water off the coast. Virgil was fishing beneath an umbrella and Puppy was working on a car. And Omar, the black bull, stood in the breaking waves and plowed them with his nose, lifting his head to the wind, his hide shining wetly and the curly hair blowing on his face.

*forshadowing*

*~ looking beyond basic roles as men*

t was late and Puppy knew he needed to get on home, but he hated to fold his hand. He was out of beer and he'd written a check to get into the game and it was lying out there now in the center of the table with greenbacks crumpled in piles, low mounds of quarters and dimes. There was a blue chip in front of him, two red ones, and a white one. Twenty-one dollars. He was holding two pair, jacks and eights, all different suits, and a three that he couldn't match up with anything. And he knew better than to try and draw to a possible full house with it this late, and with this much money lying on the scuffed table, and twenty-one dollars in front of him that he could still stick back in his pocket. All he had to do was fold and go home. But he'd been losing all night, off and on, and knew it was time for his luck to change.

"What about you, Puppy?"

He glanced over at Wayne, who was holding the deck in his hand, leaning back in his wooden chair. A small cloud of smoke hovered over the table, a vague smell of musty furniture and rat poison that seeped from the corners of the room.

"I'm thinkin about it," he said.

"Well don't think all night. Some of us got to work tomorrow."

He started to say something back but he'd already taken too long to decide. Good sense told him to get out, have money for gas and buy a few groceries. Trudy was going to be waiting up on him and if he came in broke again she wouldn't even let him go to sleep.

"Bet's to you, Puppy," Tolliver said.

"I know it."

"We gonna play or what?" Jimmy Jackson said. They were all looking at him and Wayne gave out a long sigh. There was an open half pint of whiskey sitting in front of him and he picked it up and took a small sip. He cleared his throat and set it down.

"What damn time is it anyway?" Tolliver said.

Wayne lifted his wrist and looked at his watch.

"Five till twelve," he said. "Shit, I need to go after this hand."

"I should have done gone," Jimmy said.

It was two dollars to him and they could see how much money he had left, and they probably knew too that he didn't have any more in his pocket. If he could just draw a jack or an eight. But Wayne probably had him beat anyway. Still, he hated to fold. All that money was out there on the table. If he could give her all that she might even treat him right for a change.

"Come on, Puppy, shit," Wayne said.

"I'm out," he said, and he dropped his cards on the table and pushed his chair back.

"Bout goddamn time," Tolliver said. "Bet's to you, Jimmy."

Puppy got up from his chair and picked up his chips, walked over to the table where the kitty was, and brought it back over and set it on top of his cards. He stood and watched them finish the hand, watched Jimmy rake it all in with a small flush. He got his twenty-one dollars back when they cashed their chips in and then they put in three dollars apiece for the light bill and the snacks they kept in the old icebox and then it was time to go home. They put the cards away and the chips and Wayne waited for them all to get out on the front porch before he pulled the chain on the light that hung over the table. Puppy waited on the porch and then Wayne came out and locked the door.

The grass was high in the yard and the big black trees were full of dark leaves that waved gently over the silent cars parked in the grass.

"You got a beer, Wayne?" Puppy said. "I done run clean out."

"They's some in my cooler, Puppy. Help yourself."

He walked over to Wayne's truck and lifted the lid on the cooler. The others were coming off the porch and lighting cigarettes and going to their cars. He waved, said, "See y'all later."

"Take it easy, Puppy."

"Holler at me when you ready to lose some money."

Wayne came on over and put his moneybag up on the roof of his truck and fished for his keys. The rest of them got into their vehicles and left. The yard was silent again after the cars went down the road.

"Thanks for the beer, Wayne."

"Aw, you welcome. How much did you lose?"

Puppy turned around and leaned his back against the truck and took another drink of the beer. "About twenty dollars. Glad I got out when I did."

He heard Wayne's keys land on the fender of the truck and Wayne said, "I believe I'll get me one for the road."

Wayne moved down beside him and Puppy looked at the roof of the old house, stained near black with the sap from the trees. The stars were out and shining brightly and he could see them just beyond the ridge of the house. He heard Wayne rattling around in the cooler, heard him pull one out. Wordlessly he reached in his pocket for the opener and handed it to him.

"Thanks," Wayne said. He opened the bottle and passed the opener back. Puppy slipped it in his shirt pocket. They stood there drinking under the dark trees. He felt bad about losing money again, didn't know why he kept on doing it when good sense told him not to. He loved to play, but it cost to play, and sometimes it cost too much. But he had to get out sometimes, get away from that blaring television and all the racket everybody made. Some nights he thought he might explode if he had to sit there one minute longer. Some nights he just wanted to go play cards. Leaving like that didn't make it easy to go home. But he had to go back home. He had to go to work in the morning.

"Shit," he said. "I guess I better get on in."

"Yeah, it's late. I got to be on that dock at seven o'clock."

Neither of them made a motion to move. The night breeze was cool and the beer was cold.

"I guess you heard Glen was home," Puppy said.

Wayne took a drink of his beer and leaned against the truck. Puppy heard him rattle the change in his pocket.

"Yeah, I did. I guess he's glad to be out. Three years would be a long time, locked up in a place like that."

"I guess so."

The beer was about half gone and he hated to ask Wayne for another. Sometimes he had good plans, solid plans, work hard and save his money and do better in general. But the weekends always rolled around and there was always something inside him that cried out for a little freedom even if it was only fleeting, like this: a little beer, a few games of cards. And it almost always ended up on Sunday night, just like it was now, out of beer, almost out of money.

"Get you another beer, Puppy, if you want one."

"Okay. Thanks."

He finished the one in his hand and set the bottle in the back of Wayne's truck, then groped around in the melting ice of the cooler and fished out another one.

"I guess you heard about Frankie Barlow," Wayne said.

The words came with no warning and Puppy felt dread deep inside himself. Something bad was coming and it wasn't going to surprise him much.

"Naw. I ain't heard nothin about him," he said.

Wayne lifted his bottle and drank from it, then leaned his elbows back on the truck bed.

"I went across the river to get this beer this afternoon," he said. "Couldn't get in the drive over there. Cops had the road blocked off."

Puppy wished suddenly that he didn't have to go to work in the morning. He wished he had a whole case of beer and a tank full of gas so that he could just ride and drink beer all night and not have to worry about tomorrow or any other man, surely not his brother.

"I talked to some fellers over there at the other store. They said somebody went in Barlow's place and killed him last night. I just thought you might have heard about it."

"Naw," Puppy said. "That's the first I've heard."

Their words were soft in the black and gently moving air and he wondered why Wayne hadn't brought it up in front of the others. Maybe it was because they had been friends for so long. He stood there and sipped his beer. A fox barked and a whippoorwill was calling somewhere off in the woods that surrounded them.

"When did Glen get in?"

"Yesterday. I got up early and went down and got him."

After yesterday he should have expected this. He thought about all those nights and days when he had wondered about his brother down there in that place, what he was feeling, what he was missing. All that time of knowing it was just a break in time and events, that they were only going to hold him back for a while from doing the things he said he'd do, that when it was over he would come on home and start doing them.

"They had some pretty bad blood between em, didn't they?"

"Who?"

He heard Wayne pause and take a drink of his beer. "Hell. Glen and Barlow. Wasn't that the cause of all that trouble he got into?"

He felt far apart from Glen here, close to midnight, standing in this cool black yard. But he had been so far away from him for so long that it was not a new feeling, and he took another sip of his beer.

"He went to the pen cause he run over that little boy of Ed Hall's."

It was quiet for a moment, and he hoped Wayne wouldn't say anything else about it, or think anything about his silence. He felt a little sick to his stomach, and it was going to be a long ride home now.

"Well," Wayne said. "I guess I better get on home. Six o'clock's gonna come early. I'll see you, Puppy."

Puppy fished in his pocket for his keys as Wayne started past him. "Take it easy, Wayne."

"You be careful, Puppy."

He said that he would. He got into his car and started it and pulled out ahead of Wayne. He turned the lights on and wished he had just one more beer. He thought he might be able to get to sleep if he had just one more. But he was out. And it was time to go home.

There were only a few patrons left in This Is It, it being near midnight and only the drunk and the jobless remaining. Glen was perched on a stool at the end of the bar and he'd been talking to an old man named Reeves who had been trying to sell him a car and had bought him a few beers. The old man had gone now and Glen was sitting there nursing the last one and wondering how much money he had left in his pocket. He'd convinced himself that he hadn't done anything wrong with the girl, that she'd asked for it, that it was all a misunderstanding and there was nothing they could do to him. He didn't much want to go home, but he knew he had to be in the probation office bright and early in the morning.

He looked at the clock on the wall behind the bar and saw the hand pointing to ten till. Nobody had fed any money into the jukebox in a while and the bartender was boxing up the empty bottles and counting his dough.

"How about one more over here," Glen said, then turned up his bottle and finished it. The man behind the counter reached into a cooler beside him and opened a beer and set it up on the bar.

"One dollar," he said. "Better drink up there."

Glen took his time reaching into his pocket for the money and he pulled out a crumpled wad of bills and slowly extracted a mangled single from it. He laid it on the bar and the bartender picked it up and stuck it in his pocket.

"What's your hurry?" Glen asked him.

The bartender only glanced over his shoulder for a moment, stacking the money in little piles before him. Glen figured he had a good bit back there. A right smart.

"I ain't in no hurry. I close in ten minutes."

"Aw hell." He took a sip of beer. "Maybe you better give me one more for the road then."

The bartender kept on counting his money. He did nod his head, though. Glen wondered just how much he had back there. The way he was kind of hiding it with his body as if he didn't want anybody to see it. He sipped his beer and watched the man's back. He was a pretty big man. But he thought he could probably take him.

"I said how about one more for the road here."

"I heard you."

He still didn't turn his head. He was flicking bills through his fingers and stacking them. He stopped doing that and picked up a pencil and wrote something down on a piece of paper and reached for a bank bag to his right. He bundled the money with rubber bands and unzipped the bag and put it all in there. When he set it aside and turned around he saw Glen looking at it, a little blue bag of canvas with a big brass zipper. He reached toward Glen and under the counter and brought out a little hammerless revolver with a big bore and put it on top of the money. He stood there for a moment and looked at Glen.

"You ain't finished the one you got," he said.

Glen pulled another dollar from his pocket and put it on top of the bar. It lay there between them. "I want one to take with me."

"You look like you've had about enough."

Glen looked at the clock. It said five till. He turned his head for a moment. There was a man sitting four stools down whose head was almost on the bar.

"What about him?"

"I done cut him off."

"What you gonna do with him?"

"What's it to you?"

Glen straightened up. The bartender was smiling at him.

"It ain't a goddamn thing to me. I just want another beer to take with me."

The bartender chuckled and stepped back to the cooler, brought out a beer, and opened it and set it on the bar.

"This one's on me, buddy. But it's time to go."

The bartender had folded his arms and was standing before Glen to see how things would go. Glen took another drink of the beer in his hand and looked at the money again. Then he slid off his stool and captured the other beer and went across the floor to the door. He turned around and looked back. The bartender was moving down the bar, cutting the lights off, the small neon signs that hung in the windows. Glen saw him coming around the corner of the bar and he pushed open the door and went on outside. The door locked behind him. He looked back. The bartender was watching him through a small window set into the door. He went on out to his car. There were two other vehicles out there. A small light high on a pole shed some light over the cars and the small beads of dew gathered on the hoods and the roofs. His keys were in his pocket and he got them out and opened the door and slid in behind the wheel. The motor turned over slowly when he twisted the key but it caught and he sat there revving it. He turned the lights on and read the fuel gauge. Bad news there, too, almost on E from his riding around and beer drinking. But enough to get home probably. He was pretty drunk but it wasn't that far. The tires crunched over the gravel as he backed the car around and pointed it out toward the road. He had been thinking about Jewel and the lushness of her body, the softness of her mouth, the way it looked when she unbuttoned her blouse or slid her panties down over her legs. He'd seen her naked in the moonlight, had kissed her on his knees while she lay stretched and ready on a blanket in the woods. He pulled out into the road, checked a little late to see that nothing was coming, and then eased down the road, shifting slowly, holding one beer in his hand, the other between his legs.

It was a little hard to see. The road would get unfocused on him if he stared at it too long, so he had to close one eye sometimes to get it back on track.

He fumbled in his shirt pocket for a cigarette and fished one out and got it into his mouth. The window was down on the other side and the wind was whipping the flame of his Zippo but he finally got it lit. He tried to find some music on the radio, fiddling through the static left by closed stations and the fuzz that came over the airwaves. On a nice clear night you could get a station out of Chicago, but this night it eluded him, only brief patches of music and a lot of roaring and whining. The dial was lit, a bright red line straight across the numbers, and he kept turning the knob, trying to keep the car on the road. He almost ran off it a few times, trees and ditches suddenly veering up into the windshield.

He drank the beer he was holding, gripping the cigarette and the steering wheel with the other hand. She wouldn't care what time it was. As long as he'd been gone, she wouldn't care. What she wanted anyway.

The road was crooked and sometimes the car would slide over to the shoulder, where the dirt was lumped up from the grader blades. Then he'd have to wrench it back with a violent motion of the wheel and the rear end would slide in the gravel.

"Goddamn road," he said.

He wondered if his drunkass daddy was home. Go by there and see him, tell him what a sorry son of a bitch he is. Let him know a few things. Like what a sorry son of a bitch he is and things like that.

The road climbed up over some steep hills and it was like riding a roller coaster down into the bottom of them, rocks and gravel flying. Becoming airborne. As he himself would be if he didn't watch it. But it leveled out a little and followed the backs of ridges, their wooded hills and vast hollows full of lush green growing things. Crickets singing in places to deafen the ears almost. What did it matter if he didn't even report? What could they do to him? Send him back? They wouldn't do that. They didn't want him back, and had told him so at the gate. Don't come back. We don't want your kind around here no more. Because you can't pick enough cotton. Because we have to wash your clothes and things, fix your meals. Wasting the tax-payers' money.

He knew she wouldn't be gone anywhere this late. She'd be home, sleeping soundly in her bed, or maybe even waiting up on him, a small light burning in the front room where she sat just yearning for him again. Before the weekend got over. Get one more fuck in before she had to start cooking all those hamburgers again. A little last happiness before all those hamburgers, that might be good. Lie naked and hold each other against a world that was so hard. And no talk of marriage again. He'd explain to her that it wasn't good, that it promised things it couldn't deliver, that it led to people hating each other and doing bad things to each other and then there were children and things could happen to them so that what you wound up having was not what you'd hoped for to start, a long life, happiness, good times, no. You could rock along for a while and think everything was just fine and then turn around and you were in the goddamn penitentiary. Then you'd be out there chopping cotton. Then you'd be out on the roadside in the hot sun cutting grass with a sling blade and people looking at you when they drove by in their nice cars.

She didn't realize all that. She didn't realize what all he'd been through. She didn't have any idea because nobody had ever told her because he'd never told anybody and the only other one who knew it was dead. Rotted by now. And not even a damn flower. It hit him that what he ought to do was just stop the damn car and turn it around and go over there and just kick his ass. He should have unloaded the damn gun. If he was going to load the damn gun and go out there and see about his damn chickens then he should have unloaded it when he came back in and he probably would have if he hadn't been drunk but he hadn't and how was *he* to know that it was loaded, it never had been before.

He remembered what he had said: "If you don't go out there and feed them damn chickens, I'm gonna blow your damn head off."

He remembered what Theron had said: "I done told you I'll go feed em in a minute."

Sitting there eating his breakfast. Chopping his eggs up the way he did and sprinkling black pepper all over everything and wiping his nose with the back of his thumb and biting into a biscuit and ignoring the gun that was leveled at his head while the same old screaming and arguing went on up in the front room.

"Feed them chickens."

"Fuck them chickens."

"I'm gonna tell Daddy you fucked a chicken."

"You better put up Daddy's gun."

And then when he pulled the trigger, expecting it to click.

He shivered again thinking about it and drank from the beer and wobbled over the road trying to see where to go. Things were getting really blurry now and hard to see but he didn't think he had a whole lot farther to go and he thought he could make it if he could just keep it in the middle of the road. Keep it between the ditches. That was all you had to do. A lot of people didn't know how to drive drunk and they were the ones who caused all the wrecks. It wasn't that he was so drunk when he ran over that kid, it was simply the fact that the kid ran out in front of him and he didn't have time to stop. It happened too fast and he thought it would have happened if he'd been drunk or not because you couldn't do anything when a kid ran out in front of you like that. Little bastard ought not been playing so close to the road and his parents should have been watching him a little closer or his grandparents or somebody should have been watching him and at the very least they should have told the little fucker not to play so fucking close to the fucking road cause that's where the fucking cars were. Dumb parents was all it was. Couldn't even watch a kid long enough to keep somebody from running over him.

Bad breaks Bobby Blanchard said. What did he know about bad breaks? He'd been born with a silver spoon up his ass and had good clothes and lunch money and a nice car waiting at the curb to pick him up after school everyday. Him and her both. Having to look at them all the time and see her sitting on her stool at the front of the class like she was as good as anybody else but people just didn't know how she was, what she'd done, what a whore she was. She could fool some people but she couldn't fool him. Couldn't fool his mother either. She told him where he went, who he saw, how long it had been going on and still was probably. She needed her ass whipped too. Or worse. That breeze when it came in the windows lifted the edges of her dress where she sat on the stool and he could almost look up in there and see where his father had been.

When he came to the car was still running. It was up against a tree and the lights were shining and the beer was still between his legs. He lit a cigarette and looked everything over with a kind of calm detachment and a feeling of omnipotence. No problem that could not be solved. The lights were bright in the dash and the gas gauge was sitting below empty. He found the door handle after a few tries and opened the door. When he stepped out, the sky was dusted with specks of white light. He used the left front fender to guide himself around there to where the damage was. His hand found the spotted chrome rim of one headlight and he stood there, smoking, sipping his beer, looking at the front bumper, the tree that had ground itself up against it. He was in somebody's driveway, who knows whose?

He got down on one knee next to the hood and looked at it. Somebody had made a mistake and evidently they had made it at the factory where the car had come from and it was funny he'd never noticed it before, the big emblem with the V8 hanging upside down.

"Drunk motherfuckers," he said, and stood up.

"Whew," he said.

Back the son of a bitch out of here. What did they mean having their goddamn driveway here? He looked up at the lights of the house on the hill. They probably needed a good talking to. But Jewel was waiting, still waiting beside that light, baby he's coming, he's coming baby but the Ford Motor Company has fucked up his car and it may take a few minutes.

He got back in and revved it up. He lifted his right hand in one motion and revved it up. It didn't move. Damn tree had it. He felt around on the floor with his foot for the clutch in some dim memory of remembering and pushed it in. He shoved his hand up. He let his foot out. A tire whined and the car backed away from the tree. Tiny bugs warred in flames of dust.

He got it pointed straight and backed out into the road once more. The gas gauge was flat on the bottom. Could he make it over for one more love? He could walk if he had to. He could swim if he had to. He could do anything he had to to get over there one more time.

He sang a little dirge:

All the little devils
up against the wall
yellin kill him Paw
fore he fucks us all.

A long time later, or so it seemed, he came to in a yard. He was on his back on the wet grass and the sky above him had not changed. He rolled over onto his side and looked at the car. A bush was hanging out from behind the back wheel. He found an empty beer bottle in his hand and lifted it and sucked at it, but nothing came out. The world did not love him and he knew it. He sucked at the bottle and then he laid it down.

It was hard to get up on his knees but he did. Dogs barked far off. He knelt at the edge of a gravel drive where a house sat a few dozen feet off, looming a strange subdued white in the dark. Open windows and a black porch. The house of his loved one now wrapped in slumber. It would be okay to wake her now. She had rested, waiting for him. And maybe dreamed.

He got up onto his feet and bent over for a moment. Touching his head almost to the ground. Then he did a kind of flip and was lying again on his back. Where was the whiskey? Oh God, left behind at the house. Did she have anything to drink? Would she mix him a drink? He remembered the small clipped black hairs on the backs of her thighs. When she put him in her mouth he said he was in heaven but he went to hell and stayed for a while and he didn't want to go back because they don't treat him nice like she does, gives her magnificent tits to his mouth and the milk that spurts when she squeezes the nipple kneeling over him while the baby sleeps.

He got up to the door and it was black and inside there was no noise. A pair of chains where a swing had hung. A pair of tennis shoes. A slight wind blowing that heralded maybe at long last the coming of rain. The clouds were drifting across the stars in dark bunches and he attempted some way inside the house. The door was locked and he knocked softly. Maybe she waits in a dream of screaming sex. The times he'd rocked on her like that, the way her eyes looked big enough to fall into and rimmed with something like tears and the whimpers she made and the soft animal sounds that had no description to them, so natural and pure they were. He knocked at the windows on the front porch and made his way past the swing chains and no lights came on inside. Like a cat burglar he dropped off the end of the porch into the flower bed and crept softly around the side of the house, looking for her bedroom window. House-creeping with a hard-on. He would go to her where she lay sleeping and lift her nightgown and she would awake pleasantly surprised to find him buried deep within her, orgasms beginning to melt the insides of her, how she'd moan. A shuffling curmudgeon hand-walking past the windows and tripping on the bricks she'd hauled from a dump and made her flower beds with one sunny May morning.

"Jul," he said, and then he said it again, flat, tuneless, devoid of emotion: "Jul."

The windows were open to her room and he could look through the screen but everything was black inside. He panted that same litany to the screen but no light came on. Nothing to do but go on in there. Welcome at any hour. He knew that.

Something told him not to do it but another thing did and he got his pocketknife out and unfolded the blade. It wasn't very sharp but he hooked the tip into the edge of the screen and began sawing away at it, working his way up. The stars were still up there and he mused as he worked on how pretty they were, how they should have been lying out on a beach blanket on a fern-covered forest road somewhere or on the beach at Sardis or anywhere that would be better than this, her in, him out, having to saw his way inside to her as if she were a prisoner.

He got it ripped out of the right side and then it was too high over his head for him to reach the top of it. He gave it a good pull with the knife in the other hand and the whole thing ripped away from the window frame. It fell to the ground. He looked at the knife and then folded it and put it back in his pocket. Time to get in there to the lushness of those loins. He lifted one knee first, but it didn't reach the sill. He thought maybe he should just turn around and boost himself up onto it. There wasn't any glass, was there? Not cut your ass to ribbons, what blood there'd be then. But probably not as much as Theron had coming out of his head. That boy had a lot of blood in his head. Poured it all over the kitchen he did, up under the chairs and down beside the door and out onto the porch so that they had to use mops and buckets and all that water in the buckets was bloody and they had to keep wringing the mops.

He lifted the other knee up. It didn't reach either.

"Well fuck me nekkid runnin backwards."

He ended up hoisting himself in on his belly and rolling onto the floor. He imagined himself soundless although one of his feet kicked a tall floor lamp and made it sway. On his hands and knees he crept to her bedside and laid his hand on her hip atop the covers. She moaned in her sleep and turned over. He felt around for a while, couldn't tell which end was which, where the important stuff was. And then he felt something next to her, a small body, complete with hair and legs and arms. He felt the hair and knew who it was. It caused him to stop quite suddenly.

He drew back. He could see her head on the pillow and the way she was balled up in her sleep. A light snoring that sawed through the black room. And he had not forgotten those nights nuzzling at the breasts of his mother long after he was too old to and the mammoth heat that came from her body and it soft, warm, the milk that came and how she rubbed him and held him close to her whenever the other side of the bed was empty, which was often. He said he was fishing. She said different. *That whore of his, that's where he goes.* He remembered how she looked when she was stretching in front of the window, the nightgown pulled right across the top of her, the thin morning light coming through the fabric of her gown so that her legs were planted like tree trunks for just one moment and her toes unpainted and cold on a linoleum floor.

He sat there on the rug for how long he didn't know, just listening to them breathe. Little breaths and big breaths, the faint smell of the shampoo with which they'd washed their hair. Little toys and stuffed things scattered all over the room. After a while he turned his head and saw the cat watching him, crouched in the corner like a speaker or a bookend, down on its legs. Not like a dog that would bark. Just a hateful thing with eyes that seemed to pierce the gloom and bore into the depths of his soul.

He got up after a bit, after he'd thought about everything, and quietly slid across the floor and over to the window, where he eased himself out and went across the grass to his car. It was cooling in those early morning hours, the motor not even ticking now, the car just sitting there laden with dew. He swiped his hand across the hood, lifted it to his mouth, licked at it.

He got in and the car started. He pulled on the lights and swung out of the yard, the headlights sweeping the side of the house and a small white face coming suddenly to the window to lie vanquished by the passing beams and left behind, on down the road where they lighted an owl perched on a fence post, a frozen and then bounding rabbit, a slowly trotting cow loose from somebody's pen with her sharp hipbones and her mouth trailing a mix of grass and weeds and stems.

Bobby woke early. The sun was not yet up but it was daylight. In his mother's yard the trees were standing still under their burden of leaves and the grapevines at the side of the house were likewise laden with their clusters of fruit. All of it standing in a kind of gray mist that was neither light nor dark but a halfway meeting of the two, and it felt already that the day would be hot. He turned over with his eyes open and put his head back on the pillow.

He heard Omar bawling. He heard a rooster crowing. He thought about the ham and eggs his mother would fix for him and he thought about how good it would taste, the salt on the ham, the rich yolks in the eggs. Toast with butter melting on it or biscuits with strawberry preserves. That was the last thought he had before sleep claimed him again, just before his mother knocked on the door and told him not that breakfast was ready but that Jewel was on the phone, saying she needed him, and for him to hurry and get over there.

He walked around the house a couple of times, looking here, putting his hand there. She was still shaking, sitting on the front porch, drinking coffee and smoking one cigarette after another. The tracks in the flower bed were plain, the prints of feet sunk deep in the soil and the dirt on the

166

windowsill and the dirt on her rug and her floor that he could see standing there looking in the window. He went back around to the front, carrying the piece of screen in one hand.

He tossed it down on the porch and looked up at her. She had her robe on and she was barefooted and lovely and now he was scared and mad.

"And you didn't hear nothing?" he said for the second time.

She just shook her head and sipped at her coffee without raising her face. The boards around her feet were littered with cigarette ash and she'd even thumped some on her robe.

"Well hell," he said, and stood looking at the side of the house. He looked at the drive. There was a beer bottle out there and he walked over and picked it up. He held it in his hand and studied it while she watched him from the porch. He turned the bottle upside down and not one drop came out of it. It didn't make any sense.

He walked back over to the porch and set the bottle down. There was nothing else that he could see, just the bottle and the screen and the tracks. He sat down on the top step and stared at the yard.

"Why don't you get David to come out here?" he said. "I want to talk to him."

Behind him the chair she was in creaked.

"I don't know if I should, Bobby. He's scared enough already."

He turned and looked over his shoulder at her.

"How do you expect me to do anything if I don't ask some questions?"

"He don't know nothing. He didn't move until the car started."

"You mean he just laid there?"

"That's what he said."

"Well bring him out here. I can't believe you didn't wake up."

"I can't believe it either," she said, and she got up and dropped her cigarette into one of the flower beds. Then she went to the screen door and called for the boy. She waited there for a moment and he came out in a pair of red shorts and eyed Bobby warily, looked at the gun. He sidled up against his mother's leg and hung one hand in the folds of her robe.

"Hey, David," Bobby said gently. "Come on over here and set down with me for a minute."

Still the child hung back. She bent over him and stroked his head and told him it was all right and then gave him a little push. Bobby held his arms out to him and he came over and sat in his lap. Bobby put his arms around him. He picked up one of his hands and looked at it, turning it this way and that, and then he looked at his face. That small version so much like him sitting there on his legs, the same hair, the same nose and eyes. Jewel sat down in her chair and leaned forward with her chin in her hands.

"Did you sleep good, David?" he said.

The boy shook his head. He wasn't looking at Bobby. He lowered his face and watched something on the ground.

"Did you get woke up?"

The small head nodded.

"What woke you up, David?"

He looked up at Bobby and squinted in the early morning light. "Somebody."

Bobby just held him. The thought of them lying in there like that. Not even a dog around the place to bark.

"Did you see the car, David?"

"Yes sir."

"Could you tell who it was?"

The boy looked at his mother and she put her hands together. "It's all right, David. Talk to Bobby."

The boy shook his head.

"Can I eat now?" he said.

"Sure you can," Bobby told him. He picked him up and set him on the porch. The boy went back inside the house and closed the screen door softly. She waited for a moment, until she heard him move toward the back of the house.

"You think it was Glen?" she said.

"Who in the hell else would it be?"

"It could have been anybody, Bobby."

He stood up and turned around.

"When you gonna stop making excuses for him, Jewel? Can't you see how he is by now? What's it gonna take to open your eyes?"

"If it was him he'd have knocked on the door, wouldn't he?"

"Well maybe so since he's got an open invitation here."

She stood up too.

"You don't understand nothing," she said.

"Maybe I understand a lot more than you think."

"What are you going to do?"

"What do you want me to do? I can go ask him. If I can find him. All he's gonna do is say no."

She stood there and he didn't know what else to say. He wanted to hold her but he couldn't let himself do that. Not now. He didn't want to go off and leave them but he had to get on to work sometime.

"Do your windows lock?" he said.

"Yes," she said quietly. "They lock. I just had em up last night because it was hot in the bedroom."

"Well," he said. "Tonight, I suggest they get locked. I got to go home now and eat breakfast."

She took a step forward.

"I could fix you something."

"I got to get ready for work. It's gonna be a long day. Have you got a gun?"

"You know I ain't got no gun. I wouldn't know how to use one if I did."

He walked down the steps until he stood on the walk and he turned to look back at her.

"I'll see if I can find you one," he said. "I've got another pistol at the house, or the jail one. Looks like you may need one."

"Don't leave like this, Bobby. I didn't do nothing wrong. I'm just trying to . . ." She stopped. She turned and went in the house and she shut the front door. He heard it lock. He went on out to his patrol car and got in it and left.

He told Mary what had happened while she fixed his breakfast. She was strangely quiet, moving around at the stove, making biscuits. He drank coffee at the table and got up long enough to go into his bathroom and shave. He didn't like looking into his eyes in the mirror, but he watched his face watching him while he lathered the soap and put in a new blade and drew the safety razor carefully around the curves of his chin and jaw. Even so he cut himself twice. He took little pieces of tissue and plastered them there, leaning on the sink and waiting for the cuts to dry. He dressed in a clean uniform and shined his boots and went back to the kitchen for one more cup of coffee. It was only seven o'clock when she put breakfast on the table. They ate in silence, the sun continuing to rise outside the window and lighting the kitchen while the birds sang. He finished and thanked her and leaned over and kissed her on the cheek because he loved her so much and then he went out to the front room and strapped on his revolver and got his hat.

The dawn had not lied. He could feel the places where he was starting to sweat through his shirt by the time he reached the jail. The heat in the parking lot leapt up and hit him in the face when he got out and put his hat on. He took it back off as soon as he got inside.

He kept looking at his watch as he worked at papers on his desk. On

the weekdays he had a secretary named Mable and she brought him coffee when she came in. He kept working.

At nine o'clock he had to take Byers over to the courthouse and he
walked him up the sidewalk without talking, crossed the street with him,
and took him up the granite steps to the cool and dark interior, the old
high halls. He stood in the courtroom and the judge turned down the
bond as he knew he would and set a date for the trial. Byers was claim-
ing self-defense, so a county attorney was appointed and it was all over.
He walked him back to the jail and put him back in the cage himself,
then went again to his desk and worked the morning away, trying to keep
his mind off Jewel. And David. And Glen. All he wanted to do was get in
the car and go find him, but he told himself there'd be time for that later.
There were other things he had to do today.

He didn't eat lunch at Winter's. A new cafe had opened two blocks
down the street and he went there and had chicken and dumplings, sat
lingering over a cup of coffee. By one o'clock he was out at the funeral
home and he sat with Dorris and his family for a while. His mother came
in. Most of the people from the house on Sunday came in and when it
got too thick in there for him he went out and stood on the brick walk
in front of the building and smoked. The minutes dragged by and he had
to make small talk with people. Then it was time to go out to the church.

He stood in the road beside his newly washed patrol car with the
lights blinking as the procession pulled out, all the highway traffic
stopped behind his car and him holding his hat over his heart. The
downturned face of Dorris going by, suit and tie, a prisoner behind
tinted glass. After they had all gone he got in behind them and finished
out the escort. The procession drove in no particular hurry to a little
church called Wildwood Grove ten miles out in the county, a small white
building of neat wood, ancient and nestled under a canopy of old oaks.
He stood with his hat in his hands as the casket was carried in by young

boys with men helping. Then he stood against the back wall of the church while the minister said his words and wasps hung droning above the crowd, while Dorris and his family wrenched this muted gathering with their anguished noises and tried to listen to the promise of perishable flesh that would be kept forever safe. The choir sang, voices that rose to the rafters and made the hair prickle on the back of his neck. The flowers were many and they were beautiful with their ribbons of inscriptions and their little blue handwritten cards.

He stood graveside under a portable tent and saw the mound of earth with a cheap velvet robe covering it, the yawning hole in the grass.

He stood around after it was over, people trickling away in little groups and singly, the sun burning down upon the women in their black dresses and the farmers and carpenters bound up in their stifling coats and ties. The grave diggers hung back in a line of trees, smoking cigarettes and waiting to fill it back up. He saw his mother from a distance.

He talked to Dorris and promised to visit and he hugged the boy's mother. She was ashen-faced and out of it from tranquilizers. The sun flashed on the windows and the chrome of the heavy old cars as they pulled slowly down the little dirt lane and away to the blacktop road.

He stood there until everyone was gone, squatting under a big tree at the crest of the hill as the men with their shovels came forward from the woods and began to take down the tent, uncover the dirt, pack up the folding chairs and the drapes that had hung over them. Some of the flowers were trampled and trod upon now, great colorful sheaves of them bundled up on the earth where the bees and yellow jackets came to weave among them and clamber over the blossoms wilting quickly under the murderous eye of the sun.

When they started throwing the dirt in on top of the coffin he got up and walked through the graveyard, slowly, twisting a stem of grass between his thumb and forefinger, pausing here and there to read the names of the dead and regard the times in which they'd lived. Here born 1839, there died 1934 or 1899. Old tombstones carved by hand from sandstone and their crypts cracked from time and weather, little hollows of burned grass a haven for the lizards and snakes. Ancient marble or granite turned near black by rain and sun and their dates unreadable, even the stone carver who engraved them with his chisels long gone now too. Smiling dead young marines from the first wave at Iwo Jima and soldiers and sailors with their likenesses rendered in a porcelain chip, their brass forever shining. Old people he remembered just dimly from his time as a boy now only names on stone above passages of scripture. Here was Virgil's wife, dead in her grave. He stopped and studied it. He didn't know that her name was Emma Lee and he had to bend close to read the little card. And there lay Theron too. Nobody left to take care of Virgil now but Randolph. Mary if he'd let her. He remembered Theron, the tall boy with black hair and the way he made the bat crack on the field when he stood and watched him play, the swiftness of his legs rounding the bases and the old men yelling and clapping on a hot dusty afternoon. Mary had told him that Glen had climbed on top of the barn a month after he shot Theron, that his mother and Virgil saw him before he could jump and made him come down. All the fights he'd picked in school, the things he'd stolen and all the early trouble with the law, broken store windows and vandalized buildings and joyrides in cars and hurled beer bottles and the beatings he gave boys smaller than him and how they'd finally kicked him out of school and said good riddance.

He turned away from them and went on through the grass and the stones. Where babies were buried and flowers had died. A little vacation of nostalgia, idling his time away. He didn't want to go back to town but he knew he had to.

Arriving last he hadn't been able to find a tree to park his cruiser under and it had been sitting in the sun for over an hour and the seat burned his legs when he sat down in it and put the keys in the ignition. He wheeled it around and headed out, grateful for the wind that came in the open windows.

When he got back to the jail he went inside and spoke to Mable, who nodded and kept talking on her telephone. They had finally let him buy a couple of air conditioners and it was cool in the front part of the jail and in his office. He took off his revolver and placed it on top of his desk and then bent low to a drawer on the right and opened it. Among the loose papers and fishing lures and a snarled reel and a broken stapler lay a small brown leather holster. He pulled it out and unsnapped the hammer strap and seized it by the walnut grips and looked at it. He frowned at the rust on it, but he found some oil and a cloth and cleaned it, opening the cylinder and oiling the parts, adding a drop or two behind the hammer, dry-firing it in his hand over and over. In another drawer he found cartridges and loaded it. He carefully snapped the cylinder back in and left an empty chamber under the hammer. He changed his shirt and put his revolver back on and carried the other handgun with him when he walked back through the dayroom.

"You heading out, Bobby?"

He stopped to look at Mable where she was leaning up over her desk.

"Yeah. I'm going to see Dan Armstrong and then I'll be on the radio if you need me."

"Would you sign this before you go?"

She came around to where he was with a form and a pen. He put the gun down on the desk and took the pen from her.

"You get you a new gun?" she said.

"Naw," was all he said. He scribbled his name and laid the pen down. He turned and went out the door carrying one gun and wearing another.

**A**rmstrong had his office in the old library building, a small space squeezed in between the county agent and the health clinic. Small black children lined one side of the hall, their mothers in chairs stiffening visibly as he walked past them. He spoke to them, said Good afternoon and went on by them and turned in at the end of the hall. The door was open but he reached in and rapped on the glass. Dan was bent over a bookshelf crammed with files and he turned to look at Bobby with his pipe in his mouth. He had a way of looking up over his eyeglasses at people.

"You open for business?" Bobby said.

"Come on in," he said. "Have a seat."

Bobby sat down in the chair in front of the desk and took off his hat. Through some system of his own devising the probation officer selected a space among the thousands of files on the shelf and pushed the one he was holding in among the rest of them. His forearms were covered with tattoos from his years in the navy. Palm trees with hula girls and a screaming eagle diving with talons full of arrows. He sat down in his chair and reached for a pouch of tobacco and started loading his pipe.

"What can I do for you, Sheriff?"

"I'm just checking on Glen Davis. Did he come in this morning?"

He tamped the tobacco into the bowl and from his desk picked up what looked to be a hand grenade. "He was waiting on me when I got here."

"He was?"

Dan struck the lighter and held it over the bowl of the pipe, making wet sucking sounds as he puffed and tried to get it going. Bobby set his hat on his knee.

"Standing out there in the hall."

"How's his attitude?"

"All right, I guess. Better than a lot of em come in here."

"What did he say?"

Dan had the pipe going by then and he set the lighter back on the desk, held the pipe near his jaw.

"Nothing much. Said he'd learned his lesson. Didn't want to go back. He was highly cooperative. I was impressed."

Bobby leaned back in his chair and looked out the window. He could see some leaves on a tree and part of the courthouse.

"You want to see his papers, Sheriff?"

"Yeah, I guess."

He handed them over and swiveled around in his chair to look at his files while Bobby scanned down the field report. Glen was supposed to come in weekly, every Monday at 8:00 A.M. Released early on good behavior. Served two years and eleven months. Two prior convictions for simple assault. One drunk driving. Outstanding warrants: none. Everything seemed to be in order. Except now he was crawling around in people's houses.

Bobby closed the file and handed it back. Dan took it and dropped it on his desk.

"Well," Bobby said. "How did he look?"

"About like everbody who comes in here. A little nervous. I probably would be, too. Some come in with a chip on their shoulder. Want to blame me for their troubles I guess. But no, he was fine. I gave him the regular speech. You know. Get a job, stay out of the bars. Stay out of trouble."

"And what about a job. Is he looking for one?"

"I believe he said he was going out to Chambers. Said that was where he used to work. I told him he could go by the unemployment office too and sign up to draw until he gets on somewhere. He should, really."

Dan seemed serene. His day's work was probably over. His eyes flicked back up. "Have you got some concern about him?"

"I was just checking," Bobby said, and he stood up. "Just like to keep my eye on em when they come home."

"Well I certainly appreciate your interest, Sheriff. Makes my job easier."

"Let me know if he gives you any trouble, okay?"

"I'll do that. And you have a good afternoon."

Bobby put his hat on and got out of there. Some of the children were still in the hall and some of them couldn't walk too good yet and he almost got a few of them tangled up in his legs. He lifted his arms and kind of waded through them and then he was back out on the street in the sunshine and the traffic of the town and most of the day was gone. He looked at his watch. Jewel wouldn't get off until six but there would be a couple of hours of daylight left after that. He figured she was probably still pissed off at him. He walked back up the sidewalk to the jail but he didn't go in. He got his keys from his pocket and got into the car and started it. There was still a load of paperwork on his desk but he didn't want to mess with it now. He backed out of the parking lot and drove around the square and headed south, down the wide street lined with big oaks and old fine houses, just driving. Looking in particular for Glen. He didn't know what he'd say to him this time if he found him. There wasn't much left.

He turned the volume up on the radio and put his hat on the seat. He couldn't just stay up all night or watch him twenty-four hours a day waiting for him to do something. Or even try to keep up with his comings and goings. And what if he was wrong about everything? The only thing he knew for sure was that he'd been to see Jewel one time. But no matter what Armstrong said, he knew the pen hadn't changed him. Not him. If anything it had probably made him worse. Armstrong didn't know him like he did. Armstrong hadn't grown up with him.

He drove down toward DeLay on a back road, cruising along about forty and looking at the crops, the cotton and the corn. Four-thirty. Still another hour and a half before Jewel got off. Somebody was building a new barn, a bright arch of pale lumber that rose up into the air where men stood handling shining sheets of tin that flashed in the sun. He slowed, looking at it. He thought that probably wouldn't be a bad job, being a carpenter. You could work with your hands. You wouldn't have any problems with your job after you finished working each day. Go home, drink a beer, eat supper, read the paper. Let somebody else worry about all the headaches. Just drive the nails and saw the lumber. You wouldn't have to be on call and you wouldn't always be seeing the bad side of people.

He almost didn't see the car. He was driving slowly over the river bridge and he just happened to glance down to the right. It was nosed up into a stand of cane on top of the bank and he could see a man and a woman struggling against the hood. Bobby slammed on the brakes and shoved his car up in reverse, squalling a tire and going quickly back across the bridge and a little past it, where a sort of dirt trail led down beside the bridge. It was deeply rutted but he pulled off down in there, dust rolling over and through the car. They had stopped what they were doing by the time he pulled up beside them but the woman was crying. He left the car running and got out. The man was just standing there, weaving unsteadily. He had on a ripped shirt and a pair of cutoff jeans. Beer cans were scattered over the ground. Two small children squatted beside the remains of a fire.

"What's going on here?" Bobby said.

"Arrest this son of a bitch," the woman said as she wobbled toward him. Her black hair was knotted and tangled and her bare feet were dusty. She had on a baggy pair of shorts and some kind of elastic top that stretched over her breasts. He could see her rotten teeth.

"This ain't none of your goddamn business," the man said. "This between me and her." He put one hand on the car to steady himself but it didn't do much good. He seemed to be trying to effect a casual air now that they weren't alone.

"You better watch your mouth, mister," Bobby told him. "I'm gonna ask you again. What's going on here?"

The woman had come up beside him by then and he could smell her. One little whiff that almost took his breath away. It was not the first time he had seen folks like these running loose out in the county.

"He's botherin us," she said, and she stumbled and almost fell. She grabbed Bobby by the arm but he pushed her hand away.

"I ain't bothered nobody," the man said. "I was mindin my own business. You goddamn whore."

"All right. That's enough of that. What about these kids here?"

"They mine," the woman said, and lifted a finger and pointed to the man. "And his. But he won't help me feed em and he comes around botherin me all the time and I'm sick of it. I want his ass arrested."

Bobby looked at both of them and then he looked at the kids. They had not moved. Then he looked a little closer.

"Both of you stay right where you are. You hear me? Don't make a move."

"I ain't goin nowhere," the man said, and he started walking toward a cooler next to the car. Bobby took four steps and pushed him hard against the fender.

"I said freeze. You know what *freeze* means?"

The man didn't say anything but he stayed where he was, glaring at him with drunken intensity. Bobby took his hands off him and walked toward the children. They were a boy and a girl about three or four years old. They looked like they wanted to run.

"It's okay," he said. "I'm not going to hurt you."

He could see their fear so he moved slowly, watching their lowered faces and sidelong eyes. He knelt next to them. There were tin cans in the rubble of the fire, a crude circle of rocks with the blackened stubs of sticks, the skeletons of small fish charred and dusted with ash. He looked back at the man and the woman. They were watching him, poised for flight.

"You better not move," he said.

"Can I set down?" the woman said.

He didn't answer. He reached out for what he'd already seen, the little girl's arm. A shriveled stick of flesh in his hand, the nails on the fingers deeply rimmed with dirt and the bowed arch of the two bones that run from elbow to wrist. The break had been set badly or maybe not set at all. He turned it over, this way and that. He looked into her eyes. A feral child with bright eyes shining in a bleak face and her hair home-cut and lying in long ragged waves close to her ears.

"What happened to this kid's arm?" he said.

Nobody said anything. He got up and walked behind the girl and over to the boy, a trip of a few steps, and he knelt again. He put his amazed hand gently on the boy's naked back. All his ribs showed and he was badly blistered. He touched the peeling skin with the pads of his fingers. The boy's belly was swollen. One of his eyes was matted almost shut like hounds Bobby had seen and his right arm and leg were covered with clustered bruises scattered up and down those limbs in blue and yellow hues. He stood up and stepped away from them and put his hand on his gun.

"You people are under arrest. If you move one step I'll shoot you where you stand. If you don't believe me, try me."

They didn't move. Not one muscle.

"You sit down right there where I can watch you. Go on."

The woman started crying and she covered her face with her hands. She was shaking her head and she turned and pointed to the man still frozen against the car like a rabbit caught in a pair of bright headlights.

"It's all his fault," she said. "He does it to me, too, comes in drunk and if supper ain't ready starts hittin everbody I told him he was gonna get caught you son of a bitch I told you."

"Shut up and sit down," Bobby said, and when she didn't he walked closer and pushed her hard to the ground. She landed on her ass in the dirt and rolled over onto her side, beating at the ground with her fist in her outrage and weeping as if her heart had broken in half.

"Turn around," he told the man. The man didn't want to do it. He started trying to say something, maybe words in his own defense, but Bobby just went to him and got him by the arm and turned him around and wrenched it up. The man struggled against him until Bobby laid the muzzle of the revolver into the soft place behind the lobe of his ear and leaned close to whisper through gritted teeth: "You can go easy or you can go hard and it don't matter to me. I'd like to shoot you anyway."

The man quit moving. Bobby holstered the gun and got his cuffs off his belt and shackled him tight, then led him over to the car and made him stand there while he got on the radio and started calling for some people to come help him.

They acted as if they were starving, and he guessed they were. He sat at the kitchen table with them and watched them clean up two plates apiece of hamburger patties and vegetables. Mary had given both of them a bath and borrowed clothes from a neighbor. Dr. Connor had come over and had seen to the boy's eye. He had a white patch over it now and their hands were clean and their hair was clean and they were giggling and whispering to each other and they looked a lot better.

Mary was washing dishes at the sink and she kept turning to smile at them over her shoulder. She finally hung up her dish towel and motioned for him to step out on the back porch with her.

"I'll be back in a minute," he told them, and they nodded and kept eating. When he went outside she was sitting in a chair near the railing. He hoisted one leg up on it and leaned back against the post. It was nearly dark.

"Why don't you just let them stay here tonight?" she said. "I can fix their breakfast in the morning."

"I told those people I'd meet them at eight-thirty. I need to get on down there before long. I appreciate you helping me with em, though."

He looked through the screen door at them. The boy leaned over and said something to the girl and she squealed and covered her mouth.

"What's gonna happen to them, Bobby?"

He looked at her. She was rocking gently, staring out across the yard where night was coming to the trees and the grass in ever-softening shades, creeping toward them where they sat. Night things beginning to call. The unhurried lowing of a cow calling to her baby and the little cow voice that answered.

"I can tell you what ain't gonna happen to em. They not going back to what they were living in. Right now they're in my custody. The foster home'll see after them until the court decides what to do. That may take a while, though."

"I don't understand how people can treat children like that," she said.

He let out a big sigh and turned his face toward the pasture. The cows had all gone down behind the barn.

"I don't know either. They'd be better off adopted than where they were."

"And how would that happen?"

"The court has to rule that they're unfit parents. I'd have to testify. It ain't easy to get em took away from the parents but I can talk to the judge."

"You going to?"

"Yeah. I got to."

She sat there rocking for a bit. He watched her. He'd caught her crying one time earlier, when she was dressing them in their new clothes and having to look at their bodies. They still didn't have any shoes but he could find some for them somewhere.

"Did you know those people?"

"Naw. I'd seen somebody down there fishing before by that car. They live back up around Old Union somewhere. I'm gonna take him out to their house sometime, maybe tomorrow or the next day. I want to see what it looks like so I'll have a little information before I go in front of the judge. I need to know what I'm talking about."

He got off the railing and stood up. She got out of her chair slowly.

"Are you ready?" she said.

"I guess so. I'll take em on down to the jail and meet those people. We've got some papers to sign. I got to tell the mother and daddy what's going on."

She went into the house ahead of him and was talking to the children while he picked up his hat and got his keys. He stood there waiting for them. Mary herded them toward the front door with her hands on their shoulders and he went out behind them and got them into the car. He let them both sit in the front seat. She leaned in the window and he saw her trying not to cry.

"Y'all come back and see me sometime," she said. They didn't say if they would or not. They didn't say anything. They looked at her and then they looked at him.

"I'll see you later, Mama," Bobby said, and he pulled out. They were quiet in the seat beside him. He turned the scanner up and let them listen to that. He found some gum in the glove box and they each got a piece of that. He smoked a cigarette and drove slowly and asked them if they liked to fish. They began talking to him a little. After a bit he pulled his headlights on. And after a bit the children moved closer to him on the seat and began to hold on to him and tell him of the wonders they had seen.

Virgil was sitting on the front porch working on one of his reels, an old Zebco 33 on a taped-up Eagle Claw rod that he'd owned for twenty years. He'd pulled the handle off and had been squirting some sewing machine oil behind the shaft to try and get it to work a little smoother. The line was strung out between his knees and the front face of the reel was lying on the porch when he heard the car coming down the road.

The Redbone puppy raised his head from his front paws beside him as the crunching of the gravel got louder. The blue Buick was slowing down and then it seemed to make a quick decision and pulled into the yard. Mary drew up beside the porch with the driver's side closest to him. He stopped what he was doing and put the rod and the reel down. She was smiling a shy smile and she asked him if he wanted to take a little ride. He got up for his cigarettes and then went down the steps to the car.

There was a place on the back side of her land. A POSTED sign that guarded a wire gap that stayed chained and locked. It was dark enough to use the headlights to guide them through the sunken woods' road littered with leaves that whispered under the tires. At the top of a small hill she pulled into a clearing where the trees were spread out a little and there was room enough to see the sky. She shut off the lights and the motor and they got out. She opened the trunk for him and he got out the quilt.

In near full dark he stood holding her and opened the buttons of her dress to find her naked beneath it as always in the past. He knelt in the pooled fabric of her dress at her feet and kissed her stomach while she held his head in her hands. Tree frogs were singing and through the trees the faint flare of fireflies moved slowly in the air. And she lowered herself to him with the moon beginning to come up through the trees. It hung there for a long time, soft rays shining down among the leaves.

When the dust she'd left had settled over the road, he eased back into his chair and the puppy came over. He petted him. The puppy whined and nuzzled deeper into his hand. The sound of the crickets came back, lulling him in the cooling evening air and taking him back to the last time he had made love to her, in the dark of a hot summer night, beneath that old oak tree, in 1941.

David was in his little chair rocking and watching the television while she ironed some clothes in the front room. She saw the headlights pull into the yard out past the curtains and she set the iron down and turned it off. All the doors were locked and she went to the window and looked out, saw the big star on the side and saw him cut the headlights off.

There was a switch for the porch lights beside the door and she turned it on, unlocked the door, and stepped out holding the screen door open. He was reaching back to get something out of the car and she sat down in a chair to wait on him.

"I'm runnin late," he said, and she could see something in his hand. He came up the steps and sat down in the chair next to her, holding the gun in both hands.

"What am I supposed to do with that?" she said.

"Use it if you have to."

"I don't know how to use it."

"I'm gonna show you."

He took it from the holster; to her it was an ugly thing, short and deathly. He made her take it and hold it.

"This is a double-action revolver," he said. "That means you don't have to cock it. All you got to do is point it and squeeze the trigger."

She looked at the thing. It was very heavy to her. She couldn't imagine using it on anybody or what it would do to a person.

"What is it?" she said.

"It's a .44 magnum."

She turned it over in her hands. Through the side of the cylinder she could see the ends of the brass cartridges nestled snugly in their chambers.

"I'm scared of it, Bobby. And David in the house, where am I going to put it?"

He reached over and took it back and slid it into the holster, put the strap behind the hammer, and snapped it down. Then he put it back in her lap.

"Put it somewhere you know he can't get to it. Might be better if you don't even let him see it so he don't know it's in the house. If you've got a shoe box or something, put it up high on a shelf in your closet. Keep it in one place. That way if you need it you'll always know where it is. Like if you wake up in the middle of the night or something. You hear me?"

She rubbed her hand over the holster.

"All right," she said. "Have you seen him?"

"No. Have you?"

She shook her lead a little. "No."

The bugs had started coming into the light and some of them had landed on the porch and were crawling over it. Bobby put his foot out and crushed one with his boot. A thin dry crackling.

"How's David?" he said.

"He's okay."

"He said anything about it?"

"Not much. I had to leave him with Miss Henderson today and I had to work late. I fixed his supper and he's been watching TV. He's all right."

That seemed to satisfy Bobby.

"Well," he said, and he got up. "I guess I better get on. It's been a long day."

She sat holding the gun and looking up at him.

"Why don't you come on in? I can fix you a cup of coffee."

There was something in the way he watched her that made her afraid a little. They both heard the car coming and turned their heads as it slowly went by. There under the bright light on the front porch they watched it go by in plain sight and saw his car and saw for a brief moment Glen looking out at them and then flipping a cigarette butt into her driveway. The car neither sped up nor slowed down, just kept traveling at the same rate on down the road and out of sight.

She didn't say anything. He didn't either. He just ran down the steps and got into his car and cranked it and pulled away.

He was thinking of the little sand road just beyond the next hill and he kept his eyes on the rearview mirror for as long as he could see the straight part of the road behind him. Once over the hill he sped up and then spun the car into the side road and rocketed down through a gully of dust and gravel and sailed up the next hill and powered it into a sliding drift that took him around the next curve and his only hope was that he wouldn't meet anybody at that speed. At the T in the road he took the right turn and shifted into second and kicked hard down on the gas and wound it up tight, dropped it back into third and looked back for Bobby. He took the old car fast up the patched blacktop past rusted fences and a crumbling barn, black cows on green grass, into the woods that began there and into a vast cavern of trees and hanging grapevines, the headlights boring a tunnel that he followed. He stuck one hand out the window and waved at nothing.

"Adios, motherfucker," he said.

Late that night in her bed she held David close and stroked his sleeping head. It was hot with the window down and she could feel a thin film of sticky moisture in the folds of skin at her throat. She rubbed at it with the web of her hand and looked at the dark ceiling. A small fan was casting waves of humid air over the single sheet that covered them. David had been asleep for over an hour but tonight it wouldn't come to her. Not now. Not with it this hot.

She got her arm from around him and eased out of the bed. He didn't stir. She covered him back up with the sheet and went across the floor, her bare feet padding softly, out the bedroom door and down the short hall to the kitchen. There were some little Cokes in the icebox and she opened one and went out to the living room where she'd left her cigarettes, turned on the lamp, and sat down in the chair that faced the television. She didn't turn it on.

The cigarettes were on the table there and she shook one loose from the pack and lit it with a match and then blew the match out, dropped it into the ashtray. It was very quiet with David asleep. He was growing up fast and he didn't understand about the things grown people did. He didn't understand why his daddy didn't live with them and it was hard for her to make him see why. Virgil had been good to spend time with

him and she was grateful for that. David always came back happy from
their little fishing trips.

The cat came out of the bedroom, hugging the wall, rubbing against
a chair and the lamp. It stopped and stood whipping the tip of its tail,
watching her. Then it walked across the floor and jumped up on the
couch and stretched out.

She knew it was cool out on the porch. She got up and went over to
the front door and unlocked it, pulled it open so that maybe a little air
would come in through the screen door. A slight breeze was weaving
through the ferns that were hanging on the front porch. There was no
sound coming from the bedroom. She went back and got her Coke and
picked up her cigarettes and went out, holding the screen door and not
letting it slam behind her.

The floorboards were cool on her feet. She sat in a dark chair on the
dark porch and looked out at the road shining under the moonlight. Out
there beyond the fence the trees stood humped in black and silver tones.
Clouds were drifting over the face of the moon. It felt like it used to
when she slept on the screened-in porch at her father's house. He'd been
gone a long time now and she barely remembered him. The red ember
of her cigarette brightened and glowed when she put it to her mouth
and drew on it. She could hear the smoke whistling out of her lungs
when she exhaled. She could hear the slow crunching of gravel under
tires, almost like somebody walking but louder than that. And then she
saw that a car was creeping down the road above her house, the lights
off, moving just barely above an idle. She stubbed the cigarette out
quickly on the leg of the chair and sat perfectly still. Maybe it was darker
under the overhang of the porch roof where she sat. The car came on
not moving any faster than a person could walk, maybe not that fast. She
began to hear the sound of the motor. The car slowed and it looked like
Glen's. It stopped in front of the house and sat there. A match flared

inside the car, a face was briefly lit. And then a hand came out the window and an arm hung down the side of the car. The hand moved the cigarette back and forth to the face. Somebody watching her as she watched him.

The wind picked up a little and wafted the leaves of the ferns up and down. They rocked a bit in their pots, turning and swinging on their chains.

And then the car started moving again. The hand that held the cigarette still trailed down the side of the door. It went away as slowly as it had come, not hurrying, not making very much noise at all. She sat there and watched it. It went on down the road and she couldn't hear it for very long, thought maybe it might have stopped. But then down the road some distance she couldn't judge, through the trees a pair of lights came on and the car picked up speed and ran away through the night, a fading roar in the vastness of the land lying around her that died away in gradually diminishing bits of sound until there was nothing left to hear but the quiet of the darkness and the crickets still speaking out there in the wet grass.

She got up, grabbed her cigarettes, and locked herself back inside the house. She turned off the light in the living room and when she went back to the bedroom she reached high into the closet and found the handgun in its cardboard shoe box and put it under the mattress, a hard lump she could feel beneath her for a long time until finally worry and weariness closed in, took over, conspired together to take her to a land of dreams where dark things moved and shadows rustled.

He lay there alone in his black bed in the blackness of the house with the dark walls around him. The wind was blowing a little and the weak moonlight made shapes and forms that roamed up and down the torn wallpaper when the leaves on the trees in the yard moved and swayed. He'd stripped the bloody sheets off and they lay piled in a pale white bundle in one corner. There was just the rough ticking of the mattress against his skin, a loose button that dug into his ribs if he turned the wrong way. He'd had neither drink nor the comfort of another's hand. Just the endless roaming over the roads and the ceaseless cigarettes and the music that he was already tired of hearing. And how many nights had he lain like this already? In the saw and whine of a thousand sleeping throats he'd imagined a world different, a better place than the one that had been his for so long, as if stepping out those iron gates would free more than his physical body and allow him to regain some sort of balance, quell his anger, drive away the bad memories, make possible all the things he wished could be. But he saw now that it wasn't going to be like that. He'd been gone too long.

The back door was loose on one hinge and he could hear it flopping, rattling, a soft and steady bang bang that was keeping him awake. That's

LARRY BROWN

what he told himself. He knew now what she'd meant in the cafe when she said that things had changed. She must have meant for herself only, because for a long time now his heart had been darkening and hardening within his chest and he had felt it and felt it again now like stone, cold and lost to him and his eyes would not close.

Tuesday morning it was cramped and small inside the well house. The door was open and the overhead light was on and the puppy was keeping Virgil company by lying right outside. A few tools lay in the damp dirt between his feet, a chipped screwdriver, a small adjustable wrench, a hammer, some Allen wrenches. He was sitting on an over-turned bucket. He could make the pump run for a few minutes but he thought it had lost its prime. And even if he had a new contact switch, it wouldn't matter unless he had about five gallons of water to prime it.

He tapped on a pipe with the screwdriver, looking at it. He turned around to the puppy.

"She's tore up," he said.

The puppy raised its head and looked at him. The red tail thumped halfheartedly on the ground and he whined a little.

Virgil tapped the pipe some more. The joints of the brick walls in the well house hadn't been finished smooth on the inside and the mortar had squeezed from between the bricks and dried like cake icing. Herman House had laid them one pretty fall day and he'd been gone a long time now. Virgil dropped the screwdriver.

"Yep," he said softly. "Long time now."

He reached in his pocket for his rolling papers and the little red tin of

Prince Albert and rolled one, glancing at the Redbone watching him. He lit his smoke and waved the match out, let it fall to the dirt. It was kind of nice to be in the well house. It was always cool in there from the moisture of the pipes.

"Need a new contact switch," he told the puppy. The puppy lowered his head and regarded him from his paws with his eyes rolled up mournfully.

"Know what that costs?"

The puppy didn't move. He closed his eyes.

"Fifteen bucks. Fifteen bucks, buddy."

The puppy didn't appear to be listening anymore. Virgil looked at the pump a little while longer.

"And you ain't gonna pump no water till you get one, are you?" he said to it.

The full heat of the sun hit him when he crawled from the little brick building on his hands and knees and stood up, slapping the dust from his hands. The puppy was standing there waiting as if they were going somewhere. Even if he had the switch, he needed that water to prime it. A barrel to haul the water. A pickup to haul the barrel.

"I ain't got shit," he told the puppy, and then he walked up on the porch.

It was the middle of the morning before anybody came by. He was sitting under the shade tree in a steel porch chair reading a story about grizzly bears in an old hunting magazine. He'd made some coffee and was sipping that and he'd brought the whiskey out with him and was sipping that too. The man in the story had been hunting grizzly bears but had accidentally surprised one and had been mauled for a while, dragged around over the ground screaming, then buried alive beneath leaves and twigs and dirt and bear shit. He'd lain there for a while, playing dead, bleeding from two dozen places, fading in and out of shock, waiting for the bear to go away, and after a long while when things had gotten totally quiet and he was absolutely sure the bear had gone away, he'd crawled out from under the pile of nastiness the bear had buried him beneath only to find the bear waiting, and it had begun to maul him and drag him around screaming again.

"Goddamn," Virgil said. "I believe I'da climbed a tree."

He heard something coming and looked up. The sun was bright on the gravel road and he saw a pickup coming down it, a greasy tank in the back end, a small emblem on the door. It was the truck Puppy used to haul fuel and parts and grader blades to the backhoes and tractors and road machines the county owned. He slowed down and swung in and pulled up right beside Virgil in his chair. He got out. He hadn't shaved in three or four days and his shirt was already soaked through with sweat.

"What are you doing?" he said, and he plopped down on the ground there beside him.

Virgil closed his magazine after bending down one corner of the page. He dropped it under his chair. It was getting too hot to sit out there much longer.

"I'm still messin with this well. It ain't dried up. But it's lost its prime I reckon. I need to get a part on it and try to haul me some water over here some way."

He reached down for the whiskey and took a small sip. He offered the bottle but Puppy put one hand up.

"Not when I'm on duty. W.G. would fire me in a second. What are you doing hitting the hard stuff this early?"

He held it in his lap and grinned. "I don't know. I ain't got nothing else to do."

"Damn, Pop. You feeling good today, ain't you?"

"I guess I am."

"I wish to hell I did. They workin my ass off today."

He sat up and looked around. "You still got that barrel in the back-yard?"

"Yeah."

"You got a lid to go on it?"

"I think so. Pretty sure I do."

"Well come on and let's load it up and I'll run you by the parts store. I got to pick up a carburetor and we'll find some water somewhere and I'll bring you back over here. Will that fix you up?"

Virgil got the bottle from the grass and stood up.

"It ought to. You sure you got time?"

"Shit yeah. I'm going anyway, come on."

Puppy backed the truck around in the yard and they put the barrel in. Then they went inside and Puppy fixed himself a glass of water from the little that was left in the wine jug while Virgil changed his shirt and combed his hair. In a few minutes they were going down the road.

Virgil chewed a piece of gum while the water ran from the hose inside the service station into the barrel. It was very hot out there on the con-crete and he watched the traffic as cars pulled in and rang the bell on the pumps. Boys in blue clothes wiped windshields and pumped gas. Puppy was inside in the air-conditioning, smoking cigarettes in the cool com-fort. It took a long time to fill the barrel up. He let it run until he figured he had about forty gallons in it and then he walked inside the shop and cut the faucet off. He took the hose from the barrel and coiled it back neatly and hung it on the rod where it had been.

Standing in front of the big panes of glass he waved to his son, and Puppy came on out and they got back in the truck.

"Wait a minute," Virgil said. He got out and went back and put the lid on the barrel, clamped the band around it so the water wouldn't spill. Then he got back in. Puppy pulled out to the edge of the concrete apron and then swung out into light traffic. Trucks and cars were parked against the curbs and some workmen were putting a new sign up on a little grocery store where produce sat on the sidewalk, striped watermelons and bushels of tomatoes.

"Damn it's hot," Puppy said.

Virgil wiped at the sweat on his forehead and hung his elbow out the window.

"Where y'all working at today?"

"Over there on Bell River Road. We had to put in some culverts so we can blacktop that road. We gonna blacktop yours next."

"It's about time. How long's that gonna take?"

"We'll be through by September we hope. Then we'll start on em again next spring. Looks like he wants to blacktop the whole damn county before election time rolls around."

Virgil rubbed at some grease on his hands. "How's he to work for?"

"Aw, he's all right if you don't ask him too many questions. He gets upset if you ask him a bunch of questions."

Puppy pulled up at a stop sign and waited for a woman pushing a baby buggy to come across. "You seen anything out of Glen?" he said.

"Not since Sunday. He slept at my house Saturday night. I got up and made us some coffee. Tried to talk to him for a while."

Puppy turned his face a little. The woman and the baby got across to the sidewalk and he pulled out into the square.

"How come him to spend the night with you?"

"I don't know."

"Huh."

"What?"

"Nothin. I figured he'd stay with her. Didn't he go see her?"

Virgil looked out the window at the shops and the stores. "Yeah. He went to see her."

They drove around the square where shiny automobiles were parked in rows alongside shabby junkers. A concrete truck was parked on one corner and men in black knee boots were finishing forms for new sidewalks.

The parts store was just on down the street and Puppy started looking for a place to park. He stopped in front of a furniture store and backed into a space there and shut off the truck. They got out and went down the sidewalk together, Puppy hitching at his pants with both hands. They turned in at the double glass doors and a little bell rang when they pushed through them. Sporty steering wheels were hung on the walls, brake shoes and packets of spark plugs and tools of every sort all shiny and chromed. People were sitting on stools at the counter and men with pen clips in their pockets were moving slowly behind the counter filling orders. Puppy and Virgil stood there for a moment.

"Damn they're busy today," Puppy said. "Let's grab us a stool and set down."

They found a pair and sat down and put their feet up on the rungs.

"Be with y'all in a minute," a man said.

"We ain't in no hurry," Puppy said. "Y'all got it good and cool in here."

He got out a smoke and lit it, then swiveled around on the stool to face Virgil.

"I can't get over him spending the night with you. It just ain't like him. Maybe he's gonna settle down now that he's home."

"I doubt it. I took a ride with Bobby other night."

"Bobby? What for?"

"He wanted to talk about Glen. Did you know somebody killed Frankie Barlow?"

Puppy's eyes shifted away from Virgil until they were looking down at the floor. He glanced back up. "I heard about it."

"You know anything about it?"

Puppy let out a big sigh. "I took him over there Saturday afternoon before we come to see you. But Barlow wasn't there. We met him on the road heading back. I don't know nothin else about it. And don't want to."

Virgil sat there for a moment, thinking things over.

"Did you tell him about Bobby and Jewel?"

"It ain't my place to tell him. Besides. I don't want him pissed off at me."

"Why in the hell should he care? He ain't gonna marry her anyway. I knew that before he ever come home."

"Well," Puppy said. "You know how he is about Bobby. He can't stand the ground he walks on. All it's gonna be is just more trouble."

They sat there quietly for a while. Virgil looked at his fingernails.

"When you gonna fix my car?" he said.

"I'm gonna get around to it."

"You've had it two months."

"I know it."

"I get tired of walkin."

"I know it."

Somebody finally came down and waited on them. They ordered their parts and waited a few minutes and the man came back out and placed a big gray box on the counter. Puppy opened it and pulled out the carburetor and turned it over in his hands.

"That looks like her," he said, and put it back in the box. He scratched the back of his neck and leaned his elbow on the counter. The man made a note on a piece of paper and left again.

"There ain't no need in worrying about him, Daddy. It ain't gonna do no good."

"I can't help but worry about him," Virgil said. "I always knew he was gonna wind up in the goddamn penitentiary."

They waited some more and smoked another cigarette apiece and then the man came out with a small green box and set it down. "Look at it and see if that's it," he said.

Virgil slid the bottom of the box from under its lid and picked up the contact switch. He opened and closed it, looked at the shiny new points.

"That's it," he said.

"Good. That's the last one we got."

Puppy signed a ticket on the county for his part and Virgil paid for his. They picked up their stuff and Puppy crammed the flimsy copy of the ticket in his pocket as they went out the door.

"I'll run you back over to the house and then I need to get on back to work," he said. "I'll come by this evening and see if you got it runnin."

"I'm gonna need that water to prime it. Can you stick around long enough for me to put it on?"

Before he could answer, Ed Hall stepped from the cleaners with some shirts and dresses in a plastic bag and he was concentrating so intently on a little piece of paper in his hand that he bumped into them. Virgil stopped.

"Excuse me," Puppy said, and started around him.

Ed looked up to see them suddenly and his face turned red. "You ought to watch where you going," he said.

Puppy stopped and turned around. He hadn't heard him plain evidently. Virgil took a few more steps and got up beside him.

"What?" Puppy said.

Ed Hall was standing there with his clothes in his little plastic bag. Small and enraged. It was very hot there on the sidewalk. Cars were going up and down the street beside them.

Ed Hall looked at Virgil and jerked his head toward Puppy. "Is he yours too?" he said. "Or do you even know?"

Virgil started walking toward Ed Hall but Puppy stepped in front of him.

"What'd you say?" said Puppy.

Virgil caught Puppy by the arm but he snatched it away. He walked up to Ed Hall and stood very close to him. "You little sawed-off mother-fucker you better shut your mouth."

"Wait a minute, now," Virgil said, and tried to get between them, but there wasn't any room between them by then. Puppy didn't even look at him.

"Stay out of this, Daddy." He stepped a little closer to Ed Hall. "You want me to slap the shit out of you?"

Puppy still had the carburetor in one hand and he was poking Ed Hall in the chest with a greasy finger, little dark spots appearing on Ed's white shirtfront as his face got redder and redder.

"You people ain't nothing but trash," Ed Hall said.

Puppy bent over to set the carburetor on the sidewalk. "I'll show you some trash," he said.

Ed Hall dropped his dry cleaning on the sidewalk and drew back and kicked Puppy in the side of the head. Puppy landed on the concrete on his hands and knees and his cap came off. Virgil bent over to help him but Ed Hall kicked Puppy again.

"You little asshole," Virgil said. He swung wild and Ed Hall leaped out of the way and jumped back and tattooed Virgil on his right ear. It felt like a boxcar had slammed into his head. He fell up against a pickup. People were starting to come to their windows to watch. Ed Hall was dancing around, his fists up.

"Come on," he said. "I'll whip both of you right here."

Puppy got up off the sidewalk. He was almost crying with his rage. "Why you son of a bitch, you hit my daddy."

Ed Hall jumped in and popped Puppy twice on the nose, then danced out of the way. He had pretty good footwork. Puppy reached up for his nose and then looked at the blood on his fingers. He seemed amazed by it. Virgil tried to get off the pickup but he had an awful pain in his ribs. It almost took his breath away. He couldn't believe what was happening. Puppy was following Ed Hall around on the sidewalk, swinging and missing. Ed Hall was jumping in and out like a banty rooster, hitting Puppy whenever he wanted to. People were coming up the sidewalk and from across the street to watch.

"Somebody call the law," Virgil said weakly, not loud enough for anybody to hear him.

Puppy was starting to breathe hard and his legs weren't steady under him. Blood was running into his mouth and it spewed out in little flecks as he talked.

"Why don't you stand still?" he said.

"Why don't you make me?"

It didn't go on much longer. Ed Hall made a misstep and Puppy got his hands on him. He bent him backwards like a dancer and the tiny fists drummed on his broad back and the side of his head but Puppy bore him relentlessly to the concrete so that Virgil could see his eyes wide with fear as the bulk of the huge body that was hugging him so tightly began to smother him from sight. Puppy had him down, flat on his back, choking the shit out of him and beating his head senseless against the base of a parking meter when the city police arrived.

They sat in chairs at the jail with their bandages on. Virgil had scraped his ear somehow and his hand too and they'd wrapped them at the hospital. Puppy had numerous skinned places and bruises. They heard steps coming but they didn't look around, just sat there staring at the wall. Bobby stopped in front of them and stood there for a second, then folded his arms over his chest and shook his head.

"Well?" he said. "Y'all able to walk?"

"I'm all right," Puppy muttered. "Little son of a bitch."

"What happened?"

"He started it," Puppy said. "We wasn't doing nothing but minding our own business."

"That right? He says you cussed him."

"He's a lying bastard, too."

Bobby looked down at them reproachfully. "Well. Whatever. I think you got more to worry about right now than the city police. W.G. called up here a while ago and wants to know what the hell's going on. I've got a patrolman to take you back to your truck. He's got your carburetor, too. Hope you ain't lost your job over this, Randolph."

"I hope I ain't, too," he said. He got up slowly from the chair. "I better not have."

Bobby unfolded his arms and put his hands on his hips. He glanced at Virgil. "And what does that mean?" he said to Puppy.

Puppy gave him a look that Virgil didn't like to see. Puppy was slower to rile than Glen but Virgil had always known the waters in him ran deeper.

"It don't mean nothing, Bobby. You gonna take Daddy home?"

Bobby ducked his head and nodded. They could see just the brim of his hat bobbing up and down.

His voice was low. "Yeah. I'm gonna take your daddy home."

"Okay then." Puppy half turned for just a second, swung one hand out wide from his body, and looked back at Virgil, already beginning to move away. "Watch out for them left hooks, Pop." And then he was gone.

Bobby dropped into the chair beside him. Virgil had his hands folded in his lap and he just looked at him. He'd probably have to listen to some more shit now. And still didn't have his damn well running.

"What do you mean getting in a fistfight, at your age, right in front of God and everybody?"

Bobby was looking at him like he was a child and he expected the right answer.

"What'd he say to you?"

"What's it matter what he said? He said something, we got in a fight, it's over. I'll pay my damn fine or whatever. I ain't gonna whine to you. I don't need you to take up for me. We took up for ourself."

Bobby studied him for a little bit. Then he smiled a very small smile. "Don't look like you did too good a job to me. How bad you hurt?"

"I'm all right. Just bruised some ribs a little. I just got to take it easy for a while."

Bobby stood up. "All right, then. Let's get you somewhere you can take it easy for a while."

He put his hand out. Virgil looked at the hand and then he looked up at the face. A gentle smile, a big strong arm. He knew it was more than he deserved, and he was grateful for it.

"Thanks," he said, and he let Bobby help him up out of the chair. His ribs were hurting and he guessed stuff like this was always worse when you got older. He didn't know how he was going to get his well fixed now.

The man across the desk from Glen had been studying the application for a long time, much longer than it should have taken to read it. There wasn't much on there. He'd worked here for two years before he'd gone to Parchman, and he'd seen this office before. Drab green walls and a crooked set of venetian blinds. A chipped tile floor and squeaky wooden chairs. He'd been wanting a cigarette but he didn't see an ashtray and he was intimidated about asking. But it shouldn't have taken this long anyway. The man in the chair behind the desk had not raised his head for several minutes. Glen cleared his throat but the man didn't look up.

Wait around on this asshole all day to make up his mind. He didn't even want the job anyway, but he had to have one somewhere. And no telling what they'd put him to doing. They might stick him back in the paint room or somewhere, have to wear one of those masks all day long, be in some cramped little place doing the same thing over and over. He was hoping maybe he'd get on in the stockroom or at the shipping dock, someplace where he could drive a forklift or fill orders and not be stuck on the assembly line putting screws in holes on stove frames forty hours a week. Handling insulation. There were a lot of bad jobs in this place, and some people had been doing them for twenty years. This was just temporary. This was just for the probation officer. And he needed the money anyway. What he'd taken out of Barlow's register was just about gone. A few more nights of drinking and eating drive-in hamburgers and it would be gone. He wished the guy would hurry and make up his mind.

The man didn't put the application down. He just kind of released it from his hand and let it float down to the desk. It spun a little and turned, sliding across the desk, and slipped over the edge and wafted down to the floor. Glen looked at it. When he raised his eyes the man was watching him and not kindly. The man didn't seem to fit behind the desk. He was too big for his clothes. His eyes were cold with the look of a hawk, unblinking, steady, not cruel but not caring either. Indifferent then. As if Glen's livelihood and his request for employment once again at the Rangaire Corporation didn't matter one whit.

"You thow everbody's application on the floor like that?" Glen said.

The man leaned back in his chair and crossed his arms over his belly. The chair squeaked. Outside the room there was the slam of presses and the tortured whine of metal being torn and ground away. A palpable hum of noise and the dim shriek of shouting voices.

"You don't know me, do you, Mr. Davis?"

Glen studied him. He knew he'd never seen him before. But the man knew him, that was plain.

"Naw. I don't know you. Am I supposed to?"

"You knew my son briefly. He's gone now. Overseas. Fighting in another goddamned war they've got started."

"What's that got to do with me?"

The man leaned forward slightly in his chair for a pencil that was on the desk. He held it by the eraser and turned sideways in the chair and began tapping the lead on the edge of the desk. Just gently tapping it. Making tiny little noises that mixed with the sounds from the factory behind them.

"There was a basketball game at the high school. One night years ago. You might not even remember it. I think you were drunk."

"I been to a lot of basketball games," Glen said.

"My son was sixteen," the man said. "A boy. He accidentally bumped into you coming out of the bathroom and you hit him in the face and broke his nose. Do you remember that, Mr. Davis?"

He remembered a fight. He'd been drinking and fucking in a parked car and he'd gone inside to use the bathroom. In those days he used to pick up girls at the ball games. It wasn't even a fight. The boy had never even seen the punch coming. He had bumped into him and said he was sorry almost simultaneously and had started turning to walk away and Glen had hit him with a straight left hand without thinking, automatically, and the boy had gone down hard.

The man was waiting for an answer. Glen shrugged.

"Barely. It was a long time ago. Look, mister, I'm just trying to get me a job."

"You're not going to get one here. You're lucky I didn't come after you myself. Now don't let the door hit you in the ass on the way out."

Seventeen dollars and sixty cents. He held it in his hand and laid it on the seat of the car and looked at it. He had a full tank of gas in the car, but it was drinking it pretty fast. He didn't know if it was because it had set up for so long or what. He thought about riding over to Puppy's and getting him to take a look at it, but he was probably working today.

He looked at the money again and put the bills back in his wallet and slipped it into his hip pocket. Sitting in the parking lot he looked out over the concrete walls of that big cage and thought about the lives going on inside it, how they were strapped into this place almost like he had been strapped into that other one. But they could go home at night. Their cars and pickups were waiting for them on the hot asphalt. He cranked up his own car.

"Fuck all of you," he said out the window. "I didn't want to work here anyway."

He headed back up the little blacktop road he had come down and then halted at the stop sign and looked both ways. A truck was coming, stacked high with mangled pine logs, their limber ends wagging and swaying. The truck rolled past in a grind of dust and falling bark that landed in the road. Glen pulled out behind it. The car wasn't running very well.

"Come on, you son of a bitch," he said, watching the speedometer and listening to the motor. "Goddamnit," he muttered. He pressed harder on the gas and it smoothed out a little, but it made him uneasy. He didn't want to get broken down on the road somewhere. If he just had some money everything would be all right for a while. He wondered if Virgil had any. Maybe, maybe not. The little bit of Social Security he drew each month probably didn't go too far. But he didn't have to pay any rent, and he didn't have to take care of anybody besides himself. His light bill probably wasn't much. He bought a little food and whatever he drank and his cigarettes. A little dog food for that puppy. It looked like he was still raising his own vegetables. So if he was saving some, where would he stash it? Would he have it in the bank? Or would he have it stuck back in some drawer, or under a mattress? He'd never been one to use the bank very much. Glen had never even seen him write a check. His mother had kept a small account, had sent him money from time to time when he was in the pen, little ten- and fifteen-dollar checks that he cashed to buy cigarettes and 7UPs.

The log truck slowed ahead of him, turned left, and went down another road. The car smoothed out some. He guessed it was probably around ten o'clock or so. Puppy would be at work, but the old man was probably home. He didn't feel much like spending the whole day looking for a job. It was probably going to be the same story everywhere he tried when they saw that missing three-year gap and found out he'd been in the pen. He'd have to answer all their questions, humble himself to a bunch of pencil-pushing assholes with their little chickenshit paychecks and rules and hours. Their time clocks to punch. He didn't want any of that anyway. He just needed about a hundred dollars. That would keep him going for a while, just until he got on his feet. He thought he'd drive by the old man's house and see if he was home.

He pressed harder on the gas and listened to the motor. It seemed to be sounding stronger and stronger.

There was a chair in the yard beneath the small tree, a magazine lying under it whose pages had been riffled by the wind. He walked over and looked down at it. He knelt and reached under the chair and picked it up, turned back the pages and gazed at the cover. A spotted trout leaped there with a hairy fly imbedded in its jaw and a line stretching back to a tiny man standing far away on the bank of a stream. The date on the cover was March 1959. He used to love to read these things and he remembered this one because there was a story in it about bears. The subscription label bore the name Emma L. Davis. One more remnant of his mother. One more thing she had done for them.

He dropped the magazine in the chair and looked around. The Redbone puppy was lying under the porch watching him. He walked toward the house. The puppy came out wagging its tail but he paid no mind to it. When it came up and tried to lick his hand he just kicked casually at it and told it to get away. It seemed puzzled, standing there watching him go up the steps and over to the screen door.

He pulled it open and stuck his head inside.

"Hey. Daddy. You here?"

A house full of silence answered him. He stepped inside and took a few steps down the hall.

"Hey. Old man. You asleep?"

The bed in the front room was empty, the sheets rumpled and swept halfway to the floor. The television dead and black. There was no telling where he was. Probably over there fucking that old woman again. It looked like he would have had enough by now. All those nights he'd stayed gone. What had they done about Bobby? Had they met somewhere? Had they done it in a car or a motel or out in the woods? All the arguments and the screaming when he came home, all his mother's tears. Sad times and the weight of them still pulled at him. And now Bobby carrying on with Jewel. Somebody was going to pay for that. Nothing but a bunch of sorry son of a bitches around him his whole life.

He walked on down the hall, calling out a few more times. By the time he got to the kitchen he knew there was nobody home. The empty cups they'd used were still in the sink, the coffeepot sitting where he had left it on the dead stove eye. But now there was a pint bottle of whiskey on the kitchen table. He picked it up and opened the screen door. Some chickens were walking around on the back porch. He stepped out there, watchful where he put his feet. He shooed and kicked at the chickens and they fluttered squawking. The old cars baked under the sun in the yard. Some of them had been sitting there for as long as he could remember, junkers hauled in and never hauled out, cannibalized for parts, rusting lower and lower into the ground each year, his mother's beggings to his father to remove them falling on deaf ears.

He sat down in a chair and took the cap off the whiskey and turned the bottle up. It burned going down and his eyes watered a little. He put the cap on the arm of the chair and studied the faded hulks before him.

"Why don't you clean this damn place up?" he asked softly. He shook his head and took another drink. After a while he got up and put the cap back on the whiskey and stuck it in his back pocket and began moving through the house, looking for money.

The first place he tried was Virgil's bedroom. He was loath to go in there, more so after he saw his mother's clothes hanging in the closet. Standing there in front of the opened double doors he touched a white dress with small blue spots, a matching belt that hung in braided loops at the waist. He could see her walking in it, her purse in her hand. He rubbed the material between his fingers, felt the smoothness of it slide on his fingertips. He let it drop. Her shoes were there on the closet floor in a pile. Her one good coat stuffed in between the dresses. Why did his father keep all this stuff? He guessed he had loved her at one time. He didn't know when things had gone so wrong between them. Things had gotten jumbled together in his mind. Times and events. After she'd gotten sick he'd thought of trying to escape, but it always seemed so hopeless to him, standing at the back of a truck loading or unloading with other prisoners and looking off into the distance at the fields burning under the hot air, the thousands of acres of Delta land that stretched away to the far tree lines and somewhere out there ending in twelve-foot razor wire. The guards rode horses and carried shotguns for those who would run. Nights locked into the camps and everything outside alight with the beams from the fence and the invisible guards with their bolt-action deer rifles. He never had tried them, never formed a plan. Three years sometimes didn't seem that long. Sometimes it seemed an eternity. He had missed her cooking. And missed it now this moment he stood looking at her clothes.

He turned away from the closet and looked at the things in the room. A dressing table like Jewel's, small white bottles and jars still sitting there. A hand mirror facedown on an embroidered doily. Walking closer he saw envelopes addressed to his mother in his own hand. He pulled back the chair and sat down at the table and picked one from the pile, turned it over in his hand, looked at the postmark. It had been written nearly two years before. With something like dread he opened the flap and pulled out the thin folded pages. That time came back to him as he read the first lines. He was saying how much he wanted to be home and how hot it was and he could remember being on his bunk with his pillow turned sideways and propped against the angle iron that formed the headboard, a tablet on one raised knee and radios playing, the babble of voices around him and the blue pants with the white stripe down the side of each leg. Sock-footed and the overhead light smoky and dim and home seeming so far away. It all came back to him, how it smelled down there, how it sounded at night with that constant talking and shouting and radio music and how he could write a letter to his mother and make it go away for small bits of time. In the letter he never mentioned his father or Jewel. He talked about working in the fields, told her he was sorry for what he'd done, that when he got out he was going to do better. Things he wrote to make her feel better, things he knew she wanted to hear. Little lies that maybe buoyed her heart up some. In those spaces of time when he wrote the letters he felt that he was somehow with her, somehow sharing her presence across the distance that separated them from each other.

After a while he stopped seeing the words he had so painfully scrawled on the cheap pulp paper and folded the letter back up, stuck it inside the envelope, and put it where it had been.

He went through the drawers in Virgil's dresser quickly, flipping through socks and underwear, a meager assortment of near-threadbare things. Not much of a place to hide anything to begin with. There were no sheaves of money in there. He turned away from the dresser and looked at the room again, saw a cardboard box of old magazines, the bed, a tall wastebasket that held umbrellas and canes. He went to the bed and lifted the mattress from one side, ran his hand under it and looked, repeated the search from the other side. Nothing. He was reluctant to go through his mother's things, but he did. The pockets of her dresses, the drawers of her dresser, becoming more irritated and feeling more desperate at what he was doing. He felt in the pockets of her coat. Got down on his knees and looked into the toes of her shoes for bills wadded and crammed. He searched every possible hiding place in the closet and it yielded him nothing except a bite on the end of one finger from a large brown spider that was up in the toe of one shoe.

"Son of a bitch!" he said, then shook the spider out and smashed it with the shoe.

He looked at the room again. A small bedside table was filled with pictures that he rummaged through, pausing to look at them, Virgil and fish, his mother in a blue dress, Theron on a horse, Puppy on a bicycle, infants sprawled on blankets. There were younger versions of his parents sitting on the hood of a shiny car holding hands. There was no money in those images of times gone by. He shut the drawer and stood up, almost in a panic. He walked quickly from the room and went into the kitchen and started going through the cabinets. Behind the third door he tried he found a white teapot with a lid and he pulled it from its resting place and removed the top. U.S. currency was hiding in there, folded crisp twenty-dollar bills packed in a wad.

"All right," he said quietly, then set the teapot on the table and went to the front door and looked out. The road was deserted. Virgil wasn't walking into the yard. The puppy was lying on the porch. It lifted its head at his step and began to get up wearily to greet him but he turned away and hurried back to the kitchen. The whiskey was still in his pocket and he pulled it out and sat down in the chair and got another drink of it. He was hurrying now, anxious to be away and done with it. Out of here and no trace of his coming and going left for the old man to find. And maybe he didn't even know how much was in there. He reached in and pulled the wad out and straightened the bills and counted them, sliding them quickly through his fingers and flattening each bill on the table. There was six hundred and forty dollars in the little teapot and he kept a hundred and put the rest back, took another drink of the whiskey and left it on the table where it had been. Then he was up the hall and out the door and into the car, going down the road glancing up at the rearview mirror until he could get to the turnoff and the woods that would hide him. Once he got there he relaxed, lit a cigarette, feeling the weight of the money in his pocket not as a tangible thing like ounces or pounds but with a steady reassurance that the day was looking a lot better.

He turned up the radio and drove leisurely, riding in and out of the sunshine where the machines were busy mauling the forest and where trucks stood waiting to be loaded by knucklebooms that lifted handfuls of logs in their giant claws and dropped them splintering each other into the waiting uprights of the trucks that swayed and shook with the weight. There might be a job and probably a bad one, running a chain saw all day long dropping trees. But he had money in his pocket now. He wasn't going to worry about a job for a while.

He drove on past the loading sites and turned down a sand road about a mile past there. He was in the national forest once he drove past a brown sign made of wood and yellow letters proclaiming it so. The hand of man had not touched these woods. None of it was posted or could be. He and Jewel had parked in this refuge a lot of times early on and he drove down through the sandy lane, a little breeze blowing through the trees that lined the road, by giant leaning pines that were the last of their kind, limbless for sixty or seventy feet and then bushed heavily with branches and cones. Hollows of old hardwoods where the sunlight broke into shafts of white intensity and the floor of the forest was clean of scrub stuff and smooth with its carpet of dead leaves, eighty and ninety years of them lying packed and dense upon the ground so that you could see a deer moving a quarter mile away between the gray trunks if your eyes were good. A curve in the road where there were minerals in the ground and the deer had pawed and licked out a hollow two feet deep and sometimes when you rounded that curve at night you might see ten or a dozen of them grouped there, bucks, does, fawns. He drove by a little creek that fed into a lake of forty acres. They had parked there, too, summer nights on the backseat with the radio playing and the car pointed toward the road so that if anybody came up he could turn on the headlights and blind the driver until they could get their clothes on, but nobody ever came up. How many times with the stars bright above as he caressed her body on a quilt in the woods with the moon showing through the limbs overhead? Uncounted the times she had moved over him and swung her heavy breasts to an unheard rhythm that she carried in her head and her womb. Long nights of lovemaking with her dark hair in a tangle and the tiny freckles on her shoulders visible in the pale light that shone down on them from above. He eyed the woods he drove through and almost wished it could be that way again. Wondered how long it had been going on between them, what they'd done, if they did it in her bed, if they took his son on picnics, and if he knew who his father was.

He wished now that he'd brought the whiskey with him. He could have sipped it, driving this lane of timber, his lane of memories, listening to the radio. There seemed to be no answers. She'd always talked about love but she didn't know what she was talking about. She didn't know what kind of trouble love could get you in. It could ruin everything and turn into hate. He didn't want love. He only wanted things to be easier somehow, for his life to not be so wrong. It had been a long time since it hadn't been that way and he didn't think it had just started with Theron. Something had always been wrong at his house, way back when he didn't understand what his father drank that made him fall in the house or the yard and cry the way he did, say the strange things he said. Why they fought and why his mother wept alone in her bed at night. So many things he didn't understand back then, the long absences of his father, the cars towed into the yard burned or smashed beyond repair, the bandages he wore on his face sometimes and the whiskey always sitting on the kitchen table as it had been today. Once in a while in a rational moment he would ask himself why he drank after he'd seen what it did to his father, to his whole family. But there was no answer for that either.

The woods were lush and deep green and the limbs were alive with birds. A banded woodpecker rapped hard and staccato on a standing dead tree near the road and then flew, a bright dart weaving through the leaves. He drove slowly, guiding the car around the curves and over the hills, cool winds wafting through the opened windows of the car. At a three-way intersection he slowed and downshifted and turned right, then gaining speed, moving it up into third, his arm resting on the sill of the window. After a few more miles he came to a stop sign and halted at the edge of the highway. He waited on one car and then a dump truck topped the hill behind it and he had to wait on it too. But he wasn't in any hurry now. It came by dropping gravel that bounced in the road. He swung out behind it and trailed it for a few miles, until it turned off. He kept going, driving south now, the tires slapping at the highway. It was hot again now that he was out of the woods. When the news came on he knew it was noon. He kept driving, looking for the sign. Maybe it wasn't even there anymore. In three years things could change. Some things could. On a long straightaway a car came up behind him rapidly and shot around, cutting back in close. He held up his middle finger but the car went on up the road very fast. Then he saw the old sign. He put his blinker on and slowed, turned to the right with a lazy spin of the steering wheel. The road was rough with patched asphalt and potholes and the worn shocks on the car didn't do much for the ride. He drove up the hill and put on his blinker again even though there was nobody behind him. It was a dirt road he turned into, washboarded and rutted and grass standing up in places. It looked as if it hadn't been used for a long time. The road got narrower and rougher and there was a half-filled mud hole he had to ease through carefully, the bottom of the car dragging until he goosed it and splashed on through.

A treacherous bridge of old timbers and planks spanned a ditch of black stagnant water and he rattled over it quickly, a trifle uneasy at the nail heads sticking up. Somebody had dropped a car through it once, some drunk who had to be winched out with a dozer. He turned right where the road forked and went beside a cotton patch and a wooden pen that sat listing to one side, made of small logs, the spaces chinked with mud and raw cotton and almost covered with briars and honeysuckle vines. Behind it loomed the big levee of the lake, a mile long, high with weeds, straight as a plumb line across the line of his vision. It was very green in the sun and he turned to the right, following the trail through the tall grass, easing along now because he couldn't see what holes there might be. The grade was gradual and it had gravel on it and the car climbed it easily. At the top where it leveled off he was in timber again and he drove through it and looked out over the water, the clean black expanse of it, tiny waves riffling over the surface and the far side dotted with cypress trees that towered into the sky, their spiky limbs furred a deep green, and beyond that small clouds that hung unmoving in a pale blue void. The house came into view and he pulled up in the yard and parked beside a new Ford pickup sitting there. A man more than twice his age was on the front porch cooking split chickens on a grill. There was a bottle of beer beside his foot and Glen got out and shut the door, walked over toward the porch.

"Well look here," the man said, and got up and came down the steps.

Glen grinned and went up with his hand out and took the one that was offered. He squeezed hard but not as hard as the hand that shook his.

"Looks like I got here just in time," he said. "How you doing, Brother Roy?"

"I'm doing all right. You hungry? I got some chicken on here. You want a beer?"

They climbed the steps together and Glen looked at the grill. The chickens were slathered with a red sauce and little droplets of reddish water ran from the holes that had been pierced in their skins.

"Hell yeah," he said.

"Well just grab you a seat. I'll go in here and get you one."

"All right."

He sat down in a kitchen chair and turned it sideways. He looked out over the lake. There were bluffs of hardwood timber above the east side and the trees stood mirrored in a small cove where the land came out and formed a spot protected from the wind. He could see two boats tied up on the far bank. Just looking at the lake made him feel better. Roy didn't own it; he just took care of it for a rich man who rarely visited. There were five hundred acres to hunt on. In pens at the back lived Llewelyn setters and Roy was free to run them on birds, which were in abundance in the fields below the levee. He killed three or four deer every year and there were wild hogs in the woods. The lake was heavily stocked with crappie, bass, catfish.

Roy came back out with a dripping Budweiser bottle and handed it to him already opened.

"Thanks a lot, Roy. I just thought I'd come up here and see if you's home."

His friend sat back down and took up his long-handled fork and his own beer again. Smoke was rising up to the porch rafters, where it flattened and rolled out from under the edge of the roof.

"Well I'm glad you did. I heard you was gettin out. Thought you might come by. I won't ask you how it was."

"Well," he said, and took a drink of his beer. It was very cold and slightly bitter. He felt all his nerves unwinding, something smoothing out within himself. He lit a cigarette and held the beer between his knees as he leaned forward. "You still got it made, looks like."

Roy poked at the chicken and it sizzled on the grill.

"Aw yeah. Mr. Duvall came out about two weeks ago, stayed two days."

"He have another one of those good-looking women with him?"

"Shoot. You ought to seen this one. Made Marilyn Monroe look like a milk cow. I don't see how he stands it."

"He's pretty old, ain't he?"

"Yep. It don't slow him down none I don't reckon though. He was happy with everything. Told me I's doing a good job. I don't do nothin. Set out here and fish and hunt and drink beer."

Glen lifted his beer and took a long swallow. When he lowered it he said, "You ever get tired of it, tell him I want to put my application in."

They both smiled at that. Roy turned the chicken over and set his beer back on the porch. "How's your daddy?"

Glen paused for a moment, thinking about what he had in his pocket. Thought of his mother's dresses. Those old pictures.

"He's all right I guess. I've seen him a few times."

Roy nodded and picked up a Pepsi bottle filled with water and sprinkled droplets over the flames that were climbing up through the wire rack the chicken was laid on. The flames hissed and receded.

"I ain't seen him in a while. He still fish like he used to?"

"I guess. I guess he does. He always did."

"He loves it about as good as anybody I've ever seen. You see him again, tell him I said hi, okay?"

"I'll tell him."

Roy sat there for a bit, looking at the birds. He lifted his eyes toward the lake and then turned back to Glen.

"I hate it about everything, Glen. I didn't come to the jail to see you I know. Didn't want to see you in there like that. I hope you understand about that."

"I do. I'm glad you didn't."

Later Roy brought out some paper plates and forks and a bag of potato chips and they ate on the front porch, looking out over the water, marking where fish leaped and dimpled small pools. When the sun began to lower in the sky they loaded a cooler into the pickup and drove across the levee and put the rods and reels and the beer into one of the boats and sculled out along the edge of the hardwood bluff, under the trees that reached shadows out into the water. Glen took off his shirt and took a great joy in the wind and the sunlight on his skin. In the little cove they cast their lures beside a log that lay in the water and the water swirled around Glen's lure and the rod bowed hard.

"Oh shit," he said.

A green body flashed out there and the drag screamed as the fish peeled off line. It made one run toward the boat and the rod bent nearly double. Glen thought the line would surely break. But it held and the fish made hard circles deep in the water. Roy had put his rod down to watch. The fish pulled so hard that the little boat turned and moved.

"Damn, Glen. I knew they was some big ones in here."

Glen didn't say anything. He kept the rod tip up and the old familiar pleasure came back into him like those distant mornings on the river with his old man. He smiled now, feeling the fish weaken.

"Watch him, now, he's liable to jump."

He did jump. He leaped completely free of the water, an enormous chunk of shining living flesh, wet scales and wildly bowing body, rattling the plug in his head so hard they could hear the hooks shaking in their fasteners. He landed sideways with a big splash and water erupted and shot into the boat. Glen felt a drop land on his bottom lip. But he thought he had him now. The circles were smaller and he kept coming to the top but he never did jump again. Glen leaned forward and backward, taking in the line, and now he could see the fish and the plug in his mouth as he swam back and forth in front of the boat.

"Good God, what a fish, Glen."

"You got a net?"

"It's at the house. I didn't think to bring it."

"That's all right."

Roy knelt in the boat and Glen towed the fish closer. Ten feet. Six feet. It was swimming slowly but he knew it could make another surge. Only when it turned on its side did he know that it was whipped. He lifted hard on the rod and Roy reached and caught it by the underjaw and pulled it dripping from the water and laid it gently in the bottom of the boat. It flopped around some at first but then it lay there heaving, the red gills exposed, the tail wider than Glen's hand. He reached to it and took the plug from its jaw. One hook had held it. For a few moments they just looked at it.

"How much you think?" Glen said.

"God, I don't know. Ten pounds maybe? I never seen one this big. We got to take it somewhere and try to weigh it."

Glen looked up. He saw the trees above the water and the way the wind was moving through the branches. He looked at the dark water and the small ripples that lapped at the bank. He looked at a hawk soaring lazily by the cypresses on the other side of the lake, the beds of water lilies floating in their mats of stems.

"You know who'd get a kick out of this?"

"Who's that, Glen?"

✓"My daddy. I lost one about this big when I was ten and he like to never got over it."

"Well, shit, carry it home and show it to him. Let me find that stringer."

Roy started to open his tackle box but Glen told him to hold it. Roy looked up at him. "What?"

"Let's turn him loose."

"Turn him loose? Hell, Glen, lot of people fish all their lives and don't never catch a fish like this. You may have the state record here. You can't turn him loose."

The fish lay in the bottom of the boat, the gill plates rising and falling. His dark green color was starting to fade under the merciless sun.

✓"I just don't want to kill him," Glen said. "He never done nothin to me."

Roy leaned back on the boat seat and put his hands down beside him. He looked at the fish. "I don't understand what you're talkin about, Glen."

There wasn't much time to explain it. The fish would die if he wasn't put back in the water soon. "It's like this. I never killed a deer that I didn't wish was still alive after I looked at it. This thing's too pretty to kill. I'd rather have him back in here instead of hung up on some wall."

Roy nodded, looking down at the thing. "He's pretty."

"Let's turn him loose, then."

"All right."

Glen still had the rod in his hand and now he reeled the lure in to the tip and laid it aside. He knelt in the boat and got one hand under the belly of the fish and held its head by the lower jaw and eased it over the side and immersed it in the water. It lay there breathing weakly and he watched its eyes. He released it. It turned slowly on its side, the gills working, then with one enormous spasm of its tail it righted itself and vanished into the deep gloom of the water. He knelt there looking after where it had gone.

"You're a good man, Glen," Roy said to him.

"No I ain't," he said to the water.

A couple of cold beers were still in the icebox, left over from Sunday night. Virgil hobbled back there after Bobby left and got one and found an opener. He dropped the cap on the table and looked at the whiskey sitting there. The level of it was lower than what he remembered. In the old days if he left it out Emma would water it down while he was drunk. He stood there looking at it for a minute, then set the beer down and picked it up. It was an inch or so lower. He wondered if Glen had been by. He didn't know who else would come into his house and drink his whiskey. It didn't matter. He didn't need it anyway. He just liked it was all.

His ribs were still hurting but the doctor had given him some little red pills for pain. He set the whiskey down and pulled the plastic bottle from his pocket and washed two of them down with a couple of swallows of beer. Then he walked slowly back up to the front room and eased himself down onto the bed, pulled a chair closer and set the beer on it, put his ashtray on it, then started taking off his socks. After he got them off he pulled a couple of pillows together and lay back against the headboard. The window was open and a small breeze was drifting into the room. He hated to be laid up. The damn well. No water in the house. Just a hell of a mess. He didn't want to call Puppy and worry him with it. He was afraid that W.G. might have fired him over all this. But he hoped he hadn't. He started to get up and call him, but it seemed too much trouble. And he might be back at work anyway. He could always do it later. Right now he just wanted to rest.

The puppy was whining out on the porch.

"Settle down," he called to it. He heard it go down the steps and into the yard. It was probably going around back so it could get in through the screen door. He needed to fix that one of these days. He couldn't do anything without his car, couldn't get to town to get anything. He hated to worry Puppy about it.

The beer was dripping water onto the chair and he reached up painfully and got it, leaned back, held it against his belly. He guessed he was lucky he hadn't hurt himself any worse than he had. Little son of a bitch. Saying things like that. But still hurt over his kid. In a way he didn't blame him for being the way he was. He was never going to get over it. There was no way he could. Not if you got to thinking about how things could have turned out. Virgil could see that even though none of it was his fault, Ed Hall somehow held him responsible. Probably for nothing more than bringing Glen into the world. You couldn't reason with people when they got to thinking like that.

All that thinking wearied him even more, so he just rested on his bed, listening to the puppy scratch at the back door. And it was only a little while before he walked into the front room and came up next to the bed. Virgil reached a hand out and patted him on the lead.

"I'm laid up, little buddy," he said. "Got my damn ass whipped." The puppy sniffed up and down Virgil's legs, wagging his tail, as if in agreement.

"Don't you take a shit in this house. I ain't up to cleaning it up today."

The puppy walked to the window and looked out. Virgil eased back and sipped his beer. He wished he had the hunting magazine to read. But it would be too much trouble to go out and get it. Best to just lay here and rest. He felt old, and his bones were tired.

He woke to soft knocking on the screen door, a timid voice calling his name. The puppy was standing at the door to the hall, looking out inquisitively to the porch. Part of his beer had spilled against him and he set it on the chair.

"Come on in," he said. He heard her ask if the dog would bite and he got up from the bed and made his way to the hall. Mary was opening the screen door, a basket in her hand. He grinned at her.

"He won't bite. Nothin but a biscuit. Come on in."

He sat back down on the edge of the bed. The puppy sniffed around her legs, nosed at her dress. She set the basket on the couch and then sat beside him on the bed. The puppy went to the basket and she got up.

"I've got some sandwiches in there," she said. "Where can I put em?"

"Just let him out," Virgil said. "Just get him by the collar and take him out."

She did and then came back.

"Now go back to the kitchen and shut that wood door or he'll come back in."

She went down the hall and he heard her close the door. Her steps in the hall coming back to him. Her smile at the door, looking in at him for just a moment before she came in and sat down beside him again. She picked up his hand and held it. He leaned over clumsily and kissed her, the taste of her mouth sweet and warm.

"How bad you hurt?" she whispered against his lips.

"I didn't hurt that part."

She got up and shut the hall door and undressed slowly in front of him, smiling the whole time, and then when she was naked she came to him and helped him remove his clothes, carefully, her eyes looking into his and touched with that small warm way she had and the fine wrinkles etched into her face and her body imbued with a soft light, her face shy of makeup and her hands free of any rings, until she lay next to him on the bed with her head on his chest, the good scent of her hair in his nose, until he turned her over and kissed her again and was wrapped in the familiar and fragrant embrace of her and knew that if he died in this moment he would die happy.

After it was over she lay naked next to him talking. He rubbed her shoulder, scratched her back.

"How'd you know about it?" he said.

"Bobby came home for lunch and told me. You didn't care for me coming over, did you?"

He turned his face and looked at her. Her eyes were so calm, her little smile constant.

"I'm glad to see you. I'm always glad to see you, Mary. What about Bobby?"

"What about him?"

"What would he say if he came by here and saw your car?"

She leaned to kiss him on the cheek and one of her nipples touched his arm and the weight of her breast stuck to his skin by the friction between them. He loved her smell. He reached out and hefted the other breast, lifted it, rolled the nipple under his thumb and watched her close her eyes.

"Bobby's got his own life," she said, and moved on top of him again.

It was midafternoon when they finally stopped. She put her clothes back on and dressed him and fluffed up his pillows. She brought him a thick ham sandwich and another beer and set to cleaning up the house. While he ate he could hear her in the kitchen, in the hall. She went around his bed picking up bottles and old newspapers and she swept the floor. Just listening to her tired him out.

"You need to hire you a maid," she said once, passing down the hall.

"You interested in the job?"

"Maybe part-time," she said, then winked and went on down the hall.

After a while he got up and went down the hall to the kitchen. It didn't look the same. All the pots of dead plants were gone and he could hear her doing something out in the backyard. He pushed open the screen door and went out there. The empty pots were all stacked up in one corner of the porch and she had dumped the potting soil and the dry stalks over the fence at the side. She was just bringing the last one back and she put it on the stack and dusted her hands off. She looked up at him.

"I hope you don't care," she said. "A year's plenty long, Virgil."

He sat down in the chair and reached for his cigarettes. He lit one and leaned back, crossed his legs.

"I don't care. Should have done it a long time ago. I still got all her clothes."

She stepped up on the porch and sat in the other chair, then pulled it a little closer to him.

"I know. I went in there but I didn't touch anything. You want me to clean them out?"

He thought about it. There didn't seem to be much point in keeping them. They were a constant reminder and he didn't even sleep in there anymore. In the past he could feel her in there at night and so he had moved to the other room. But sometimes she came in there too. Not in a while now though. He hoped she wasn't agonized in some place where she could see him. See them.

"I don't know. What would you do with them?"

"Take it to town. Give it to the Salvation Army. I know there's somebody who could get some use out of all those dresses. They're good as any you buy in a store."

"She used to make me shirts," Virgil said. "She made Glen a huntin coat one time. It was the damnedest thing I ever seen. Bought some brown canvas and some corduroy. Lined it with a wool blanket she cut up. It even had a padded shoulder for a shotgun. You couldn't tell it from one that came from Sears and Roebuck."

She lowered her eyes and rocked for a bit, then looked out across the yard where the chickens were scratching in the dust.

"She never got over hating me, did she?"

"Naw. She never did. She thought I was still seeing you right up to the day she killed herself. I never could convince her any different. And after a while I guess I just got tired of trying."

"Let me know what you want to do about all these clothes," she said. "I'll come back and haul them off if you want me to."

"Okay."

"What do you need? I don't want you to have to be up and down fixing something to eat all the time."

"I got some stuff to eat."

She laughed at that.

"Oh yeah. I saw what you've got to eat. Chili and beef stew. You can't live on that."

"I've lived on a lot worse. Raw fish and coconuts. Try that sometime and a bowl of beef stew looks pretty good. Main thing I need is to get some water in the house."

"What would it take to fix it?"

"Just some water now. The part's up there in the front room. Puppy was going to help me. We'd already loaded up the water when all this happened."

"How much water would it take?"

"Bout five gallons."

She got up. "Well come on then."

"Where we going?"

"Get you some water. You can't even flush your toilet. Me and you can fix it."

They did. She got him in the car and drove him to her house and loaded a barrel into the back end of Bobby's old pickup and filled it with water. Back at his house she handed him wrenches and they got the part on and then with a five-gallon bucket they poured water down the long shaft that went into the well and when he flipped the switch manually they could hear it surging and bubbling. It ran for two or three minutes and then shut itself off. When they walked into the house all the taps had water. She made him sit down and she started washing all his dishes as soon as there was some warm water. He watched her for a while and then he got up and told her he was going back to the front room to lie down.

He was tired again and he stretched out on his bed. Music started up in the kitchen when she turned the radio on. He put his head back on his pillow and listened to it. The boys had always played it when they were growing up, and he hadn't realized that he'd missed it until now. Mary was singing and he smiled. His eyelids were heavy and he thought he'd close them for just a minute, just until she got through washing the dishes. It was nice of her to do that. And she was right about the clothes. No need to hang on to all that stuff. Not when somebody else might be able to get some use out of it. He needed to get those cars hauled off, too. Puppy probably knew somebody with a wrecker. He'd ask him soon. He hoped Puppy was all right. Little son of a bitch. He was fast as lightning though.

When he woke up it was almost dark and she was gone. He checked the house. She'd put all the sandwiches into the icebox and the dishes were stacked beside the sink and there was a note with two words: *Call me.*

He walked out on the porch and sat down in his chair. The puppy heard him when he came out and climbed up on the porch to stay with him while the sun dropped down through the trees on the other side of the road. The last of the birds winged their way through the darkening air and then everything was still. He rocked slowly, watching. The puppy put his head down on his paws and slept. A deep solid peace settled into Virgil's bones. His ribs were still hurting a little but it was just a minor thing, a thing a man could easily bear. Night came and he didn't move.

The sun was hanging at the tops of the cypresses that stood by the lake and the fish were hitting everywhere, but by now they had caught so many they were tired of catching them. They rowed back to the levee and untied a stringer of eight fat bass and put them in the back of Roy's pickup. Glen got the rods and reels and lifted the last two beers from the cooler and they drove back across the levee with the western sky reddening in the retreat of the sun and watched the last of the light shatter up through the pale clouds.

"It's been a nice day, Glen. I'm proud you came out to see me."

Glen looked out across the water and trailed the hand that held his cigarette out the open window.

"You got a pretty place out here," he said.

"Yep. I don't know what I'd do if he decided to run me off. I've gotten so used to it. Listen here, why don't you stick around and help me dress these fish? I got some peanut oil and a bunch of french fries. We'll fillet these bass and cook us up a feast after while."

Glen took a long drink of the beer and eyed the bottle. The truck bumped gently over the grass on the levee.

"I'd love to. I guess I better get on, though. I got some stuff to do."

Roy smiled as he drove. Of all the people Glen had known in his life, he'd never had a cross word with this one. Had never heard him speak badly of another person. He had offered words of quiet comfort about Theron in that bad time. And he knew he wouldn't judge him about Jewel.

"Now what you got to do that's more important than a good fish fry? We can have em in the pot in thirty minutes. I got some more beer in the frigerator."

"I better get on. I'm kinda thinking about going to see somebody."

Roy just nodded. He drove to the end of the levee and pulled up and parked next to the porch. They got out and looked at the fish in the back end. Glen hooked his arms over the side of the truck and nodded to them.

"That's a nice mess of fish."

"It's a lot more than I can eat. I wish you'd just stay on with me. But I know you probably got stuff to do. I don't blame you. You seen Jewel?"

Glen frowned a little. Took a swallow of his beer.

"Yeah. I've seen her." He looked up at Roy. "I don't know what to do about her," he said. "Daddy thinks I ought to marry her. But I done tried that one time Roy and it didn't work. Besides. I think she's been messing around with Bobby Blanchard."

Roy looked uneasy then. He shook his head slowly and stared at the fish.

"I don't know nothing about that, Glen. But a lot of stuff can go on in three years. Things can change. People can, too. Look at me. I baptized you when you were ten years old. I was pretty young then myself. I never figured I'd ever do anything else but preach. Marry somebody and settle down, have a family, get a church of my own. But it didn't work out that way. I ain't give a sermon now in five years."

"Why'd you quit?"

"Lots of reasons. I did wrong with a woman I wasn't married to." He showed Glen his beer bottle. "Got to liking this stuff a little too much. Didn't figure I had any more business being up in a pulpit trying to tell other folks how to live. So I quit."

"Well. At least you're honest about it."

"Everybody sins, Glen. They ain't a one of us that don't."

"I guess that's right. But I thought she was gonna wait on me. She said she would. First day I saw her she said things had changed. Then I drove by her house and seen him over there."

"Have you talked to her since then?"

"Naw."

"Maybe there's a reason he was over there. Maybe she had some trouble."

Glen didn't say anything. He'd been trying to forget about Sunday night. He couldn't remember most of it anyway. Except that he'd gone in and found the boy in the bed with her. He remembered that.

"Maybe you ought to just go talk to her, Glen. I ain't trying to tell you what to do. Your daddy means well I know. He ain't never forgive himself for what happened to your brother. He never will."

"He blames me."

"He don't blame you, Glen. It was a long time ago."

Roy turned around and put his hand up on the tailgate and fixed Glen with a look that was all kindness. "I know you've had a hard time. But try to put all this bad stuff behind you. I don't want to see you get in no more trouble. If you ever need somebody to talk to I'm always here. I can loan you some money if you need it, too. You can even stay out here if you want to."

Glen set his beer in the bed of the truck and slipped his shirt on and started buttoning it. He unbuckled his pants and tucked it in and then fastened the belt back together and ran one hand through his hair and picked up the beer. He took another swallow and turned his head to look one last time at the lake. If he could stay out here everything might be okay. If he could stay away from people. If he could live his life in a way that other lives couldn't mess up. He turned back to face Roy.

"That's mighty nice of you, Roy. Thanks for taking me fishing."

"We'll go again. Any time you want to."

They shook hands again and Glen went to his car. As he backed it up Roy was taking the fish around the side of the house, out of sight. Dark was falling and all the light had gone out of the lake. He glanced at it again, going down the hill, and now it lay flat and black and brooding, the solemn cypresses melting together into a thick mass forming at the backwaters. Owls would be coming soon out of the high woods on the bluff, their silent soaring shapes slanting down across the water and rifling toward the grasses on the far side where mice crouched fearless and unaware.

He took a bath when he got home and combed his hair and shaved. He'd spent part of the day before cleaning up, knocking down cobwebs and dirt dauber nests. Bottles had been sitting in corners and on tables and he'd boxed them up and set them on the back porch. He went out there now that he'd cleaned himself up, washed the fish smell from his hands. Somebody had come out to turn the electricity on after he'd gone by there and paid the bill, and now he had lights, hot water, an icebox to keep things cold. Hot dogs and baloney and mustard in there with a six-pack of Pepsis.

The porch had been built years ago from sawmill oak and it had gone unpainted and now was rotten in places. There was one chair in the yard, overturned he guessed from some storm, and he stepped down and got it and set it up on the porch. There was an old swing set out there left behind by a former owner but no child of his had ever played on it.

Standing in the yard he looked down toward the river and the dark banks of trees that lined it. There was a big field of cotton at the end of his backyard, over a hundred acres, lush now with cotton plants, their ordered rows stretching away to invisibility under the blankets of clouds. It was hot and humid and he could see heat lightning flaring in the distance, something that seemed dark and ominous moving toward him. The trees began to bend a little in the wind that was rising up. He wanted to go see her but that image of Bobby on her front porch still burned inside him. He was feeling worse and worse about the little boy and he had begun to feel a yearning to see him, hold him, know him. He thought it might be better for all of them if he just went away somewhere, but the thought of Jewel was a magnet forever pulling him toward her. Those nights in his mind would not go away and he told himself to just go talk to her. He'd gotten a cheap wristwatch in town the day before and he struck his lighter over the face of it to read the time: eight o'clock.

He could go drink a few beers, give her time to put the boy to bed. Then he could go over. His sins were beginning to weigh on him and if what he held within was not remorse it was something close to it. He knew that he needed to slow down on his drinking but he needed a drink. So he went through the side yard, not bothering to lock the house, and out to his car and down the road somewhere to get it.

M ost of the fear had gone with the passage of another day and Jewel
had cooked pork chops on the grill for the two of them. They'd
finished eating and she had let him play in the yard until dark and mosquitoes had driven them in. He was watching television on the floor in
the living room and she was drinking a rare beer in the chair behind
him. She was wondering if Bobby was going to come by tonight to
check on them. She hadn't decided whether to tell him about the car
coming by the night before. And she hadn't decided what she would do
if Glen came by. Talk first for sure.

"Bedtime before long, honey," she said.

He was petting his cat where it lay stretched out in his lap and he
looked at her over his shoulder.

"Can I have a Coke?"

"You already had one."

"Please?"

"Can you get it?"

"Yes ma'am."

He set the cat on the floor and it walked to Jewel and leapt easily to her
lap. David got up and went down the hall and she heard him open the

icebox door. She petted the cat for a little bit and then it jumped down and trailed after the boy.

There was not much traffic on the road tonight. She'd been listening. There were a lot of times when she wished she could get out of the house at night and this was one of those times. But David needed her at night. She thought she'd let him stay up for another thirty minutes and then she would lie in her bed with her eyes open and try to think again of where she had gone wrong. Her body would turn and twist in the sheets and the sweat would come again and she would remember those nights in the woods on a blanket and wonder if he did.

David came back with his drink and sat on the floor again, watching the characters on the fuzzy television screen. The antenna needed fixing but she was scared to get up on the roof by herself. There were so many things she needed a man for, a leaky faucet, a stuck door, and more than anything the warmth of another hand. She thought about calling Bobby. She looked down at her legs, her painted toes propped on the footstool. She drew a deep breath and sighed. David got up and came over to her. He climbed up in the chair with her and she got him up under her arm and hugged him.

"Who is that man?"

"What man?"

He pointed toward the television. "That man."

"That's Andy."

"Where's Barney?"

"Barney's not on there now."

"I want to see Barney."

"He'll be on there after while."

He was quiet then, watching the show. From time to time he lifted his bottle and took a drink from it. The cat had come back in and was stretched out on the floor, paws twitching. She watched the show without really listening to it. She guessed she could call up to the jail and see where he was. He might be there, or he might be on the road. He moved around so much. Slept at odd hours and ate sometimes when most people were sleeping. It wasn't nine o'clock yet. And she could always take a bath and forget about it. Stretch out in the tub and turn the water on warm and later try to get a good night's sleep. She hated sleeping with the window down because it was so hot. But now a breeze was lifting the curtains from the front windows and she could hear thunder far off. Rain coming. It would be welcome, the garden was so dry. The grass. The road in front of her house so dusty.

"You sleepy?" she said.

"Not yet."

"You can stay up thirty more minutes. Then you've got to go to bed."

"Okay."

He climbed down from her lap and went to sit beside the cat again. Stroking it and drinking his Coke. She got up too.

"I'm going out on the front porch and smoke a cigarette."

He looked up. "Ain't nobody gonna bother us is it?"

"No baby. Ain't nobody gonna bother us."

She hoped that was true. She picked up her cigarettes and lighter and grabbed the beer and pushed open the screen door. She stood for a moment leaning against a post, watching the clouds sliding rapidly over the moon, light and dark showing, the wind rising and the trees waving a little. She sat down in the chair and put the bottle on the porch and lit a cigarette. With her legs stretched out in front of her she watched the sky and the road. She wanted to call him. Glen could always drive by again. She wished she knew if it was him in the car the second time. She wished it hadn't been so dark.

She turned and looked in the window at David. He was still on the floor with the cat. If she left him alone he'd go to sleep in there. She got up and walked to one end of the porch and looked out into the blackness. Then she walked to the other end and did the same thing there. She sat down in the chair again and put her feet up on the post. You're worse than a damn cat in heat, she told herself. She smoked, rocking back and forth, reaching down once in a while to take a sip from the beer. She got to thinking about her mother and all that she'd said, what she'd called David. It still hurt to think about all that and she wished again that her father had lived. He would have talked to her about it. It would have hurt him too but he wouldn't have turned his back on her. But at least David had Virgil. He was always glad to see them, was always happy to take David fishing. She didn't know why Glen couldn't be more like him. They were so different. Bobby was more like Virgil, but most of the time they seemed like strangers to each other. She was afraid there was going to be trouble between Glen and Bobby and she didn't want to be the cause of it, never had meant to be. Her promise was the only thing that had kept her from letting Bobby in. And it looked like that promise hadn't been worth much to her anyway.

She took another drink of the beer and looked out into the darkness. All this time waiting for him. All those nights when she couldn't sleep for thinking and worrying. The times alone when David was sick and crying. Or happy and growing and such a joy to look at and hold and bathe and feed. All that time by herself. One night with him in her bed didn't make up for all that.

The thunder rolled again and the sky split its dark underbelly with flashes of lightning. The breeze was coming steady now, cool and strong. It wafted under the limbs of the trees in the yard and the leaves danced on the edges of the wind. She heard the first few drops hit the roof. A smattering like a handful of shotgun pellets on a tin plate. She hugged her knees and laid her cheek on one of them. She kept sitting there, waiting for whatever would come. She was lonely all the time now, and the nights had become too long. It began to rain harder and the earth seemed to revel in it, the clouds moving into a steady black mass. The thunder cracked closer and the rain began to roll in beads from the edge of the roof. She rocked in the chair and listened to the television. There was no way she could go and get into her bed. Not yet. The night had not brought what she wanted yet. She sat there and listened to it rain. It came down and down and pounded on the roof and swept in sheets along the edges of the yard where little pools of flowing water formed and glistened. It drowned out the noise of the television and she sat there for a while longer, then looked through the window and saw the little boy lying on the floor, his head along one out-flung arm, the cat next to him. She got up and went into the house and picked him up and put him in his bed with his clothes on. Pulled the single sheet up over him. Went back to the front porch to watch it rain some more. It was dark out there, black with the rumblings of the night. She watched for lights coming down the road.

B obby had given up on finding Glen. The rain started down on his windshield ten minutes after he left the jail and now his wipers were going at it, sweeping the water from the glass in little cascades. His headlights showed it slanting down on the highway and he was still heartsick with the things the children had told him. He'd been putting off doing what he had to do, knowing it wasn't right but not wanting to face it this soon either. Now it had started raining and his task would be worse. Tomorrow he would have to face it, rain or not.

He turned down the road that led to Virgil's house and drove by it in the rain. The house was dark except for a dim light in the front room. Lying in there listening to the radio probably. There was no need to stop. He probably didn't know where Glen was. And all his driving hadn't turned up a trace of him. It was like he had vanished somehow. And Virgil was probably all right. In a few weeks he'd be healed up okay. He could stop and check on him later and see how he was doing.

The rain came down and he could see the drops of it bouncing off the hood. Nobody much was out. He did meet a few cars, their lights bleary and water-streaked in the rain, and it looked like a good night to stay home. He thought about Jewel in the storm alone. At least he hoped she was alone. He could drive by there too. See how she was doing. See if he

244

was over there or had been. He had already told them at the jail that he might be in the car for a while.

He'd had no supper yet but he wasn't hungry for food.

It took him ten minutes to get over to Jewel's house. When the headlights swept the yard and the porch he could see her sitting in the chair, the tip of her cigarette a tiny red neon light. He pulled up close and shut off the lights and the motor, walked fast with the rain pelting him up to the porch and then he was standing beside her. She got up and kissed him and he held her tight, not saying anything, just holding her and rubbing his hands over her back. But then for the first time she pulled his hands around to the places he had wanted to touch for so long and she started breathing harder. The lightning flashed and the thunder called and she took him by the hand and led him inside, into the darkened house and down the hall to her room. It was hard to see and he followed by holding on to her as a blind man might.

D avid watched from a crack in the door after the lightning woke him up. Mama and that man.

*Was that his daddy?*

At first they pulled at each other's clothes and then the lamp went off and there was just the noise of them in there, the things they were whispering, the sounds they made. The cat watched, too, silent beside him, its eyes almost luminous in the dark hall where the two of them crouched soundless, listening.

Virgil lay in his bed and listened to the rain whisper on the roof of a house that he did not own. The puppy was in there, too, curled in a red ball on the floor, tail tucked and muzzle on his paws. The television was playing silently to give a little light to the room but he had the radio on, Johnny Cash and Cowboy Copas, Patsy Cline and Ernest Tubb. The rain danced against the roof and poured down the posts on the front porch, where it blew in under the eaves. He lay back on his nest of pillows and heard the rain drip down into the dead flower beds that ringed the house and knew that the chickens were snug in their rusted cars.

He could feel Emma again now in the dark corners and could almost hear her steps in the hall. The air was infused with a cool and soothing moisture that had settled on his skin. There was someone else in there, too, and he felt his presence and knew that it was Theron come to see him again as he always had. He felt him in the way the curtains moved and the way the wind whistled outside the windows, the way it was whistling now through hollows of hardwood timber and dark river bottoms where the trees stood dripping water into the black sloughs that surrounded and nurtured them. He felt him in the creaking timbers, in the rafters above, his step on the boards of the house where he had died.

The wind hushed, the curtains stood still as if something had passed out-side them. Then it was gone. The wind picked up, and it rattled the screens, and he took a last drink of the whiskey. The puppy whined uneasily in his sleep and he told it to hush. He wished he could see Glen. He remembered how small his hands were when he held him on his knee by the river and put a cane pole into his fingers.

F or some the night was not over. In a gathering of the drunk and happy Glen sat nursing a glass of straight whiskey and brooding over the remains of his food, barely touched on a red china plate. It was a catfish place with open-air tables but the rain had driven everybody inside. Music was playing loud but he barely heard those laughing voices and those country tunes of heartbreak and loss. He drank the whiskey and stared at the table. The cheap watch said it was 10:30 and he knew it was time to be moving out.

He got up from the booth none too steady and went to stand at the bar. Faces surrounded him, wide smiles and cracked teeth and missing teeth and it seemed that everybody in there was having a good time that hadn't rubbed off on him. He drank some more of the whiskey. Time was slowing down. He watched the second hand on a dusty clock hanging on the wall.

It was still raining outside. He could hear it on the windows and the roof. The storm had moved in bringing with it lightning and crashes of thunder that he could hear pealing outside the cinder-block walls of the joint. The smell of fried catfish hung over everything. It was on his clothes, his skin. He was drunk enough now to be able to start feeling bad about taking the money from his father and to wonder if it was still a good idea to go over and try to see Jewel.

He drained the glass and rapped it on the counter. The barman came down and refilled it, and he paid. The air seemed to be cooling, the outside night pressing in. His mood kept swinging. He wanted to be in her bed, see her face, touch her skin. Breathe in the stillness with her lying naked beside him, the rain coming down. Then he'd start feeling there was nobody to turn to, just like the way it had been after Theron died in all his blood. That long period of grief when he felt that he might go out of his mind from having to remember it over and over every day and knowing that his good strong brother was lying under six feet of dirt and wilted flowers and that the rain would fall on him and the sun would burn down on him and that his spirit would move lost in this world maybe forever, rootless and drifting, watching them, hovering around the edges of the house and the yard where he felt him many times and did not want to feel him anymore.

His mother had never blamed him. She had just borne it, carried it around with her. Her grief was so deep and personal she could never share it with anybody, not even his father. And he had watched them drift farther and farther apart until they were no more than strangers who had to live in the same house, take meals together, raise him and Randolph for the good of them. And always Bobby too, the outside child, standing on the outside edges looking in.

The lights seemed to dim in the place for a moment. Talk waned, the jukebox skipped, then something hummed and the lights came back on bright and the music picked up and people started laughing and talking again. He sipped his whiskey and looked at his watch. It was getting late. If he was going he needed to go now. But something still held him back. He didn't know what she would say if he went back now. So much time had gone by. There would be those questions again and he knew there were no answers he could give her that would satisfy her. He knew she'd probably already made plans but they weren't his plans. It was too soon, and too much had happened. She probably wouldn't put up with much more because all the promises he'd made had not been kept. She might not even let him in this time. Not unless he made some more promises.

"Hey Glen," a voice said. He turned his head to see who'd spoken so nicely. A woman was standing there and he didn't recognize her. Red hair, tight jeans, a pair of bright red lips. A fuzzy sweater that outlined her small pointy breasts.

"You don't remember me, do you?"

He smiled with effort, waved his whiskey at her with a vague motion of both agreement and indifference.

"Not right off. You look a little familiar."

She grinned and moved up closer and lowered her voice.

"Well I hope I do. Maybe you just don't recognize me with my clothes on."

He searched his memory with nothing coming and then a dim bulb came on deep in the besotted depths of his brain. He pointed to her. "Linda?"

"Brenda. You a little drunk, ain't you?"

"I ain't sober, that's for damn sure. Don't want to be. Come on and let me buy you a drink."

She got up next to him and she smelled good. She never stopped smiling. He signaled the bartender and suddenly he stood before them.

"What you want?" Glen asked her.

"Tom Collins."

"Gimme another one too," he said to the bartender.

The bartender turned away to make the drinks and she put her hand on his forearm. Pink nails with cheap rings garnishing her fingers. She had on a lot of makeup and eye shadow. A whore's disguise.

"So," she said. "I heard you been gone for a while."

"Yeah. Had to take a little vacation down in the Delta."

"Well. I've missed seeing you. You back for good now?"

He rattled the ice in his glass and drank some more of the whiskey. It was watery now, tasted flat.

"Yep. I'm home to stay. Gonna straighten up and fly right."

"Oh yeah? I remember when you didn't use to. I done been married and divorced since I seen you. You ought to come on and go out to the lake with me. They having a dance out there tonight. I'll pay your way in."

The bartender brought their drinks and looked warily at Glen but he didn't notice. He pulled out some money and put it on the bar.

"What time is it?" he said, and then he looked at his watch. It was fifteen minutes till eleven.

"We got plenty of time," she said. "They don't close till two. We can catch up where we left off if you want to."

She was still smiling at him and she had moved in closer and put one of her knees between his legs and she was looking into his eyes and rubbing the side of his waist. She lifted her drink without looking at it and sipped it, watching him.

He remembered her now, or at least a smaller and younger version of her laboring beneath him in a motel outside town on Highway 7, dark nights going from the parking lot to the lights outside the room and drinking whiskey at the door, oral acts performed on top of the bedcovers and the way she could pull her knees almost up beside her ears. She had a false nipple low on her left breast and she used to go into a state of near catatonia when the orgasms shuddered through her body.

"I was thinking about going to see somebody," he said.

"Go see em later. I want to get my hands on you again."

She moved her hip against him and turned it so that it shielded the movement of her hand when she reached down and touched the front of him. He started rising up against her fingers. She sipped her drink, gave him her little knowing smile.

"Hell yeah," he said. "Drink up."

In a cavern of wood and dim lights he staggered around with her over the floor, bumping other patrons, his feet dragging, a loud band up on a plywood stage and clusters of people at tables along the walls. They stopped serving him and she had to get their drinks. Kissing her in the corner, mauling her breasts with his hands, people watching them, him unaware or just not caring who saw. Finally somebody came over and told them to be nice or leave and they left.

He fell once in the rain but they just laughed about it and she got him back into her car and he reached for her when she got in on her side, pushing her back against the door with the rain coming down and the heat of their bodies and their breath fogging up the windows to where nobody could see in.

She didn't want to there but he locked all the doors and pulled her sweater over her head and got her pants off and they managed it on his side of the car, her head bumping against the headliner sometimes, a cramped and sweaty encounter, their bodies slick and shining in the weak light that came from the front of the club. He rested, drank whiskey from a flask in her purse. She stretched out on the seat and tried to revive him with her mouth. Later he dimly remembered a few minutes here and there of sex and when he woke he was back at the catfish place and she was trying to pull him out of the car, screaming at him. He tried to fend her off with one hand, batting at her, but she dragged him out and he fell in the mud. The rain poured down on him and plastered his hair to the back of his head while he cussed her and tried to get up. It was hard for him to get up. Everybody had left and there was just his car in the parking lot. He made his way to it and crawled into the backseat and put his muddy head down on the mildewed upholstery. He spoke a last unintelligible plea for something, death or release or maybe just for the rain to stop so that he could find his way to Jewel's. That was the last thing he knew until he woke up in the morning hearing voices. His head badly overripe and feeling swollen, his tongue thick and furred with some disagreeable taste as if somebody had shit in his mouth. He sat up and rubbed his eyes. Two black women in cook's clothes were looking at him.

"That white boy drunk," one said.

"Shoo," the other one said. "Look what a mess. He done been crawlin around in the mud."

"Oh God," he said, and put his head back down on the seat, trying to ignore the sun that was beginning to fill the car with light.

Jewel woke him just before daylight and stepped from the room in her robe to check on David. He was asleep in his bed, lying on top of the covers. She worked the sheet from beneath him and put it over him and went to the kitchen to put on coffee. When she walked back into the bedroom Bobby was lying back against the pillows. He was smoking a cigarette and looking out the window. He turned his face at her step and she bent over him, kissed him.

"Good morning," she said.

"Mornin. How you feel?"

She sat down and he scooted over a little for her.

"I feel good. I feel a lot better."

He nodded and drew on his cigarette.

"He asleep?"

"Yeah."

"You think he heard anything?"

"Naw. He sleeps like a log. Like you."

He smiled at her and turned in the bed. "Did I snore?"

"I started to get up and go sleep in the living room one time."

"Well. I should have gone on home I guess."

She reached out and put her hand on his stomach. Ran her nails through the black hairs there. "Why?"

"Hell. Mama."

"I can't tell if she approves of me or not."

"That don't matter."

"You got to live with her, though."

"No I don't."

She smiled at that, bent down and kissed him again. Then she got up and took off her robe and let him watch her dress. After a while he got up and put his clothes on, got his hat, grabbed the gun in its holster, and by then the coffee had finished perking and he drank a quick cup at the kitchen table. She eased him out the front door and kissed him by the side of the car with the sun just up. He cranked the car and she leaned down to kiss him again and told him to call her.

"I will."

She turned around and went back into the house and into David's room. He was still sleeping. She sat on the bed for a while watching his face, the soft chin, the hair a little too long, the little dimples on the backs of his knuckles where they lay slack over the sheet. Something had changed now. She wasn't worried anymore. She got up and went into the kitchen to start making their breakfast. The cat came in and sat watching her and she talked to it as if it knew what she was saying.

The top edge of the sun was beginning to rise from the trees on the river. Bobby splashed through holes of water in the road as he drove along. He had to have a shower, fresh clothes, a shave. The rain had drenched the trees and the leaves stood bright and shining and the rows of cotton held long trenches of muddy water, the little creeks he crossed over swirling foam and sticks and sucking at the limbs that trailed down from the banks.

He drove with his hand resting lightly on the wheel and the memory of her giving him a peace he had never felt. He'd slept little but he didn't feel tired. And there were things to do.

It was 6:30 when he looked at his watch and Mary was probably up by now, making biscuits, making coffee. She would already have gone to his room.

He turned off onto his road and the sun kept rising through the windows on the right side of the car. Mist was lifting from the fields and the sun flashed on the weeds still wet from the rain.

He slowed, turned into the yard, and parked the car in front of the porch. He left his keys in it and when he got up to the door it was open. He walked in and found her in the kitchen, standing at the sink and looking out the window.

"Good morning," he said.

"Morning."

That was all he got out of her and he couldn't read her mood. She'd probably been worried about him. She always worried about him.

"Is there any coffee?"

"Over there in the pot."

She kept looking out the window. He set his hat on the table and took off his revolver and put it on a chair. He looked down at the mud on the heels of his boots, saw where he'd tracked it on her nice clean floor. She hadn't noticed. He sat down and took his boots off and then went across the floor in his stocking feet to the corner cabinet and took down two cups.

"Want me to pour you some?"

"I've already had some."

He put one cup back and poured the other one full of coffee, stirred in some sugar, and reached inside the icebox for the milk.

"What'd you do?" she said. "Work late?" She'd turned around and she didn't look happy.

"Not exactly," he said, and took the coffee and the milk back to the table with him.

"You sleep at the jail?"

He poured some milk into his coffee and reached inside his pocket for a cigarette. Once he had it lit he looked up at her.

"I spent the night with Jewel."

"You mean you slept with her?"

"Yes."

She looked down at the floor.

"I knew that was going to happen," she said. "Don't you care what people think?"

The anger came quickly and he was surprised at the level of it. He wasn't going to hurt her if he could help it. Their fights had been few, but when they came they had always been bad. So he tried to head it off.

"Tell you what, Mama. I'm gonna drink this coffee and take a shower and shave and I'll get me some breakfast in town. I got a lot to do today and I don't want to start my day off having an argument with you. So let's just be nice, and I'll sit here and drink my coffee, and I'll be out of here in about twenty minutes. We can talk about it tonight if you want to."

He lowered his face and took a sip of his coffee. It was rich and hot and sweet. He hoped she'd hush. All she had to do was behave.

"That girl," she said, and he held up one hand.

"Hold it. Don't say nothing about her."

"That boy's not yours. He's Glen's and you know it. What are you gonna do, marry her?"

She was looking at him with eyes he hadn't seen before, and she took a few steps toward him.

"If she'll have me I'm going to. This has gone on long enough."

"What about the way she ran wild with him for years? Do you think people are just going to forget about that? Don't you want to get elected again? Don't you care anything about your career?"

"This ain't the only job in the world. I can raise cows. Or drive nails if I have to."

"Drive nails? You're the sheriff. Did you work this hard to give it all up?"

She came closer to the table and he forgot about his coffee and set it down.

"Listen, Mama," he said. "I grew up without a daddy. David ain't going to."

He saw the tears well up in her eyes and it was too late to take it back. But he would have given almost anything not to have said it. She put one hand up to her face and covered it. She looked old and small and weak.

He started to get up and put his arms around her, but she took the hand away from her face and came closer to the table.

"Why do you think it's up to you to marry her? Why don't you ask yourself why Glen never married her?"

"Because he's sorry, Mama."

He looked down at the table for a moment. He had to make her see, and he looked back up into her eyes.

"I don't give a damn about what happened before," he said. "She made some mistakes, yeah. She was young. I was too at one time. It don't mean people can't change and straighten up their lives."

She leaned over the table to him like some wraith descending upon him and her eyes were filled not with anger but with worry, the faded blue of them searching over his face in something like awe.

"What if you marry her and he starts coming around again? What will you do then?"

"That ain't gonna happen."

"How do you know?"

"Because I ain't gonna let it."

She straightened up and rubbed her hands along her arms. The light was coming through the window and she turned to look at it as she moved away from the table. She went to stand at the sink, still hugging herself. Some birds were singing out there in the wet leaves.

"Wild," she said. "I know about that. I was always crazy about Virgil. But my father didn't like him. Wouldn't let him come around. So I had to see him in other places. Sometimes I slipped out. There was a place we'd meet when they thought I was asleep."

"I think I'd just as soon not hear this," he said. He reached to pick up his coffee but his hand was shaking. He spilled some trying to take a sip. He looked at her and could see the gray strands in her hair. He could imagine what she looked like in her youth and he knew that had to be a hard thing for her to turn loose of, like everybody had to one day. He could remember her face leaning into him when he was a child and she held his chin in her hand and combed his hair and how young and pretty her face was in that dim memory. He imagined her the way that Virgil had first seen her.

"You never know what the future's going to bring," she said. "I just don't want to see you hurt. I'm sure she's a nice girl."

She turned around to him and he sat silent in the chair watching her. She wiped at the wetness on her cheeks with the backs of her fingers.

"Look at me," she said. "Like I'm the one to try and give you any advice."

"It's okay, Mama. Everything's going to be all right. You'll see."

"Have you asked her yet?"

"Not yet. I don't know what she'll say yet. And I wanted to talk to you."

"Well," she said in a low voice. "I hope everything will be okay. I just want what's best for you."

And then her voice broke and she came to him. He got out of the chair and put his arms around her and he hugged her tight. She was so small under his arms. She cried a little more and then she quit. He turned loose of her and watched her face.

"You going to be okay?"

"Of course I will. I'm sorry for acting like that. I just want you to be happy."

"Just give me a little time. I've got to work things out with Jewel. And probably Glen, too."

She took a step away and turned halfway to the window, rubbing one hand with the other.

"Glen's what I'm worried about. The whole time he was in school he always looked at me like he hated me. I guess he does." She glanced back at him, and to him she looked scared. "Be careful with him. You don't know what he might do."

"I'll worry about that later," he said. "I got to get on to work. There's something I've got to do today."

"What?"

He picked up his hat and put on his gun and took a last sip from the coffee on the table.

"I'll tell you tonight," he said.

Puppy was sitting on a five-gallon bucket he had turned over and he was taking a starter apart with a screwdriver and an adjustable wrench while having his morning coffee. Engine blocks and hubcaps and the crushed fenders of cars and trucks lay about him. A hoist for hauling up motors hung from a limb on a big tree in the yard. He was trying to get the bendix off and put a new one on and his tennis shoes were wet from the dew.

He dropped the screwdriver in his lap, picked up his coffee, and eyed the road. He had to get his sign out there today so that people would know he was open for business again. In a way he was glad. He liked working for himself and setting his own hours.

He looked toward the trailer and wondered if she was awake yet. Sometimes she didn't get up until nine or ten, depending on when the television woke her. He sipped his coffee and noticed that it was getting a little cold in the cup, so he thought he'd ease back inside and see if she was awake.

He put his tools and the starter on the ground on a rag and got up and walked to the steps, concrete blocks stacked against the sill of the door. He'd been meaning to build a front porch but there was always too much to do. He didn't look at Virgil's car as he went past it. It was just another reminder of things that needed to be done. He knew his daddy needed his car. Some days he just couldn't seem to get going. But now that he had all this time maybe he could get around to it. His daddy didn't need to walk everywhere with that bad leg. It probably wouldn't take him over half a day to fix it.

There was a screen door but the screen was gone from the frame. It rattled when he pulled it open, banged against his knee shutting as he went in. The living room floor was littered with clothes and empty potato chip bags. He set the coffee cup on the counter and went down the hall toward the bedrooms. It was already hot in the trailer. He stopped at the door to the boys' room and looked in. Walt and Johnny were piled up in the bed in a tangle of arms and legs, sleeping soundly. He eased the door shut and went to the next room. Henrietta was under the covers, just her head sticking out. He pulled her door closed, too. He smiled a little and tiptoed back to his own bedroom, shut that door as well, turned the knob, and locked it.

Trudy was a solid lump of sleeping womanhood, her mouth slightly open. She was snoring lightly and the trick was not to wake her suddenly. He took off his cap and laid it on top of the dresser, removed his shirt, slipped off his tennis shoes, and took off his pants. He was not wearing any underwear since he had risen early with this deed in mind and he lowered himself down on the bed next to her and began to slide himself under the covers. She was right in the middle of the bed and he got up next to her. Mornings were about the only chance he got, and sometimes he got lucky. But she was sleeping heavily and didn't respond to his quiet and subtle insinuations. He laid his head back on the pillow and looked at the ceiling. Then he turned over on his side and watched her. One hand crept out and touched the rounded haunch of her tremendous ass. She had on her panties. Her nightgown had bunched up around her waist. He lifted the covers and peered at her breasts. White watermelons.

He felt himself stiffening. He reached down and got it, slid closer to her, rubbed it along her leg. She didn't notice. She didn't do anything until he put his tongue in her ear. Then she reared up wildly, turned over, flopped down with her back to him. Her snoring filled the quiet little room. He knew those kids were going to wake up any minute and start hollering for their breakfast. He hadn't thought to set out the cereal and the bowls and the spoons when he came through.

He listened, but there was no sound from the hall. He wormed his way deeper under the covers, as close to her as he could get. His hand went slowly over her ribs and tried to find one of her nipples beneath the weight of her arm. All that skin made it hard to find. His fingers roamed over the expanse of flesh, soft, warm, slightly damp. His straining member poking straight into the crack of her ass. He began to try and work her panties down and her voice came out disembodied, quietly vicious through her clenched teeth: "What the goddamn hell you think you're doin?"

He stopped. It was important to give the right answer.

"You just look so good I can't help it," he said. "Why don't you roll over?"

"Why don't you get to work you lazy son of a bitch?"

And she pulled the covers up over her head.

"Hell, I done got started. Just thought I'd come in here and take a little break. The kids are all asleep. I done checked. They won't hear us."

She didn't answer. Was she agreeing to it or thinking it over? He thought she might have gone back to sleep. He reached out for her again.

"Quit it," she said.

He stopped where he was. He hated to give up this soon. But if he pissed her off she might stay that way for three or four days.

"You sure?" he said. She didn't answer. In a little while she started snoring again. He rolled over onto his back and studied the ceiling again.

He gave out a long plaintive sigh, a gasp of air filled with anguish for what could have been. He closed his eyes to try and remember how it used to be. And after a while he got up and put his clothes back on.

He was up under the truck putting the bolts back into the starter when he heard somebody pull up. A door slammed and he turned his head and saw two feet coming toward him.

"Be out in a minute," he said. There was a noise beside him and he looked over to see Glen down on one knee with his head sideways watching him.

"What in the hell are you doing up this early?" Puppy said, and kept turning the ratchet handle.

"Shit. I ain't been to bed."

"Where'd you get all that mud on you?"

"It's a long story. You got any coffee made?"

"Yeah. It's in there in the kitchen. Go on in and help yourself. I got to finish this and get these wires on. They's some cups in the cabinet."

"Thanks."

Glen got up from the dirt and Puppy heard him open the screen door, go inside. The door flopped shut behind him. Puppy got the bolts tightened, then put the wires over the posts and picked up a small nut and a washer from where he'd laid them on top of the idler arm and threaded them on. He got them hand-tight, then slipped the little wrench from his shirt pocket and tightened them down. He wormed his way out from under the truck and stood up, opened the door, sat down behind the wheel, and reached for the keys. But then he remembered that the battery cables were still off and he got back out and leaned under the open hood and put them back on, tightened them. Then he got back behind the wheel and turned the key. The engine coughed over and cranked, and he sat there revving it. He saw Glen come back out holding a cup of steaming coffee and blowing on it. He shut off the truck and got out, slammed the hood, and picked up his wrenches from the ground.

"Let's go set in the shop," he said, and went over and pulled the doors open. There were a couple of wrecked chairs in there on the greasy sand and he lowered himself into one and lit a cigarette. He watched his brother come in, look around, take the other chair. The shop was half filled with parts and junk, old bed frames, a broken television, half of an old Ford pickup. Glen crossed his legs and sipped on the coffee. He had mud in his hair, mud on his shirt and pants. Puppy eyed him critically.

"What'd you do, get in another fight?"

"Naw. Got drunk was all. Some old girl picked me up down at Wallace's. I don't remember much of it."

"You got a job yet?"

"Not yet."

"What are you gonna do?"

"I don't know. I got to do something. How come you ain't at work?"

Puppy looked out across the road. "I don't work there no more."

"Since when?"

"Since yesterday. I don't guess you've been to see Daddy, huh?"

"Not in a couple of days."

"What you been doing?"

"Hell. Nothin. Went fishin yesterday."

"Fishin?"

"Yeah."

"When you gonna get out and look for a job?"

"What the hell is it to you?"

Puppy sat there for a little bit, rocking the toe of one tennis shoe up and down. Finally he turned to Glen.

"Smart-ass. Me and Daddy got in a fight cause of you yesterday. So don't ask me what the hell it is to me."

Glen's face was streaked with mud and he gave Puppy an incredulous look.

"What'd you get in a fight with Daddy about?"

"Damn it, I didn't get in a fight with Daddy. Me and Daddy got in a fight with somebody else."

"Fight with who? What are you talking about?"

"Ed Hall. Right on the goddamn sidewalk uptown. Daddy's laid up in the bed right now. Trying to take up for your sorry ass. And you ain't even worth it."

Glen set his coffee down and leaned forward in the chair. "Now before I get pissed off why don't you just explain to me what the hell you're talking about?"

Puppy cooled off a little. He scratched at the sand with his foot. "Hell. It wasn't just you. He said something about all of us. And we got into it."

"Well?"

"Well what?"

"Did you whip his ass?"

"I like to choked the little son of a bitch to death. They took me and Daddy to jail and W.G. fired me yesterday afternoon."

"Is that what's the matter with your nose?"

"Yeah."

"Did he hit the old man too?"

"He did one time. He's bruised up a little. Bobby took him home."

Glen's face clouded up. He sat back in the chair and stared out at something ahead of him, or maybe at nothing. He muttered a few words.

"What?" Puppy said.

"I'm just talking to myself." He turned his head and fixed Puppy with a steady glare. "Has he been seeing Jewel while I been gone?"

"How the hell would I know?"

"Cause you been here and I ain't."

Puppy shifted in his chair and patted his leg impatiently. "What would it matter if he had? Best thing for you would be for somebody else to take care of her anyway. You ain't gonna marry her, and if you ain't gonna marry her and you keep messing around with her, it ain't gonna be nothing but trouble."

"You're just full of advice, ain't you? You and Daddy both."

"And you're so goddamn hardheaded you won't listen to anybody."

They sat quietly for a few moments. Glen took another sip of his coffee. "What are you gonna do?" he said.

"About what?"

"About a job. You said he fired you."

Puppy drew on his cigarette and let the smoke trail out through his nose. He watched a wasp fly into the shop over his head.

"I'll go back to fixin cars. All I got to do is put my sign back out front."

"How come you quit before? That's what you were doing when I went in."

"Hell. I couldn't get people to pay me. They run me out of business when they cut off my credit at the parts store. I had to have a paycheck. That's why I went to work for the county."

"People still owe you money?"

"Hell yeah. Sorry son of a bitches."

"How much?"

"You mean for everything? Or just labor?"

"For everything."

Puppy thought about it for a little bit. It had been a while since he'd looked at his books but he knew what Trudy had said. She'd taken bookkeeping in high school. He scratched the side of his jaw.

"About three thousand dollars."

"You're shittin me."

"No I ain't either. They always gonna pay you some next week, you know. And next week don't never roll around."

Glen drank the rest of his coffee and set the cup in his lap. He fanned at a fly circling his face.

"So why you gonna get back into it?"

"Cause. There's money in it."

"It ain't if they won't pay you."

"Well. I'm gonna do things different this time. Somebody brings a car in here they're gonna hand me the keys. I'm gonna look at the car and figure up what it'll cost to fix it and call em up and let em know. And then when they come to pick their car up if they ain't got the money they don't get their keys back."

"Why didn't you do that before?"

"Aw hell. Everybody's got a sob story. You do work for friends. Relatives too, by God. This time it's gonna be different. Have you looked for a job?"

"I went out to the stove factory. That ain't no job."

"It's a paycheck. Hell, Glen, you got to do something. You got to eat. Why don't you try to get on working construction somewhere?"

"Shit," Glen said. "I don't know nothing about no construction."

"Well damn, Glen, you may have to learn how to do something. You can't just sit around on your ass and wait for something to come along."

"I applied for my unemployment."

"Yeah? And what's that? Twenty dollars a week?"

"Twenty-eight."

"Shit. I'm gonna go in and get me another cup of coffee. You want one?"

"Naw."

Puppy got up from the chair and flipped his cigarette out onto the gravel. "I'll be back in a minute," he said.

He went across the yard and opened the door again and stepped into the living room. All the kids were up watching television and eating cereal, sprawled on the couch or the floor, and they seemed hypnotized by the images on the set, their slack mouths vaguely chewing their food like some memory of eating they once might have had. They were all still in their underwear.

"Why don't y'all put some clothes on," he said, but he got no answer. He set his cup on the counter to pour some more coffee. He heard a door open and looked up to see Trudy in front of the bathroom in her robe, one finger crooked and moving rapidly to summon him to her. He stepped down the hall to where she was.

"What the hell's he doing here?" she said.

He knew who, but he said it anyway. "Who?"

She glared at him and he guessed he'd put her in a bad mood, waking her up like he had.

"I don't want him around my kids," she said. "He's a bad influence."

"He's my brother. What you want me to do, run him off?"

"If you don't, I will."

A slow burn started inside him as it sometimes did. He spoke very slowly. "He's just having a cup of coffee. He'll be gone after while."

"He better be," she said, and she stepped back into the bathroom and slammed the door in his face.

Another fight. He didn't know why they always had to fight. He had almost forgotten the time when they didn't. He was tired of it, God knows he was tired of it, and his whole fucking sorry life with greasy hands all the time and working on some piece of junk or other for somebody, it didn't matter who, looked like he'd always be doing that, always be on his hurting back on gravel reaching up into the dark oily undersides of vehicles skinning his knuckles.

He looked at the cheap wood-grained door for a moment and then drew back and drove his fist into it and it jumped open to reveal Trudy's big white hips overswallowing the maw of the green commode, where she was perched with her robe up around her waist, her eyes wide open in alarm. She didn't say anything and he could hear her dripping down into the water. He stood there and looked at her.

"Don't say nothing else about my brother," he said. She didn't move and she stopped peeing. He shut the door and went back up the hall and poured his cup of coffee. The kids were still facing the television.

"I said put some clothes on," he told them, and when he went out the door they were going toward their rooms.

Glen was still sitting in the chair looking out at the morning when he sat down again. He lowered his mouth to his coffee and sipped at it.

"Why don't you go see Daddy?" he said. "I meant to go check on him but I need to get to work."

"What are you working on?"

"That pickup there. I just fixed the starter on it and I got to put a new muffler on it. I got to get my sign back out on the road so folks'll know I'm open for business again."

Glen sat there looking at the ground. "What did he say to you?"

"Who?"

"Ed Hall."

He wished now he hadn't even told it. He didn't know why he had. It probably wouldn't do anything but stir up more trouble.

"It don't matter what he said. Only reason he said it was cause you run over his kid."

"So you're blaming me for it."

"Naw, Glen, I ain't blaming you for it. What good would that do?"

It was quiet for a while. They sat in the chairs with the heat rising around them. Glen looked up toward the trailer and nodded at it. "She still hate my guts?"

"You ain't her favorite person in the world I don't guess."

"Well," he said. "She never did like me anyway." He got up from his chair. "I'm gonna get on down the road."

"Why don't you go by there and see about Daddy?"

Glen put his hands in his pockets and kicked at a rock. His eyes were red and he looked rough. "I don't know. Hell, he's probably all right, ain't he?"

Puppy took another sip of his coffee. He hated to have to beg him like this. "He's getting pretty old, you know?"

"Yeah, I know."

"I mean, wouldn't you want your kids to come see you when you get old?"

"Wouldn't make no damn difference to me," Glen said. "I'm gonna go talk to Jewel."

"You better leave it alone."

"Fuck leavin it alone. I'm gonna find out what's going on."

Glen walked to his car and Puppy got out of his chair. He wanted to say something else to him but he didn't know what it should be. He knew Glen wouldn't listen to him anyway. So he didn't say anything. He just wondered if his own children would visit him when he got old. And if Glen was the one who killed Frankie Barlow. He was pretty sure that he was. He didn't watch his brother leave, didn't see him turn up the whiskey bottle. He went around the side of the shop, trying to remember where he had put that muffler. His hand was beginning to hurt a little.

Bobby thought he knew every pig trail in the county, but he didn't know this one. The road was more like a path through the woods, shaded and relatively cool, and it sloped up the hill to a clearing where he could see the roof of the trailer in the morning sun. Once they got close he began to see things abandoned by the edge of the road and half reclaimed by creeping vines and nests of briars, old refrigerators and discarded lawn mowers, bedsprings and rotted sheets of plywood, cans buried in leaf mold, piles of bottles, a rusted-out Ford pickup riddled with bullet holes as if people had been shot standing beside it.

His prisoner had not spoken since he'd turned off the main road and Bobby could sense a growing uneasiness in the backseat where he sat with his hands cuffed. He stank. The children had, too, before Mary gave them a bath.

He slowed the car and pulled up over the hill and turned down into what he guessed they called the yard. He stopped in front of the trailer and looked around. Overturned chairs and scattered beer cans. Broken tree limbs were hanging from the roof of the trailer and panes of glass were patched with masking tape. Milk crates and soda bottles and wheel rims and blown-out tires. He shut the car off and turned in the seat.

"Just stay in here. You got that?"

The man eased himself to rest against the back of the seat and his eyes were hooded and dark and they mocked Bobby. "I need to get some more clothes," he said. "You said you'd let me get my clothes."

"I will. I'm gonna have a look around first. You stay in the car. You hear?"

"I hear."

"I can always handcuff you to the car if you're thinking about running."

The prisoner looked away.

Bobby got out and took the keys with him. The sky was beginning to cloud over and a small wind was whistling through the tops of the pines. He stepped around the stuff in the yard and walked over to the door. He looked at the concrete blocks stacked there and went up them cautiously and glanced back once at the prisoner before he tried the knob. It turned stiffly in his hand and he stepped into the trailer.

The first thing that hit him was the smell. Mildew and rot. The floor was buckled and water stains in strange brown shapes had spread out over the ceiling. The furniture was piled high with clothes. It was damp in there and a small puddle of water lay on the floor. He stood in the middle of the living room for a moment. Beneath the couch he spotted something and he went closer and then knelt and reached under it for the thing that lay there. It was a child's shirt, spotted with dried blood. He smelled it but it had no odor at all. He laid it aside and stood back up. There were rooms at either end and he went down the narrow hall with a vague distress consuming him. He didn't want to be in this place, neither as visitor or intruder. He kept thinking of the children.

His boots pressed spots of water from the soiled carpet in the hall and he stopped at the back door to look and see what was out there. A small pane of glass was set into it and he looked through it to a bleary world outside. There was a loose aluminum knob set into the door and he twisted it. The door was jammed in its frame and he had to push hard on it. The top sagged out but the bottom was hung up on the threshold. He pushed harder and it wobbled open and he let it sway away from the trailer. There was an odd light in the woods out there. He looked down but there were no steps. The ground was two feet below the floor. He left the door open and went on down the hall.

A bathroom with no door was on the left. He studied the rusted tub, the torn shower curtain. A few cans of shaving cream and some shampoo and soap were on the sink. Wet towels were piled up. The commode was leaking and water had pooled around it and run down the hall and he was standing in it. He moved out of there and walked into the bedroom. It was dark in there, the windows shuttered against the light with venetian blinds. A rumpled bed dusted with cigarette ashes, record albums on the floor, and a player set on top of a dresser whose drawers were hanging open. He looked behind the door and the shotgun was leaning there in the corner just where they said it would be. He picked it up. The gun was rusted and the stock was full of scratches. He found the release and pulled down on the slide to see if it was loaded. It was. He pumped the slide three times and the shells kicked out and landed on the floor with small clatters. He stooped and picked them up, turned them over in his hand in the dim light. Birdshot, some green, some red. He put them in his pocket and cleared the action on the gun one more time, looked into the chamber to see that it was empty. Then he put it back where it had been and moved the door over it. He stood there listening but he heard nothing.

The open back door was letting light into the hall and he walked back to it and grabbed hold of the door frame and took a long step down into the backyard. The woods were close and he could see more junk scattered down through there. An old Dodge car was resting in the weeds and he walked over and looked inside. The seats had rotted and the hood was up and the motor was missing. He glanced up. Clouds were pushing fast across the sky and he heard a low rumbling.

There seemed to be some kind of path down through the woods, not exactly well worn, more like a trail. He looked back up the hill. The door was still hanging against the outside wall. He eased into the woods. Evidently people had used this place as a dumping ground for years. The stands of scrubby trees were littered with the cast-off items of so many households, cardboard boxes of Mason jars and old crates, broken washing machines. He moved past these things and watched the ground for snakes. Little oak trees with their broad leaves carpeted the ground, thin pines swayed in the breeze, nests of honeysuckle and vines tangled with piles of wooden skids. The ground was still damp from the rain and he stepped around the holes of water, trying to keep his feet dry. He kept glancing back at the trailer until it was out of sight and then he went deeper into the woods. He walked and walked, remembering what they'd said. There was the white stump. And then he saw it: a low mound of earth on the other side of a pile of downed timber, fresh spadings of earth still in chunks with bits of shattered rock embedded in the blue bits of clay. He walked closer to it until he stood over it. It was such a small thing. He went to his knees and started digging with his hands. The clay stuck to his fingers. No worms had turned in this earth.

He knelt, unmindful of the wetness that was spreading over his knees, and he began to breathe a little harder just as Byers had, and it was not lost on him. When his hand struck a bone he stopped. Leaned back on his haunches with the gun hanging heavy at his side and raised his face to the sky that was swirling and arguing with its own elements and closed his eyes for a second. A thunderbolt barked far off. A dry rumbling cracking that seemed to be heading his way with one purpose and that to split the heavens open and devour him and everything in the world that was under it. He could hear it forming up in the distance and thunder building on thunder and it began to rain. He took his hat off and let the drops pepper his shoulders, his forearms. He sank his fingers back into the cheap and worthless red dirt and it rose up between his knuckles as he pawed it back or cast it to one side or the other. The cloudhead moved above him and the trees swayed hard in the wind it brought and the noise like a long sighing rose up all around him.

The lightning moved in and it began to arc down to the land. He heard a bolt explode nearby. He felt that he was about to be struck and with one quick movement he stood up and unbuckled the gun and pitched it away running and dove to the ground and in the report and clash that followed, from one corner of his eye, he saw a tall pine tree illuminated in a bright flash of blue light, a halo of electric fire, and the bark sliding away in curved shells as the resin boiled out in black bubbles and slid hissing down the white pale length of the naked tree all bent and smoking and its limbs in ruins.

He lay on his face in the mud with both hands over his ears and thinking his eardrums were burst while from the sky a torrent of water settled over him and poured down into every inch of ground. It poured ceaselessly and it roared with a sound that drowned out every nuance of hearing he might have had left. He stood up in the midst of it and saw the water flowing into the shallow depression he had made with his hands and he moved toward it even in the midst of what was coming from the sky. Little rivulets of packed dirt were shearing away from the edges of the hole and mud and water were being borne away down the hillside and while he stood there half blind and near deaf he saw the thin bones coming yellow into the gray light and the femurs rising out of the sludge and the hips and what lay there was not over two feet long. He staggered through the soggy leaves and recovered his gun and strapped it on and didn't look anymore. He found his hat and went back up the path as the storm began to move away, the rumbling fading, the lightning spearing down to the earth at other points, a dying message talking, God uneasy, maybe, but he'd seen all he needed to.

Dripping onto the soaked carpet at the back door he stood poised and listening for the repeat of a small noise and when he turned the barrel of the shotgun was looming up and the clenched hands still bearing the handcuffs were what he looked at before the face, the finger on the trigger, the other hand gripping the shotgun just short of the pump slide, and then he looked at the face, the wet hair hanging down into the smiling eyes and a single drop of rainwater depending from the chin and it seemed to happen in slow motion, how the barrel moved up and how he looked deep into the black nothingness contained there and peered up almost detached into the eyes that smiled and then the finger bent and the firing pin snapped on the empty chamber and all the light went out of those eyes. He would remember it for years, his own gun coming into his hand, the rustle of the leather against the steel and the horror in the eyes that had fixed on his when he brought the heavy revolver up and leveled it, that moment so quiet and still when they both listened to the chamber rotate up as he cocked it and how the little black iron tooth moved back under his thumb with a dead dry click.

The gun did not waver as it moved toward the face and it was almost comical the way the eyes crossed to try and keep that small black bore in focus. But Bobby didn't laugh. In that tiny second when he decided not to kill him he became very sad.

"You're under arrest for murder now, you son of a bitch," he said.

Jewel got to work early and let herself in through the back door that faced the alley where the delivery trucks parked, putting the key into the lock over the hasp and swinging the hasp back and going into the kitchen. It was dark until she swung the door back and propped it with a brick. She hooked the spring into the screen door and let it close.

She set her purse on a table and went to the wall switch and turned on the lights. They hummed and blinked a few times and then came on all over the ceiling. She made some coffee and went out to the front where the same quiet lay over everything, the dark tables and chairs, the ceiling fans hanging still and dusty.

One by one she raised the blinds in the windows and looked out onto the street. It was cloudy and the pavement was wet. She called back the night and the crashings of thunder and the intermittent flashes of light, the bristles of his jaw, the gentleness of his hands. How soft his words in her ear and the things he had said. Those wasted three years, all that time waiting because she'd said she would. If Glen came by now she'd have to think of what to tell him. She couldn't let things go back to the way they had been. When that time came she'd have to be strong enough to send him away, to tell him that it was over, that she had to think about David. She had to think about the rest of her life.

She unlocked the front door and turned on the lights in the front room. Customers would be coming in by eleven and the phone would start ringing for orders before long. She went to the grill and turned it on, walked back to the kitchen and put on a fresh apron and started getting things from the coolers and freezers. It helped to keep her hands busy with things, to work, to get started on the day and not worry about what might happen later or what he might do when he found out. Too much time had gone by. She had wasted too much of her life on him already. She had to let him go.

When she walked out to the front to draw herself a Coke from the fountain there was nobody sitting at the counter but Glen. She stopped suddenly. He didn't look good and she could tell he'd been drinking by the way his eyes were. And he was just sitting there with his hands folded together as if he had been waiting for her to appear.

"Well," she said, and went to the rack of glasses and got one and reached into the bin and scooped it full of ice. She could feel him watching her as she filled the glass from the dispenser. She didn't know what she was going to say, but she turned around to him and set the glass on the counter and crossed her arms.

"You want something?"

He pulled his hands apart and watched the counter for a moment, then looked up at her.

"Cup of coffee, maybe?"

"Okay."

She had to go back to the kitchen for it, through the double doors and past one of the stoves where an old black crone named Nell was mindlessly stirring something in a big pot with a long wooden spoon. A couple of the cooks had come in and she was glad she and Glen weren't alone. She got a saucer and a cup and a spoon and filled the cup with coffee from one of the urns and carried it all back out front and set it before him, slid over the sugar shaker and pulled a tin of milk from an icebox below the counter. She watched him tend to his coffee. He swung the spoon back and forth in it for a long time.

"How you been doing?" he said, and took the spoon out and laid it down.

She leaned back against the table she used to fix the hamburgers and studied him. "If you'd come around you'd know how I'm doing."

"Yeah, well, I hate to have to get in line."

He picked up his coffee and sipped it, set it back down.

"I saw you come by," she said. "You been watching me. I don't like it. Did you cut that hole in my screen?"

"I don't know what you're talkin about," he said, and kept his eyes on his coffee.

"You're lying, Glen."

One of the cooks came to the doors and poked her head out and watched what was going on and then withdrew.

"What the hell does she want?" he said.

"Why don't you look at me, Glen? Where you been since Saturday night?"

He gave a little shrug and turned his head to one side, then looked back.

"Just around. Hell. I've had things to do. Looks like you have, too."

"You're talking about Bobby?"

"Who else would I be talkin about? I come by to see you and he's over there. You think I's gonna stop?"

"Somebody come in my house and I called him," she said. "We wasn't doing nothing but talking."

"What you two got so much to talk about all of a sudden? But I don't guess it's all of a sudden, is it?"

It hit her then what he had done, how he had looked at a thing and decided what it was. He had probably driven around thinking about it while he was drinking and brooded over it. She'd spent enough time with him to know how his mind worked. No grudge ever forgiven, no wrong ever allowed to be righted. And he'd always hated Bobby. But none of that was her fault. All that had happened a long time ago.

"You think I been slipping around with him behind your back, is that what you think?"

"How the hell would I know? I been gone three goddamn years, remember?"

"I ain't forgot where you been," she said. "What you think I been doing but raising David and working here and waiting for you to get out and come see me?"

"I come to see you."

"You think one hour in my bed makes up for all that? What do you reckon I say to that baby when he keeps asking where his daddy is?"

He picked up the coffee and she stepped back in case he decided to throw it on her. But he just lowered his head and took a sip of it. She could see dirt under his fingernails. His hair hadn't been combed and there was dried mud all over him.

"What have you been doing, Glen?"

He didn't give her any answer for that. It was rumbling thunder outside and the air had darkened again. Cars were going along the street with their wipers sweeping at a misting rain that had started falling. Behind her was a clatter of things in the kitchen and the cooks talking, a radio playing with muted and indistinct voices. It was time for people to start coming in.

"I done told you I don't want to get married," he said. "It ain't nothin but trouble and I don't want no more of it."

"And where does that leave me and David?"

"I don't know," he said.

She had her answer now, but she'd always known what it would be. She walked a little closer to him.

"I don't want you to come around no more, Glen. You don't care who you hurt and you don't care nothing about me. David either. All you want is one thing."

"Same thing he got?"

"That ain't none of your business."

"You probly been fuckin him the whole time I was gone."

She felt the hot rush of blood wash up through her cheeks.

"That's a lie," she said. "I waited on you. But I want you to go now. I got to get back to work."

He didn't get up, only sat there staring at her with the same look she had seen him use on other people. It was a bad thing to see it turned on her.

"You ain't nothin but a goddamn whore," he said. "I bet he ain't even mine."

She thought of all the nights with him and the years that were now thrown away so fast that they were worth nothing. She didn't want to cry in front of him, but if he didn't leave soon she was afraid she would. He didn't even look the same now. His face had thinned and the way he was looking at her caused her to start to back away from him, her hand going out to find whatever she might use to defend herself against him because he was getting up from the stool and bending over the counter with a hard glint coming into his eyes. She had seen it once before, on that summer night so far back, when he had moved toward Frankie Barlow with the knife in his hand and murder on his face. The voice that came out of him was more of a hiss than words.

"He'll be sorry," he said. "And you will, too."

"Get out of here, Glen. Before I call the police."

She started to move toward the telephone and when he saw that, he stepped down from the stool and turned away and started walking out with a quick step, not looking back. The door slammed hard and then she couldn't see him anymore. She walked to the counter and picked up the cup and the saucer and the spoon and carried it all back to the kitchen and set it down gently in the sink. Outside she heard a tire squeal, a horn blare. She stood there at the sink and just looked at the wall for a little while. Nobody said anything to her. The radio was still playing and steam was rising from the big pots on the black iron stove. After a while she went back out front and leaned against the counter, waiting for the first customer to come in. It was still raining and in the distance she could hear the storm gathering in a voice that was low and angry.

All that morning Mary thought about Virgil. It was too wet to work in the yard, but after Bobby left she cleaned up the breakfast dishes and put on an old dress and went out there to see about hanging out some clothes. It was still cloudy and she decided she'd just wait until it cleared off. She was glad for the rain. The farmers needed it.

She went back in and gathered a load of clothes to wash and got her little sharp paring knife and stepped into the muddy rows of the garden to gather some okra and tomatoes. She put the okra in her pockets but she didn't get all of it. When they'd planted it Bobby told her they didn't need that much. Her pockets were bulging with it and there was still half a row to cut. She picked all the tomatoes she could hold in her arms and unloaded it all on the kitchen counter. While she was in there she got to thinking that Virgil might want something good for lunch, so she started making some spaghetti sauce in a skillet and left in on low to simmer. If Bobby came in he could eat with her, and then she could take the rest of it over to Virgil. She knew he didn't eat right half the time and wouldn't unless he had somebody to take care of him. And it was more than just that. It wasn't good for either one of them to spend so much time alone. A long time ago it hadn't mattered as much, when Bobby was growing up and needed her and there wasn't as much time to think about all that. But he was home so rarely now. He stayed so busy. Getting up and going at all hours of the night whenever the phone rang to wake her long enough to listen to part of a sleepy conversation and then he would call to her and tell her he was going and she would drift back to sleep hearing his car go down the road. All the trouble on the weekends, all the drunks and the fights and the wrecks. All the bad stuff always happened then. People got to drinking and they went crazy.

She went back to the garden and gathered some more of the okra, but it was so muddy at the far end of the row that she thought she'd just leave the rest of it for later. Going back across the yard she saw her wheelbarrow beside the door of the barn with her little tomato plants in it. All that rain, it was probably full of water, drowning those tiny plants. Her old tennis shoes squeezed liquid mud from the grass as she walked down the hill.

The wheelbarrow was half full of water and just the tops of the tomato plants were sticking up above it. She slipped the knife into her pocket carefully because it was so sharp and then walked around behind the wheelbarrow and picked up on the handles to tip it forward and let the water drain off. It poured out the front onto the ground and she eased it up a little bit at a time, trying not to slide the plastic pots out with it. She was going to set them out before long so they'd have fresh tomatoes right on into the fall. Bobby loved them so much. And everything would probably work out okay about him and Jewel. It was just Glen she was worried about. He'd been in so much trouble and she knew it was because of what happened to his brother. A child like that, he couldn't help but be affected by something bad like that. And all this time later, for Emma to do what she'd done. She'd never understood that, people thinking they were ending all their troubles without ever thinking about the trouble they were leaving for the people behind them. She wondered if they'd ever told Glen the truth about that. It was just as well if they hadn't. But he'd probably find out the truth one day anyway. You couldn't keep a thing like that a secret forever. You might keep it for a long time, years might even go by, but somebody would eventually tell it.

She couldn't understand why he wouldn't claim that little boy. He was a nice little boy. Always behaved in church. And he was Virgil's grandchild. Hers if Bobby married Jewel. And there might be other children later. It was so nice to think about. She was almost scared to think too much about getting back with Virgil after all this time. She hoped he would call her.

The hoe handle struck her above the left eye—she saw it looming, swinging in, hands gripping it—and she had a vague impression of tumbling sideways over the tipping wheelbarrow. Then the ground rushed up to her face and smacked her into a black place with a soft *whump*.

Bobby got back to the jail around the middle of the morning and he parked the car next to the steps. He left the keys in it and got out, opened the back door and waited for his prisoner to get out. There had been no words said on the way back and he wouldn't even look at Bobby now.

Bobby got him by one arm and shut the door behind him. They turned toward the jail and stood there for a moment, and then he turned him loose.

"All right," he said. "You know the way in."

He never expected him to run then. He wasn't even paying that much attention to him. He had mud all over him and he wanted to get inside and change clothes. There was a quick movement beside him and then his prisoner was running hard across the wet parking lot, holding his cuffed hands to his chest. In a way it didn't surprise him. That was the thing of it. They never wanted to pay for what they did.

He didn't have to chase after him or even draw his gun. A city police car turned in at the end of the parking lot and Bobby just watched as the officer behind the wheel realized what was happening. The car slid to a quick halt and the prisoner washed up against it, rolled over against the grill one time, and tried to go around the other side. But he slipped on the pavement and the officer stepped out and collared him. His knees almost went out from under him and he sagged against the city cop. Bobby walked over there slowly, reaching for a cigarette, and he stopped for just a moment to light it. Then he walked on up there.

The officer was still holding him, and Bobby nodded and the officer turned him loose. They watched him. He leaned against the fender of the patrol car, his face twisted, and he laid his manacled hands on the shiny hood of the car where drops of water from the morning rain were beaded, and he seemed to be praying as the tears began to roll out of him. His eyes squeezed shut hard and deep sobs began to wrack his frail body. He confessed it all, and it only took a minute, a deed done with a walking cane to a little boy who was sick and would not stop crying. Bobby and the officer stood there in the street under the cloudy sky with their heads down and listened to it.

He seemed to feel better after he did that. He got off the hood and stood up, sniffling loudly through his nose and trying to wipe his eyes with the cuffs on his hands. Then he straightened himself and started walking briskly back across the parking lot toward the front door of the jail, as if he had some high purpose, some destination other than the one that was his.

Bobby had him back in the cell and he was looking around the office to see if there was any coffee made when Mable came over and stopped. He was doubtfully eyeing the dregs of some evil-looking fluid he had poured into his cup that was dark and thick and smelled rank.

"Somebody called for you a while ago, Bobby."

"Who was it?" he said, and poured the stuff into the sink.

"Jewel Coleman. Said she wanted to talk to you."

He rinsed the cup and looked up at Mable. "She say what she want?"

"Naw. Just wanted to know if you were in. Said to tell you she called."

He set the cup back onto the towel where they kept them. It seemed like somebody should keep some coffee made for him. He guessed he'd have to make it himself and he started looking for the stuff.

"She want me to call her?"

"She didn't say. What you looking for?"

"The coffee. I wish y'all would keep it someplace I could find it or keep some made."

It wasn't like Jewel to call up there. She probably wanted to know what his mother said. But he didn't really have time to go by there or get into all that on the phone. He could give her a call later on this evening.

"I'll make you some coffee. Go on back there and change your clothes. You look like you've wallered in a mud hole."

"Holler at me when it's ready, okay?"

"Okay."

He turned and went down the hall. He thought maybe they could take David out sometime, maybe this weekend if things settled down. He had to find Glen and have a talk with him. A calm talk. Get everything straight with him.

Mable called after him, "We gonna keep him a while longer?"

He stopped and turned around. "Who's that?"

"That one you just brought back in."

"Oh yeah. He's gonna be here for a while."

He went on back to his office and sat down at his desk. Then he got back up and locked the door for a few minutes and changed into a clean uniform and got another pair of boots. When he opened the door Mable was bringing him a cup of coffee up the hall. He thanked her and went over to his desk again and leaned back in the chair. There was a lot to do yet. Somebody would have to take his confession down and then take him over to the courthouse and get him charged. More paperwork. More time in court. The main thing he had to do was go back out there and dig that child up as soon as he could. That might take most of the afternoon and it could always start raining again, but he hoped not. He had to call the coroner and he had to call Jackson and let them know he had to have an autopsy done. Mable could probably do some of that for him.

He picked up his coffee and slid the telephone closer and dialed his house. He hated to have to tell her about this one. She wouldn't understand it any better than she had about the others. But he didn't understand it himself. The phone rang in his house and he put one boot up on the desk. Probably drunk when he did it. Probably no money to go to the doctor. There was no telling what time he'd be through tonight. He might not even have time to go see Jewel. It rang again. He couldn't let that baby keep lying in that ground out there. They'd need shovels, a body bag. He needed to round up somebody to help him. It rang again and he figured she was probably out in the yard. Out there doing something, always was. Come on, Mama, answer the phone. It rang three more times and he pulled it away from his ear and started to hang it up, but she was probably trying to get to it, had her hands covered with flour or something, so he let it ring a few more times. On the tenth ring he knew she wasn't home and he hung it up.

He started pulling forms out of his desk drawers, the telephone numbers he needed.

"Hey Mable?" he called.

"Yes sir," she said when she appeared at the door.

"Would you mind runnin out to get me a sandwich?"

"Not a bit. What you want?"

"I don't care. A hamburger. Anything. I got so much to do I ain't got time to go get it myself."

"I'll find you something."

"Thanks, Mable. And would you raise Harold on the radio and tell him I'm gonna need him pretty soon? Please ma'am?"

"Sure will."

She went back down the hall and he scanned with his finger down the list of numbers. He wondered briefly where his mother could be at this time of day and then he thought no more of it. He had a lot of things on his mind just then.

He dragged her by the arms and she was lighter than he would have thought. There was a little runnel of blood coming down over her left eye and sliding off her cheek, and he had to hold up on her arms to keep her head out of the mud as he was going into the barn with her.

It was dark in there, cool and quiet. An old wagon stood backed in between posts, fat bags of musty corn encrusted with dust. A hay rake with one flat tire sat at the rear, the claw tines frozen with rust and disuse. An old smell of horses and fertilizer and cow shit through which he dragged her, breathing heavily from exertion and the weight of this deed. Some okra fell out of her pockets as he dragged her along.

He stopped for a moment to rest and to look for a place to put her. Some fitting niche where the thing could be done without wallowing in any nastiness. He dropped his hold on her arms.

Some carpenter long ago had erected poles of peeled oak and had hammered the joists to them. Glen looked up through the rafters and could see specks of light through the tin roof even though it was still cloudy and the promise of more rain was in the sky. A loft at the back held stacked bales of hay. There was a ladder standing up against it and he walked over and looked at it. He shook it with one hand. It seemed rickety and he didn't think he could get her up there by himself. He turned and looked at her. Her eyes had not opened and one of her tennis shoes had come off. She lay like one braced against sleep, her arms out to her sides and flat on her back with her legs slightly spread and her face turned to one side in a soft grimace.

He walked around, feeling somehow like a burglar or a lecher, a voyeuristic bent inside him that had never been his intention. But some wounded piece of him still cried out for the need to punish Bobby, and she was the one who could cause him the most hurt. She was the easiest.

He wandered among dusty relics, an old icebox whose chromed hinges had barnacles of corrosion encroaching. Cigar boxes stacked on a shelf. He lifted some of the lids and peered in to see: ancient fishing lures, goggle-eyed wooden minnows and silver spoons, a busted padlock, tarnished shotgun shells. A single round for a .50-caliber machine gun that felt like it weighed half a pound. She lay sleeping quietly in the hall of the barn whenever he looked her way.

It was still overcast when he walked to the door of the barn. A few clouds had parted and dark shafts of vapor hung down through a hole in the gray center of the sky and the thunder rumbled far off. He looked back at her but she had not moved.

Standing there at the entrance he lit a cigarette and stepped back out of sight of the house to kneel with one knee up and smoke and watch her. She had aged. He could remember her writing on the blackboard, could remember her at her desk and going down through the aisles handing out papers and reading from her books with her feet propped on a drawer and the wind coming through the windows billowing her dress up. Now thin strands of gray had settled in her hair and her face was devoid of makeup and her lips were pale. He put his head down on his arms and held the cigarette, rocking gently, waiting for this day to be over.

After a while he got up and toed a clean place in the scattered hay that lined the floor of the barn and dropped the cigarette and pressed the butt firmly into the black dirt and made sure that it was out. Then he walked to the back of the barn. There was one stall in the corner where hay was piled up beneath a window set into the rear wall. It looked dirty. It looked damp. He didn't want her to have to lie in that.

He took another look at her and then walked to the ladder, shaking it one more time, and then he put his foot up on it and began to climb, watchful for the little nails that might pull out, and he went up carefully until he came to the top and stopped. He looked out at the floor of the loft. Fifty or sixty bales of hay were up there. The uprights extended five feet above the floor and he climbed on up and stepped off. Old sea grass ropes had been hung from the timbers. He walked to the nearest bale and bent over, grabbed the strings, carried it to the end of the loft. Looking down to judge its impact with a careful eye he turned loose of it and saw it fall in front of the stall. He went back for another one, dropped it, too. He went back for one more. It hit the other two and bounded across the floor, bouncing once on its end and landing near her. He stood looking down. He could see her stretched out on her back. She still had not moved and he began to wonder if he had hit her too hard. But then he realized that she should have thought about that whenever she was fucking his old man and he climbed back down.

He pulled the strings off one of the bales and started taking the charges apart, separating the little blocks of hay and scattering them about, the dusty components of stem and seed floating in the air and settling over the floor. He worked calmly, tearing the hay apart and smelling its clean fragrance, it wafting down around his knees and over his shoes, piling up. He kept working and spreading it and he looked through the dirty window to see her garden and her flowers in the yard, her neat back porch.

When he had all the hay scattered and spread out he bent down to it, spread his hand out to test its resilience. A nice soft bed to lay her upon. He went back to her and got her by the arms again.

He dragged her into the little stall and he dropped her arms. She lay as before, but now nested in fresh clean hay. It was like something he might have dreamed a long time ago.

There were rags for a blindfold hanging over a brace and he took some of them down and knotted them together and tied them around her head, blinding her eyes so she could not see him. Another trip to the loft brought down bale strings with which to bind her arms. He wrapped them around her wrists but not tightly enough to cut off her circulation. He tied them to the posts that flanked the stall. And then he sat down beside her and waited for her to wake up. He wanted her to know what was happening, and he kept telling himself that he could really do this.

He thought it might rain again, looking out the barn door. And sitting there he saw the overturned wheelbarrow and got up and went out there and righted it. He looked up at the house. Nothing was stirring up there. Not even the wind riffling the leaves in the trees. All was still.

He went back into the gloom beside her and tried to think where he would go when this was over. But he already knew that.

Mable brought his sandwich and Bobby kept working. When Harold finally came in, he got his papers gathered up and stacked on his desk and they got into the cruiser and drove out into the county to meet the coroner and his helpers at a lonely and rain-swept crossroads where the hawks had folded their wings to sit on the fence posts and regard the sky with their cold bright eyes. Shoals of water were riffling off the fields and the day was gray and dark, the creeks rising, foaming, the beavers swimming strongly with sticks in their mouths as the men crossed the little bridges in their cars and cast a glance down into the muddy currents. In a small procession they drove to that place where he had already been and unloaded their shovels, and then they went down through the woods.

The storm had passed and the weeds were wet with that passing. The little pullings of mud at the soles of their boots and the trees dripping water down on them in their sorrow. A small caravan of officials bearing the weight of the law with them. Bobby directed them and at last they stood beside the opened grave with the bones still showing, flies hovering, the short blue flight of a jay over their heads as it dipped and swayed. They started digging the child up and Bobby walked off some distance where he wouldn't see what was going on and smoked a cigarette. He could hear them talking quietly. He could hear the clay sucking at the blades of the shovels as they pressed their feet down on them. He could remember his mother shushing him and rocking him in her lap one time when he had skinned his knee. He could remember the taste of Jewel's nipples and the sweet smell of her breath. He wondered if she was thinking of him now.

After a while they came back up, the black zippered bag slung between two of them, and they started out of the woods with their little pile of bones seeming so small to Bobby, so insubstantial. He walked quickly, leading them. The sky was still dark and he watched for it to come up blue again, but it never did.

They placed the tiny corpse on the backseat of his car and then single file they drove out to the main road back toward town. Bobby was thinking of the father again across the hood of the car and how the tears had rolled out of him too late. Harold was beside him but they didn't talk. They drove on, through the gray and cloudy day and past the hawks that had not moved.

The sky was still and dark when Virgil walked out on his front porch and sat down in the chair. He was out of cigarettes again and he had to roll one, taking the tobacco from his pocket and getting the papers and working at it, glancing up from time to time to look across the road at the sky and what it was doing. When he had it rolled he stuck it between his lips and lit it, leaning back in the chair and rocking a little, the smoke drifting out across the porch and into the yard where it dissipated. He felt uneasy somehow.

After a while he tossed away the burnt nubbin of it and sat there. There was no traffic on the road and he wished he had his car again. He didn't want to walk all the way over to the store for some more cigarettes. The road was muddy now, and he was still tired.

The puppy came around the end of the porch and angled up the steps, and he stopped near Virgil's knee and wagged his tail.

"Hey little buddy," Virgil said, and the dog sat. He twisted his head up on one side and sneezed. Then he stretched out beside the chair and closed his eyes. Virgil rocked, watching him. He had some hope that maybe Glen would come by. After a while he folded his hands together and just sat in the chair, waiting for something to tell him to move.

The chair creaked slowly on the boards of the porch. He pushed it back and forth with a little motion of his knees. The dog slept on his side. The yard was wet and the puddles were visited by drinking birds. It was hushed and quiet. He rocked slowly, sitting on his porch alone except for a dog and watching his world, wishing he could see his son come driving up the road.

Mary smelled hay and knew she was in the barn. She could feel the little sharp points of stems lightly sticking the skin of her arms, the backs of her knees, and as she shifted she could hear it rustle beneath her, could feel the dust rise around her in little clouds that settled in her throat and made her want to cough.

There was a large dull pain over her left eye and her face on that side felt swollen. The thing over her eyes smelled of something like paint thinner, a light odor of petroleum like the faintest whiff of coal oil or lighter fluid. She was afraid to speak. She could tell that she was not alone. Somebody was near, maybe crouched, maybe sitting, listening and watching.

Her wrists were up in the air and she pulled down to see if she could move her arms. She couldn't move them much. She was tied and she could feel something like thin ropes wrapped around her wrists, but not tightly, not painfully.

She was trying to remember what she had been doing. Looking at the little tomato plants, and then she had fallen it seemed. But she couldn't figure out what that had to do with this. It was confusing, and trying to figure it out made her head hurt, so for a while she just lay quietly and listened.

There wasn't any sound. She couldn't tell which part of the barn she was in. It was cool where she was but she had no indication of light or dark, just the clean smell of the hay and the memory of the day she and Bobby had stacked it in the loft. That was June, last year, a day and a half of work in the pasture and the barn, a Friday and a Saturday, Bobby with his work clothes and a baseball cap. She wore her overalls and tennis shoes and her wide straw hat. The old truck grinding through the stubble and how the wind cooled the sweat on her body when they stopped for a break under the trees by the fence. Ice water in a gallon jug kept in a wrinkled paper sack, and iced tea on the back porch still in their work clothes as dusk moved in, a few minutes of rest before she started fixing their supper. That was right after Emma killed herself and she remembered thinking about Virgil and his pain while she drove the truck, and then later, that night, lying forever alone in her bed and not being able to sleep for thinking about him. She didn't go to the funeral. Bobby did. He didn't want to talk about it much when he came back. He just said that Virgil looked bad.

There was a slight rustle in the hay not far away, as if someone had moved his foot or sat up or turned his body in some small way. But nothing after that.

"Who's there?" she said, but there was no answer. Somehow she knew there wouldn't be an answer in the same way she knew that her face was covered so that she wouldn't be able to see who was doing this to her.

"Why are you doing this to me?"

It seemed foolish to listen to her own voice in the quietness of the barn. It was almost as if she were talking to herself. Her mouth was dry. She licked her lips. A little dust had settled in her mouth but she didn't want to spit. She swallowed it and cleared her throat.

When she began to imagine what was going to happen to her, it didn't scare her. Things like this happened, you heard about them, saw them in the paper. She only hoped that whoever it was wouldn't think it necessary to take her life because there was still too much she had to do. She hated she'd argued with Bobby about Jewel. What did he want but his own family and what did anybody ever want but their own family and love and a safe place to stay. And she'd had almost all of that. She'd had Bobby all this time. She'd watched him grow and become a man and run for office and get elected. She'd watched him act decent all his life and that comforted her even now. If today was the day she had to die, she could at least go knowing that Bobby had turned out okay. She'd worried about him so much. But she didn't have to worry about him now.

She let her head sag back into the hay and she felt it cushioning her. It was hard to breathe in it for the dust but it was a strain to hold her head up with it hurting the way it was. She had no idea how long she'd been lying tied like this. It might have been a long time. She wondered if he was going to say anything. It had to be a man, didn't it? But what man? She tried to think of somebody she had harmed but she couldn't think of anybody. She had no enemies that she knew of. But it seemed unlikely that some stranger had wandered in and found her and watched her and done this to her.

"Is somebody there?" she said. That soft rustle answered again, and it sounded like it was near her right foot. Her wrists were beginning to hurt a little now from the strain, and she could feel pinpoints of pain in her fingertips. Going to sleep. Circulation getting cut off.

"Please talk to me," she said. "I can't do anything. I'm tied up. You could untie me and I'd keep my face covered up until you could get away. I don't have any way of knowing who you are. I'd promise not to uncover my eyes. I'll swear it on the Bible if you'll go in my house and get it. It's on the coffee table in the living room."

Still there was no answer, but she heard the click of something metallic, and then a tiny sound like a piece of sandpaper rubbing against something, and she heard the outrush of breath and knew that somebody had lit a cigarette. She thought about the hay in the barn and the hay she was lying on and fire for a moment, but that was too bad to think on for long. Somebody was watching her and smoking a cigarette. It seemed almost impossible that somebody could do that, that somebody could be calm enough to sit there watching her tied up and blindfolded and ignore her pleading and just light a cigarette. Relax like that.

"Won't you please say something? Are you somebody I know?"

At first she wasn't aware that it was pain, and then she felt the heat on her shin and she screamed and snatched her leg back as the cigarette burned into her skin. She whimpered then. It was going to be worse than she'd thought.

Now there was a louder rustle in the hay, and she drew back as far as she could, not knowing what to expect. Suddenly there was somebody beside her ear bending close and she could smell hair tonic, cigarette smoke, sweat, and whiskey.

"Shut your damn whore's mouth," a voice said, the lips very close to her ear. The noise, the slow gentle rasp of the whisper, was almost comforting, coming as it did so low and near. But in the voice was a bad memory that had always bothered her, of a dark-haired boy in a classroom who watched her with sullen eyes, insolent and full of contempt, his face filled with hate.

"My mama told me all about you," the voice said, just before she heard him pull back. She knew who he was then, and she was very afraid.

He tied a rag around her mouth so she couldn't scream anymore. After that he got up and moved away from her, back up to the door of the barn where the light was, looking out to the road to see if anything was coming. He crossed the yard quickly and went up the steps to the back porch and smelled something burning as soon as he opened the door. A skillet full of meat and sauce was smoking on the stove. He stepped over to it, looked around for a pot holder, found one hanging on a hook, and put it around the handle of the skillet. He moved it to a cold eye and cut off the one that was lit. A counter was piled full of tomatoes and okra. He picked up one of the tomatoes and looked at it. It was a pretty nice tomato. He set it down.

Her kitchen was neat and all the dishes had been washed. Just like his mother. He started opening cabinets and saw pots and pans, glasses and all manner of small appliances. In the cabinet next to the sink he found a bottle of whiskey and pulled it out and looked at it. It was a fifth of Evan Williams and it was nearly full. He thought about moving her car so that it would look like she was gone, but he was afraid he would meet somebody on the road and he didn't figure he'd be able to find her keys. But as he twisted the cap off the bottle and turned it up, he saw a ring of keys sitting beside the toaster on the counter.

He walked over to the refrigerator and opened the door to see if there were any Cokes in there. A small carton of six bottles rested within. He got one out and found the opener nailed to the wall beside the garbage can and he opened it and took a sip from it. He shook it the way some people do and made it fizz, then drank a little more of it. Then he filled it all the way up with whiskey and drank the whole thing in one long swallow. It heated his belly. He capped the whiskey and walked over and looked at the keys. He was wondering what the chances were of some-body picking just that time to come along, just as he got ready to move the car. He hated to chance anything, but if the car was gone nobody would think of looking around the place for her, and he would have more time. He wanted plenty of time.

He leaned against the counter, considering it. He picked up the keys and looked at them. One of them was an ignition key for a Buick. Still shiny, not worn down to the brassy metal by fingertips yet. A new car, maybe. He hefted the bottle in his hand.

"Well shit," he muttered. Bobby was the only one to worry about coming along. He didn't know what the chances were but he thought it was worth the risk. It wouldn't take but a minute to find out.

He walked up the hall to the front door and looked out. The road was deserted. He pushed open the screen door and stood on the porch lis-tening. He couldn't hear anything but the wind. He could see the back end of the car sticking out of the car shed, a chrome bumper, a blue trunk. When he moved he moved fast.

He ran to the end of the porch and jumped off and landed running, crossed the yard at a lope and turned the corner of the shed and went down the side and yanked open the driver's door. He threw the bottle onto the seat and slammed the door while he was cranking the car. When it fired to life he shoved it into reverse and stepped down hard on the gas. It spun gravel at first and he could hear the rocks clattering against the walls of the wooden shed and then back into the sides of the car and he let off the gas and it lurched backward. As soon as it cleared the shed he spun the wheel hard to the right and turned it around, hit the brakes, shoved it into drive, and swung out of the yard with mud and gravel flying. He pushed the pedal to the floor and raced toward the side road a half mile beyond the house, and he didn't meet anybody. And after he was on that road he knew he probably wouldn't.

He drove slower then, sipping on the whiskey, looking for a place to hide one more car.

Things were quiet at the jail now. The coroner had taken care of the body and Harold had gone off to patrol some more. Bobby sat in the dayroom and waited for the coffee to brew and watched part of a game show with the sound off. There wasn't anything pressing to do now and he just wanted to rest for a while. He thought about calling Mary to see if she was back. He didn't like it when they argued and he wanted to see if she was all right. But he thought he'd just drive out there after a while.

When the coffee was ready he got up and poured a cup and took it back to his office and sat down, more to keep from answering all of Mable's questions than anything else. At least it was over now. He'd done what he had to do. But he should have done it yesterday. Shouldn't have let that baby lay out there another whole day. He told himself that it had just been because of what Virgil and Puppy got into, but that wasn't it. He hadn't wanted to go out there, hadn't wanted to see what the children told him was out there. But now he had done it and now it was over.

He looked up at the open door to his office. If it were closed, Mable wouldn't come back there and bother him unless it was something she thought was important. He got up and closed it, then sat back down.

There was always plenty of noise and meanness out in the world and it was nice to be able to get away from it for short periods of time. Like now. He put his feet up and reached in his pocket for his cigarettes.

He felt bad for the two kids who were left. They'd be shunted off to somebody else forever now probably. He didn't figure the mother was much better than the father. She hadn't told on him. Maybe they'd done it together. Maybe he'd just scared her into staying quiet. Maybe he was in the process of killing her when he drove up on them the other day. And those kids there watching it. He hoped for a better life for them.

He eased back in his chair and lit his cigarette. Smoke drifted over his desk. His boots were muddy again and he was getting some of it on his desk. But it was his desk and he could get mud on it if he wanted to.

All he had to do was sit here, finish his coffee and his cigarette, and then he could get up and go home and take a shower, see what Mary was fixing for supper. Maybe there wouldn't be any more trouble for a while. Maybe Glen would stay out of the way and leave Jewel alone. And if he wouldn't he could always take his badge off for that five minutes. Five minutes. You could hurt somebody real bad in five minutes. But he hoped it wouldn't come to that. All he wanted was for Glen to leave Jewel alone. He'd had his chance. It was all over now and he didn't want to have to worry about him anymore.

He kept sitting there, sipping on his coffee. After a while he finished it and got up and found his hat and put it on. He opened the door, turned the light off, and pulled the door closed behind him. Mable was still working on some papers up front. He told her where he was going and then he left.

It was still cloudy outside and he wondered if the rain was over. He got into his car and pulled out into the street.

The town was still wet and there were few people about, no idlers on the benches under the oaks of the courthouse. He drove by it slowly, looking up at the high windows set into the white masonry and saw someone peering down at him, a judge, a lawyer, a juryman, maybe a shoplifter. The man lifted a hand and Bobby nodded to him across the height and distance.

He stopped at the red light and put his blinker on. Cars and trucks passed through the intersection and he waited for the light to turn green. Tapping his hand idly on the steering wheel, watching a woman next to him in a car speaking to her child. The light changed and he went through it and turned down the hill, picking up speed and moving over into the right lane past gas stations and grocery stores and a bank and a tire shop. He had to wait for another light at the bottom of the hill and then he pushed down hard on the gas and drove to the other side of town and left the city limits. He dreaded telling Mary.

He slowed once for some puppies playing near the highway, weaving wide of them and going by carefully. Children were in yards and old people sat in chairs on their porches. Some of them waved. He waved to some of them.

Once he got deeper into the county he could see water lying everywhere, pooled in the ditches and flowing through the creeks, rain-drenched yards with their sodden trees standing guard beside the road. He felt dirty and he couldn't remember when he'd ever been so tired. It seemed to have seeped into his bones and it felt as if it were pushing him down into the seat with its weight. His eyes drooped a few times and he weaved a little and snapped out of it. For a little while. Staying awake with Jewel almost all night. He couldn't get the way she'd looked and the way she'd felt out of his mind and he knew he wouldn't be able to stay away tonight either but he had to have some sleep. An ache had settled into his backbone and his shoulder blades. He guessed he needed some more coffee.

He turned off the highway and slowed a little, splashing through a few low places that still held water. The road was lined with big trees and the pastures were wet, the cows grazing in the deep grass and the little frogs that had come out of the ditches hopping across the blacktop. He'd seen them come out of the road at night in the rain, thousands of them, and he wondered where they came from in such masses, why they did that.

He pulled up in his yard and parked the cruiser. He got out and looked at the empty car shed and went across the gravel to the steps. He had his key out to put it in the door but he saw that it was open. That stopped him. She never left it unlocked. He stood there looking at it from the bottom step. He stared at the car shed as if that would tell him why the door was open.

"Well hell," he said, and went on up the steps. Maybe she'd gone to the grocery store. Maybe she was quilting a quilt with some of her friends. He didn't blame her for not wanting to stay by herself at home all the time. The thought crossed his mind that she might have gone to see Virgil now that he was hurt. He didn't care, kind of even hoped that she would. He didn't want her to be lonely. Everybody needed somebody.

He pushed the door open and let the screen door flap behind him, took off his gun and dropped it in the chair and sat down and took his boots off. Took his wet socks off, too, stuck them down inside the boots and carried them back to his room and dropped them beside the bed. There were clean boots inside the closet and more uniforms. He undressed and balled up all his clothes and grabbed some clean underwear from a drawer, went down the hall and tossed the clothes into the utility room and went into the bathroom and closed the door just out of habit.

They'd remodeled the bathroom two years before and he liked the shower. He turned the water on and stepped in under the spray, feeling the heat soak into his skin. He put his hands against the stall and just stood there under the spray with his head down. It felt so good he didn't want to get out from under it, but after a few minutes he shut it off and stepped out.

Back in his room he found an ironed pair of uniform pants and put them on, found some fresh socks and put them down on the bed. He combed his hair in front of the mirror and slipped on a ribbed undershirt and patted at his hair again, then went down the hall into the kitchen and looked around. The first thing he noticed was the pan of spaghetti sauce on the stove. He frowned a little when he walked over to it. The stove was cold. He stuck his finger into the sauce and it was cold, too, but burned around the edges. A faint trace of something acrid still hung in the room. It wasn't like her to forget about something on the stove and let it burn. Unless maybe she was out in the yard. But she wouldn't have been out in the yard with it this wet. He picked up the pan and felt around on the bottom of it. There was no trace of heat there. He set it back and turned slowly around in the kitchen. Nothing was out of place. All the dishes were washed. He began to be just a little worried about her. He looked at his watch and saw that it was time for her soap operas to come on. It was strange for her not to be home at this time of day. She never missed her soap operas, never forgot to lock the door, never burned anything on the stove. He thought he ought to walk out in the yard.

He stepped out on the back porch and tried to remember what time he'd tried to call her. It looked like she'd be back by now. It just wasn't like her to go off and not tell him.

"Damn, Mama," he said softly. "Where the hell you at?"

The yard was wet and her flowers were bending from the weight of the rain that had fallen on them. He looked down toward the barn. But her car was gone. If her car was gone she was gone. Wasn't she?

He didn't have his boots on, was still barefooted, but he went down the steps and stood at the edge of the yard and looked out over that old familiar place. He couldn't imagine where she could be. And she shouldn't have gone off like this without letting him know where she was. Maybe she was over at Virgil's and didn't want him to know. But wherever she was, it wasn't any big deal. For once in her life she'd left something on the stove and she'd forgotten to lock the door. She was a grown woman, not some child he had to take care of. She'd probably be in after a while. He went up the steps and back into the house.

He found the coffee in the cabinet and poured some water into the pot and fixed it all and put it on the stove to start it. While it was warming up he went back to his room and put on his socks and his boots and got a clean shirt. He pinned some brass on it at the kitchen table while a cigarette smoked in the ashtray. He hung the shirt on the back of his chair and waited impatiently for the coffee to be ready. He kept listening for her car. He crossed his legs in the chair and leaned back and looked at the walls, tapped the ashes into the ashtray. The coffee perked quietly on the stove. After a bit he got up and found a cup and poured it full, spooned in some sugar, and reached into the icebox for the milk and poured a little in it. He sat at the table and sipped his coffee. He didn't want to go back to the jail now unless something came up. What he really needed was a nap. Needed one bad. He got up and walked up the hall to the little table where the phone sat and called Mable. He told her he was going to be at home for a while, that if she needed anything to call him there.

In the kitchen he found a pen and a piece of paper and wrote her a note and left it on the table: *Wake me up when you get in Love Bobby.* He stretched and yawned and went back to his bedroom and took off his boots.

The bed he slept in was the one he'd slept in all his life. It was an old cord bed with high wooden posts at the corners and the spread over it was white and laced with little fuzzy knots of yarn. On the walls hung a few pictures of a young Bobby standing in jeans and cowboy boots in the sawdust of showrings holding black bulls with leather harnesses on their muzzles, first-place ribbons in his hand, staring blankly into the eye of the camera. Sharp old black-and-white photos that had been in the local paper years back. His mother had gone to every event, had helped him wash the bulls like cars in the yard, soaping their black hides and running the water hose over their backs as the soap foamed up and ran down their sides, their legs, both of them combing out the hair and brushing it until it gleamed, leading them into the covered cattle trailer that was his high school graduation present a year early for the rides to the livestock barns in Jackson and Tupelo and Grenada.

He sat down on the bed and took off his socks, then leaned back with a long sigh and put his head down on the pillow and looked at the ceiling. This room had been his for as long as he could remember, his and his alone. But he wanted to sleep in another bed now, forever and always. He closed his eyes and the good memories came back. Anybody watching would have seen the small smile that curved into his mouth, the utter peace and serenity that seemed to seep into his body, would have heard the light snoring that began to rise and fall in the room while the clock ticked its slow minutes and the afternoon crept on by.

He found a grassy road on the back side of her place and drove the car up in there, sliding in a few spots but not caring if he got it stuck once he got it out of sight of the road. He made it up to a wire gap with a POSTED sign hanging on it, locked with a chain. That was far enough. He got out and left the keys in it, took only the whiskey with him. He figured he was at least a hundred yards off the road. Nobody was going to drive up in there and find it. Not today.

The grass he walked in was wet and little seeds stuck to the cuffs of his pants. He climbed over the gap with the whiskey in his hand, carefully, trying not to snag his pants on the wire. The road went up through the woods and he followed it, trying to stay in the drier places, but it was all wet, just like before when he'd gone to the barn the first time to wait for her. He stopped in a little clearing up in the woods and knelt there, uncapped the whiskey and took a drink. He was sweating and he could feel his shirt sticking to his back. He almost took a few minutes to rest and smoke a cigarette, but he thought he'd better get on back and make sure she hadn't gotten loose. She hadn't seemed to notice him leave, but he wasn't sure. He got up and capped the whiskey and started walking again.

Once he got down the hill he could see the pond, patches of water through the trees now brown and stirred up by the rain. A few cows were down there in the brush surrounding it and they looked at him as he went by. A huge black bull stood among them, flicking his ears at flies. There was a mud hole at the foot of the hill that he had to walk around, tall grass that he had to put his feet down in, a place where it would be easy to step on a snake. He was glad when he was able to get out of the grass and back on the pasture road.

There was another big patch of woods to walk through where stands of oak and sweet gum and beech trees were hung with muscadine and scuppernong vines, the fruit hanging in clusters among the green and yellow leaves. He kept walking and sweating, worrying about her getting loose and going for help, maybe call somebody. He could have cut the phone lines. But if Bobby tried to call her and the line was dead, he might think something about it and come home. He knew then that hiding the car was the right thing to do. He felt better then. It eased his mind.

He opened the whiskey still walking and turned a drink down his throat. It was starting to get to him and it was making everything easier. There was still plenty of it left and he was glad of that.

When he came out of the woods he could see the back side of the barn again. He stopped for a moment and looked at everything. It all looked just as it had before. The sweat was rolling down his temples and he mopped at it with the back of his hand and took another drink of whiskey. His legs and feet were wet and his hair was hanging down over his forehead. He started climbing up through the nests of blackberry bushes that dotted the hilly pasture behind the barn. The thorns tore at his arms and hands, cutting lines in his skin that raised tiny welts of blood not much thicker than hairs. They stung and then his sweat seeped into the cuts and they stung even more. He cursed constantly and fought his way through the worst of the bushes and skirted around some of them and finally made his way up to the fence. He could see the house from there and he stopped again. Everything looked as before. He went over the fence quietly and through the back door of the barn to stand in the dim light once again. He was almost afraid to look into the stall, fearing that she had somehow gotten away, that some trap was waiting to be sprung. But when he took a deep breath and stepped around the edge of the stall, she was lying there on the hay, her head turned to one side, her breasts rising and falling gently with each breath, her arms still suspended in the air. She stirred when she heard him and her head moved. He hoped she wouldn't try to talk to him anymore if he took the gag off. She looked as if she were having a hard time breathing, but he didn't want to talk to her. He only wanted to do what he had to do. In a way he felt sorry for her. She had made a mistake a long time ago and now it was time for her to pay for it. He knew about mistakes. He'd had to pay for his, and his father's too. Now Bobby had made a mistake and his mother was going to have to pay for it. This one and the other one, might as well make her pay for both of them at the same time. He wondered when people would learn not to mess with him. Somebody always had to be messing with him and he was tired of it. He was sick of it. You couldn't just let people run over you. They'd get to thinking they could do it all the time and they'd keep on doing it if you didn't do something about it. And he'd had about enough of her shit. His mother had told him about her all his life. He was just taking up for his mother. It was time somebody did.

He went closer, and she heard him and tried to scoot backwards. Her feet pushed at the hay and she went back a little, but stopped when the sea grass strings stretched out tight. He could see the bottom of her slip behind her knees and he could see partway up one of her thighs. He could see that her legs were still good. She was even kind of pretty to be so old, and that was good too. That would make it easier.

Her whole body was braced, and with the blindfold over her eyes he was reminded of a picture he'd once seen in school of the Statue of Liberty. And something a teacher had said—was it her?—about justice being blind. But he knew better than that. He knew the guilty always got punished. That was how things were supposed to be in the real world. You did something wrong, you got punished for it if you were around to punish.

He knelt next to her and set the bottle in the hay. He untied the gag and pulled it away. His feet were wet. He started taking off his shoes, the same cheap lace-ups he'd worn out of the gate at the prison. They were soaked and he had to pick at the laces with his scabbed hands, those monkey bites still there. That seemed so long ago now. The briar cuts were still stinging. He raised his head from time to time and watched her listening to him. Her head was still up, her mouth open slightly, but as he pulled his left shoe off his foot she gave out a little groan and let her head fall back into the hay. He stripped off the wet sock and hung it on a board in the stall and bent to the right shoe. It was very quiet in the barn. It felt nice to him, just the two of them sharing this space, not having to talk. He worked his foot out of the other shoe and laid it aside, pulled off the sock and hung it beside the other one. He wiggled his toes and looked at them. They were wrinkled, looked like he'd been taking a bath. But he stretched them out in the hay and the dry warmth of it felt good on his feet. He looked at her. She turned her head away from him. Now he could have a drink in the cool darkness and smoke another cigarette, sit here for a while and just relax before he got started.

He got out a cigarette and lit it, watching her. She raised her head when she heard the lighter strike, held it up for a moment, then put it back down. He twisted the cap off the whiskey and took a drink, then decided he'd give her a drink. He raised up on his knees, not saying anything, and saw her draw back as she felt him come near. He tilted the neck of the bottle carefully, brought it near her lips, and poured a little onto her mouth. He poured too much and some of it went up her nose. She reared up and choked and strangled but the ropes wouldn't let her come all the way up and she sagged back, coughing, slinging her head and trying to shake the whiskey off her face. He thought she might ask him not to do that again but she didn't. He guessed she didn't like whiskey. He took another drink for himself and she lowered herself back to where she had been, slowly rubbing the side of her face against the hay. Some of it stuck to her cheek and he reached out and brushed it away. She let him do that. She cleared her throat and then lay still.

He looked at her legs again, put the cigarette in his mouth and reached out and rubbed the top of her shin. She didn't move but he felt the muscles in her leg tense up. He trailed his fingers down to her ankle slowly, then back up to her knee. He let his hand rest there for a moment, and then ran it up to the middle of her thigh, cool and smooth. She started trembling and her mouth creased downward and he could tell that she was trying not to cry. He let it rest there, felt the silkiness of her skin, and he wondered how many times his father had felt it too. His hand rubbed back and forth, almost as if he were trying to soothe her, let her know that everything was going to be all right. She stopped trembling and he patted her thigh in reassurance. She lay unmoving in the hay and he looked at the fine wrinkles of skin at her throat and remembered her in bright dresses, with a ribbon in her hair, remembered her grading papers at her desk with her glasses low on her nose. He finished the cigarette. When the car pulled in they both heard it at the same time and he lunged over her body, spilling some of the whiskey on her, covering her mouth with his hand and crushing back the rising scream and bottling it in her throat. His knee was beside her head and he pushed harder on her mouth until she stopped trying to scream.

Outside somewhere a car door slammed and he knelt there in the hay, breathing hard, listening. But there was nothing else to hear. He knew it was Bobby, had to be.

He leaned close to her ear, put his lips right up against her hair, spoke in a whisper: "You better be quiet." Her head nodded beneath his hand and he let off the pressure a little. Her nostrils flared and she took in a big breath of air. But still he didn't move his hand. He was listening for the sound of a door slamming, and finally he heard it. After that there was nothing. He was probably inside the house by now.

"Is that him?" he said.

She nodded. She was trying to say something and he lifted the pressure of his hand so that when she spoke the sound of her voice was muffled against his palm. "I guess so."

"What's he doing home?"

She paused for another breath. "He comes in at different times."

He looked out toward the front of the barn, but he couldn't see the house from where he was. He would have to get up and leave her, find a crack in the wall or something, look out. But she might scream if he left her. So he set the whiskey on a timber at the base of the wall and reached into his pants for the little pocketknife he'd used on Jewel's screen. He held his hand over her mouth and watched her. He couldn't tell if she was going to do anything or not. She didn't move when he lifted his hand a little. He took his hand away from her mouth and opened the knife quickly and then turned it in his hand and pushed the tip of the blade into the soft skin just beneath her jaw, right into the side of her throat. It made a small dent in her skin and she stopped breathing, held it in. He spoke to her again. "I can kill you and go out the back door and he'll never catch me. If you make any noise, you'll get this in you. You hear me?"

He waited for her answer. She nodded slowly.

"You believe me?"

She nodded again, very slowly.

"You better."

He pulled the knife away and she took a breath. He kept watching her. She didn't move or anything, just lay there like before. He got up, still watching her, and slowly began to back away from her. He didn't think she was going to try anything. The knife, she was scared of that. He kept easing toward the entryway until he got to a place where he couldn't see her anymore. The boards that formed the walls of the barn were old and full of cracks where they had shrunk and pulled loose and he knelt next to a small split place and put one eye up against it. There were some flowers out there, some grass and a tree. He backed away and moved on up the wall, looking for another crack. There was one about waist high and he got down on one knee and looked out. He could see the whole back side of the house, the porch and steps. Now he just had to wait. Long slow minutes with everything quiet and then suddenly there he was, coming out the back door. He had on a pair of pants and an undershirt. He was barefoot. He walked to the end of the porch and stood there for a moment, put his hands on his hips and looked out over the yard.

"You bastard," Glen said softly. He watched Bobby standing on the porch and he saw him look directly at the barn. But it was only for a second. His heart gave a leap when Bobby came down the steps, and he gripped the knife in his hand. Bobby stopped at the edge of the yard and just stood there looking around. Didn't want to get his feet wet Glen guessed. After a while he saw him turn around and go back up the steps and inside the house. The door closed behind him. He kept watching for a few more minutes, waiting to hear him leave, but he never heard the car crank up. He guessed he was looking for her. And he could always put his boots on and come on down there.

He didn't know what to do now. Maybe it wasn't too late to just leave.

He didn't think she knew who he was. He hadn't spoken to her in years. Never had spoken to her much to begin with. Never had wanted to. But maybe she remembered his voice. Maybe his voice sounded like his daddy's, and she wouldn't have forgotten that. He looked at the knife again and stood up and turned. They would never knew who had done it. All he had to do was to do it and leave back across the pasture the way he had come, get his car, go find a beer joint somewhere. Sit in there and drink all evening, have a good alibi, just like the one he had for Barlow: *I spent the night with my daddy.* They couldn't prove anything if he said: *I was in a beer joint all evening, ask anybody.*

But he didn't want to leave just yet because she hadn't paid yet, not for what she had caused between him and his mother. It was too late to fix that now, too late to fix anything. They might have been able to work everything out if she had just lived until he could get out and come home and try to repair the things that had gone so wrong, but now she was dead and nothing was going to bring her back and now he couldn't tell her again that he didn't mean to shoot his brother or that he didn't mean to run over that little boy. It all rose up in him and choked him and he fell against a stall with hot tears blinding him, knowing full well about love and the pull of it and the way of flesh and how weak it was, how it could turn you away from the path of what was right and good. He knew that was true because Brother Roy had stood up in the pulpit and shouted those things back on those summer nights when he was caught up in the fever of it and knew that he was saved by Jesus and would be forever clean and washed of his sins, even the one of killing his brother. But then there were those other nights when his daddy was gone and Puppy had run away again, and he was all alone in the house with her. He remembered how scared he was, too scared to tell anybody, and how it went on all that summer until the day he climbed to the barn roof and went across it and walked its ridge with his hands out for balance and came to the edge of the eaves and stood there looking down at the yard so small and the little house and how they came out and called for him to come down, and how he obeyed only because he could not bear to face what Theron already had.

He went to his knees in the barn, crying and knowing she was hearing it, knowing that she was afraid and thinking of all the nights when he had been afraid, and he went forward on all fours to where she lay in her nest of hay. He saw then that she was indeed beautiful. She was almost as beautiful as his mother, and he began to undress slowly, quietly, taking a great pleasure in it, thinking of how it was going to be, how fine to finally join with that flesh. When he was naked he went to her and once again laid his hand upon her leg. She didn't move. She didn't do anything at all. This was so wonderful. This was so right. He had been waiting for it for so long. He knelt there, touching her, smiling in the dim light that came in through the door of the barn. He saw a mouse run across the floor. He heard a distant rumble of thunder that promised more rain.

Bobby had curled onto his side. The noise of his light snores sawed through the room and the old ceiling fan turned over him, cooling him, rocking him deeper into sleep. Nothing moved in that room except for the fan whisking its blades around and around, a soft white blur that spun above him, making a current of air that stirred the hairs on his head. He dreamed in quiet, his face crushed into the bedspread and his hands drawn up between his knees and his eyes closed tightly against the world. Maybe he moved with Jewel in her bed again, or drove over the country road, walked again the woods where the buried child had lain.

The phone began ringing in the hall, a little cheery musical tingling that went unheard. He slept on in the quiet room, the telephone ringing, the house still. It sat on the table and rang and rang and the sound of it echoed lightly up and down the hall, small, insistent, slightly shrill, unheard. It rang and rang and then it was silent. It was so quiet in the house that you could have heard the mouse that had come from the barn run across the polished hardwood floor, its little feet scrabbling for purchase on the waxed surface, rounding the curve outside Bobby's room, leaping down the hall, the little tail waving and making a tiny squeak as it hopped into the bag of yarn where Mary sat nights knitting an afghan for a neighbor's child.

J ewel put the phone back into the cradle and sat there looking at it. They'd told her at the jail that he was at home but she guessed he had left again. She still had her work clothes on and she went back to her room to change. She found some shorts and a sleeveless blouse and slipped out of her uniform and put on the other clothes, slid her feet into a pair of sandals. David had gone out into the backyard and she walked through the kitchen and out the back door. He was out there climbing on the swing set.

She looked up at the sky and wondered if the rain would stop now. But it had been nice last night to see Bobby's headlights coming through that rain and up into the yard. She wanted to cook supper for him if she could just find him. She wanted to talk to him about Glen coming by. And she wanted him to spend the night again.

She went down the steps and out into the yard. It was still wet but a lot of it had soaked into the ground. She tipped the grill over and poured the water out of it and set it back. David was swinging now. His shoes were muddy. There was somebody else she wanted to see, too. It was still early enough that she could go by there. She just hoped Glen wouldn't be there. But she knew they didn't get along. It was sad, but she didn't guess anything was going to change it.

"You want to go see Papaw?" she said.

He stopped swinging immediately and climbed down and ran across the grass to her.

"Papaw," he said. "Let's go see Papaw, I want to go fishin."

"I don't think we can go fishing today. We got to come back home and cook supper after while. We'll just go see him a little bit. Okay?"

"Okay," he said. "But I want to tell him I want to go fishin again."

She took his hand and smiled at him and they turned together and went across the yard holding hands. The birds were in the trees again and there were puddles of water in the driveway.

"You need to put on some clean clothes," she said.

"I ain't dirty, Mama."

"Yes you are too. You've got mud on your shorts and you need to put on some clean shoes if you're gonna go see Papaw."

"Papaw don't care if my shoes are muddy."

"I know he doesn't. But I do."

She took him in the house and helped him change and she found her car keys. She stuck a pack of cigarettes in her pocket and thought about trying to call him one more time, and then she thought she could do it later. Or maybe just stop by there. There was plenty of time. It was nowhere close to dark yet. The sun hadn't even started down.

She told David to wait just a minute and she went back through the kitchen and fastened the latch on the screen door and locked the wooden one. She heard the front screen door slam and David was sitting in a chair on the porch when she went out there.

"You ready?" she said.

"Yep."

She locked the front door and got him into the car. She was still a little worried about Glen, that look he'd had on his face. And she saw his face in David every time she looked at him, and more than once she had wondered what Glen had looked like as a little boy. He'd never shown her any pictures from home, never had seemed to want to talk about his family, had always dismissed them with a few words. All that anger that had always been inside him. What had happened to his brother. How bad things must have been for him when he was growing up. It wasn't any wonder that he'd always stayed in trouble.

"Did you call Papaw?" David said.

She pulled the car into gear and headed down the driveway, easing through the mud holes. She'd have to wash her car now.

"We're just gonna drop by," she said. "We probably won't stay long. I just want to see how he's doing."

"What if he's not home?"

"I think he's probably home."

She pulled to the end of the driveway and looked out at the road. The tracks of tires were embedded in the mud and she'd never liked driving when it was wet. Somebody had told her they were going to blacktop all the roads soon and she was glad of that.

She swung out and passed one hand through her hair and rested her elbow on the windowsill. David got up in the seat and walked across it to stand beside her. He put his arm around her shoulder and leaned his head against hers.

"Sit down, now," she said. "Be careful."

He slid down in the seat but he stayed next to her. She smiled, driving with him close to her, the clouds still hanging in the sky and the fields drab and laden with water.

"I want to play with Papaw's dog," he said.

"We can't stay long. We'll just visit for a little while. I need to talk to Bobby sometime."

"You mean Daddy?"

"No. I mean Bobby. You remember Bobby. He came over to the house the other day. The sheriff. That's Bobby."

He turned his small face up to her. "That's not Daddy?"

"No, honey. That's Bobby."

He had that look of confusion on his face that he always wore whenever she got to talking about Bobby or Glen. She never had all the answers for his questions. He saw things on television, he picked up things from conversation. Virgil had told her that David asked him about things on their little fishing trips. She knew it hadn't been easy on David and that she was to blame for it. But she hoped that most of this would be something he wouldn't remember much of when he got older. There would be plenty of time to explain things then.

The red mud sucked at the tires as they drove along. She thought of all the letters she'd written Glen and how few she'd gotten back. They were more like notes, scribbled things she could hardly read sometimes. She would tell him how David was growing and what he was doing, but he wouldn't say anything about all that. He'd just talk in his notes about how hot it was, how hard they were working him, how much he hated them, what he'd like to do to them. She knew now that she never should have let him back in her bed that first night. But it had been such a strange time. Such a lonely time. The good times with him were what she'd thought about, not that last night across the river when she saw again how he could be. She had hoped those three years would change him, that he'd come home and do the right thing, marry her, claim David, give him his name. But all that was gone now. And Bobby was a good man. With enough time she'd be able to forget about Glen. It might not be easy but she had to think about David. She wanted to try and explain all that to Virgil, to let him know that nothing had changed between them just because she wasn't going to see Glen anymore. He was still David's grandfather. There wasn't any way around that.

The old house was streaked dark with rain when she pulled up and parked. David was out the door almost before she could get the car stopped.

"Wait a minute," she said, but he didn't wait. He ran across the muddy yard toward the front porch while she was getting out of the car, but Virgil had already heard them pull up and he was coming out with a grin on his face. David ran up the steps and Virgil knelt to hug him instead of picking him up as he usually did. He had him in his lap in a chair by the time she got up on the porch.

"Hey Papaw," she said, and she bent over and gave him a hug that he returned with one arm, the other one holding David.

"It's about time y'all came to see me," he said. "Pull you up a chair and set down."

"I told David we couldn't stay long," she said. She got the other rocker and pulled it up next to the edge of the porch. "How you been doing?"

"I been doing all right. What about you?"

She sat down in the chair and got her cigarettes and lighter out of her pocket.

"We're doing okay," she said. The puppy came up from the yard snuffling and sniffing at everything, and David climbed down and started petting him. The puppy slapped his long bony tail against the leg of Jewel's rocker.

"Why don't you go out in the yard and play with him, honey?" she said.

"Come on, puppy," David said, and the puppy followed him down the steps. She watched Virgil watching them, smiling a little, rocking slowly in his chair.

"You want a cigarette?" she said, and held the pack out to him.

"Thanks." He reached and got one and pulled some matches from his pocket. She got one for herself and lit it and crossed her legs.

"That rain cooled it off good, didn't it?" he said.

"Feels good out here."

"I was just fixin to drink me a beer, Jewel. You want one?"

"I might drink one with you," she said, and he got up and went in to get them. David started around the corner of the house with the puppy trotting behind him.

"Don't get off too far, now," she called after him. He waved and went out of sight. She heard Virgil coming back up the hall and he pushed open the screen door and handed her a bottle of beer.

"Boy that's cold," she said, and took a drink of it.

"I had em in the freezer."

He sat back down and she saw him wince just a little.

"You all right?"

"Aw yeah. I just slipped down the other day. You seen anything out of Glen lately?"

She rocked slowly and held the beer on the arm of the chair. "Well. That's what I wanted to talk to you about. He came by the cafe this morning."

"Was he drunk?"

"Not exactly."

"But he wasn't sober either?"

"No sir. He wasn't sober. I asked him what he was going to do about David and he said he didn't know."

She'd been looking at the floorboards but now she raised her face and watched Virgil. He took a long pull on his beer and then held it on his knee.

"I asked him the same thing," he said. "That was Sunday. That's the last time I've seen him."

331

The wind was blowing just a little and riffling through the trees at the edge of the road. Virgil's rocker made little squeaks on the boards of the porch.

"I tried to talk to him Saturday night," Jewel said. "But he said he had to leave. I kept thinking he'd come back that night, but he never did. Did you know somebody broke in my house?"

Virgil seemed stunned.

"Naw," he said. "When was that?"

"Sunday night. I called Bobby to come over the next morning and then he come back that night and brought me a gun. We were out on the porch and Glen drove by and saw us. Now he thinks . . . he called me a whore and said David wasn't his. But I'm afraid it was him that come in my room. I've got to do something."

Virgil didn't seem to be listening to her. He was looking at something out across the road. "What do you mean?"

"I waited on him, Virgil," she said. "I guess it was crazy but I thought maybe things would be better when he got out. That's what I was hoping for. But he ain't gonna marry me. And I don't even want him to now. I can't believe how he looked at me. It was like he hated me. I'm sorry to have to say all this to you."

Virgil rocked and didn't answer. He seemed to have withdrawn into some place deep inside himself.

"David don't even know who his daddy is," she said. "And Glen wouldn't talk to me about him. So I told him not to come back. I just wanted to let you know. I don't mean to hurt you. You been good to us and we both love you. You know that."

He finally turned his head and she could see the pain on his face. He leaned forward and winced again.

"I don't blame you," he said. "You got yourself to think about. And that boy. You've give him every chance in the world to do right by you."

"This don't change nothing between you and me and David. He's still your grandson. I want you to see him."

"I appreciate that," he said. "You gonna marry Bobby?"

"I am if he asks me. He's a good man."

Virgil nodded and lifted his beer again. "I imagine he'll ask you."

"I was afraid you'd get upset. I know you've worried about all this as much as I have."

"I can't do nothing with Glen. Ain't been able to for a long time."

"I tried to call Bobby," she said. "They said he was at home but I never did get an answer. I guess he must have left. I was all upset. I wanted to tell him about Glen. Let him know it was over. But I wanted to see you first."

He took a last drag from his smoke and threw the butt out into the wet yard, lifted the beer again but then set it back on his knee.

"You might as well go see if you can find Bobby and tell him. He might be home by now."

She looked out across the road to the muddy field beyond the fence. The leaves on the trees were trembling in a slight breeze.

"I don't know," she said. "I kind of hate to go over there. I wouldn't have even called if I hadn't been so scared. I don't know Miss Mary that well. I've talked to her a little at church. But I don't know what she thinks about all this."

"Maybe you need to set down and have a talk with her," he said. "You gonna have to get to know her sooner or later, sounds like."

"I guess so. She might know where Bobby's at anyway. I'm just nervous about going over there. I hate to take David over there just yet."

"Leave him here with me," Virgil said. "I been wantin to see him anyway."

"I hate to ask you to babysit him."

"I don't care. I'll go around back and watch him," he said, and he got up from the chair. "Go on over there and stay awhile if you want to. We'll watch some TV or something. I'll let him feed my chickens again."

She guessed it wouldn't hurt anything. And it had been a while since they'd gotten to see each other. She knew David would stay over here with him all the time if she'd let him.

She took a last drink of her beer and set the bottle on the porch, then got up from the rocker.

"Well. If you don't care I think I'll let him stay a little while, then. I didn't know if Glen would be over here or not. You think he'll come by?"

"I don't know why he would. But it won't matter if he does."

"He was mad when he left the cafe. He said I was gonna be sorry. He scared me bad."

"Don't worry about him. He stays mad. And he ain't gonna come over here anyway."

There was something in his voice that she hadn't heard before. He was standing there holding the beer bottle down beside his leg and looking vacantly out across the yard.

"I had a lot of hopes, too," he said. "And I ain't turned my back on him. I know he thinks I have. A lot of it's my fault. I stayed drunk for a long time there. Me and Emma fought all the time. It ain't good for kids to grow up in stuff like that."

"Why does he hate Bobby so bad?"

He turned his face and looked at her, sadness marked deep in his eyes.

"His mama," he said. "She was always jealous of Mary. It was crazy. She couldn't stand the idea of knowing I had another child with some-body else. Something happened to her after Theron died. She started telling Glen things about me and Mary. Wasn't none of it true. But I reckon he believed it."

"What kind of things?"

"You don't want to hear all that. I guess I should have took her somewhere and got her some help. She never was right after that. It got worse when Glen got sent off. I made some bad mistakes."

"We all make mistakes," she said.

"Yeah," he said, and lifted the bottle to take a drink. "Some of us just make worse ones than others. I'm gonna go around here and see about David. I'll see you when you get back."

He went down the steps and she watched him, standing there for just a moment on the porch by herself, and she almost said his name again, but there was nothing left to tell him and nothing left to ask him, and she went on down into the yard and opened the door of her car and got in and drove away.

She heard him taking his clothes off and when she felt him come near, she knew that it would soon be over. She knew, too, that Bobby was probably sleeping in his room. He'd looked tired this morning, and then he'd worked all day. Now he was probably in his room, sleeping. She could almost see him in there. Even if she screamed for help now he wouldn't hear her, so there was not going to be any help. She wished it didn't have to be like this, but she understood it now. It was because of what she had done with Virgil so long ago, and that made it about Bobby, too, so there was nothing to be done. Her life was going to change now, become something different. Everything else in her whole life had been leading up to this.

She felt something touch her leg and knew what it was. It was soft but firm, a warm piece of living flesh being pressed against her leg.

She thought about trying to talk to him again, but she knew it wouldn't do any good. He had made up his mind to do this and there was nobody to stop him. And if he had made up his mind to do this, he had probably made up his mind to take her life some way. She hoped it wouldn't be the knife. And then she remembered that she had her own knife. She had slipped it into her pocket after she finished cutting the okra. It was down in the pocket of her dress. And it was very sharp.

"Untie me," she said suddenly, and she felt him stop what he was doing. She could hear him breathing close to her and she could imagine him kneeling naked in the hay. She was aware of her own breath coming very fast and shallow from her chest. There was a faint rumble of thunder far off to the north. Other than that it was very quiet. She wished she could see his face. She wanted to see what he looked like now.

For a moment nothing was said. One of his hands was on her leg. And then one word came out of him, soft, inquisitive, full of wonder: "What?"

"Untie me," she said. "And take the blindfold off. I'm not going to fight you. But I don't want it like this. Not tied. Not blind so I can't see."

He didn't say anything for a minute. She lay on her back in the hay and smelled the dust of years and wondered what he would do. She thought if she could only look into his eyes it might change something, because in that face she would see that other face she loved so much, that face she had given up so much for, the years of waiting, the nights of loneliness with only her pillow to go to sleep against. She thought that if he would only look at her before he did this, he would see that she wasn't scared, and that it would be okay to cut her loose.

"What are you doing?" he said. "What are you trying to do to me?"

Mary could hear something in his voice that wasn't quite right, a small quavering that shook in his words, a rising little pitch of something unsteady that sounded almost like fear. She tried to calm her own voice, and she spoke very slowly.

"Untie me," she said. "Cut my hands loose and I'll take my clothes off. You won't have to rape me."

He was quiet again for a bit. She moved a little, trying to ease the dull pain that had started growing between her shoulder blades.

"Please," she said. "It doesn't have to be like this. You don't have to hurt me. I don't deserve this."

"Yes you do," he said, and there was no fear in his voice now. It was flat and final, and it sounded to Mary like a judgment. She wanted desperately to be able to see him, and it was maddening to have to lie in the blackness that covered her eyes, choking in the dusty hay. She struggled and pulled but the ropes didn't give and she heard his laughter at her feet and knew that he had to be kneeling there, watching her, and then she felt his hands on her legs. They were hard hands and she could feel the calluses on his palms sliding up over her shins, touching her knees. She tried to pull back but she had already gone as far as she could go.

"Don't do this," she almost whispered, and she turned her head from side to side, feeling the stems scratching her cheeks and her temples. It became harder to get her breath because she was raising more dust with her struggling, but she couldn't lie still either, not with those hands creeping farther up her legs, past her knees, up the insides of her thighs like a snake sliding, exploring each new inch of skin, touching and resting and then moving again bit by bit. She didn't want to let him see her cry but it was hard not to cry. She was ashamed and she felt the heat in her cheeks and she knew that her face was turning red under the rag he had put over her face.

"Please, Glen," she said. "Think about what you're doing. You could go back to prison for this."

The hands were going higher and higher and they were squeezing the skin of her thighs and she was trying to think of something to say that would make him stop because they were almost up to the place she didn't want them to be and her head was reeling and the hands were still climbing and she said the next thing she thought of.

"You just stop this," she said. "You just stop this right now. Your mother wouldn't want you to do this."

He stopped. His weight was leaning on her thighs. She could almost see him, bent forward, his face almost over hers.

"What did you say?" he whispered. "Did you say somethin about my mother?"

She heard the threat in his voice, the anger that was climbing into it, and she was suddenly scared to speak again. But his voice demanded an answer, so she answered him. "I said stop this."

She felt him bending low over her and it seemed that his lips were almost against hers when he spoke again.

"You goddamn bitch," he whispered. "You don't know nothin about my mother. You ain't even fit to say her name."

She didn't know what to say to him then. He was right on top of her and she could smell the whiskey on his breath even stronger now. And then his fingernails were at the side of her head, working at the knot in the cloth. She could smell him thick and strong in her nostrils, and she could hear him panting as he clawed at the knot. Then the cloth slipped away from her eyes and she was looking at him kneeling over her with the cloth in his hand and she had never seen a face like that. She looked deep into his eyes and swallowed hard at the hate and the lust showing there. His eyes were cold, glinting bits of light, so dark brown and shining and absolutely devoid of anything resembling human compassion that she could not look into them for long. She turned her face downward as she knew she must and saw with a shock that made her heart wilt the thick and blue-veined length of rigid flesh that trembled slightly between his legs. He wasn't going to just let her go when this was over. He couldn't. She'd seen his face now.

"Untie me," she whispered.

Nothing mattered now but what would happen next. Nothing she would do for the rest of her life was as important as what was happening now. She waited for him to move, and like somebody who cannot wake from the blackest dream she watched him drop the cloth and fumble in the pocket of the crumpled pants beside him and draw out the small folded Case knife. He never took his eyes from her and she watched that little blade come into the light when he opened it. It fascinated her how he never looked at it, just turned it in his hand and moved up closer to her, holding the blade pointed down toward her chest and in that one small moment when she knew that he was not going to cut the ropes that held her, when she realized that she had made a bad mistake, she just pulled her breath in and closed her eyes and waited for it, wondering how it was going to feel when it went into her heart. She thought about Virgil, almost wept for all that could have been and never would be now, and she was thankful that she had gone to see him that one last time.

There was a slight pressure on her left wrist and she opened her eyes to see him sawing through the little sea grass rope. The tiny strands parted one by one and suddenly her left hand was free. He wasn't looking at her. He was cutting the rope on her right wrist now and when it was free he dropped the knife in the hay behind him and leaned back with his buttocks against his heels and his hands flat on his thighs.

"Do what you said," he told her. His eyes on her were hot and she had to obey.

She reached down for the hem of her dress and pulled it up and started opening the buttons over her breasts. But he couldn't wait. He reached for her roughly and stripped her panties down and over her feet and tossed them away. He looked at her for just a moment and then he was on her, his hands going everywhere, smothering her mouth with hard kisses, trying to push his way inside her, pulling at her hair, her shoulders, burying his face in her throat. His unshaven jaw scraped her skin. She felt him slide inside her and he was huge and it hurt. She put one arm around the back of his neck and he began panting faster and she felt the rope trailing from her wrist as she reached into the pocket of her dress for the little paring knife and her hand closed over it. He was heavy on her and he was pushing her deeper into the hay and she opened her eyes to see his teeth gritted and his lips bared in what looked to be almost a snarl. She hoped that Virgil would be able to forgive her one day for this.

When he started shivering and shaking and moaning into her ear she raised the knife and turned it to his throat and pushed it all the way in. Suddenly blood was pouring down onto her face and she felt him pull out of her, heard him groan. She wiped at her eyes with the back of her free hand and his blood was hot on her face. He got off her and she sat up. He was back on his knees and blood was pumping from the hilt of the knife and leaking down his chest and there was semen on her thighs. His hands had gone to his throat and he was trying to pull the knife out. He seemed to be choking there on his knees and he was shaking his head to show that he could not believe she had done this to him.

He pulled the knife out and dropped it in the hay. He turned and put his hands down and he arched his back and coughed out a great gout of blood that ran down his chin and spattered on the hay and soaked quickly away. He looked up at her, a sidelong glance over his shoulder, and then on all fours he began to try and move away from her. He moved very slowly, like a child trying to learn how to crawl, the motions of his body ebbing down. She wished then that she could take it back, undo it somehow, because she knew there was not much time left for him now. When he turned for the last time and looked back at her for just a moment, she heard very clearly what he said. The words were soft and on his face and in his eyes she saw a great regret.

"I'm sorry," he said, and she believed him.

He eased himself down into the hay and moved onto his side and lay there, and it seemed to her that he was trying to find a comfortable place to rest his head. He breathed a few more times and then he was still. It was quiet once again in the barn. She felt his semen cooling on her thighs. She pulled herself up slowly, painfully, sat up, wiped her legs off, and shook the hay from her panties and put them on. After a bit she was able to get to her feet, but she was still dizzy from the place on her head. She held on to a post and stood there until she was able to walk over to him. She stood looking down at him for a long time. His eyes were half open and all the light had gone out of them. They saw nothing.

Her hands were still shaking when she buttoned her dress. She found an old mildewed quilt and covered his nakedness so that no part of his body could be seen. She heard a car pull up in the front yard and wondered who it could be. And then she walked out of the barn and back out into her wet yard, under the cloudy sky, trying to find her son.

Puppy's day was nearly done. He was working on his daddy's car when he heard the front door of the trailer open and close. He was bent under the hood, pulling the cover off the timing chain, and he drew back and peered around the side of the car to see who it was. Trudy was coming across the yard toward him and he guessed she was still mad at him, but he hoped she wasn't. He hated it when they fought. It wasn't good for the kids. It made it harder to stay home. It made everything harder. He bent back to his socket wrench and broke another bolt loose, then started taking it out. He didn't want to fight with her anymore, and he felt bad about putting his fist through the door. He knew he needed to spend more time with her, stop staying gone so much. But it wasn't too late to fix that. She was probably upset about him losing his job and everything. Then Glen came along and that didn't help anything. She'd probably get over it pretty quick and it wouldn't be any trouble to take her out to eat sometime, maybe go to the drive-in and watch a movie like they used to. She'd like that.

He was waiting to see what she was going to say when she came around to where he was, smiling a little, and put her hand on his shoulder.

"Hey," she said.

He glanced up at her. She didn't look mad at all.

"Hey, baby. How you doing?"

"Fine."

He got the bolt out and put it with the others on top of the breather, then laid the ratchet on the fenderwell. He leaned both hands on the radiator and looked down at the motor. It was leaking some oil from the valve covers and he figured he might as well put some new gaskets on while he was working on it. Save his daddy from having to do it later. It wouldn't take ten minutes. Go ahead and get everything fixed while he had it over here.

"You fixing your daddy's car?" she said. "I know he'll be glad of that."

"Well, I thought I would. Go ahead and get it runnin for him, take it on over to him when I get it ready. It ain't much wrong with it. He needs his car. I should have done fixed it."

"I'm glad it quit raining," she said.

"Yeah, me too. It's faired off right nice."

She moved a little closer and put her hand on his back and rubbed it slowly.

"You gonna get all dirty," he said. "I got grease all over me."

"I don't care. What you want for supper?"

He looked up into her eyes and he saw a soft light there that made him feel better.

"I don't care. Whatever you want to fix'll be fine."

"I'm sorry about this mornin," she said. "I didn't mean to be ugly."

"That's all right. I didn't mean to either."

She leaned closer and kissed him. Her voice was low and happy when she spoke. "Why don't you come on in the house and take you a long hot bath and I'll fry you some pork chops. I put some beer in the freezer for you."

Puppy smiled.

"That sounds pretty good," he said. "Let me just let the hood down on this thing in case it rains again."

He reached up and lowered the hood over the motor and his tools, pulled it down just short of the latch and left it. She stood there waiting for him.

"I cleaned up the house," she said.

"Good."

He walked over to her and she put her hand around his arm and turned with him. A little breeze was stirring and it cooled his sweating back. He was tired from working all day but he felt good. He was glad to be back on his own again. He thought things would work out. People would probably start bringing their cars in when they heard that he was open again.

"I put clean sheets on our bed, too," she said. "Mama wants the kids to spend the night with her."

"What'd you tell her?"

"I told her I'd bring em over after while."

"Why don't we just go out?" he said. "We could go eat some catfish." She looked up at him and he smiled at her.

"That sounds good," she said.

They walked and she kept holding on to his arm. It had been a long time since she'd done that and he was glad she was doing it now.

I t was one of those evenings when it clears off just before sundown and you know that the rain is finally gone. The sky is filled with scattered clouds and the last sinking tip of the sun sends light up to brighten the back side of them in hues of orange and pink and the light falls bit by bit until there is only a faint trace of where it has gone before night.

Virgil sat there with David on his lap and they watched it together. The birds had come back out and they lit in the yard and from the porch he pointed out to him mockingbird and sparrow, cardinal and jay. He told him fishing stories and in a little while the boy's eyes closed and Virgil nestled his head with his arm and saw again how the flesh there had wrinkled and sagged. He wanted another smoke but he would not disturb this child to roll it and was content to look down on his face. The puppy dozed beside the chair and he watched the last light fade out of the sky.

Just before full dark he heard cars coming down the road in the mud. They swung in one by one with their parking lights on, and he turned his head to see them getting out. The doors closed and he held his precious bundle a little tighter when he saw who it was. He rocked, watching them come closer. Bobby was there and Mary and Jewel, and he held David close to him as if to protect him from any harm. He looked at their faces and the old boards creaked softly as he pushed the chair to and fro. When they came near enough to hear him he told them to be quiet, that the boy was asleep.